MASTERFUL STORIES FROM 17 DISTINGUISHED IMAGINATIONS

In Isaac Asimov's "Hell-Fire," man's power to destroy unleashes the ultimate evil.

Ray Bradbury's "Asleep in Armageddon" features a crashed spaceman fighting invisible enemies who are battling for his mind.

"Orange Is for Anguish, Blue for Insanity," by David Morrell, has an artist following his friend down a psychotic path to suicide.

An experimental aphrodisiac turns a man's lust for life into uncontrollable animalistic urges in Clive Barker's "Age of Desire."

... and thirteen other tantalizing stories by bestselling authors who know all about fear.

BETWEEN TIME AND TERROR

If you and/or a friend would like to receive the *ROC Advance*, a bimonthly newsletter featuring all the newest and hottest ROC books and authors, on a complimentary basis, please fill out this form and return it to:

ROC Books/Penguin USA
375 Hudson Street
New York, NY 10014

Your Address
Name _____
Street _____ Apt. # _____
City _____ State _____ Zip _____

Friend's Address
Name _____
Street _____ Apt. # _____
City _____ State _____ Zip _____

BETWEEN TIME AND TERROR

EDITED BY

Robert Weinberg,
Stefan Dziemianowicz,
and Martin H. Greenberg

A ROC BOOK

ROC
Published by the Penguin Group
Penguin Books USA Inc., 375 Hudson Street,
New York, New York 10014, U.S.A.
Penguin Books Ltd, 27 Wrights Lane,
London W8 5TZ, England
Penguin Books Australia Ltd, Ringwood,
Victoria, Australia
Penguin Books Canada Ltd, 10 Alcorn Avenue,
Toronto, Ontario, Canada M4V 3B2
Penguin Books (N.Z.) Ltd, 182-190 Wairau Road,
Auckland 10, New Zealand

Penguin Books Ltd, Registered Offices:
Harmondsworth, Middlesex, England

First published by Roc, an imprint of Dutton Signet,
a division of Penguin Books USA Inc.

First Printing, April, 1995
10 9 8 7 6 5 4 3 2 1

Contents

Introduction

On first consideration, science fiction and horror fiction appear to represent opposite extremes of the spectrum of fantastic fiction. At the most basic level, science fiction is concerned with the rational, and horror fiction with the irrational. Science fiction extrapolates the scientific advances of enlightened civilizations, while horror fiction explores the darkness of primal fears. Even the trademark symbols for the two genres seem to contradict each other: for science fiction, the sleek rocket ship thrusting spaceward; for horror, the disintegrating House of Usher collapsing inward upon itself.

Yet ever since 1818, when Mary Shelley conjured a frightening monster with the scientific theories of her day in *Frankenstein,* countless writers have demonstrated that the separation between horror and science fiction is neither so simple nor so clear. In their stories one does not find the optimism of future worlds made better by technological perfection, but rather the pessimistic speculation that scientific progress will only amplify human imperfection and misery. Beneath the science fiction patina of their writing, one sees the lineaments of supernatural horror: aliens from outer space cut from the same cloth as the demons and devils of superstition, chemical formulae that do the work formerly performed by magic spells and incantations, scientists who resemble wizards and warlocks in their reckless disregard of limits. The moral of their stories is not that there are things man was not meant to know, but that often there are terrible consequences of scientific curiosity that man cannot responsibly foresee.

Shelley's legacy of scientific skepticism extended to a number of nineteenth- and early twentieth-century writers, including Edgar Allan Poe, H. G. Wells, Sir Arthur Conan

Doyle, and Ambrose Bierce. However, their work tended to be read in the context of philosophically and sociologically speculative fictions in the literary mainstream. "Science fiction" was not perceived as a genre distinct from any other type of fiction until 1926, when *Amazing Stories,* the first magazine devoted exclusively to science fiction, appeared at the newsstands. Three years before the advent of *Amazing,* however, *Weird Tales,* the first magazine devoted exclusively to fantasy and horror fiction, began offering its readers a story type known as the "weird scientific" tale. The most basic difference between the science fiction and weird scientific story was the latter's typically bleak outlook: it portrayed a universe openly hostile to human endeavor, which man could never master but only hope to defend himself against.

The weird scientific tale became a staple of both the weird fiction magazines and, to a lesser extent, science fiction magazines. Most weird scientific stories were little more than conventional terror tales tricked out in high-tech garb, featuring the stock props of horror fiction: mad scientists, flesh-eating monsters, and bookish dilettantes prying foolishly into the unknown. In the hands of a few writers, though, the weird scientific story became a vehicle for exploring man's relationship with an incomprehensibly vast and alienating universe.

The greatest of these writers was H. P. Lovecraft. Although acknowledged today as the most important American writer of horror fiction in the twentieth century, Lovecraft wrote stories strongly informed by the scientific understanding of his time. A staunch materialist, he believed that the increased knowledge that science yielded would only impress upon the human species its insignificance in the cosmic scheme of things. Lovecraft expressed the indifference of the universe to human needs and concerns by distilling the cosmic forces that shape existence into alien creatures who wreak havoc whenever they enter our sphere. His 1927 story, "The Colour Out of Space," is a fine example of this philosophy of "cosmic indifferentism": essentially a tale of extraterrestrial invasion, it eschews any attempt to explain the alien visitor or its motives, and focuses instead on the devastating impact of alien contact with human beings.

Many of Lovecraft's *Weird Tales* colleagues shared his skepticism of scientific progress. "The Vaults of Yoh-Vombis" is one of several stories in which Clark Ashton Smith envisioned the dangers awaiting human travelers to other worlds as those of the charnel house. In "The Man with a Thousand Legs," Frank Belknap Long saw science as a dangerous tool in the hands of flawed human beings.

It was partly in response to morbid extrapolations of science like these that John W. Campbell turned *Astounding Science Fiction* into a bastion of rationalism when he began editing the magazine in 1937. Campbell had spent his salad days writing super-science epics, which typically featured scientist heroes saving the universe through their technological prowess. As a science fiction editor, he asked writers to set their stories in worlds where scientific sophistication shaped the characters and their adventures. By denying the hysterical responses to science in the weird science story, Campbell helped science fiction evolve from a mere offshoot of the fantasy tale to a discrete fiction with ideas of its own. Horror did not disappear entirely from the genre while Campbell ruled the science fiction roost, but tended to manifest in a manageable form, as in his own "Who Goes There?" wherein an alien life form with shape-shifting capabilities equal to those of any supernatural monster's is vanquished with the help of the scientific method.

Campbell did openly invite horror into the pages of *Unknown,* the fantasy companion to *Astounding* that he edited between 1939 and 1943. His only caveat was that the premise for any horror story be developed with the same rigorous logic that went into plotting science fiction. Not surprisingly, *Unknown* attracted more science fiction than weird fiction writers, and yielded stories whose modern settings and situations provided a credible counterpoint to their twisted probabilities. A prime example is Robert A. Heinlein's masterpiece of paranoia, "They," which inflates the simple rationale of a conspiracy theory to literally universal proportions.

Paranoia is, of course, one of the basic building blocks of horror fiction, and despite Campbell's efforts to separate the two genres, it became an integral part of science fiction in the years following World War II. The timeless paranoia of unseen things that go bump in the night is at the heart of Arthur C. Clarke's "A Walk in the Dark," a well-told science fiction campfire story, and Ray Bradbury's "Asleep in Armageddon," a spooky space age bedtime story whose objective is to scare the reader into not wanting to go to sleep. But a different kind of paranoia growing out of contemporary social anxieties darkens much science fiction from this period, presaged by Robert Bloch's 1943 revolt-of-the-machines story "It Happened Tomorrow," a cautionary tale about mankind's displacement by his own technology. Science fiction is never about the futures it projects so much as the time in which it is written, and this is fairly obvious from the apprehension of nuclear armageddon addressed in Isaac Asimov's "Hell-Fire," the horrors of mutation expressed in Richard Matheson's "Born of Man and Woman," and the fear of "The Other" that permeates Philip K. Dick's "The Father Thing," and allows one to read it as both a story of body-snatching aliens and an allegory of America's Red Scare paranoia.

Within the last twenty-five years science fiction has increasingly come to serve as a modern mythology by which writers devise novel embodiments of humanity's fears and concerns and offer them up for our analysis. Some of their stories deal with timeless fears: physical violation in Dean Koontz's "Nightmare Gang," loss of personal control in David Morrell's "Orange Is for Anguish, Blue for Insanity," and subjugation of the powerless by the powerful in John Shirley's "Ticket to Heaven." Others speak more directly to the bewildering and frightening incursion of modern science into the most intimate areas of human life: the family in F. Paul Wilson's "Soft," the hospital room in Dan Simmons's "Metastasis," and the very genetic code that makes us human in Clive Barker's "The Age of Desire." If the persistent fears these stories address tell us anything, it's that for every fear scientific progress allays it creates entirely new ones.

The stories in *Between Time and Terror* were selected to shed light on this dark side of science fiction. Some are classics of their kind, others lesser-known works by writers renowned for their straight science fiction or horror fiction. As many appeared originally in science fiction books and magazines as in horror publications. Taken as a whole, they describe a venerable twentieth-century tradition of speculative fiction writers looking ahead to the future with the same dread they feel when looking back over their shoulders.

—Stefan Dziemianowicz
New York, 1995

The Colour Out of Space
H. P. Lovecraft

Although acknowledged as the greatest American writer of horror fiction since Edgar Allan Poe, H. P. Lovecraft (1890–1937) based many of his best-known stories on science fiction concepts: time travel in "The Shadow Out of Time," extraterrestrial life in "At the Mountains of Madness," and alien invasion in "The Colour Out of Space." Invariably, Lovecraft used science fiction motifs to suggest worlds and forces that defied human understanding. "The Colour Out of Space" was published in the July 1927 issue of the science fiction magazine *Amazing Stories,* where it was lauded as an instant classic even though lacking any hard scientific substance. It has been filmed twice as *Die, Monster, Die* in 1965 and *The Curse* in 1988.

West of Arkham the hills rise wild, and there are valleys with deep woods that no axe has ever cut. There are dark narrow glens where the trees slope fantastically, and where thin brooklets trickle without ever having caught the glint of sunlight. On the gentler slopes there are farms, ancient and rocky, with squat, moss-coated cottages brooding eternally over old New England secrets in the lee of great ledges; but these are all vacant now; the wide chimneys crumbling and the shingled sides bulging perilously beneath low gambrel roofs.

The old folk have gone away, and foreigners do not like to live there. French-Canadians have tried it, Italians have tried it, and the Poles have come and departed. It is not because of anything that can be seen or heard or handled, but because of something that is imagined. The place is not good for imagination, and does not bring restful dreams at night. It must be this which keeps the foreigners away, for old Ammi Pierce has never told them of anything he recalls from the strange days. Ammi, whose head has been a little

queer for years, is the only one who still remains, or who
ever talks of the strange days; and he dares to do this because his house is so near the open fields and the travelled
roads around Arkham.

There was once a road over the hills and through the valleys, that ran straight where the blasted heath is now; but
people ceased to use it and a new road was laid curving far
toward the south. Traces of the old one can still be found
amidst the weeds of a returning wilderness, and some of
them will doubtless linger even when half the hollows are
flooded for the new reservoir. Then the dark woods will be
cut down and the blasted heath will slumber far below blue
waters whose surface will mirror the sky and ripple in the
sun. And the secrets of the strange days will be one with the
deep's secrets; one with the hidden lore of old ocean, and all
the mystery of primal earth.

When I went into the hills and vales to survey for the new
reservoir they told me the place was evil. They told me this
in Arkham, and because that is a very old town full of witch
legends I thought the evil must be something which gran-
dams had whispered to children through centuries. The name
'blasted heath' seemed to me very odd and theatrical, and I
wondered how it had come into the folklore of a Puritan
people. Then I saw that dark westward tangle of glens and
slopes for myself, and ceased to wonder at anything beside
its own elder mystery. It was morning when I saw it, but
shadow lurked always there. The trees grew too thickly, and
their trunks were too big for any healthy New England
wood. There was too much silence in the dim alleys between
them, and the floor was too soft with the dank moss and
mattings of infinite years of decay.

In the open spaces, mostly along the line of the old road,
there were little hillside farms; sometimes with all the buildings standing, sometimes with only one or two, and sometimes with only a lone chimney or fast-filling cellar. Weeds
and briers reigned, and furtive wild things rustled in the un-
dergrowth. Upon everything was a haze of restlessness and
oppression; a touch of the unreal and the grotesque, as if
some vital element of perspective or chiaroscuro were awry.
I did not wonder that the foreigners would not stay, for this
was no region to sleep in. It was too much like a landscape
of Salvator Rosa; too much like some forbidden woodcut in
a tale of terror.

But even all this was not so bad as the blasted heath. I knew it the moment I came upon it at the bottom of a spacious valley; for no other name could fit such a thing, or any other thing fit such a name. It was as if the poet had coined the phrase from having seen this one particular region. It must, I thought as I viewed it, be the outcome of a fire; but why had nothing new ever grown over those five acres of grey desolation that sprawled open to the sky like a great spot eaten by acid in the woods and fields? It lay largely to the north of the ancient road line, but encroached a little on the other side. I felt an odd reluctance about approaching, and did so at last only because my business took me through and past it. There was no vegetation of any kind on that broad expanse, but only a fine grey dust or ash which no wind seemed ever to blow about. The trees near it were sickly and stunted, and many dead trunks stood or lay rotting at the rim. As I walked hurriedly by I saw the tumbled bricks and stones of an old chimney and cellar on my right, and the yawning black maw of an abandoned well whose stagnant vapours played strange tricks with the hues of the sunlight. Even the long, dark woodland climb beyond seemed welcome in contrast, and I marvelled no more at the frightened whispers of Arkham people. There had been no house or ruin near; even in the old days the place must have been lonely and remote. And at twilight, dreading to repass that ominous spot, I walked circuitously back to the town by the curving road on the south. I vaguely wished some clouds would gather, for an odd timidity about the deep skyey voids above had crept into my soul.

In the evening I asked old people in Arkham about the blasted heath, and what was meant by that phrase 'strange days' which so many evasively muttered. I could not, however, get any good answers, except that all the mystery was much more recent than I had dreamed. It was not a matter of old legendry at all, but something within the lifetime of those who spoke. It had happened in the 'eighties, and a family had disappeared or was killed. Speakers would not be exact; and because they all told me to pay no attention to old Ammi Pierce's crazy tales, I sought him out the next morning, having heard that he lived alone in the ancient tottering cottage where the trees first begin to get very thick. It was a fearsomely ancient place, and had begun to exude the faint miasmal odour which clings about houses that have stood too long. Only with persistent knocking could I rouse the aged man, and when he shuffled timidly to the door I could tell he was not glad to see me. He was not so feeble as I had expected; but his eyes drooped in a curious way, and his unkempt clothing and white beard made him seem very worn and dismal.

Not knowing just how he could best be launched on his tales, I feigned a matter of business; told him of my surveying, and asked vague questions about the district. He was far brighter and more educated than I had been led to think, and before I knew it had grasped quite as much of the subject as any man I had talked with in Arkham. He was not like other rustics I had known in the sections where reservoirs were to be. From him there were no protests at the miles of old wood and farmland to be blotted out, though perhaps there would have been had not his home lain outside the bounds of the future lake. Relief was all that he showed; relief at the doom of the dark ancient valleys through which he had roamed all his life. They were better under water now—better under water since the strange days. And with this opening his husky voice sank low, while his body leaned forward and his right forefinger began to point shakily and impressively.

It was then that I heard the story, and as the rambling voice scraped and whispered on I shivered again and again despite the summer day. Often I had to recall the speaker from ramblings, piece out scientific points which he knew only by a fading parrot memory of professors' talk, or bridge over gaps where his sense of logic and continuity broke down. When he was done I did not wonder that his mind had snapped a trifle, or that the folk of Arkham would not speak much of the blasted heath. I hurried back before sunset to my hotel, unwilling to have the stars come out above me in the open; and the next day returned to Boston to give up my position. I could not go into that dim chaos of old forest and slope again, or face another time that grey blasted heath where the black well yawned deep beside the tumbled bricks and stones. The reservoir will soon be built now, and all those elder secrets will be safe forever under watery fathoms. But even then I do not believe I would like to visit that country by night—at least not when the sinister stars are out; and nothing could bribe me to drink the new city water of Arkham.

It all began, old Ammi said, with the meteorite. Before that time there had been no wild legends at all since the witch trials, and even then these western woods were not feared half so much as the small island in the Miskatonic where the devil held court beside a curious stone altar older than the Indians. These were not haunted woods, and their fantastic dusk was never terrible till the strange days. Then there had come that white noontide cloud, that string of explosions in the air, and that pillar of smoke from the valley far in the wood. And by night all Arkham had heard of the great rock that fell out of the sky and bedded itself in the ground beside the well at the Nahum Gardner place. That was the house which had stood where the blasted heath was to come—the trim white Nahum Gardner house amidst its fertile gardens and orchards.

Nahum had come to town to tell people about the stone, and dropped in at Ammi Pierce's on the way. Ammi was forty then, and all the queer things were fixed very strongly in his mind. He and his wife had gone with the three professors from Miskatonic University who hastened out the next morning to see the weird visitor from unknown stellar space, and had wondered why Nahum had called it so large the day before. It had shrunk, Nahum said, as he pointed out the big brownish mound above the ripped earth and charred grass near the archaic well-sweep in his front yard; but the wise men answered that stones do not shrink. Its heat lingered persistently, and Nahum declared it had glowed faintly in the night. The professors tried it with a geologist's hammer and found it was oddly soft. It was, in truth, so soft as to be almost plastic; and they gouged rather than chipped a specimen to take back to the college for testing. They took it in an old pail borrowed from Nahum's kitchen, for even the small piece refused to grow cool. On the trip back they stopped at Ammi's to rest, and seemed thoughtful when Mrs. Pierce remarked that the fragment was growing smaller and burning the bottom of the pail. Truly, it was not large, but perhaps they had taken less than they thought.

The day after that—all this was in June of '82—the professors had trooped out again in a great excitement. As they passed Ammi's they told him what queer things the specimen had done, and how it had faded wholly away when they put it in a glass beaker. The beaker had gone, too, and the wise men talked of the strange stone's affinity for silicon. It

had acted quite unbelievably in that well-ordered laboratory;
doing nothing at all and showing no occluded gases when
heated on charcoal, being wholly negative in the borax bead,
and soon proving itself absolutely non-volatile at any pro-
ducible temperature, including that of the oxy-hydrogen
blowpipe. On an anvil it appeared highly malleable, and in
the dark its luminosity was very marked. Stubbornly refusing to grow cool, it soon had the college in a state of real excitement; and when upon heating before the spectroscope it
displayed shining bands unlike any known colours of the
normal spectrum there was much breathless talk of new elements, bizarre optical properties, and other things which
puzzled men of science are wont to say when faced by the
unknown.

Hot as it was, they tested it in a crucible with all the
proper reagents. Water did nothing. Hydrochloric acid was
the same. Nitric acid and even aqua regia merely hissed and
spattered against its torrid invulnerability. Ammi had difficulty in recalling all these things, but recognized some solvents as I mentioned them in the usual order of use. There
were ammonia and caustic soda, alcohol and ether, nauseous
carbon disulphide and a dozen others; but although the
weight grew steadily less as time passed, and the fragment
seemed to be slightly cooling, there was no change in the
solvents to show that they had attacked the substance at all.
It was a metal, though, beyond a doubt. It was magnetic, for
one thing; and after its immersion in the acid solvents there
seemed to be faint traces of the Widmänstätten figures found
on meteoric iron. When the cooling had grown very considerable, the testing was carried on in glass; and it was in a
glass beaker that they left all the chips made of the original
fragment during the work. The next morning both chips and
beaker were gone without trace, and only a charred spot
marked the place on the wooden shelf where they had been.

All this the professors told Ammi as they paused at his
door, and once more he went with them to see the stony
messenger from the stars, though this time his wife did not
accompany him. It had now most certainly shrunk, and even
the sober professors could not doubt the truth of what they
saw. All around the dwindling brown lump near the well was
a vacant space, except where the earth had caved in; and
whereas it had been a good seven feet across the day before,
it was now scarcely five. It was still hot, and the sages stud-

ied its surface curiously as they detached another and larger piece with hammer and chisel. They gouged deeply this time, and as they pried away the smaller mass they saw that the core of the thing was not quite homogeneous.

They had uncovered what seemed to be the side of a large coloured globule embedded in the substance. The colour, which resembled some of the bands in the meteor's strange spectrum, was almost impossible to describe; and it was only by analogy that they called it colour at all. Its texture was glossy, and upon tapping it appeared to promise both brittleness and hollowness. One of the professors gave it a smart blow with a hammer, and it burst with a nervous little pop. Nothing was emitted, and all trace of the thing vanished with the puncturing. It left behind a hollow spherical space about three inches across, and all thought it probable that others would be discovered as the enclosing substance wasted away.

Conjecture was vain; so after a futile attempt to find additional globules by drilling, the seekers left again with their new specimen—which proved, however, as baffling in the laboratory as its predecessor. Aside from being almost plastic, having heat, magnetism, and slight luminosity, cooling slightly in powerful acids, possessing an unknown spectrum, wasting away in air, and attacking silicon compounds with mutual destruction as a result, it presented no identifying features whatsoever; and at the end of the tests the college scientists were forced to own that they could not place it. It was nothing of this earth, but a piece of the great outside; and as such dowered with outside properties and obedient to outside laws.

That night there was a thunderstorm, and when the professors went out to Nahum's the next day they met with a bitter disappointment. The stone, magnetic as it had been, must have had some peculiar electrical property; for it had 'drawn the lightning,' as Nahum said, with a singular persistence. Six times within an hour the farmer saw the lightning strike the furrow in the front yard, and when the storm was over nothing remained but a ragged pit by the ancient well-sweep, half-choked with a caved-in earth. Digging had borne no fruit, and the scientists verified the fact of the utter vanishment. The failure was total; so that nothing was left to do but go back to the laboratory and test again the disappearing fragment left carefully cased in lead. That fragment lasted a week, at the end of which nothing of value had been learned of it. When it had gone, no residue was left behind, and in time the professors felt scarcely sure they had indeed seen with waking eyes that cryptic vestige of the fathomless gulfs outside; that lone, weird message from other universes and other realms of matter, force, and entity.

As was natural, the Arkham papers made much of the incident with its collegiate sponsoring, and sent reporters to talk with Nahum Gardner and his family. At least one Boston daily also sent a scribe, and Nahum quickly became a kind of local celebrity. He was a lean, genial person of about fifty, living with his wife and three sons on the pleasant farmstead in the valley. He and Ammi exchanged visits frequently, as did their wives; and Ammi had nothing but praise for him after all these years. He seemed slightly proud of the notice his place had attracted, and talked often of the meteorite in the succeeding weeks. That July and August were hot; and Nahum worked hard at his haying in the ten-acre pasture across Chapman's Brook; his rattling wain wearing deep ruts in the shadowy lanes between. The labour tired him more than it had in other years, and he felt that age was beginning to tell on him.

Then fell the time of fruit and harvest. The pears and apples slowly ripened, and Nahum vowed that his orchards were prospering as never before. The fruit was growing to phenomenal size and unwonted gloss, and in such abundance that extra barrels were ordered to handle the future crop. But with the ripening came sore disappointment, for of all that gorgeous array of specious lusciousness not one single jot was fit to eat. Into the fine flavour of the pears and apples had crept a stealthy bitterness and sickishness, so that even the smallest bites induced a lasting disgust. It was the same with the melons and tomatoes, and Nahum sadly saw that his entire crop was lost. Quick to connect events, he declared that the meteorite had poisoned the soil, and thanked Heaven that most of the other crops were in the upland lot along the road.

Winter came early, and was very cold. Ammi saw Nahum less often than usual, and observed that he had begun to look worried. The rest of his family too, seemed to have grown taciturn; and were far from steady in their church-going or their attendance at the various social events of the countryside. For this reserve or melancholy no cause could be

found, though all the household confessed now and then to
poorer health and a feeling of vague disquiet. Nahum himself gave the most definite statement of anyone when he said
he was disturbed about certain footprints in the snow. They
were the usual winter prints of red squirrels, white rabbits,
and foxes, but the brooding farmer professed to see something not quite right about their nature and arrangement. He
was never specific, but appeared to think that they were not
as characteristic of the anatomy and habits of squirrels and
rabbits and foxes as they ought to be. Ammi listened without
interest to this talk until one night when he drove past Nahum's house in his sleigh on the way back from Clark's Corners. There had been a moon, and a rabbit had run across the
road, and the leaps of that rabbit were longer than either
Ammi or his horse liked. The latter, indeed, had almost run
away when brought up by a firm rein. Thereafter Ammi
gave Nahum's tales more respect, and wondered why the
Gardner dogs seemed so cowed and quivering every morning. They had, it developed, nearly lost the spirit to bark.

In February the McGregor boys from Meadow Hill were
out shooting woodchucks, and not far from the Gardner
place bagged a very peculiar specimen. The proportions of
its body seemed slightly altered in a queer way impossible to
describe, while its face had taken on an expression which no
one ever saw in a woodchuck before. The boys were genu-
inely frightened, and threw the thing away at once, so that
only their grotesque tales of it ever reached the people of the
countryside. But the shying of horses near Nahum's house
had now become an acknowledged thing, and all the basis
for a cycle of whispered legend was fast taking form.

People vowed that the snow melted faster around Nahum's than it did anywhere else, and early in March there
was an awed discussion in Potter's general store at Clark's
Corners. Stephen Rice had driven past Gardner's in the
morning, and had noticed the skunk-cabbages coming up
through the mud by the woods across the road. Never were
things of such size seen before, and they held strange colours that could not be put into any words. Their shapes were
monstrous, and the horse had snorted at an odour which
struck Stephen as wholly unprecedented. That afternoon several persons drove past to see the abnormal growth, and all
agreed that plants of that kind ought never to sprout in a
healthy world. The bad fruit of the fall before was freely

mentioned, and it went from mouth to mouth that there was poison in Nahum's ground. Of course it was the meteorite; and remembering how strange the men from the college had found that stone to be, several farmers spoke about the matter to them.

One day they paid Nahum a visit; but having no love of wild tales and folklore were very conservative in what they inferred. The plants were certainly odd, but all skunk-cabbages are more or less odd in shape and hue. Perhaps some mineral element from the stone had entered the soil, but it would soon be washed away. And as for the footprints and frightened horses—of course this was mere country talk which such a phenomenon as the aerolite would be certain to start. There was really nothing for serious men to do in cases of wild gossip, for superstitious rustics will say and believe anything. And so all through the strange days the professors stayed away in contempt. Only one of them, when given two phials of dust for analysis in a police job over a year and a half later, recalled that the queer colour of that skunk-cabbage had been very like one of the anomalous bands of light shown by the meteor fragment in the college spectroscope, and like the brittle globule found imbedded in the stone from the abyss. The samples in this analysis case gave the same odd bands at first, though later they lost the property.

The trees budded prematurely around Nahum's, and at night they swayed ominously in the wind. Nahum's second son Thaddeus, a lad of fifteen, swore that they swayed also when there was no wind; but even the gossips would not credit this. Certainly, however, restlessness was in the air. The entire Gardner family developed the habit of stealthy listening, though not for any sound which they could consciously name. The listening was, indeed, rather a product of moments when consciousness seemed half to slip away. Unfortunately such moments increased week by week, till it became common speech that 'something was wrong with all Nahum's folks'. When the early saxifrage came out it had another strange colour; not quite that of the skunk-cabbage, but plainly related and equally unknown to anyone who saw it. Nahum took some blossoms to Arkham and showed them to the editor of the *Gazette*, but that dignitary did no more than write a humorous article about them, in which the dark fears of rustics were held up to polite ridicule. It was a mistake of Nahum's to tell a stolid city man about the way the great, overgrown mourning-cloak butterflies behaved in connection with these saxifrages.

April brought a kind of madness to the country folk, and began that disuse of the road past Nahum's which led to its ultimate abandonment. It was the vegetation. All the orchard trees blossomed forth in strange colours, and through the stony soil of the yard and adjacent pasturage there sprang up a bizarre growth which only a botanist could connect with the proper flora of the region. No sane wholesome colours were anywhere to be seen except in the green grass and leafage; but everywhere were those hectic and prismatic variants of some diseased, underlying primary tone without a place among the known tints of earth. The 'Dutchman's breeches' became a thing of sinister menace, and the bloodroots grew insolent in their chromatic perversion. Ammi and the Gardners thought that most of the colours had a sort of haunting familiarity, and decided that they reminded one of the brittle globule in the meteor. Nahum ploughed and sowed the ten-acre pasture and the upland lot, but did nothing with the land around the house. He knew it would be of no use, and hoped that the summer's strange growths would draw all the poison from the soil. He was prepared for almost anything now, and had grown used to the sense of something near him waiting to be heard. The shunning of his house by neighbours told on him, of course; but it told on his wife more. The boys were better off, being at school each day; but they could not help being frightened by the gossip. Thaddeus, an especially sensitive youth, suffered the most.

In May the insects came, and Nahum's place became a nightmare of buzzing and crawling. Most of the creatures seemed not quite usual in their aspects and motions, and their nocturnal habits contradicted all former experience. The Gardners took to watching at night—watching in all directions at random for something—they could not tell what. It was then that they all owned that Thaddeus had been right about the trees. Mrs. Gardner was the next to see it from the window as she watched the swollen boughs of a maple against a moonlit sky. The boughs surely moved, and there was no wind. It must be the sap. Strangeness had come into everything growing now. Yet it was none of Nahum's family at all who made the next discovery. Familiarity had dulled them, and what they could not see was glimpsed by a timid windmill salesman from Bolton who drove by one night in ignorance of the country legends. What he told in Arkham was given a short paragraph in the *Gazette;* and it was there that all the farmers, Nahum included, saw it first. The night had been dark and the buggy-lamps faint, but around a farm in the valley which everyone knew from the account must be Nahum's, the darkness had been less thick. A dim though distinct luminosity seemed to inhere in all the vegetation, grass leaves, and blossoms alike, while at one moment a detached piece of the phosphorescence appeared to stir furtively in the yard near the barn.

The grass had so far seemed untouched, and the cows were freely pastured in the lot near the house, but towards the end of May the milk began to be bad. Then Nahum had the cows driven to the uplands, after which this trouble ceased. Not long after this the change in grass and leaves became apparent to the eye. All the verdure was going grey, and was developing a highly singular quality of brittleness. Ammi was now the only person who ever visited the place, and his visits were becoming fewer and fewer. When school closed the Gardners were virtually cut off from the world, and sometimes let Ammi do their errands in town. They were failing curiously both physically and mentally, and no one was surprised when the news of Mrs. Gardner's madness stole around.

It happened in June, about the anniversary of the meteor's fall, and the poor woman screamed about things in the air which she could not describe. In her raving there was not a single specific noun, but only verbs and pronouns. Things moved and changed and fluttered, and ears tingled to impulses which were not wholly sounds. Something was taken away—she was being drained of something—something was fastening itself on her that ought not to be—someone must make it keep off—nothing was ever still in the night—the walls and windows shifted. Nahum did not send her to the county asylum, but let her wander about the house as long as she was harmless to herself and others. Even when her expression changed he did nothing. But when the boys grew afraid of her, and Thaddeus nearly fainted at the way she made faces at him, he decided to keep her locked in the attic. By July she had ceased to speak and crawled on all fours, and before that month was over Nahum got the mad notion that she was slightly luminous in the dark, as he now clearly saw was the case with the nearby vegetation.

It was a little before this that the horses had stampeded. Something had aroused them in the night, and their neighing and kicking in their stalls had been terrible. There seemed virtually nothing to do to calm them, and when Nahum opened the stable door they all bolted out like frightened woodland deer. It took a week to track all four, and when found they were seen to be quite useless and unmanageable. Something had snapped in their brains, and each one had to be shot for its own good. Nahum borrowed a horse from Ammi for his haying, but found it would not approach the barn. It shied, balked, and whinnied, and in the end he could do nothing but drive it into the yard while the men used their own strength to get the heavy wagon near enough the hay-loft for convenient pitching. And all the while the vegetation was turning grey and brittle. Even the flowers whose hues had been so strange were greying now, and the fruit was coming out grey and dwarfed and tasteless. The asters and golden-rod bloomed grey and distorted, and the roses and zinnias and hollyhocks in the front yard were such blasphemous-looking things that Nahum's oldest boy Zenas cut them down. The strangely puffed insects died about that time, even the bees that had left their hives and taken to the woods.

By September all the vegetation was fast crumbling to a greyish powder, and Nahum feared that the trees would die before the poison was out of the soil. His wife now had spells of terrific screaming, and he and the boys were in a constant state of nervous tension. They shunned people now, and when school opened the boys did not go. But it was Ammi, on one of his rare visits, who first realized that the well water was no longer good. It had an evil taste that was not exactly foetid nor exactly salty, and Ammi advised his friend to dig another well on higher ground to use till the soil was good again. Nahum, however, ignored the warning, for he had by that time become calloused to strange and unpleasant things. He and the boys continued to use the tainted supply, drinking it as listlessly and mechanically as they ate their meagre and ill-cooked meals and did their thankless and monotonous chores through the aimless days. There was something of stolid resignation about them all, as if they

walked half in another world between lines of nameless
guards to a certain and familiar doom.

Thaddeus went mad in September after a visit to the well.
He had gone with a pail and had come back empty-handed,
shrieking and waving his arms, and sometimes lapsing into
an inane titter or a whisper about 'the moving colours down
there.' Two in one family was pretty bad, but Nahum was
very brave about it. He let the boy run about for a week until
he began stumbling and hurting himself, and then he shut
him in an attic room across the hall from his mother's. The
way they screamed at each other from behind their locked
doors was very terrible, especially to little Merwin, who fancied they talked in some terrible language that was not of
earth. Merwin was getting frightfully imaginative, and his
restlessness was worse after the shutting away of the brother
who had been his greatest playmate.

Almost at the same time the mortality among the livestock
commenced. Poultry turned greyish and died very quickly,
their meat being found dry and noisome upon cutting. Hogs
grew inordinately fat, then suddenly began to undergo loathsome changes which no one could explain. Their meat was
of course useless, and Nahum was at his wits' end. No rural
veterinary would approach his place, and the city veterinary
from Arkham was openly baffled. The swine began growing
grey and brittle and falling to pieces before they died, and
their eyes and muzzles developed singular alterations. It was
very inexplicable, for they had never been fed from the
tainted vegetation. Then something struck the cows. Certain
areas or sometimes the whole body would be uncannily
shrivelled or compressed, and atrocious collapses or disinte-
grations were common. In the last stages—and death was always the result—there would be a greying and turning brittle
like that which beset the hogs. There could be no question
of poison, for all the cases occurred in a locked and undisturbed barn. No bites of prowling things could have brought
the virus, for what live beast of earth can pass through solid
obstacles? It must be only natural disease—yet what disease
could wreak such results was beyond any mind's guessing.
When the harvest came there was not an animal surviving on
the place, for the stock and poultry were dead and the dogs
had run away. These dogs, three in number, had all vanished
one night and were never heard of again. The five cats had
left some time before, but their going was scarcely noticed

since there now seemed to be no mice, and only Mrs. Gardner had made pets of the graceful felines.

On the nineteenth of October Nahum staggered into Ammi's house with hideous news. The death had come to poor Thaddeus in his attic room, and it had come in a way which could not be told. Nahum had dug a grave in the railed family plot behind the farm, and had put therein what he found. There could have been nothing from outside, for the small barred window and locked door were intact; but it was much as it had been in the barn. Ammi and his wife consoled the stricken man as best they could, but shuddered as they did so. Stark terror seemed to cling round the Gardners and all they touched, and the very presence of one in the house was a breath from regions unnamed and unnameable. Ammi accompanied Nahum home with the greatest reluctance, and did what he might to calm the hysterical sobbing of little Merwin. Zenas needed no calming. He had come of late to do nothing but stare into space and obey what his father told him; and Ammi thought that his fate was very merciful. Now and then Merwin's screams were answered faintly from the attic, and in response to an inquiring look Nahum said that his wife was getting very feeble. When night approached, Ammi managed to get away; for not even friendship could make him stay in that spot when the faint glow of the vegetation began and the trees may or may not have swayed without wind. It was really lucky for Ammi that he was not more imaginative. Even as things were, his mind was bent ever so slightly; but had he been able to connect and reflect upon all the portents around him he must inevitably have turned a total maniac. In the twilight he hastened home, the screams of the mad woman and the nervous child ringing horribly in his ears.

Three days later Nahum burst into Ammi's kitchen in the early morning, and in the absence of his host stammered out a desperate tale once more, while Mrs. Pierce listened in a clutching fright. It was little Merwin this time. He was gone. He had gone out late at night with a lantern and pail for water, and had never come back. He'd been going to pieces for days, and hardly knew what he was about. Screamed at everything. There had been a frantic shriek from the yard then, but before the father could get to the door the boy was gone. There was no glow from the lantern he had taken, and of the child himself no trace. At the time Nahum thought the lan-

tern and pail were gone too; but when dawn came, and the
man had plodded back from his all-night search of the
woods and fields, he had found some very curious things
near the well. There was a crushed and apparently somewhat
melted mass of iron which had certainly been the lantern;
while a bent handle and twisted iron hoops beside it, both
half-fused, seemed to hint at the remnants of the pail. That
was all. Nahum was past imagining, Mrs. Pierce was blank,
and Ammi, when he had reached home and heard the tale,
could give no guess. Merwin was gone, and there would be
no use in telling the people around, who shunned all
Gardners now. No use, either, in telling the city people at
Arkham who laughed at everything. Thad was gone, and
now Merwin was gone. Something was creeping and creeping and waiting to be seen and heard. Nahum would go
soon, and he wanted Ammi to look after his wife and Zenas
if they survived him. It must all be a judgment of some sort;
though he could not fancy what for, since he had always
walked uprightly in the Lord's ways so far as he knew.

For over two weeks Ammi saw nothing of Nahum; and
then, worried about what might have happened, he overcame
his fears and paid the Gardner place a visit. There was no
smoke from the great chimney, and for a moment the visitor
was apprehensive of the worst. The aspect of the whole farm
was shocking—greyish withered grass and leaves on the
ground, vines falling in brittle wreckage from archaic walls
and gables, and great bare trees clawing up at the grey No-
vember sky with a studied malevolence which Ammi could
not but feel had come from some subtle change in the tilt of
the branches. But Nahum was alive, after all. He was weak,
and lying on a couch in the low-ceiled kitchen, but perfectly
conscious and able to give simple orders to Zenas. The room
was deadly cold; and as Ammi visibly shivered, the host
shouted huskily to Zenas for more wood. Wood, indeed, was
sorely needed; since the cavernous fireplace was unlit and
empty, with a cloud of soot blowing about in the chill wind
that came down the chimney. Presently Nahum asked him if
the extra wood had made him any more comfortable, and
then Ammi saw what had happened. The stoutest cord had
broken at last, and the hapless farmer's mind was proof
against more sorrow.

Questioning tactfully, Ammi could get no clear data at all
about the missing Zenas. 'In the well—he lives in the

well—' was all that the clouded father would say. Then
there flashed across the visitor's mind a sudden thought of
the mad wife, and he changed his line of inquiry. 'Nabby?
Why, here she is!' was the surprised response of poor Nahum, and Ammi soon saw that he must search for himself.
Leaving the harmless babbler on the couch, he took the keys
from their nail beside the door and climbed the creaking
stairs to the attic. It was very close and noisome up there,
and no sound could be heard from any direction. Of the four
doors in sight only one was locked, and on this he tried various keys of the ring he had taken. The third key proved the
right one, and after some fumbling Ammi threw open the
low white door.

It was quite dark inside, for the window was small and
half-obscured by the crude wooden bars; and Ammi could
see nothing at all on the wide-planked floor. The stench was
beyond enduring, and before proceeding further he had to retreat to another room and return with his lungs filled with
breathable air. When he did enter he saw something dark in
the corner, and upon seeing it more clearly he screamed out-
right. While he screamed he thought a momentary cloud
eclipsed the window, and a second later he felt himself
brushed as if by some hateful current of vapour. Strange colours danced before his eyes; and had not a present horror
numbed him he would have thought of the globule in the
meteor that the geologist's hammer had shattered, and of the
morbid vegetation that had sprouted in the spring. As it was
he thought only of the blasphemous monstrosity which confronted him, and which all too clearly had shared the nameless fate of young Thaddeus and the live-stock. But the
terrible thing about the horror was that it very slowly and
perceptibly moved as it continued to crumble.

Ammi would give me no added particulars of this scene,
but the shape in the corner does not reappear in his tale as
a moving object. There are things which cannot be mentioned, and what is done in common humanity is sometimes
cruelly judged by the law. I gathered that no moving thing
was left in that attic room, and that to leave anything capable of motion there would have been a deed so monstrous as
to damn any accountable being to eternal torment. Anyone
but a stolid farmer would have fainted or gone mad, but
Ammi walked conscious through that low doorway and
locked the accursed secret behind him. There would be Na-

hum to deal with now; he must be fed and tended, and re-moved to some place where he could be cared for.

Commencing his descent of the dark stairs, Ammi heard a thud below him. He even thought a scream had been sud-denly choked off, and recalled nervously the clammy vapour which had brushed by him in that frightful room above. What presence had his cry and entry started up? Halted by some vague fear, he heard still further sounds below. Indubi-tably there was a sort of heavy dragging, and a most detest-ably sticky noise as of some fiendish and unclean species of suction. With an associative sense goaded to feverish heights, he thought unaccountably of what he had seen up-stairs. Good God! What eldritch dream-world was this into which he had blundered? He dared move neither backward nor forward, but stood there trembling at the black curve of the boxed-in staircase. Every trifle of the scene burned itself into his brain. The sounds, the sense of dread expectancy, the darkness, the steepness of the narrow steps—and merci-ful Heaven!—the faint but unmistakable luminosity of all the woodwork in sight; steps, sides, exposed laths, and beams alike.

Then there burst forth a frantic whinny from Ammi's horse outside, followed at once by a clatter which told of a frenzied runaway. In another moment horse and buggy had gone beyond earshot, leaving the frightened man on the dark stairs to guess what had sent them. But that was not all. There had been another sound out there. A sort of liquid splash—water—it must have been the well. He had left Hero untied near it, and a buggy-wheel must have brushed the coping and knocked in a stone. And still the pale phospho-rescence glowed in that detestably ancient woodwork. God! how old the house was! Most of it built before 1670, and the gambrel roof no later than 1730.

A feeble scratching on the floor downstairs now sounded distinctly, and Ammi's grip tightened on a heavy stick he had picked up in the attic for some purpose. Slowly nerving himself, he finished his descent and walked boldly toward the kitchen. But he did not complete the walk, because what he sought was no longer there. It had come to meet him, and it was still alive after a fashion. Whether it had crawled or whether it had been dragged by any external forces, Ammi could not say; but the death had been at it. Everything had happened in the last half-hour, but collapse, greying, and disintegration were already far advanced. There was a horrible brittleness, and dry fragments were scaling off. Ammi could not touch it, but looked horrifiedly into the distorted parody that had been a face. 'What was it, Nahum—what was it?' he whispered, and the cleft, bulging lips were just able to crackle out a final answer.

'Nothin' ... nothin' ... the colour ... it burns ... cold an' wet, but it burns ... it lived in the well.... I seen it ... a kind of smoke ... jest like the flowers last spring ... the well shone at night ... Thad an' Merwin an' Zenas ... everything alive ... suckin' the life out of everything ... in that stone ... it must a' come in that stone ... pizened the whole place ... dun't know what it wants ... that round thing them men from the college dug outen the stone ... they smashed it ... it was that same colour ... jest the same, like the flowers an' plants ... must a' ben more of 'em ... seeds ... seeds ... they growed ... I seen it the fust time this week ... must a' got strong on Zenas ... he was a big boy, full o' life ... it beats down your mind an' then gets ye ... burns ye up ... in the well water ... you was right about that ... evil water ... Zenas never come back from the well ... can't git away ... draws ye ... ye know summ'at's comin' but tain't no use ... I seen it time an' agin senct Zenas was took ... whar's Nabby, Ammi? ... my head's no good ... dun't know how long since I fed her ... it'll git her ef we ain't keerful ... jest a colour ... her face is gittin' to hev that colour sometimes towards night ... an' it burns an' sucks ... it come from some place whar things ain't as they is here ... one o' them professors said so ... he was right ... look out, Ammi, it'll do suthin' more ... sucks the life out ...'

But that was all. That which spoke could speak no more because it had completely caved in. Ammi laid a red checked tablecloth over what was left and reeled out the back door into the fields. He climbed the slope to the ten-acre pasture and stumbled home by the north road and the woods. He could not pass that well from which his horses had run away. He had looked at it through the window, and had seen that no stone was missing from the rim. Then the lurching buggy had not dislodged anything after all—the splash had been something else—something which went into the well after it had done with poor Nahum....

When Ammi reached his house the horses and buggy had

arrived before him and thrown his wife into fits of anxiety. Reassuring her without explanations, he set out at once for Arkham and notified the authorities that the Gardner family was no more. He indulged in no details, but merely told of the deaths of Nahum and Nabby, that of Thaddeus being already known, and mentioned that the cause seemed to be the same strange ailment which had killed the live-stock. He also stated that Merwin and Zenas had disappeared. There was considerable questioning at the police station, and in the end Ammi was compelled to take three officers to the Gardner farm, together with the coroner, the medical examiner, and the veterinary who had treated the diseased animals. He went much against his will, for the afternoon was advancing and he feared the fall of night over that accursed place, but it was some comfort to have so many people with him.

The six men drove out in a democrat-wagon, following Ammi's buggy, and arrived at the pest-ridden farmhouse about four o'clock. Used as the officers were to gruesome experiences, not one remained unmoved at what was found in the attic and under the red checked tablecloth on the floor below. The whole aspect of the farm with its grey desolation was terrible enough, but those two crumbling objects were beyond all bounds. No one could look long at them, and even the medical examiner admitted that there was very little to examine. Specimens could be analysed, of course, so he busied himself in obtaining them—and here it develops that a very puzzling aftermath occurred at the college laboratory where the two phials of dust were finally taken. Under the spectroscope both samples gave off an unknown spectrum, in which many of the baffling bands were precisely like those which the strange meteor had yielded in the previous year. The property of emitting this spectrum vanished in a month, the dust thereafter consisting mainly of alkaline phosphates and carbonates.

Ammi would not have told the men about the well if he had thought they meant to do anything then and there. It was getting toward sunset, and he was anxious to be away. But he could not help glancing nervously at the stony kerb by the great sweep and when a detective questioned him he admitted that Nahum had feared something down there—so much so that he had never even thought of searching it for Merwin or Zenas. After that nothing would do but that they empty and explore the well immediately, so Ammi had to wait trembling while pail after pail of rank water was hauled up and splashed on the soaking ground outside. The men sniffed in disgust at the fluid, and toward the last held their noses against the foetor they were uncovering. It was not so long a job as they had feared it would be since the water was phenomenally low. There is no need to speak too exactly of what they found. Merwin and Zenas were both there, in part, though the vestiges were mainly skeletal. There were also a small deer and a large dog in about the same state and a number of bones of small animals. The ooze and slime at the bottom seemed inexplicably porous and bubbling, and a man who descended on hand-holds with a long pole found that he could sink the wooden shaft to any depth in the mud of the floor without meeting any solid obstruction.

Twilight had now fallen, and lanterns were brought from the house. Then, when it was seen that nothing further could be gained from the well, everyone went indoors and conferred in the ancient sitting-room while the intermittent light of a spectral half-moon played wanly on the grey desolation outside. The men were frankly nonplussed by the entire case, and could find no convincing common element to link the strange vegetable conditions, the unknown disease of live-stock and humans, and the unaccountable deaths of Merwin and Zenas in the tainted well. They had heard the common country talk, it is true; but could not believe that anything contrary to natural law had occurred. No doubt the meteor had poisoned the soil, but the illness of persons and animals who had eaten nothing grown in that soil was another matter. Was it the well water? Very possibly. It might be a good idea to analyse it. But what peculiar madness could have made both boys jump into the well? Their deeds were so similar—and the fragments showed that they had both suffered from the grey brittle death. Why was everything so grey and brittle?

It was the coroner, seated near a window overlooking the yard, who first noticed the glow about the well. Night had fully set in, and all the abhorrent grounds seemed faintly luminous with more than the fitful moonbeams; but this new glow was something definite and distinct, and appeared to shoot up from the black pit like a softened ray from a searchlight, giving dull reflections in the little ground pools where the water had been emptied. It had a very queer colour, and as all the men clustered round the window Ammi gave a violent start. For this strange beam of ghastly miasma was to him of no unfamiliar hue. He had seen that colour before, and feared to think what it might mean. He had seen it in the nasty brittle globule in that aerolite two summers ago, had seen it in the crazy vegetation of the springtime, and had thought he had seen it for an instant that very morning against the small barred window of that terrible attic room where nameless things had happened. It had flashed there a second, and a clammy and hateful current of vapour had brushed past him—and then poor Nahum had been taken by something of that colour. He had said so at the last—said it was like the globule and the plants. After that had come the runaway in the yard and the splash in the well—and now that well was belching forth to the night a pale insidious beam of the same demoniac tint.

It does credit to the alertness of Ammi's mind that he puzzled even at that tense moment over a point which was essentially scientific. He could not but wonder at his gleaning of the same impression from a vapour glimpsed in the daytime, against a window opening on the morning sky, and from a nocturnal exhalation seen as a phosphorescent mist against the black and blasted landscape. It wasn't right—it was against Nature—and he thought of those terrible last words of his stricken friend, 'It come from some place whar things ain't as they is here ... one o' them professors said so. . . .'

All three horses outside, tied to a pair of shrivelled saplings by the road, were now neighing and pawing frantically. The wagon driver started for the door to do something, but Ammi laid a shaky hand on his shoulder. 'Duon't go out thar,' he whispered. 'They's more to this nor what we know. Nahum said somethin' lived in the well that sucks your life out. He said it must be some'at growed from a round ball like one we all seen in the meteor stone that fell a year ago June. Sucks an' burns, he said, an' is jest a cloud of colour like that light out thar now, that ye can hardly see an' can't tell what it is. Nahum thought it feeds on everything livin' an' gits stronger all the time. He said he seen it this last week. It must be somethin' from away off in the sky like the men from the college last year says the meteor stone was. The way it's made an' the way it works ain't like no way o' God's world. It's summ'at from beyond.'

So the men paused indecisively as the light from the well grew stronger and the hitched horses pawed and whinnied in increasing frenzy. It was truly an awful moment; with terror in that ancient and accursed house itself, four monstrous sets of fragments—two from the house and two from the well—in the woodshed behind, and that shaft of unknown and unholy iridescence from the slimy depths in front. Ammi had restrained the driver on impulse, forgetting how uninjured he himself was after the clammy brushing of that coloured vapour in the attic room, but perhaps it is just as well that he acted as he did. No one will ever know what was abroad that night; and though the blasphemy from beyond had not so far hurt any human of unweakened mind, there is no telling what it might not have done at that last moment, with its seemingly increased strength and the special signs of purpose it was soon to display beneath the half-clouded moonlit sky.

All at once one of the detectives at the window gave a short, sharp gasp. The others looked at him, and then quickly followed his own gaze upward to the point at which its idle straying had been suddenly arrested. There was no need for words. What had been disputed in country gossip was disputable no longer and it is because of the thing which every man of that parts agreed in whispering later on, that the strange days are never talked about in Arkham. It is necessary to premise that there was no wind at that hour of the evening. One did arise not long afterward, but there was absolutely none then. Even the dry tips of the lingering hedge-mustard, grey and blighted, and the fringe on the roof of the standing democrat-wagon were unstirred. And yet amid that tense, godless calm the high bare boughs of all the trees in the yard were moving. They were twitching morbidly and spasmodically, clawing in convulsive and epileptic madness at the moonlit clouds; scratching impotently in the noxious air as if jerked by some allied and bodiless line of linkage with subterrene horrors writhing and struggling below the black roots.

Not a man breathed for several seconds. Then a cloud of darker depth passed over the moon, and the silhouette of clutching branches faded out momentarily. At this there was a general cry; muffled with awe, but husky and almost identical from every throat. For the terror had not faded with the silhouette, and in a fearsome instant of deeper darkness the

watchers saw wriggling at that tree-top height a thousand
tiny points of faint and unhallowed radiance, tipping each
bough like the fire of St. Elmo or the flames that come down
on the apostles' heads at Pentecost. It was a monstrous constellation of unnatural light, like a glutted swarm of corpse-
fed fireflies dancing hellish sarabands over an accursed
marsh; and its colour was that same nameless intrusion
which Ammi had come to recognize and dread. All the while
the shaft of phosphorescence from the well was getting
brighter and brighter, bringing, to the minds of the huddled
men, a sense of doom and abnormality. It was no longer
shining out; it was *pouring* out; and as the shapeless stream
of unplaceable colour left the well it seemed to flow directly
into the sky.

The veterinary shivered, and walked to the front door to
drop the heavy extra bar across it. Ammi shook no less, and
had to tug and point for lack of controllable voice when he
wished to draw notice to the growing luminosity of the trees.
The neighing and stamping of the horses had become utterly
frightful, but not a soul of that group in the old house would
have ventured forth for any earthly reward. With the moments the shining of the trees increased, while their restless
branches seemed to strain more and more toward verticality.
The wood of the well-sweep was shining now, and presently
a policeman dumbly pointed to some wooden sheds and bee-
hives near the stone wall on the west. They were commencing to shine, too, though the tethered vehicles of the visitors
seemed so far unaffected. Then there was a wild commotion
and clopping in the road, and as Ammi quenched the lamp
for better seeing they realized that the span of frantic greys
had broken their sapling and run off with the democrat-
wagon.

The shock served to loosen several tongues, and embarrassed whispers were exchanged. 'It spreads on everything
organic that's been around here,' muttered the medical examiner. No one replied, but the man who had been in the
well gave a hint that his long pole must have stirred up
something intangible. 'It was awful,' he added. 'There was
no bottom at all, just ooze and bubbles and the feeling of
something lurking under there.' Ammi's horse still pawed
and screamed deafeningly in the road outside, and nearly
drowned its owner's faint quaver as he mumbled his formless reflections. 'It come from that stone—it growed down

thar—it got everything livin'—it fed itself on 'em, mind and body—Thad an' Merwin, Zenas an' Nabby—Nahum was the last—they all drunk the water—it got strong on 'em—it come from beyond, whar things ain't like they be here—now it's goin' home—'

At this point, as the column of unknown colour flared suddenly stronger and began to weave itself into fantastic suggestions of shape which each spectator later described differently, there came from poor tethered Hero such a sound as no man before or since ever heard from a horse. Every person in that low-pitched sitting room stopped his ears, and Ammi turned away from the window in horror and nausea. Words could not convey it—when Ammi looked out again the hapless beast lay huddled inert on the moonlit ground between the splintered shafts of the buggy. That was the last of Hero till they buried him next day. But the present was no time to mourn, for almost at this instant a detective silently called attention to something terrible in the very room with them. In the absence of the lamp-light it was clear that a faint phosphorescence had begun to pervade the entire apartment. It glowed on the broad-planked floor and the fragment of rag carpet, and shimmered over the sashes of the small-paned windows. It ran up and down the exposed corner-posts, coruscated about the shelf and mantel, and infected the very doors and furniture. Each minute saw it strengthen, and at last it was very plain that healthy living things must leave that house.

Ammi showed them the back door and the path up through the fields to the ten-acre pasture. They walked and stumbled as in a dream, and did not dare look back till they were far away on the high ground. They were glad of the path, for they could not have gone the front way, by that well. It was bad enough passing the glowing barn and sheds, and those shining orchard trees with their gnarled, fiendish contours; but thank Heaven the branches did their worst twisting high up. The moon went under some very black clouds as they crossed the rustic bridge over Chapman's Brook, and it was blind groping from there to the open meadows.

When they looked back toward the valley and the distant Gardner place at the bottom they saw a fearsome sight. All the farm was shining with the hideous unknown blend of colour: trees, buildings, and even such grass and herbage as had not been wholly changed to lethal grey brittleness. The boughs were all straining skyward, tipped with tongues of foul flame, and lambent tricklings of the same monstrous fire were creeping about the ridgepoles of the house, barn and sheds. It was a scene from a vision of Fuseli, and over all the rest reigned that riot of luminous amorphousness, that alien and undimensioned rainbow of cryptic poison from the well—seething, feeling, lapping, reaching, scintillating, straining, and malignly bubbling in its cosmic and unrecognizable chromaticism.

Then without warning the hideous thing shot vertically up toward the sky like a rocket or meteor, leaving behind no trail and disappearing through a round and curiously regular hole in the clouds before any man could gasp or cry out. No watcher can ever forget that sight, and Ammi stared blankly at the stars of Cygnus, Deneb twinkling above the others, where the unknown colour had melted into the Milky Way. But his gaze was the next moment called swiftly to earth by the crackling in the valley. It was just that. Only a wooden ripping and crackling, and not an explosion, as so many others of the party vowed. Yet the outcome was the same, for in one feverish kaleidoscopic instant there burst up from that doomed and accursed farm a gleamingly eruptive cataclysm of unnatural sparks and substance; blurring the glance of the few who saw it, and sending forth to the zenith a bombarding cloudburst of such coloured and fantastic fragments as our universe must needs disown. Through quickly reclosing vapours they followed the great morbidity that had vanished, and in another second they had vanished too. Behind and below was only a darkness to which the men dared not return, and all about was a mounting wind which seemed to sweep down in black, frore gusts from interstellar space. It shrieked and howled, and lashed the fields and distorted woods in a mad cosmic frenzy, till soon the trembling party realized it would be no use waiting for the moon to show what was left down there at Nahum's.

Too awed even to hint theories, the seven shaking men trudged back toward Arkham by the north road. Ammi was worse than his fellows, and begged them to see him inside his own kitchen, instead of keeping straight on to town. He did not wish to cross the blighted wind-whipped woods alone to his home on the main road. For he had had an added shock that the others were spared, and was crushed forever with a brooding fear he dared not even mention for many years to come. As the rest of the watchers on that tempestuous hill had stolidly set their faces toward the road, Ammi had looked back an instant at the shadowed valley of desolation so lately sheltering his ill-starred friend. And from that stricken, faraway spot he had seen something feebly rise, only to sink down again upon the place from which the great shapeless horror had shot into the sky. It was just a colour—but not any colour of our earth or heavens. And because Ammi recognized that colour, and knew that this last faint remnant must still lurk down there in the well, he has never been quite right since.

Ammi would never go near the place again. It is forty-four years now since the horror happened, but he has never been there, and will be glad when the new reservoir blots it out. I shall be glad, too, for I do not like the way the sunlight changed colour around the mouth of that abandoned well I passed. I hope the water will always be very deep—but even so, I shall never drink it. I do not think I shall visit the Arkham country hereafter. Three of the men who had been with Ammi returned the next morning to see the ruins by daylight, but there were not any real ruins. Only the bricks of the chimney, the stones of the cellar, some mineral and metallic litter here and there, and the rim of that nefandous well. Save for Ammi's dead horse, which they towed away and buried, and the buggy which they shortly returned to him, everything that had ever been living had gone. Five eldritch acres of dusty grey desert remained, nor has anything ever grown there since. To this day it sprawls open to the sky like a great spot eaten by acid in the woods and fields, and the few who have ever dared glimpse it in spite of the rural tales have named it 'the blasted heath.'

The rural tales are queer. They might be even queerer if city men and college chemists could be interested enough to analyse the water from that disused well, or the grey dust that no wind seems to disperse. Botanists, too, ought to study the stunted flora on the borders of that spot, for they might shed light on the country notion that the blight is spreading—little by little, perhaps an inch a year. People say the colour of the neighbouring herbage is not quite right in the spring, and that wild things leave queer prints in the light winter snow. Snow never seems quite so heavy on the blasted heath as it is elsewhere. Horses—the few that are left in this motor age—grow skittish in the silent valley; and hunters cannot depend on their dogs too near the splotch of greyish dust.

They say the mental influences are very bad, too; numbers went queer in the years after Nahum's taking, and always they lacked the power to get away. Then the stronger-minded folk all left the region, and only the foreigners tried to live in the crumbling old homesteads. They could not stay, though; and one sometimes wonders what insight beyond ours their wild, weird stories of whispered magic have given them. Their dreams at night, they protest, are very horrible in that grotesque country; and surely the very look of the dark realm is enough to stir a morbid fancy. No traveller has ever escaped a sense of strangeness in those deep ravines, and artists shiver as they paint thick woods whose mystery is as much of the spirit as of the eye. I myself am curious about the sensation I derived from my one lone walk before Ammi told me his tale. When twilight came I had vaguely wished some clouds would gather, for an odd timidity about the deep skyey voids above had crept into my soul.

Do not ask me for my opinion. I do not know—that is all. There was no one but Ammi to question; for Arkham people will not talk about the strange days, and all three professors who saw the aerolite and its coloured globule are dead. There were other globules—depend upon that. One must have fed itself and escaped, and probably there was another which was too late. No doubt it is still down the well—I know there was something wrong with the sunlight I saw above the miasmal brink. The rustics say the blight creeps an inch a year, so perhaps there is a kind of growth or nourishment even now. But whatever daemon hatching is there, it must be tethered to something or else it would quickly spread. Is it fastened to the roots of those trees that claw the air? One of the current Arkham tales is about fat oaks that shine and move as they ought not to do at night.

What it is, only God knows. In terms of matter I suppose the things Ammi described would be called a gas, but this gas obeyed the laws that are not of our cosmos. This was no fruit of such worlds and suns as shine on the telescopes and photographic plates of our observatories. This was no breath from the skies whose motions and dimensions our astronomers measure or deem too vast to measure. It was just a colour out of space—a frightful messenger from unformed realms of infinity beyond all Nature as we know it; from realms whose mere existence stuns the brain and numbs us with the black extra-cosmic gulfs it throws open before our frenzied eyes.

I doubt very much if Ammi consciously lied to me, and I do not think his tale was all a freak of madness as the townsfolk had forewarned. Something terrible came to the hills and valleys on that meteor, and something terrible—though I know not in what proportion—still remains. I shall be glad to see the water come. Meanwhile I hope nothing will happen to Ammi. He saw so much of the thing—and its influence was so insidious. Why has he never been able to move away? How clearly he recalled those dying words of Nahum's—'can't git away—draws ye—ye know summ'at's comin' but tain't no use—' Ammi is such a good old man—when the reservoir gang gets to work I must write the chief engineer to keep a sharp watch on him. I would hate to think of him as the grey, twisted, brittle monstrosity which persists more and more in troubling my sleep.

The Man with a Thousand Legs
Frank Belknap Long, Jr.

Frank Belknap Long (1903–93) was a close friend of H. P. Lovecraft and wrote Lovecraftian horror in his well-known *Weird Tales* stories "The Hounds of Tindalos," "The Space Eaters," and "The Horror from the Hills." However, Long also contributed to nearly every science fiction magazine published in the 1930s and 1940s, and this science fiction bent clearly had an impact on his weird fiction. "The Man with a Thousand Legs" is a weird scientific story from the August 1927 issue of *Weird Tales*. Essentially a mad scientist tale, its multiple story lines converge to suggest a scientific abomination more horrifying than anything that could be described directly.

1. Statement of Horace Randall, Psychoanalyst

Someone rapped loudly on the door of my bedroom. It was past midnight but I had been unable to sleep and I welcomed the disturbance.

"Who's there?" I asked.

"A young man what insists on being admitted, sir," replied the raucous voice of my housekeeper. "A young man—and very thin and pale he is, sir—what says he's business what won't wait. 'He's in bed,' I says, but then he says as how you're the only doctor what can help him now. He says as how he hasn't slept or ate for a week, and he ain't nothing but a boy, sir!"

"Tell him he can come in," I replied as I slid into my dressing gown and reached for a cigar.

The door opened to admit a thin shaft of light and a young man so incredibly emaciated that I stared at him in horror. He was six feet tall and extremely broad-shouldered, but I don't think he weighed one hundred pounds. As he approached me he staggered and leaned against the wall for support. His eyes fairly blazed. It was obvious that some tremendous idea swayed him. I gently indicated a chair and he collapsed into it.

For a moment he sat and surveyed me. When I offered him a cigar he brushed it aside with a gesture of contempt.

"Why should I poison my body with such things?" he snapped. "Tobacco is for weaklings and children."

I studied him curiously. He was apparently an extraordinary young man. His forehead was high and broad, his nose was curved like a scimitar, and his lips were so tightly compressed that only a thin line indicated his mouth.

I waited for him to speak, but silence enveloped him like a rubber jacket. "I shall have to break the ice somehow," I reflected; and then suddenly I heard myself asking: "You have something to tell me—some confession, perhaps, that you wish to make to me?"

My question aroused him. His shoulders jerked, and he leaned forward, gripping both arms of his chair. "I have been robbed of my birthright," he said. "I am a man of genius, and once, for a brief moment, I had power—tremendous power. Once I projected my personality before vast multitudes of people, and every word that I uttered increased my fame and flattered my vanity."

He was trembling and shaking so violently that I was obliged to rise and lay a restraining hand upon his shoulder. "Delusions of magnificence," I murmured, "undoubtedly induced by a malignant inferiority-complex."

"It is not that," he snapped. "I am a poet, an artist, and I have within me a tremendous force that must be expanded. The world has denied me self-expression through legitimate channels and now I am justified in hating the world. Let society beware!"

He threw back his head and laughed. His hilarity seemed to increase the tension that had somehow crept into the room.

"Call me a madman if you will," he exclaimed, "but I crave power. I can not rest until my name is on a million lips."

"A conservative course of treatment—" I began.

"I want no treatment," he shouted, and then, in a less agitated voice, "You would be surprised, perhaps, if I told you my name!"

"What *is* your name?" I asked.

"Arthur St. Amand," he replied, and stood up.

I was so astonished that I dropped my cigar. I may even add that I was momentarily awed. *Arthur St. Amand!*

"Arthur St. Amand," he repeated. "You are naturally amazed to discover that the pale, harassed and half-insane youth that you see before you was once called the peer of Newton and Leonardo Da Vinci. You are amazed to discover that the starving lad with an inferiority-complex was once feted by kings and praised by men whose lightest words will go thundering down Time. It is all so amazing and so uproariously funny, but the tragedy remains. Like Dr. Faustus I once looked upon the face of God, and now I'm less than any schoolboy."

"You are still very young," I gasped. "You can't be more than twenty-four."

"I am twenty-three," he said. "It was precisely three years ago that I published my brochure on etheric vibrations. For six months I lived in a blaze of glory. I was the marvelous boy of the scientific world, and then that Frenchman advanced his theory—"

"I suppose you mean Monsieur Paul Rondoli," I interrupted. "I recall the sensation his startling refutation made at the time. He completely eclipsed you in the popular mind, and later the scientific world declared you a fraud. Your star set very suddenly."

"But it will rise again," exclaimed my young visitor. "The world will discuss me again, and this time I shall not be forgotten. I shall prove my theory. I shall demonstrate that the effect of etheric vibration on single cells is to change—to change—." He hesitated and then suddenly shouted, "But no, I shall not tell you. I shall tell no one. I came here tonight to unburden my mind to you. At first I thought of going to a priest. It is necessary that I should confess to someone.

"When my thoughts are driven in upon themselves they become monstrous. I have an active and terrible brain, and I must speak out occasionally. I chose you because you are a man of intelligence and discrimination and you have heard many confessions. But I shall not discuss etheric vibrations with you. When you see *It* you will understand."

He turned abruptly and walked out of the room and out of my house without once looking back. I never saw him again.

2. *Diary of Thomas Shiel, Novelist and Short-Story Writer*

July 21. This is my fourth day at the beach. I've already gained three pounds, and I'm so sunbaked that I frightened a little girl when I went swimming this morning. She was building sand castles and when she saw me she dropped her shovel and ran shrieking to her mother. "Horrible black man!" she shouted. I suppose she thought I was a genie out of the *Arabian Nights.* It's pleasant here—I've almost got the evil taste of New York out of my mouth. Elsie's coming down for the week-end.

July 22. The little girl I frightened yesterday has disappeared. The police are searching for her and it is generally believed that she has been kidnaped. The unfortunate occurrence has depressed everyone at the beach. All bathing parties have been abandoned, and even the children sit about sad-eyed and dejected. No footprints were found on the sands near the spot where the child was last seen. . . .

July 23. Another child has disappeared, and this time the abductor left a clue. A young man's walking stick and hat were found near the scene of a violent struggle. The sand for yards around was stained with blood. Several mothers left the New Beach Hotel this morning with their children.

July 24. Elsie came this morning. A new crime occurred at the very moment of her arrival, and I scarcely had the heart to explain the situation to her. My paleness evidently frightened her. "What is the matter?" she asked; "you look ill." "I am ill," I replied. "I saw something dreadful on the beach this morning." "Good heavens!" she exclaimed; "have they found one of the children?" It was a great relief to me that she had read about the children in the New York papers. "No," I said. "They didn't find the children, but they found the body of a man and he didn't have a drop of blood in him. He had been drained dry. And all about his body the investigators found curious little mounds of yellowish slime—of ooze. When the sunlight struck this substance it glittered." "Has it been examined under a microscope?" asked Elsie. "They are examining it now," I explained. "We shall know the results by this evening." "God pity us all," said Elsie, and she staggered and nearly fell. I was obliged to support her as we entered the hotel.

July 25. Two curious developments. The chemist who examined the jellyish substance found near the body on the beach declares that it is living protoplasm, and he has sent it to the Department of Health for classification by one of their expert biologists. And a deep pool some eight yards in diameter has been discovered in a rock fissure about a mile from the New Beach Hotel, which evidently harbors some queer denizens. The water in this pool is as black as ink and strongly saline. The pool is eight or ten feet from the ocean, but it is affected by the tides and descends a foot every night and morning. This morning one of the guests of the hotel, a young lady named Clara Phillips, had come upon the pool quite by accident, and being fascinated by its sinister appearance had decided to sketch it. She had seated herself on the rim of the rock fissure and was in the act of sketching in several large boulders and a strip of beach when something made a curious noise beneath her. "Gulp," it said. "Gulp!" She gave a little cry and jumped up just in time to escape a long golden tentacle which slithered toward her over the rocks. The tentacle protruded from the very center of the pool, out of the black water, and it filled her with unutterable loathing. She stepped quickly forward and stamped upon it, and her attack was so sudden that the thing was unable to flip away from her and escape back into the water. And Miss Phillips was an amazingly strong young woman. She ground the end of the tentacle into a bloody pulp with her heel. Then she turned and ran. She ran as she had not run since her "prep" school days. But as she raced across the soft beach she fancied she could hear a monstrous, lumbering something pursuing her. It is to her credit that she did not look back.

And this is the story of little Harry Doty. I offered him a beautiful new dime, but he told it to me gratis. I give it in his own words.

"Yes sir, I've always knowed about that pool. I used to fish for crabs and sea-cucumbers and big, purple anemones in it, sir. But up until last week I allus knowed what I'd bring up. Once or twice I used to get somethin' a bit out o' the ordinary, such as a bleedin'-tooth shell or a headless worm with green suckers in its tail and lookin' like the devil on a Sunday outin' or a knowin'-lookin' skate what ud glare and glare at me, sir. But never nothin' like this thing, sir. I caught it on the top o' its head and it had the most human-lookin' eyes I ever saw. They were blue and soulless, sir. It spat at me, and I throws down my line and beats it. I beats it, sir. Then I hears it come lumbering after me over the beach. It made a funny gulpin' noise as if it was a-lickin' its chops."

July 26. Elsie and I are leaving tomorrow. I'm on the verge of a lethal collapse. Elsie stutters whenever she tries to talk. I don't blame her for stuttering but I can't understand why she wants to talk at all after what we've seen . . . There are some things that can only be expressed by silence.

The local chemist got a report this morning from the Board of Health. The stuff found on the beach consisted of hundreds of cells very much like the cells that compose the human body. And yet they weren't human cells. The biologists were completely mystified by them, and a small culture is now on its way to Washington, and another is being sent to the American Museum of Natural History.

This morning the local authorities investigated the curious black pool in the rocks. Elsie and I and most of the other vacationists were on hand to watch operations. Thomas Wilshire, a member of the New Jersey constabulary, threw a plummet line into the pool and we all watched it eagerly as it paid out. "A hundred feet," murmured Elsie as the police looked at one another in amazement. "It probably went into the sea," someone exclaimed. "I don't think the pool itself is that deep." Thomas Wilshire shook his head. "There's queer things in that pool," he said. "I don't like the looks of it."

The diver was a bristling, brave little man with some obscure nervous affliction that made him tremble violently. "You'll have to go down at once," said Wilshire. The diver shook his head and shuffled his feet.

"Get him into his suit, boys!" ordered Wilshire, and the poor wretch was lifted bodily upon strong shoulders and transformed into a loathsome, goggle-eyed monster.

In a moment he had advanced to the pool and vanished into its sinister black depths. Two men worked valiantly at the pumps, while Wilshire nodded sleepily and scratched his chin. "I wonder what he'll find," he mused. "Personally, I don't think he's got much chance of ever coming up. I wouldn't be in his shoes for all the money in the United States mint."

After several minutes the rubber tubing began to jerk violently. "The poor lad!" muttered Wilshire. "I knew he didn't have a chance. Pull, boys, pull!"

The tubing was rapidly pulled in. There was nothing attached to it, but the lower portion was covered with glittering golden slime. Wilshire picked up the severed end and examined it casually. "Neatly clipped," he said. "The poor devil!"

The rest of us looked at one another in horror. Elsie grew so pale that I thought she was about to faint. Wilshire was speaking again: "We've made one momentous discovery," he said. We crammed eagerly forward. Wilshire paused for the fraction of a second, and a faint smile of triumph curled his lips. "There's something in that pool," he finished. "Our friend's life has not been given in vain."

I had an absurd desire to punch his fat, triumphant face, and might have done so, but a scream from the others quelled the impulse.

"Look," cried Elsie. She was pointing at the black surface of the pool. It was changing color. Slowly it was assuming a reddish hue; and then a hellish something shot up and bobbed for a moment on its surface. "A human arm!" groaned Elsie and hid her face in her hands. Wilshire whistled softly. Two more objects joined the first and then something round which made Elsie stare and stare through the spaces between her fingers.

"Come away!" I commanded. "Come away at once." I seized her by the arm and was in the act of forcefully leading her from the edge of that dreadful charnel, for charnel it had become, when I was arrested by a shout from Wilshire.

"Look at it! Look at it!" he yelled. "That's the horrid thing. God, it isn't human!"

We both turned back and stared. There are blasphemies of creation that can not be described, and the thing which rose up to claim the escaping fragments of its dismantled prey was of that order. I remember vaguely, as in a nightmare of Tartarus, that it had long golden arms which shone and sparkled in the sunlight, and a monstrous curved beak below two piercing black eyes in which I saw nothing but unutterable malice.

The idea of standing there and watching it munch the fragmentary remains of the poor little diver was intolerable to me, and in spite of the loud protests of Wilshire, who wanted us, I suppose, to try and do something about it, I turned and ran, literally dragging Elsie with me. This was, as it turned out, the wisest thing that I could have done, because the thing later emerged from the pool and nearly got several of the vacationists. Wilshire fired at it twice with a pistol, but the thing flopped back into the water apparently unharmed and submerged triumphantly.

3. Statement of Henry Greb, Prescription Druggist

I usually shut up shop at 10 o'clock, but at closing time that evening I was leaning over the counter reading a ghost story, and it was so extremely interesting that I couldn't walk out on it. My nose was very close to the page and I didn't notice anything that was going on about me when suddenly I happened to look up and there he was standing and watching me.

I've seen some pale people in my time (most people that come with prescriptions are pale) and I've seen some skinny people, but I never have seen anyone as thin and pale as the young man that stood before me.

"Good heavens!" I said, and shut the book.

The young man's lips were twisted into a sickly smile. "Sorry to bother you," he says. "But I'm in a bad way. I'm in desperate need of medical attention!"

"What can I do to help you?" I says.

He looks at me very solemnly, as if he were making up his mind whether he could trust me. "This is really a case for a physician," he says.

"It's against the law for us to handle such cases," I told him.

Suddenly he held out his hand. I gasped. The fingers were smashed into a bloody pulp, and blood was running down his wrist. "Do something to stop the bleeding," he says. "I'll see a physician later."

Well, I got out some gauze and bound the hand up as best I could. "See a doctor at once," I told him. "Blood-poisoning will set in if you're not careful. Luckily, none of the bones are fractured."

He nodded, and for a moment his eyes flashed. "Damn that woman!" he muttered. "Damn her!"

"What's that?" I asked, but he had got himself together again and merely smiled. "I'm all upset," he said. "Didn't know just what I was saying—you must pardon me. By the way, I've got a little gash on my scalp which you might look at."

He removed his cap and I noticed that his hair was dripping wet. He parted it with his hand and revealed a nasty abrasion about an inch wide. I examined it carefully.

"Your friend wasn't very careful when he cast that plug," I says at length. "I never believe in fly-fishing when there's two in the boat. A friend of mine lost an eye that way."

"It *was* made by a fish-hook," he confessed. "You're something of a Sherlock Holmes, aren't you?"

I brushed aside his compliment with a careless gesture and turned for the bottle of carbolic acid which rested on the shelf behind me. It was then that I heard something between a growl and a gulp from the young man.

I wheeled abruptly, and caught him in the act of springing upon me. He was foaming at the mouth and his eyes bulged. I reached forward and seized him by the shoulders and in a moment we were engaged in a desperate struggle upon the floor. He bit and scratched and kicked at me; and I was obliged to silence him by pummeling his face. It was at that moment that I noticed a peculiar fishy odor in the room, as if a breeze from the sea had entered through the open door.

For several moments I struggled and fought and strained and then something seemed to give suddenly beneath me. The young man slipped from my grasp and made for the door. I endeavored to follow, but I stumbled over something slippery and fell flat upon my face.

When I got up, the young man was gone, and in my hand I held something so weird that I could scarcely believe that it was real, and later I flung it from me with a cry of disgust. It was a reddish, rubbery substance about five inches long, and its under edge was lined with little golden suckers that opened and closed while I stared at them.

I was still laboring under a fearful strain when Harry Morton entered the shop. He was trembling violently, and I noticed that he gazed fearfully behind him as he approached the counter.

"What's the best thing you have for highfalutin-acting nerves?" he asks.

"Bromides," I says. "I can mix you some. But what's the trouble with your nerves, Harry?"

"Hallucinations," he groans. "Them, and other things."

"Tell me about it," I says.

"I was leanin' 'gainst a lamppost," he says, "and I sees a big lumbering yellowish thing walkin' along the street like a man. It wasn't natural, Henry. I'm not superstitious, but that there thing wasn't natural. And then it flops into the gutter and runs like a streak of lightnin'. It made a funny noise, too. It said 'Gulp.' "

I mixed the bromides and handed him the glass over the counter. "I understand, Harry," I says. "But don't go about blowing your head off. No one would believe you."

4. Statement of Helen Bowan

I was sitting on the porch knitting when a young man with a bag stops in front of the house and looks up at me. "Good morning, madam," he says, "have you a room with bath?"

"Look at the sign, young man," I says to him. "I've a nice light room on the second floor that should just suit you."

Up he comes and smiles at me. But as soon as I saw him close I didn't like him. He was so terribly thin, and his hand was bandaged, and he looked as if he had been in a fight.

"How much do you want for the room?" he asks.

"Twelve dollars," I told him. I wanted to get rid of him and I thought the high rate would scare him off, but his hand goes suddenly into his pocket and he brings out a roll of bills, and begins counting them. I gets up very quickly and bows politely to him and takes his grip away from him, and rushes into the hall with it. I didn't want to lose a prospect like that. Cousin Hiram has a game which he plays with shells, and I knew that the young man would be Cousin Hiram's oyster.

I takes him upstairs and shows him the room and he seems quite pleased with it. But when he sees the bathtub he begins jumping up and down like a schoolboy, and clapping his hands and acting so odd that I begins to suspect that he is going out of his mind. "It's just the right size!" he shouts. "I hope you won't mind my keeping it filled all day. I bathe quite often. But I must have some salt to put into it. I can't bathe in fresh water!"

"He's certainly a queer one," I thought, "but I ain't complaining. It isn't often Hiram and I land a fish as rich as this one."

Finally he calms down and pushes me out of the room. "Everything's all right," he says. "But I don't want to be disturbed. When you get the salt, put it down in the hall and knock on the door. Under no circumstances must anyone enter this room."

He closed the door in my face and I heard the key grate in the lock. I didn't like it, and I didn't like the sounds that began to come from behind that door. First I heard a great sigh as if somehow he had got something disagreeable off his chest, and then I heard a funny gulping sound that I didn't like. He didn't waste any time in turning on the water either. I heard a great splashing and wallowing, and then, after about fifteen minutes, everything became as quiet as death.

We didn't hear anything more from him until that evening, when I sent Lizzie up with the salt. At first she tried the door, but it was locked, and she was obliged to put the bag down in the hall. But she didn't go away. She squeezed up close against the wall and waited. After about ten minutes the door opened slowly and a long, thin arm shot out and took in the bag. Lizzie said that the arm was yellow and dripping wet, and the thinnest arm she had ever seen. "But he's a thin young man, Lizzie," I explains to her. "That may be," she says, "but I never saw a human being with an arm like that before!"

Later, along about 10 o'clock I should say, I was sitting in the parlor sewing when I felt something wet land on my hand. I looked up and the ceiling was dripping red. I mean just what I saw. The ceiling with all moist and dripping red.

I jumped up and ran out into the hall. I wanted to scream, but I bit my lips until the blood begins running down my chin and that makes me sober and determined. "That young man must go," I says to myself. "I can't have anything that isn't proper going on in this house."

I climbs the stairs looking as grim as death and pounds on the young man's door. "I won't stand for whatever's going on in there!" I shouted. "Open that door."

I heard something flopping about inside, and then the young man speaking to himself in a very low voice. "Its demands are insatiable. The vile, hungry beast! Why doesn't it think of something besides its stomach! I didn't want it to come then. But it doesn't need the ray now. When its appetite is aroused it changes without the ray. God, but I had a hard time getting back! Longer and longer between!"

Suddenly he seemed to hear the pounding. His queer chattering stops and I hear the key turn in the lock. The door opens ever so slightly and his face looks out at me. He is horrible to look at. His cheeks are sunken and there are big horrid rings under his eyes. There is a bandage tied about his head.

"I want you to leave at once," I tells him. "There's queer things going on here and I can't stand for queer things. You've *got* to leave."

He sighed and nodded. "It's just as well perhaps," he says. "I was thinking of going anyway. There are rats here."

"Rats!" I gasped. But I wasn't really surprised. I knew there were rats in the house. They made life miserable for me. I was never able to get rid of them. Even the cats feared them.

"I can't stand rats," he continues. "I'm packing up—clearing out now." He shuts the door in my face and I hears him throwing his things into a bag. Then the door opens again and he comes out on the landing. He is terribly pale, and he leans against the wall to catch himself, and then he starts descending the stairs.

I watches him as he goes down, and when he reaches the first landing he staggers and leans against the wall. Then he seems to grow shorter and he goes down the last flight three steps at a time. Then he makes a running leap toward the door. I never saw anyone get through a door so quick, and I begins to suspect that he's done something that he's ashamed of.

So I turns about and goes into the room. When I looks at the floor I nearly faints. It's all slippery and wet, and seven dead rats are lying on their backs in the center of the room. And they are the palest-looking rats I've ever seen. Their noses and tails are pure white and they looks as if they didn't have a drop of blood in them. And then I goes into the alcove and looks at the bathtub. I won't tell you what I see there. But you remember what I says about the ceiling downstairs? I says it was dripping red, and the alcove wasn't so very different.

I gets out of that room as quick as I can, and I shuts and locks the door; and then I goes downstairs and telephones to Cousin Hiram. "Come right over, Hiram," I says. "Something terrible has been here!"

5. *Statement of Walter Noyes, Lighthouse Keeper*

I was pretty well done up. I'd been polishing the lamps all afternoon, and there were calluses on my hands as big as hen's eggs. I went up into the tower and shut myself in and got out a book that I'd been reading off and on for a week. It was a translation of the *Arabian Nights* by a fellow named Lang. Imaginative stuff like that is a great comfort to a chap when he's shut up by himself away off on the rim of the world, and I always enjoyed reading about Schemselnihar and Deryabar and the young King of the Black Isles.

I was reading the first part of *The King of the Black Isles* and had reached the sentence: "And then the youth drew away his robe and the Sultan perceived with horror that he was a man only to his waist, and from thence to his feet he had been changed into marble," when I happened to look toward the window.

An icy south wind was driving the rain furiously against the panes, and at first I saw nothing but a translucent glitter on the wet glass and vaguely beyond that the gleaming turmoil of dark, enormous waves. Then a dazzling and indescribable shape flattened itself against the window and blotted out the black sea and sky. I gasped and jumped up.

"A monstrous squid!" I muttered. "The storm must have blown it ashore. That tentacle will smash the glass if I don't do something."

I reached for my slicker and hat and in a moment I was descending the spiral stairway three steps at a time. Before emerging into the storm I armed myself with a revolver and the contents of a tumbler of strong Jamaica rum.

I paused for a moment in the doorway and stared about me. But from where I stood I could see nothing but the tall gray boulders fringing the southern extremity of the island and a stretch of heaving and rolling water. The rain beat against my face and nearly blinded me, and a deep murmur arose from the intolerable wash of the waves. Before me lay only a furious and tortured immensity; behind my back was the warmth and security of my miniature castle, a mellow pipe and a book of valiant stories—but I couldn't ignore the menace of the loathsome shape that had pressed itself against the glass.

I descended three short steps to the rocks and made my way rapidly toward the rear of the lighthouse. Drops of rain more acrid than tears ran down my cheeks and into my mouth and dripped from the corners of my mustache. The overpowering darkness clung like a leech to my clothes. I hadn't gone twenty paces before I came upon a motionless figure.

At first I saw nothing but the head and shoulders of a

well-shaped man; but as I drew cautiously nearer I collided
with something that made me cry out in terror. A hideous
tentacle shot out and wound itself about my leg.

With a startled cry I turned and attempted to run. But out
of the macro-carpus darkness leaped another slimy arm, and
another. My fingers tightened on the revolver in my pocket.
I whipped it out and opened fire on the writhing brutes.

The report of my gun echoed from the surrounding boulders. A sudden, shrill scream of agony broke the comparative
quiet that followed. Then there came a voluble, passionate
pleading. "Don't shoot again! Please don't! I'm done up. I
was done up when I came here, and I wanted help! I didn't
intend to harm you. Before God, I didn't intend that *they*
should attack you. But I can't control 'em now. They're too
much for me. *It's* too much for me. Pity me!"

For a moment I was too dazed to think. I stared stupidly
at the smoking revolver in my hand and then my eyes sought
the cataclysmic ocean. The enormous waves calmed me.
Slowly I brought my eyes to bear on the thing before me.

But even as I stared at it my brain reeled again, and a
deadly nausea came upon me.

"And then the youth drew away his robe and the Sultan perceived that he was a man only to his waist . . ."

Several feet from where I stood, a monstrous jelly spread
itself loathsomely over the dripping rocks, and from its
veined central mass a thousand tentacles depended and
writhed like the serpents on the head of Medusa. And growing from the middle of this obscenity was the torso and head
of a naked young man. His hair was matted and covered
with sea-weed; and there were blood-stains upon his high,
white forehead. His nose was so sharp that it reminded me
of a sword and I momentarily expected to see it glitter in the
dim, mysterious light. His teeth chattered so loudly that I
could hear them from where I stood; and as I stared and
stared at him he coughed violently and foamed at the lips.

"Whisky!" he muttered. "I'm all done up! I ran into a
ship!"

I was unable to speak, but I believe I made some strange
noises in my throat. The young man nodded hysterically.

"I knew you'd understand," he muttered. "I'm up against

it, but I knew you'd help me pull through. A glass of whisky—"

"How did that thing get you?" I shrieked. I had found my voice at last, and was determined to fight my way back to sanity. "How did that thing get its loathsome coils on you?"

"It didn't get me," groaned the young man. "I'm *It*!"

"You're what?"

"A part of *It*," replied the young man.

"Isn't that thing swallowing you?" I screamed at him. "Aren't you going down into its belly at this moment?"

The young man sadly shook his head. "It's part of me," he said again, and then, more wildly, "I must have something to brace me up! I'm all in. I was swimming on the surface, and a ship came and cut off six of my legs. I'm weak from loss of blood, and I can't stand."

A lean hand went up and brushed the water from battered eyes. "A few of 'em are still lively," he said, "and I can't control 'em. They nearly got you—but the others are all in. I can't walk on 'em."

With as much boldness as I could muster I raised my revolver and advanced upon the thing. "I don't know what you're talking about," I cried. "But I'm going to blow this monster to atoms."

"For heaven's sake don't!" he shrieked. "That would be murder. We're a human being."

A flash of scarlet fire answered him. Almost unconsciously I had pressed upon the trigger, and now my weapon was speaking again. "I'll blow it to tatters!" I muttered between my teeth. "The vile, crawling devil!"

"Don't! don't!" shrieked the young man, and then an unearthly yell made the night obscene. I saw the thing before me quiver in all its folds, and then it suddenly rose up and towered above me. Blood spurted from its huge, bloated body, and a crimson shower descended upon me. High above me, a hundred feet in the air, I saw the pale, agonized face of the young man. He was screaming blasphemies. He appeared to be walking on stilts. "You can't kill me," he yelled. "I'm stronger than I thought. I'll win out yet."

I raised my revolver to fire again, but before I could take aim the thing swept by me and plunged into the sea. It was perhaps fortunate for me that I did not attempt to follow it. My knees gave beneath me and I fell flat upon my face. When I came to so far as to be able to speak I found myself between clean white sheets and staring into the puzzled blue eyes of a government inspector.

"You've had a nasty time of it, lad," he said. "We had to give you stimulants. Didja have a shock of a sort?"

"Of a sort, yes," I replied. "But it came out of the *Arabian Nights*."

6. The Marvelous Boy

[Curious Manuscript Found in a Bottle]

I was the marvelous boy. My genius amazed the world. A magnificent mind, a sublime destiny! My enemies . . . combined to ruin me. A punctured balloon . . .

A little box, and I put a dog under it. He changed . . . Jelly! Etheric vibrations generate curious changes in living cells . . . Process starts and nothing can stop it. Growth! Enormous growth! Keeps sending out shoots—legs! arms! Marvelous growth! Human being next. Put a little girl under it. She changed. Beautiful jellyfish! It kept getting larger. Fed it mice. Then I destroyed it.

So interesting. Must try it on myself. I know how to get back. Will-power. A child's will is too weak, but a man can get back. No actual change in cell-content.

A tremendous experience! I picked out a deep pool where I could hide. Hunger. Saw man on beach.

The police suspect. I must be more careful. Why didn't I take the body out to sea?

Horrible incident. Young lady artist. I almost caught her, but she stamped on a leg. Smashed it. Horrible pain. I certainly must be more careful.

Great humiliation. Little boy hooked me. But I gave him a scare. The varmint! I glared and glared at him. I tried to catch him, but he ran too fast. I wanted to eat him. He had very red cheeks. I hate women and children.

Of course they suspect. Little boys always babble. I wanted to eat him. But I gave them all a good scare, and I got a man. He came down after me in a diver's suit, but I got him. I took him to pieces. I mean that—literally to pieces. Then I let the fragments float up. I wanted to scare them. I think I did. They ran for their lives. The authorities are fools.

I got back. But it wasn't easy. The thing fought and

fought. "I'm master!" I said, and it gulped. It gulped and gulped and gulped; and then I got back. But my hand was smashed and bleeding!

That fool clerk! Why did he take so long? But he didn't know how hungry his red face made me. The thing came back without the ray. I was standing before the counter and it came back. I sprang at him. I was lucky to get away.

Terrible trouble. I can't keep it from coming back. I wake up in the night, and find it spread out on the bed and all over the floor. Its arms writhe and writhe. And its demands are insatiable. Every waking moment it demands food. Sometimes it completely absorbs me. But now as I write the upper portion of my body is human.

This afternoon I moved to furnished room near beach. Salt water has become a necessity. Change comes on more rapidly now. I can't keep it off. My will is powerless. I filled the tub with water and put in some salt. Then I wallowed in it. Great comfort. Great relief. Hunger. Dreadful, insatiable hunger.

I am all beast, all animal. Rats. I have caught six rats. Delicious. Great comfort. But I've messed up the room. What if the old idiot downstairs should suspect?

She does suspect. Wants me to get out. I shall get out. There is only one refuge for me now. The sea! I shall go to the sea. I can't pretend I'm human any longer. I'm all animal, all beast. What a shock I must have given the old hag! I could hear her teeth chattering as she came up the stairs. All I could do to keep from springing at her.

Into the sea at last. Great relief, great joy. Freedom at last!

A ship. I ran head on into it. Six arms gone. Terrible agony. Flopped about for hours.

Land. I climbed over the rocks and collapsed. Then I managed to get back. Part of me got back. I called for help. A crazy fool came out of the lighthouse and stared at me. Five of my tentacles sprang at him. I couldn't control them. They got him about the leg. He lost his head. Got out a revolver and shot at them.

I got them under control. Tremendous effort. Pleaded with him, tried to explain. He would not listen. Shots—many shots. White-hot fire in my body—in my arms and legs. Strength returned to me. I rose up, and went back into the sea. I hate human beings. I am growing larger, and I shall make myself felt in the world.

ARTHUR ST. AMAND.

7. The Salmon Fishermen

[Statement of William Gamwell]

There were five of us in the boat: Jimmy Simms, Tom Snodgrass, Harry O'Brien, Bill Samson and myself. "Jimmy," I said, "we may as well open the lunch. I'm not particularly hungry, but the salmon all have their noses stuck in the mud!"

"They sure ain't biting," said Jimmy. "I never seen such a bum run of the lazy critters."

"Don't go complaining," Harry piped up. "We've only been here five hours."

We were drifting toward the east shore and I yelled to Bill to pull on the oars, but he ignored me.

"We'll drift in with the shipping," I warned. "By the way, what's that queer-looking tug with a broken smoke-stack?"

"It came in this morning," said Jim. "It looks like a rum-runner to me."

"They're taking an awful risk," Harry put in. "The reve-nue cutter's due by here any minute."

"There she is now," said Bill and pointed toward the flats.

Sure enough, there was the government boat, skirting the shore and looking like a lean wasp on the warpath. "She's heading the tug off as sure as you're born," said Bill. "I'll say we're in for a hot time!"

"Back water!" I shouted. "Do you want to get between 'em?"

Tom and Bill pulled sturdily on the oars and our boat swung out in the direction of the west shore; and then the current took us and carried us downstream.

A signal flag flashed for a moment on the deck of the cut-ter. Jimmy translated it to us. " 'Stand to, or we'll fire'," he exclaimed. "Now let's see what the tug's got to say to that!"

The tug apparently decided to ignore the command. It rose on a tremorless swell, and plunged doggedly forward. A vast black column ascended from its broken smoke-stack. "They're putting on steam!" cried Bill. "But they haven't a chance in the world."

"Not a chance," confirmed Tom. "One broadside will blow 'em to atoms."

Bill stood up and clapped his hands to his ears. The rest

of us were nearly deafened by the thunderous report. "What did I tell you?" shouted Tom.

We looked at the tug. The smoke-stack was gone and she was wallowing in a heavy swell. "That was only a single shot across her bows," said Bill. "But it did a lot of damage. Wait until they open fire with the big guns!"

We waited, expecting to see something interesting. But we saw something that nearly frightened us out of our shoes. Between the cutter and the tug a gigantic, yellowish obscenity shot up from the water and towered thirty feet in the air. It thrashed wildly about and made a horrible gulping noise. We could hear the frenzied shrieks of the men on the tug, and from the deck of the cutter someone yelled. "Look at it! Look at it! Oh, my God!"

"Mercy in heaven!" groaned Bill.

"We're in for it!" sobbed Tom.

For a moment the thing simply towered and vibrated between the two boats and then it made for the cutter. It had at least a thousand legs and they waved loathsomely in the sunlight. It had a hooked beak and a great mouth that opened and closed and gulped, and it was larger than a whale. It was horribly, hideously large. It towered to the mounting zenith, and in its mephitic, blasphemous immensity it dwarfed the two boats and all the tangled shipping in the harbor.

"Are we alive?" shrieked Bill. "And is that there shore really Long Island? I don't believe it. We're in the Indian Ocean, or the Persian Gulf or the middle of the Hyperborean sea . . . That there thing is a Jormungandar!"

"What's a Jormungandar?" yelled Tom. He was at the end of his rope and clutching valiantly at straws.

"Them things what live on the bottom of the arctic seas," groaned Bill. "They comes up for air once in a hundred years. I'll take my oath that there thing's a Jormungandar."

Jormungandar or not, it was apparent to all of us that the monster meant business. It was bearing down upon the cutter with incredible ferocity. The water boiled and bubbled in its wake. On the other boats men rushed hysterically to the rails and stared with wide eyes.

The officers of the cutter had recovered from their momentary astonishment and were gesticulating furiously and running back and forth on the decks. Three guns were lowered into position and directed at the onrushing horror. A little man with gilt braid on his sleeves danced about absurdly on his toes and shouted out commands at the top of his voice.

"Don't fire until you can look into his eyes," he yelled. "We can't afford to miss him. We'll give him a broadside he won't forget."

"It isn't human, sir!" someone yelled. "There never was nothing like it before in this world."

The men aboard the tug were obviously rejoicing. Caps and pipes ascended into the air and loud shouts of triumph issued from a hundred drunken throats.

"Fire!" shouted the blue-coated midget on the cutter.

"It won't do 'em no good!" shouted Bill, as the thunder of the guns smote our ears. "It won't do 'em a bit o' good."

As it turned out, Bill was right. The tremendous discharge failed to arrest the progress of the obscene monster.

It rose like a cloud from the water and flew at the cutter like a flying-fish. Furiously it stretched forth its enormous arms, and embraced the cutter. It wrenched the little vessel from the trough of the wave in which it wallowed and lifted it violently into the air.

Its great golden sides shone like the morning star, but red blood trickled from a gaping hole in its throat. Yet it ignored its wounds. It lifted the small steel ship into the air in its gigantic, weaving arms.

I shall never forget that moment. I have but to shut my eyes and it is before me now. I see again that Brobdingnagian horror from measureless abysses, that twisting, fantastic monstrosity from sinister depths of blackest midnight. And in its colossal arms and legs I see a tiny ship from whose deck a hundred little men fall shrieking and screaming into the black maelstrom beneath its churning maws.

Yards and yards it towered, and its glittering bulk hid the sun. It towered to the zenith and its weaving arms twisted the cutter into a shapeless mass of glistening steel.

"We're next!" muttered Bill. "There ain't nothing can save us now. A man ain't got a chance when he runs head-on against a Jormungandar!"

"That ain't no Jormungandar," piped Tom. "It's a human being what's been out all night. But I ain't saying we're not in for it."

My other companions fell upon their knees and little Harry O'Brien turned yellow under the gills. But the thing did not attack us. Instead with a heart-breaking scream that seemed outrageously human it sank beneath the waves, carrying with it the flattened, absurd remains of the valiant little cutter and the crushed and battered bodies of innumerable men. And as it sank loathsomely from sight the water about it flattened out into a tremorless plateau and turned the color of blood.

Bill was at the oars now, shouting, and cursing to encourage the rest of us. "Pull, boys," he commanded. "Let's try to make the south shore before that there fish comes up for breath. There ain't one of us here what wants to live for the rest of his life on the bottom of the sea. There ain't one of us here what ud care to have it out with a Jormungandar."

In a moment we had swung the boat about and were making for the shore. Men on the other ships were crying and waving to us, but we didn't stop to hand in any reports. We weren't thinking of anything but a huge monstrosity that we would see towering and towering into the sky as long as our brains hung together in our foolish little heads.

8. News Item in the Long Island Gazette

The body of a young man, about 25 years old, was found this morning on a deserted beach near Northport. The body was horribly emaciated and the coroner, Mr. E. Thomas Bogart, discovered three small wounds on the young man's thigh. The edges of the wounds were stained as though from gun-powder. The body scarcely weighed one hundred pounds. It is thought that the youth was the victim of foul play and inquires are being made in the vicinity.

9. The Box of Horror

[Statement of Harry Olson]

I hadn't had a thing to eat for three days, and I was driven to the cans. Sometimes you find something valuable in the cans and sometimes you don't; but anyhow, I was working 'em systematically. I had gone up the street and down the street, and hadn't found a thing for my pains except an old pair of suspenders and a tin of salmon. But when I came to the last house I stopped and stared. Then I stretched out a lean arm and picked up the box. It was a funny-looking box, with queer glass sides and little peek-holes in the side of it, and a metal compartment about three inches square in back of it, and a slide underneath large enough to hold a man's hand.

I looked up at the windows of the house, but there wasn't anyone watching me, and so I slipped the box under my coat and made off down the street. "It's something expensive, you can bet your life on that," I thought. "Probably some old doctor's croaked and his widow threw the thing away without consulting anyone. This is a real scientific affair, this is, and I ought to get a week's board out of it."

I wanted to examine the thing better and so I made for a vacant lot where I wouldn't be interrupted. Once there I sat myself down behind a signboard and took the contraption from under my coat and looked at it.

Well, sir, it interested me. There was a little lever on top of it you pressed and the slide fell down and something clicked in the metal box in back of it, and the thing lighted up.

I realized at once that something was meant to go on the slide. I didn't know just what, but my curiosity was aroused. "That light isn't there for nothing," I thought. "This box means business."

I began to wonder what would happen if something alive were put on the slide. There was a clump of bushes near where I was sitting and I got up and made for it. It took me some time to get what I was after; but when I caught it I held it firmly between my thumb and forefinger so it couldn't escape, and then I talked to it. "Grasshopper," I said. "I haven't any grudge against you personally, but the scientific mind is no respecter of persons."

The infernal varmint wriggled and wriggled and covered my thumb with molasses, but I didn't let up on him. I held him firmly and pushed him onto the slide. Then I turned on the lever and peeped through the holes.

The poor devil squirmed and fluttered for several minutes and then he began to dissolve. He got flabbier and flabbier and soon I could see right through him. When he was nothing but ooze he began to wriggle. I dumped him on the ground and he scurried away faster than a centipede.

"I'm deluding myself," I thought. "I'm seeing things that never happened."

Then I did a very foolish thing. I thrust my hand into the box and turned on the lever. For several moments nothing happened and then my hand began to get cold. I peeped through the holes and what I saw made me scream and scream and draw my hand out and go running about the lot like a madman. My hand was a mass of writhing, twisting snakes! Leastwise, they looked like snakes at first, but later I saw that they were soft and yellow and rubbery and much worse than snakes.

But even then I didn't altogether lose my head. Leastwise, I didn't lose it for long. "This is a sheer hallucination," I said to myself, "and I'm going to argue myself out of it."

I sat down on a big boulder and held my hand up and looked at it. It had a thousand fingers and they dripped, but I made myself look at 'em. I did some tall arguing. "Snap out of it," I said. "You're imagining things!" I thought the fingers began to shorten and stiffen a little. "You're imagining all this," I continued. "It's the sheerest bunk. That box isn't anything out of the ordinary!"

Well sir, you may not believe it, but I argued myself back into sanity. I argued my hand back to normal. The wriggling, twisting things got shorter and fatter and joined together and before very long I had a hand with fingers.

Then I stood up and shouted. Luckily no one heard me, and there wasn't anyone to watch me dancing about on my toes either. When I got out of breath I picked the infernal box up and walked away with it. I made directly for the river. "You've had your day," I said. "You won't turn any more poor critters into jelly-fish!"

Well sir, I threw the vile thing into the river, but first I smashed it against the planks on the wharf until it looked like nothing on earth under the stars. "And that's the end of you!" I shouted as it sank. I ought to have got a medal for that, but I ain't complaining. It isn't every man has the pleasure of calling himself a disinterested benefactor of humanity.

The Vaults of Yoh-Vombis
Clark Ashton Smith

Clark Ashton Smith (1893–1961) was perpetually at odds with science fiction editors for refusing to follow conventional science fiction formulas or tone down the horrors that befall his space-faring human characters. Indeed, Smith's science fiction was little different from the fantasies he contributed to *Weird Tales,* where his vivid imagination and poetic command of vocabulary helped make him one of the magazine's most popular writers. "The Vaults of Yoh-Vombis" appeared in the magazine's May 1932 issue, and features Smith's trademark blend of the awesome and the awful. Smith's science fiction appears throughout his six story collections, but the lion's share can be found in *Tales of Science and Sorcery* and *Other Dimensions.*

If the doctors are correct in their prognostication, I have only a few Martian hours of life remaining to me. In those hours I shall endeavor to relate, as a warning to others who might follow in our footsteps, the singular and frightful happenings that terminated our researches among the ruins of Yoh-Vombis. If my story will only serve to prevent future explorations, the telling will not have been in vain.

There were eight of us, professional archaeologists with more or less terrene and interplanetary experience, who set forth with native guides from Ignarh, the commercial metropolis of Mars, to inspect that ancient, aeon-deserted city. Allan Octave, our official leader, held his primacy by knowing more about Martian archaeology than any other terrestrial on the planet; and others of the party, such as William Harper and Jonas Halgren, had been associated with him in many of his previous researches. I, Rodney Severn, was more of a newcomer, having spent but a few months on Mars; and the greater part of my own ultra-terrene delvings had been confined to Venus.

The nude, spongy-chested Aihais had spoken deterringly of vast deserts filled with ever-swirling sandstorms, through which we must pass to reach Yoh-Vombis; and in spite of our munificent offers of payment, it had been difficult to secure guides for the journey. Therefore we were surprised as well as pleased when we came to the ruins after seven hours of plodding across the flat, treeless, orange-yellow desolation to the southwest of Ignarh.

We beheld our destination, for the first time, in the setting of the small, remote sun. For a little, we thought that the domeless, three-angled towers and broken-down monoliths were those of some unlegended city, other than the one we sought. But the disposition of the ruins, which lay in a sort of arc for almost the entire extent of a low, gneissic, league-long elevation of bare, eroded stone, together with the type of architecture, soon convinced us that we had found our goal. No other ancient city on Mars had been laid out in that manner; and the strange, many-terraced buttresses, like the stairways of forgotten Anakim, were peculiar to the prehistoric race that had built Yoh-Vombis.

I have seen the hoary, sky-confronting walls of Machu Picchu amid the desolate Andes; and the frozen, giant-builded battlements of Uogam on the glacial tundras of the nightward hemisphere of Venus. But these were as things of yesteryear compared to the walls upon which we gazed. The whole region was far from the life-giving canals beyond whose environs even the more noxious flora and fauna are seldom found; and we had seen no living thing since our departure from Ignarh. But here, in this place of petrified sterility, of eternal bareness and solitude, it seemed that life could never have been.

I think we all received the same impression as we stood staring in silence while the pale, sanies-like sunset fell on the dark and megalithic ruins. I remember gasping a little, in an air that seemed to have been touched by the irrespirable chill of death; and I heard the same sharp, laborious intake of breath from others of our party.

"That place is deader than an Egyptian morgue," observed Harper.

"Certainly it is far more ancient," Octave assented. "According to the most reliable legends, the Yorhis, who built Yoh-Vombis, were wiped out by the present ruling race at least forty thousand years ago."

"There's a story, isn't there," said Harper, "that the last remnant of the Yorhis was destroyed by some unknown agency—something too horrible and outré to be mentioned even in a myth?"

"Of course, I've heard that legend," agreed Octave. "Maybe we'll find evidence among the ruins to prove or disprove it. The Yorhis may have been cleaned out by some terrible epidemic, such as the Yashta pestilence, which was a kind of green mould that ate all the bones of the body, together with the teeth and nails. But we needn't be afraid of getting it, if there are any mummies in Yoh-Vombis—the bacteria will all be dead as their victims, after so many cycles of planetary desiccation."

The sun had gone down with uncanny swiftness, as if it had disappeared through some sort of prestidigitation rather than the normal process of setting. We felt the instant chill of the blue-green twilight; and the ether above us was like a huge, transparent dome of sunless ice, shot with a million bleak sparklings that were the stars. We donned the coats and helmets of Martian fur, which must always be worn at night; and going on to westward of the walls, we established our camp in their lee, so that we might be sheltered a little from the *jaar,* that cruel desert wind that always blows from the east before dawn. Then, lighting the alcohol lamps that had been brought along for cooking purposes, we huddled around them while the evening meal was prepared and eaten.

Afterwards, for comfort rather than because of weariness, we retired early to our sleeping bags; and the two Aihais, our guides, wrapped themselves in the cement-like folds of *bassa-*cloth which are all the protection their leathery skins appear to require even in sub-zero temperatures.

Even in my thick, double-lined bag, I still felt the rigor of the night air; and I am sure it was this, rather than anything else, which kept me awake for a long while and rendered my eventual slumber somewhat restless and broken. At any rate, I was not troubled by even the least presentiment of alarm or danger; and I should have laughed at the idea that anything of peril could lurk in Yoh-Vombis, amid whose undreamable and stupefying antiquities the very phantoms of its dead must long since have faded into nothingness.

I must have drowsed again and again, with starts of semi-wakefulness. At last, in one of these, I knew vaguely that the small twin moons, Phobos and Deimos, had risen and were making huge and far-flung shadows with the domeless towers; shadows that almost touched the glimmering, shrouded forms of my companions.

The whole scene was locked in a petrific stillness; and none of the sleepers stirred. Then, as my lids were about to close, I received an impression of movement in the frozen gloom; and it seemed to me that a portion of the foremost shadow had detached itself and was crawling toward Octave, who lay nearer to the ruins than we others.

Even through my heavy lethargy, I was disturbed by a warning of something unnatural and perhaps ominous. I started to sit up; and even as I moved, the shadowy object, whatever it was, drew back and became merged once more in the greater shadow. Its vanishment startled me into full wakefulness; and yet I could not be sure that I had actually seen the thing. In that brief, final glimpse, it had seemed like a roughly circular piece of cloth or leather, dark and crumpled, and twelve or fourteen inches in diameter, that ran along the ground with the doubling movement of an inchworm, causing it to fold and unfold in a startling manner as it went.

I did not go to sleep again for nearly an hour; and if it had not been for the extreme cold, I should doubtless have gotten up to investigate and make sure whether I had really beheld an object of such bizarre nature or had merely dreamt it. But more and more I began to convince myself that the thing was too unlikely and fantastical to have been anything but the figment of a dream. And at last I nodded off into light slumber.

The chill, demoniac sighing of the *jaar* across the jagged walls awoke me, and I saw that the faint moonlight had received the hueless accession of early dawn. We all arose, and prepared our breakfast with fingers that grew numb in spite of the spirit-lamps.

My queer visual experience during the night had taken on more than ever a phantasmagoric unreality; and I gave it no more than a passing thought and did not speak of it to the others. We were all eager to begin our explorations; and shortly after sunrise we started on a preliminary tour of examination.

Strangely, as it seemed, the two Martians refused to accompany us. Stolid and taciturn, they gave no explicit reason; but evidently nothing would induce them to enter Yoh-Vombis. Whether or not they were afraid of the ruins, we were unable to determine: their enigmatic faces, with the small oblique eyes and huge, flaring nostrils, betrayed neither fear nor any other emotion intelligible to man. In reply to our questions, they merely said that no Aihai had set foot among the ruins for ages. Apparently there was some mysterious taboo in connection with the place.

For equipment in that preliminary tour we took along only our electric torches and a crowbar. Our other tools, and some cartridges of high explosives, we left at our camp, to be used later if necessary, after we had surveyed the ground. One or two of us owned automatics; but these also were left behind; for it seemed absurd to imagine that any form of life would be encountered among the ruins.

Octave was visibly excited as we began our inspection, and maintained a running fire of exclamatory comment. The rest of us were subdued and silent: it was impossible to shake off the somber awe and wonder that fell upon us from those megalithic stones.

We went on for some distance among the triangular, terraced buildings, following the zigzag streets that conformed to this peculiar architecture. Most of the towers were more or less dilapidated; and everywhere we saw the deep erosion wrought by cycles of blowing wind and sand, which, in many cases, had worn into roundness the sharp angles of the mighty walls. We entered some of the towers, but found utter emptiness within. Whatever they had contained in the way of furnishings must long ago have crumbled into dust, and the dust had been blown away by the searching desert gales.

At length we came to the wall of a vast terrace, hewn from the plateau itself. On this terrace, the central buildings were grouped like a sort of acropolis. A flight of time-eaten steps, designed for longer limbs than those of men or even the gangling modern Martians, afforded access to the hewn summit.

Pausing, we decided to defer our investigation of the higher buildings, which, being more exposed than the others, were doubly ruinous and dilapidated, and in all likelihood would offer little for our trouble. Octave had begun to voice his disappointment over our failure to find anything in the nature of artifacts that would throw light on the history of Yoh-Vombis.

Then, a little to the right of the stairway, we perceived an entrance in the main wall, half-choked with ancient débris. Behind the heap of detritus, we found the beginning of a downward flight of steps. Darkness poured from the opening, musty with primordial stagnancies of decay; and we could see nothing below the first steps, which gave the appearance of being suspended over a black gulf.

Throwing his torch-beam into the abyss, Octave began to descend the stairs. His eager voice called us to follow.

At the bottom of the high, awkward steps, we found ourselves in a long and roomy vault, like a subterranean hallway. Its floor was deep with siftings of immemorial dust. The air was singularly heavy, as if the lees of an ancient atmosphere, less tenuous than that of Mars today, had settled down and remained in that stagnant darkness. It was harder to breathe than the outer air: it was filled with unknown effluvia; and the light dust arose before us at every step, diffusing a faintness of bygone corruption, like the dust of powdered mummies.

At the end of the vault, before a strait and lofty doorway, our torches revealed an immense shallow urn or pan, supported on short cube-shaped legs, and wrought from a dull, blackish-green material. In its bottom, we perceived a deposit of dark and cinder-like fragments, which gave off a slight but disagreeable pungence, like the phantom of some more powerful odor. Octave, bending over the rim, began to cough and sneeze as he inhaled it.

"That stuff, whatever it was, must have been a pretty strong fumigant," he observed. "The people of Yoh-Vombis may have used it to disinfect the vaults."

The doorway beyond the shallow urn admitted us to a larger chamber, whose floor was comparatively free of dust. We found that the dark stone beneath our feet was marked off in multiform geometric patterns, traced with ochreous ore, amid which, as in Egyptian cartouches, hieroglyphics and highly formalized drawings were enclosed. We could make little from most of them; but the figures in many were doubtless designed to represent the Yorhis themselves. Like the Aihais, they were tall and angular, with great, bellows-like chests. The ears and nostrils, as far as we could judge, were not so huge and flaring as those of the modern Martians. All of these Yorhis were depicted as being nude; but in one of the cartouches, done in a far hastier style than the others, we perceived two figures whose high, conical craniums were wrapped in what seemed to be a sort of turban, which they were about to remove or adjust. The artist seemed to have laid a peculiar emphasis on the odd gesture with which the sinuous, four-jointed fingers were plucking at these headdresses; and the whole posture was unexplainably contorted.

From the second vault, passages ramified in all directions, leading to a veritable warren of catacombs. Here, enormous pot-bellied urns of the same material as the fumigating-pan, but taller than a man's head and fitted with angular-handled stoppers, were ranged in solemn rows along the walls, leaving scant room for two of us to walk abreast. When we succeeded in removing one of the huge stoppers, we saw that the jar was filled to the rim with ashes and charred fragments of bone. Doubtless (as is still the Martian custom) the Yorhis had stored the cremated remains of whole families in single urns.

Even Octave became silent as we went on; and a sort of meditative awe seemed to replace his former excitement. We others, I think, were utterly weighed down to a man by the solid gloom of a concept-defying antiquity, into which it seemed that we were going further and further at every step.

The shadows fluttered before us like the monstrous and misshapen wings of phantom bats. There was nothing anywhere but the atom-like dust of ages, and the jars that held the ashes of a long-extinct people. But, clinging to the high roof in one of the further vaults, I saw a dark and corrugated patch of circular form, like a withered fungus. It was impossible to reach the thing; and we went on after peering at it with many futile conjectures. Oddly enough, I failed to remember at that moment the crumpled, shadowy object I had seen or dreamt of the night before.

I have no idea how far we had gone, when we came to the last vault; but it seemed that we had been wandering for ages in that forgotten underworld. The air was growing fouler and more irrespirable, with a thick, sodden quality, as if from a sediment of material rottenness; and we had about decided to turn back. Then, without warning, at the end of a long, urn-lined catacomb, we found ourselves confronted by a blank wall.

Here we came upon one of the strangest and most mystifying of our discoveries—a mummified and incredibly desiccated figure, standing erect against the wall. It was more than seven feet in height, of a brown bituminous color, and was wholly nude except for a sort of black cowl that covered the upper head and drooped down at the sides in wrinkled folds. From the size and general contour, it was plainly one of the ancient Yorhis—perhaps the sole member of this race whose body had remained intact.

We all felt an inexpressible thrill at the sheer age of this shrivelled thing, which, in the dry air of the vault, had endured through all the historic and geologic vicissitudes of the planet, to provide a visible link with lost cycles.

Then, as we peered closer with our torches, we saw *why* the mummy had maintained an upright position. At ankles, knees, waist, shoulders, and neck it was shackled to the wall by heavy metal bands, so deeply eaten and embrowned with a sort of rust that we had failed to distinguish them at first sight in the shadow. The strange cowl on the head, when closelier studied, continued to baffle us. It was covered with a fine, mould-like pile, unclean and dusty as ancient cobwebs. Something about it, I know not what, was abhorrent and revolting.

"By Jove! this is a real find!" ejaculated Octave, as he thrust his torch into the mummified face, where shadows moved like living things in the pit-deep hollows of the eyes and the huge triple nostrils and wide ears that flared upward beneath the cowl.

Still lifting the torch, he put out his free hand and touched the body very lightly. Tentative as the touch had been, the lower part of the barrel-like torso, the legs, the hands and forearms, all seemed to dissolve into powder, leaving the head and upper body and arms still hanging in their metal fetters. The progress of decay had been queerly unequal, for the remnant portions gave no sign of disintegration.

Octave cried out in dismay, and then began to cough and sneeze, as the cloud of brown powder, floating with airy lightness, enveloped him. We others all stepped back to avoid the powder. Then, above the spreading cloud, I saw an unbelievable thing. The black cowl on the mummy's head began to curl and twitch upward at the corners, it writhed with a verminous motion, it fell from the withered cranium, seeming to fold and unfold convulsively in midair as it fell. Then it dropped on the bare head of Octave who, in his disconcertment at the crumbling of the mummy, had remained standing close to the wall. At that instant, in a start of profound terror, I remember the thing that had inched itself from the shadows of Yoh-Vombis in the light of the twin moons, and had drawn back like a figment of slumber at my first waking movement.

Cleaving closely as a tightened cloth, the thing enfolded Octave's hair and brow and eyes, and he shrieked wildly, with incoherent pleas for help, and tore with frantic fingers at the cowl, but failed to loosen it. Then his cries began to mount in a mad crescendo of agony, as if beneath some instrument of infernal torture; and he danced and capered blindly about the vault, eluding us with strange celerity as we all sprang forward in an effort to reach him and release him from his weird encumbrance. The whole happening was mysterious as a nightmare; but the thing that had fallen on his head was plainly some unclassified form of Martian life, which, contrary to all the known laws of science, had survived in those primordial catacombs. We must rescue him from its clutches if we could.

We tried to close in on the frenzied figure of our chief— which, in the far from roomy space between the last urns and the wall, should have been an easy matter. But, darting away, in a manner doubly incomprehensible because of his blindfolded condition, he circled about us and ran past, to disappear among the urns toward the outer labyrinth of intersecting catacombs.

"My God! What has happened to him?" cried Harper. "The man acts as if he were possessed."

There was obviously no time for a discussion of the enigma, and we all followed Octave as speedily as our astonishment would permit. We had lost sight of him in the darkness; and when we came to the first division of the vaults, we were doubtful as to which passage he had taken, till we heard a shrill scream, several times repeated, in a catacomb on the extreme left. There was a weird, unearthly quality in those screams, which may have been due to the long-stagnant air or the peculiar acoustics of the ramifying caverns. But somehow I could not imagine them as issuing from human lips—at least not from those of a living man. They seemed to contain a soulless, mechanical agony, as if they had been wrung from a devil-driven corpse.

Thrusting our torches before us into the lurching, fleeing shadows, we raced along between rows of mighty urns. The screaming had died away in sepulchral silence; but far off we heard the light and muffled thud of running feet. We followed in headlong pursuit; but, gasping painfully in the vitiated, miasmal air, we were soon compelled to slacken our pace without coming in sight of Octave. Very faintly, and further away than ever, like the tomb-swallowed steps of a phantom, we heard his vanishing footfalls. Then they ceased; and we heard nothing, except our own convulsive breathing, and the blood that throbbed in our temple-veins like steadily beaten drums of alarm.

We went on, dividing our party into three contingents when we came to a triple branching of the caverns. Harper and Halgren and I took the middle passage, and after we had gone on for an endless interval without finding any trace of Octave, and had threaded our way through recesses piled to the roof with colossal urns that must have held the ashes of a hundred generations, we came out in the huge chamber with the geometric floor-designs. Here, very shortly, we were joined by the others, who had likewise failed to locate our missing leader.

It would be useless to detail our renewed and hour-long search of the myriad vaults, many of which we had not hitherto explored. All were empty, as far as any sign of life was concerned. I remember passing once more through the vault in which I had seen the dark, rounded patch on the ceiling, and noting with a shudder that the patch was gone. It was a miracle that we did not lose ourselves in that underworld maze; but at last we came back again to the final catacomb, in which we had found the shackled mummy.

We heard a measured and recurrent clangor as we neared the place—a most alarming and mystifying sound under the circumstances. It was like the hammering of ghouls on some forgotten mausoleum. When we drew nearer, the beams of our torches revealed a sight that was no less unexplainable than unexpected. A human figure, with its back toward us and the head concealed by a swollen black object that had the size and form of a sofa cushion, was standing near the remains of the mummy and was striking at the wall with a pointed metal bar. How long Octave had been there, and where he had found the bar, we could not know. But the blank wall had crumbled away beneath his furious blows, leaving on the floor a pile of cement-like fragments; and a small, narrow door, of the same ambiguous material as the cinerary urns and the fumigating-pan, had been laid bare.

Amazed, uncertain, inexpressibly bewildered, we were all incapable of action or volition at that moment. The whole business was too fantastic and too horrifying, and it was plain that Octave had been overcome by some sort of madness. I, for one, felt the violent upsurge of sudden nausea when I had identified the loathsomely bloated thing that clung to Octave's head and drooped in obscene tumescence on his neck. I did not dare to surmise the causation of its bloating.

Before any of us could recover our faculties, Octave flung aside the metal bar and began to fumble for something in the wall. It must have been a hidden spring; though how he could have known its location or existence is beyond all legitimate conjecture. With a dull, hideous grating, the uncovered door swung inward, thick and ponderous as a mausolean slab, leaving an aperture from which the nether midnight seemed to well like a flood of aeon-buried foulness. Somehow, at that instant, our electric torches flickered and grew dim; and we all breathed a suffocating fetor, like a draught from inner worlds of immemorial putrescence.

Octave had turned toward us now, and he stood in an idle posture before the open door, like one who has finished some ordained task. I was the first of our party to throw off the paralyzing spell; and pulling out a clasp-knife—the only semblance of a weapon which I carried—I ran over to him. He moved back, but not quickly enough to evade me, when I stabbed with the four-inch blade at the black, turgescent mass that enveloped his whole upper head and hung down upon his eyes.

What the thing was, I should prefer not to imagine—if it were possible to imagine. It was formless as a great slug, with neither head nor tail nor apparent organs—an unclean, puffy, leathery thing, covered with that fine, mould-like fur of which I have spoken. The knife tore into it as if through rotten parchment, making a long gash, and the horror appeared to collapse like a broken bladder. Out of it there gushed a sickening torrent of human blood, mingled with dark, filiated masses that may have been half-dissolved hair, and floating gelatinous lumps like molten bone, and shreds of a curdy white substance. At the same time, Octave began to stagger, and went down at full length on the floor. Disturbed by his fall, the mummy dust arose about him in a curling cloud, beneath which he lay mortally still.

Conquering my revulsion, and choking with the dust, I bent over him and tore the flaccid, oozing horror from his head. It came with unexpected ease, as if I had removed a limp rag: but I wish to God that I had let it remain. Beneath, there was no longer a human cranium, for all had been eaten away, even to the eyebrows, and the half-devoured brain was laid bare as I lifted the cowl-like object. I dropped the unnamable thing from fingers that had grown suddenly nerveless, and it turned over as it fell, revealing on the nether side many rows of pinkish suckers, arranged in circles about a pallid disk that was covered with nerve-like filaments, suggesting a sort of plexus.

My companions had pressed forward behind me; but, for an appreciable interval, no one spoke.

"How long do you suppose he has been dead?" It was Halgren who whispered the awful question, which we had all been asking ourselves. Apparently no one felt able or willing to answer it; and we could only stare in horrible, timeless fascination at Octave.

At length I made an effort to avert my gaze; and turning at random, I saw the remnants of the shackled mummy, and noted for the first time, with mechanical, unreal horror, the half-eaten condition of the withered head. From this, my gaze was diverted to the newly opened door at one side, without perceiving for a moment what had drawn my attention. Then, startled, I beheld beneath my torch, far down beyond the door, as if in some nether pit, a seething, multitudinous, worm-like movement of crawling shadows. They seemed to boil up in the darkness; and then, over the broad threshold of the vault, there poured the verminous vanguard of a countless army: things that were kindred to the monstrous, diabolic leech I had torn from Octave's eaten head. Some were thin and flat, like writhing, doubling disks of cloth or leather, and others were more or less poddy, and crawled with glutted slowness. What they had found to feed on in the sealed, eternal midnight I do not know; and I pray that I never shall know.

I sprang back and away from them, electrified with terror, sick with loathing, and the black army inched itself unendingly with nightmare swiftness from the unsealed abyss, like the nauseous vomit of horror-sated hells. As it poured toward us, burying Octave's body from sight in a writhing wave, I saw a stir of life from the seemingly dead thing I had cast aside, and saw the loathly struggle which it made to right itself and join the others.

But neither I nor my companions could endure to look

longer. We turned and ran between the mighty rows of urns, with the slithering mass of demon leeches close upon us, and scattered in blind panic when we came to the first division of the vaults. Heedless of each other or of anything but the urgency of flight, we plunged into the ramifying passages at random. Behind me, I heard someone stumble and go down, with a curse that mounted to an insane shrieking; but I knew that if I halted and went back, it would be only to invite the same baleful doom that had overtaken the hindmost of our party.

Still clutching the electric torch and my open clasp-knife, I ran along a minor passage which, I seemed to remember, would conduct with more or less directness upon the large outer vault with the painted floor. Here I found myself alone. The others had kept to the main catacombs; and I heard far off a muffled babel of mad cries, as if several of them had been seized by their pursuers.

It seemed that I must have been mistaken about the direction of the passage; for it turned and twisted in an unfamiliar manner, with many intersections, and I soon found that I was lost in the black labyrinth, where the dust had lain unstirred by living feet for inestimable generations. The cinerary warren had grown still once more; and I heard my own frenzied panting, loud and stertorous as that of a Titan in the dead silence.

Suddenly, as I went on, my torch disclosed a human figure coming toward me in the gloom. Before I could master my startlement, the figure had passed me with long, machine-like strides, as if returning to the inner vaults. I think it was Harper, since the height and build were about right for him; but I am not altogether sure, for the eyes and upper head were muffled by a dark, inflated cowl, and the pale lips were locked as if in a silence of tetanic torture—or death. Whoever he was, he had dropped his torch; and he was running blindfolded, in utter darkness, beneath the impulsion of that unearthly vampirism, to seek the very fountainhead of the unloosed horror. I knew that he was beyond human help; and I did not even dream of trying to stop him.

Trembling violently, I resumed my flight, and was passed by two more of our party, stalking by with mechanical swiftness and sureness, and cowled with those Satanic leeches. The others must have returned by way of the main passages; for I did not meet them; and I was never to see them again.

The remainder of my flight is a blur of pandemonian terror. Once more, after thinking that I was near the outer cavern, I found myself astray, and fled through a ranged eternity of monstrous urns, in vaults that must have extended for an unknown distance beyond our explorations. It seemed that I had gone on for years; and my lungs were choking with the aeon-dead air, and my legs were ready to crumble beneath me, when I saw far off a tiny point of blessed daylight. I ran toward it, with all the terrors of the alien darkness crowding behind me, and accursed shadows flittering before, and saw that the vault ended in a low, ruinous entrance, littered by rubble on which there fell an arc of thin sunshine.

It was another entrance than the one by which we had penetrated this lethal underworld. I was within a dozen feet of the opening when, without sound or other intimation, something dropped upon my head from the roof above, blinding me instantly and closing upon me like a tautened net. My brow and scalp, at the same time, were shot through with a million needle-like pangs—a manifold, ever-growing agony that seemed to pierce the very bone and converge from all sides upon my inmost brain.

The terror and suffering of that moment were worse than aught which the hells of earthly madness or delirium could ever contain. I felt the foul, vampiric clutch of an atrocious death—and of more than death.

I believe that I dropped the torch; but the fingers of my right hand had still retained the open knife. Instinctively—since I was hardly capable of conscious volition—I raised the knife and slashed blindly, again and again, many times, at the thing that had fastened its deadly folds upon me. The blade must have gone through and through the clinging monstrosity, to gash my own flesh in a score of places; but I did not feel the pain of those wounds in the million-throbbing torment that possessed me.

At last I saw light, and saw that a black strip, loosened from above my eyes and dripping with my own blood, was hanging down my cheek. It writhed a little, even as it hung, and I ripped it away, and ripped the other remnants of the thing, tatter by oozing, bloody tatter, from off my brow and head. Then I staggered toward the entrance; and the wan light turned to a far, receding, dancing flame before me as I lurched and fell outside the cavern—a flame that fled like the last star of creation above the yawning, sliding chaos and oblivion into which I descended. . . .

I am told that my unconsciousness was of brief duration. I came to myself, with the cryptic faces of the two Martian guides bending over me. My head was full of lancinating pains, and half-remembered terrors closed upon my mind like the shadows of mustering harpies. I rolled over, and looked back toward the cavern-mouth, from which the Martians, after finding me, had seemingly dragged me for some little distance. The mouth was under the terraced angle of an outer building, and within sight of our camp.

I stared at the black opening with hideous fascination, and descried a shadowy stirring in the gloom—the writhing, verminous movement of things that pressed forward from the darkness but did not emerge into the light. Doubtless they could not endure the sun, those creatures of ultra-mundane night and cycle-sealed corruption.

It was then that the ultimate horror, the beginning madness, came upon me. Amid my crawling revulsion, my nausea-prompted desire to flee from that seething cavern-mouth, there rose an abhorrently conflicting impulse to return; to thread my backward way through all the catacombs, as the others had done; to go down where never men save they, the inconceivably doomed and accursed, had ever gone; to seek beneath that damnable compulsion a nether world that human thought can never picture. There was a black light, a soundless calling, in the vaults of my brain: the implanted summons of the Thing, like a permeating and sorcerous poison. It lured me to the subterranean door that was walled up by the dying people of Yoh-Vombis, to immure those hellish and immortal leeches, those dark parasites that engraft their own abominable life on the half-eaten brains of the dead. It called me to the depths beyond, where dwell the noisome, necromantic Ones, of whom the leeches, with all their powers of vampirism and diabolism, are but the merest minions. . . .

It was only the two Aihais who prevented me from going back. I struggled, I fought them insanely as they strove to retard me with their spongy arms; but I must have been pretty thoroughly exhausted from all the superhuman adventures of the day; and I went down once more, after a little, into fathomless nothingness, from which I floated out at long intervals, to realize that I was being carried across the desert toward Ignarh.

Well, that is all my story. I have tried to tell it fully and coherently, at a cost that would be unimaginable to the sane

... to tell it before the madness falls upon me again, as it will very soon—as it is doing now. ... Yes, I have told my story ... and you have written it all out, haven't you? Now I must go back to Yoh-Vombis—back across the desert and down through all the catacombs to the vaster vaults beneath. Something is in my brain, that commands me and will direct me. ... I tell you, I must go. ...

POSTSCRIPT

As an interne in the terrestrial hospital at Ignarh, I had charge of the singular case of Rodney Severn, the one surviving member of the Octave Expedition to Yoh-Vombis, and took down the above story from his dictation. Severn had been brought to the hospital by the Martian guides of the Expedition. He was suffering from a horribly lacerated and inflamed condition of the scalp and brow, and was wildly delirious part of the time and had to be held down in his bed during recurrent seizures of a mania whose violence was doubly inexplicable in view of his extreme debility.

The lacerations, as will have been learned from the story, were mainly self-inflicted. They were mingled with numerous small round wounds, easily distinguished from the knife-slashes, and arranged in regular circles, through which an unknown poison had been injected into Severn's scalp. The causation of these wounds was difficult to explain; unless one were to believe that Severn's story was true, and was no mere figment of his illness. Speaking for myself, in the light of what afterwards occurred, I feel that I have no other recourse than to believe it. There are strange things on the red planet; and I can only second the wish that was expressed by the doomed archaeologist in regard to future explorations.

The night after he had finished telling me his story, while another doctor than myself was supposedly on duty, Severn managed to escape from the hospital, doubtless in one of the strange seizures at which I have hinted: a most astonishing thing, for he had seemed weaker than ever after the long strain of his terrible narrative, and his demise had been hourly expected. More astonishing still, his bare footsteps were found in the desert, going toward Yoh-Vombis, till they vanished in the path of a light sandstorm; but no trace of Severn himself has yet been discovered.

Who Goes There?
John W. Campbell, Jr.

Between 1937 and 1971, John W. Campbell (1910–71) edited *Astounding Science Fiction* (later retitled *Analog*), the magazine that transformed science fiction into a branch of writing distinct from fantasy and horror and that launched the careers of Isaac Asimov, Robert A. Heinlein, A. E. van Vogt, Theodore Sturgeon, and many other writers of science fiction's "Golden Age." Prior to assuming his editorial duties, Campbell wrote super-science adventures under his own name; and stories that examined the impact of scientific progress on human psychology and behavior under the pen name Don A. Stuart. "Who Goes There?" a Don A. Stuart story, is a memorable blend of scientific problem-solving and paranoid terror that has been filmed twice as *The Thing* in 1951 and 1982.

1

The place stank. A queer, mingled stench that only the ice-buried cabins of an antarctic camp know, compounded of reeking human sweat, and the heavy, fish-oil stench of melted seal blubber. An overtone of liniment combatted the musty smell of sweat-and-snow-drenched furs. The acrid odor of burnt cooking fat, and the animal, not-unpleasant smell of dogs, diluted by time, hung in the air.

Linger odors of machine oil contrasted sharply with the taint of harness dressing and leather. Yet, somehow, through all that reek of human beings and their associates—dogs, machines, and cooking—came another taint. It was a queer, neck-ruffling thing, a faintest suggestion of an odor alien among the smells of industry and life. And it was a life-smell. But it came from the thing that lay bound with cord and tarpaulin on the table, dripping slowly, methodically onto the heavy planks, dank and gaunt under the unshielded glare of the electric light.

Blair, the little bald-pated biologist of the expedition, twitched nervously at the wrappings, exposing a clear, dark ice beneath and then pulling the tarpaulin back into place restlessly. His little birdlike motions of suppressed eagerness danced his shadow across the fringe of dingy gray underwear hanging from the low ceiling, the equatorial fringe of stiff, graying hair around his naked skull a comical halo about the shadow's head.

Commander Garry brushed aside the lax legs of a suit of underwear, and stepped toward the table. Slowly his eyes traced around the rings of men sardined into the Administration Building. His tall, stiff body straightened finally, and he nodded. 'Thirty-seven. All here.' His voice was low, yet carried the clear authority of the commander by nature, as well as by title.

'You know the outline of the story back of that find of the Secondary Pole Expedition. I have been conferring with Second-in-Command McReady, and Norris, as well as Blair and Dr. Copper. There is a difference of opinion, and because it involves the entire group, it is only just that the entire Expedition personnel act on it.

'I am going to ask McReady to give you the details of the story, because each of you has been too busy with his own work to follow closely the endeavors of the others. McReady?'

Moving from the smoke-blued background, McReady was a figure from some forgotten myth, a looming, bronze statue that held life, and walked. Six feet four inches he stood as he halted beside the table, and with a characteristic glance upward to assure himself of room under the low ceiling beams, straightened. His rough, clashingly orange windproof jacket he still had on, yet on his huge frame it did not seem misplaced. Even here, four feet beneath the drift-wind that droned across the antarctic waste above the ceiling, the cold of the frozen continent leaked in, and gave meaning to the harshness of the man. And he was bronze—his great red-bronze beard, the heavy hair that matched it. The gnarled, corded hands gripping, relaxing, gripping and relaxing on the table planks were bronze. Even the deep-sunken eyes beneath heavy brows were bronzed.

Age-resisting endurance of the metal spoke in the cragged

heavy outlines of his face, and the mellow tones of the heavy voice. 'Norris and Blair agree on one thing; that animal we found was not—terrestrial in origin. Norris fears there may be danger in that; Blair says there is none.

'But I'll go back to how, and why we found it. To all that was known before we came here, it appeared that this point was exactly over the South Magnetic Pole of Earth. The compass does point straight down here, as you all know. The more delicate instruments of the physicists, instruments especially designed for this expedition and its study of the magnetic pole, detected a secondary effect, a secondary, less powerful magnetic influence about eighty miles southwest of here.

'The Secondary Magnetic Expedition went out to investigate it. There is no need for details. We found it, but it was not the huge meteorite or magnetic mountain Norris had expected to find. Iron ore is magnetic, of course; iron more so—and certain special steels even more magnetic. From the surface indications, the secondary pole we found was small, so small that the magnetic effect it had was preposterous. No magnetic material conceivable could have that effect. Soundings through the ice indicated it was within one hundred feet of the glacier surface.

'I think you should know the structure of the place. There is a broad plateau, a level sweep that runs more than 150 miles due south from the Secondary Station, Van Wall says. He didn't have time or fuel to fly farther, but it was running smoothly due south then. Right there, where that buried thing was, there is an ice-drowned mountain ridge, a granite wall of unshakable strength that has damned back the ice creeping from the south.

'And four hundred miles due south is the South Polar Plateau. You have asked me at various times why it gets warmer here when the wind rises, and most of you know. As a meteorologist I'd have staked my word that no wind could blow at −70 degrees; that no more than a five-mile wind could blow at −50; without causing warming due to friction with ground, snow and ice and the air itself.

'We camped there on the lip of that ice-drowned mountain range for twelve days. We dug our camp into the blue ice that formed the surface, and escaped most of it. But for twelve consecutive days the wind blew at forty-five miles an hour. It went as high as forty-eight, and fell to forty-one at times. The temperature was –63 degrees. It rose to –60 and fell to –68. It was meteorologically impossible, and it went on uninterruptedly for twelve days and twelve nights.

'Somewhere to the south, the frozen air of the South Polar Plateau slides down from that 18,000-foot bowl, down a mountain pass, over a glacier, and starts north. There must be a funneling mountain chain that directs it, and sweeps it away for four hundred miles to hit that bold plateau where we found the secondary pole, and 350 miles farther north reaches the Antarctic Ocean.

'It's been frozen there since Antarctica froze twenty million years ago. There never has been a thaw there.

'Twenty million years ago Antarctica was beginning to freeze. We've investigated, though and built speculations. What we believe happened was about like this.

'Something came down out of space, a ship. We saw it there in the blue ice, a thing like a submarine without a conning tower or directive vanes, 280 feet long and 45 feet in diameter at its thickest.

'Eh, Van Wall? Space? Yes, but I'll explain that better later.' McReady's steady voice went on.

'It came down from space, driven and lifted by forces men haven't discovered yet, and somehow—perhaps something went wrong then—it tangled with Earth's magnetic field. It came south here, out of control probably, circling the magnetic pole. That's a savage country there; but when Antarctica was still freezing, it must have been a thousand times more savage. There must have been blizzard snow, as well as drift, new snow falling as the continent glaciated. The swirl there must have been particularly bad, the wind hurling a solid blanket of white over the lip of that now-buried mountain.

'The ship struck solid granite head-on, and cracked up. Not every one of the passengers in it was killed, but the ship must have been ruined, her driving mechanism locked. It tangled with Earth's field, Norris believes. No thing made by intelligent beings can tangle with the dead immensity of a planet's natural forces and survive.

'One of its passengers stepped out. The wind we saw there never fell below forty-one, and the temperature never rose above –60. Then—the wind must have been stronger. And there was drift falling in a solid sheet. The *thing* was lost completely in ten paces.' He paused for a moment, the deep, steady voice giving way to the drone of wind overhead and the uneasy, malicious gurgling in the pipe of the galley stove.

Drift—a drift-wind was sweeping by overhead. Right now the snow picked up by the mumbling wind fled in level, blinding lines across the face of the buried camp. If a man stepped out of the tunnels that connected each of the camp buildings beneath the surface, he'd be lost in ten paces. Out there, the slim, black finger of the radio mast lifted three hundred feet into the air, and at its peak was the clear night sky. A sky of thin, whining wind rushing steadily from beyond to another beyond under the licking, curling mantle of the aurora. And off north, the horizon flamed with queer, angry colors of the midnight twilight. That was spring three hundred feet above Antarctica.

At the surface—it was white death. Death of a needle-fingered cold driven before the wind, sucking heat from any warm thing. Cold—and white mist of endless, everlasting drift, the fine, fine particles of licking snow that obscured all things.

Kinner, the little, scar-faced cook, winced. Five days ago he had stepped out to the surface to reach a cache of frozen beef. He had reached it, started back—and the drift-wind leapt out of the south. Cold, white death that streamed across the ground blinded him in twenty seconds. He stumbled on wildly in circles. It was half an hour before rope-guided men from below found him in the impenetrable murk.

It was easy for man—or *thing*—to get lost in ten paces.

'And the drift-wind then was probably more impenetrable than we know.' McReady's voice snapped Kinner's mind back. Back to the welcome, dank warmth of the Ad Building. 'The passenger of the ship wasn't prepared either, it appears. It froze within ten feet of the ship.

'We dug down to find the ship, and our tunnel happened to find the frozen—animal. Barclay's ice-ax struck its skull.

'When we saw what it was, Barclay went back to the tractor, started the fire up and when the steam pressure built, sent a call for Blair and Dr. Copper. Barclay himself was sick then. Stayed sick for three days, as a matter of fact.

'When Blair and Copper came, we cut out the animal in a block of ice, as you see, wrapped it and loaded it on the tractor for return here. We wanted to get into that ship.

'We reached the side and found the metal was something

we didn't know. Our beryllium-bronze, non-magnetic tools wouldn't touch it. Barclay had some tool-steel on the tractor, and that wouldn't scratch it either. We made reasonable tests—even tried some acid from the batteries with no results.

'They must have had a passivating process to make magnesium metal resist acid that way, and the alloy must have been at least ninety-five percent magnesium. But we had no way of guessing that, so when we spotted the barely opened lock door, we cut around it. There was clear, hard ice inside the lock, where we couldn't reach it. Through the little crack we could look in and see that only metal and tools were in there, so we decided to loosen the ice with a bomb.

'We had decanite bombs and thermite. Thermite is the ice-softener; decanite might have shattered valuable things, where the thermite's heat would just loosen the ice. Dr. Copper, Norris and I placed a twenty-five-pound thermite bomb, wired it, and took the connector up the tunnel to the surface, where Blair had the steam tractor waiting. A hundred yards the other side of that granite wall we set off the thermite bomb.

'The magnesium metal of the ship caught of course. The glow of the bomb flared and died, then it began to flare again. We ran back to the tractor, and gradually the glare built up. From where we were we could see the whole ice-field illuminated from beneath with an unbearable light; the ship's shadow was a great, dark cone reaching off toward the north, where the twilight was just about gone. For a moment it lasted, and we counted three other shadow-things that might have been other—passengers—frozen there. Then the ice was crashing down and against the ship.

'That's why I told you about that place. The wind sweeping down from the Pole was at our backs. Steam and hydrogen flame were torn away in white ice-fog; the flaming heat under the ice there was yanked away toward the Antarctic Ocean before it touched us. Otherwise we wouldn't have come back, even with the shelter of that granite ridge that stopped the light.

'Somehow in the blinding inferno we could see great hunched things—black bulks. They shed even the furious incandescence of the magnesium for a time. Those must have been the engines, we knew. Secrets going in blazing glory—secrets that might have given Man the planets. Mysterious things that could lift and hurl that ship—and had soaked in the force of the Earth's magnetic field. I saw Norris' mouth move, and ducked. I couldn't hear him.

'Insulation—something—gave way. All Earth's field they'd soaked up twenty million years before broke loose. The aurora in the sky above licked down, and the whole plateau there was bathed in cold fire that blanketed vision. The ice-ax in my hand got red hot, and hissed on the ice. Metal buttons on my clothes burned into me. And a flash of electric blue seared upward from beyond the granite wall.

'Then the walls of ice crashed down on it. For an instant it squealed the way dry ice does when it's pressed between metal.

'We were blind and groping in the dark for hours while our eyes recovered. We found every coil within a mile was fused rubbish, the dynamo and every radio set, the earphones and speakers. If we hadn't had the steam tractor, we wouldn't have gotten over the Secondary Camp.

'Van Wall flew in from Big Magnet at sun-up, as you know. We came home as soon as possible. That is the history of—that.' McReady's great bronze beard gestured toward the thing on the table.

2

Blair stirred uneasily, his little, bony fingers wriggling under the harsh light. Little brown freckles on his knuckles slid back and forth as the tendons under the skin twitched. He pulled aside a bit of the tarpaulin and looked impatiently at the dark ice-bound thing inside.

McReady's big body straightened somewhat. He'd ridden the rocking, jarring steam tractor forty miles that day, pushing onto Big Magnet here. Even his calm will had been passed by the anxiety to mix again with humans. It was lone and quiet out there in Secondary Camp, where a wolf-wind howled down from the Pole. Wolf-wind howling in his sleep—winds droning and the evil, unspeakable face of that monster leering up as he'd first seen it through clear, blue ice, with a bronze ice-ax buried in its skull.

The giant meteorologist spoke again. 'The problem is this. Blair wants to examine the thing. Thaw it out and make micro slides of its tissues and so forth. Norris doesn't believe that is safe, and Blair does. Dr. Copper agrees pretty much with Blair. Norris is a physicist, of course, not a biologist. But he makes a point I think we should all hear. Blair has described the microscopic life-forms biologists find living, even in this cold and unhospitable place. They freeze every winter, and thaw every summer—for three months— and live.

'The point Norris makes is—they thaw, and live again. There must have been microscopic life associated with this creature. There is with every living thing we know. And Norris is afraid that we may release a plague—some germ disease unknown to Earth—if we thaw those microscopic things that have been frozen there for twenty million years.

'Blair admits that such micro-life might retain the power of living. Such unorganized things as individual cells can retain life for unknown periods, when solidly frozen. The beast itself is as dead as those frozen mammoths they find in Siberia. Organized, highly developed life-forms can't stand that treatment.

'But micro-life could. Norris suggests that we may release some disease-form that man, never having met it before, will be utterly defenseless against.

'Blair's answer is that there may be such still-living germs, but that Norris has the case reversed. They are utterly nonimmune to man. Our life-chemistry probably—'

'Probably!' The little biologist's head lifted in a quick, birdlike motion. The halo of gray hair about his bald head ruffled as though angry. 'Heh, one look—'

'I know,' McReady acknowledged. 'The thing is not Earthly. It does not seem likely that it can have a life-chemistry sufficiently like ours to make cross-infection remotely possible. I would say that there is no danger.'

McReady looked toward Dr. Copper. The physician shook his head slowly. 'None whatever,' he asserted confidently. 'Man cannot infect or be infected by germs that live in such comparatively close relatives as the snakes. And they are, I assure you,' his clean-shaven face grimaced uneasily, '*much* nearer to us than—*that.*'

Vance Norris moved angrily. He was comparatively short in this gathering of big men, some five feet eight, and his stocky, powerful build tended to make him feel shorter. His black hair was crisp and hard, like short, steel wires, and his eyes were the gray of fractured steel. If McReady was a man of bronze, Norris was all steel. His movements, his thoughts, his whole bearing had the quick, hard impulse of a steel spring. His nerves were steel—hard, quick acting— swift corroding.

He was decided on his point now, and he lashed out in its defense with a characteristic quick, clipped flow of words. 'Different chemistry be damned. That thing may be dead—or, by God, it may not—but I don't like it. Damn it, Blair, let them see the monstrosity you are petting over there. Let them see the foul thing and decide for themselves whether they want that thing thawed out in this camp.

'Thawed out, by the way. That's got to be thawed out in one of the shacks tonight, if it is thawed out. Somebody— who's watchman tonight? Magnetic—oh, Connant. Cosmic rays tonight. Well, you get to sit with that twenty-million-year-old mummy of his. Unwrap it, Blair. How the hell can they tell what they are buying, if they can't see it? It may have a different chemistry. I don't care what else it has, but I know it has something I don't want. If you can judge by the look on its face—it isn't human so maybe you can't—it was annoyed when it froze. Annoyed, in fact, is just about as close as an approximation of the way it felt, as crazy, mad, insane hatred. Neither one touches the subject.

'How the hell can these birds tell what they are voting on? They haven't seen those three red eyes and that blue hair like crawling worms. Crawling—damn, it's crawling there in the ice right now!

'Nothing Earth ever spawned had the unutterable sublimation of devastating wrath that thing let loose in its face when it looked around its frozen desolation twenty million years ago. Mad? It was mad clear through—searing, blistering mad!

'Hell, I've had bad dreams ever since I looked at those three red eyes. Nightmares. Dreaming the thing thawed out and came to life—that it wasn't dead, or even wholly unconscious all those twenty million years, but just slowed, waiting—waiting. You'll dream, too, while that damned thing that Earth wouldn't own is dripping, dripping in the Cosmos House tonight.

'And, Connant,' Norris whipped toward the cosmic ray specialist, 'won't you have fun sitting up all night in the quiet. Wind whining above—and that thing dripping—' he stopped for a moment, and looked around.

'I know. That's not science. But this is, it's psychology. You'll have nightmares for a year to come. Every night since I looked at that thing I've had 'em. That's why I hate it—sure I do—and don't want it around. Put it back where it came from and let it freeze for another twenty million years. I had some swell nightmares—that it wasn't made like we are—which is obvious—but of a different kind of flesh that it can really control. That it can change its shape, and look like a man—and wait to kill and eat—

'That's not a logical argument. I know it isn't. The thing isn't Earth-logic anyway.

'Maybe it has an alien body-chemistry, and maybe its bugs do have a different body-chemistry. A germ might not stand that, but, Blair and Copper, how about a virus? That's just an enzyme molecule, you've said. That wouldn't need anything but a protein molecule of any body to work on.

'And how are you so sure of that, of the million varieties of microscopic life it may have, *none* of them are dangerous. How about diseases like hydrophobia—rabies—that attack any warm-blooded creature, whatever its body-chemistry may be? And parrot fever? Have you a body like a parrot, Blair? And plain rot—gangrene—necrosis if you want? *That* isn't choosy about body chemistry!'

Blair looked up from his puttering long enough to meet Norris' angry, gray eyes for an instant. 'So far the only thing you have said this thing gave off that was catching was dreams. I'll go so far as to admit that.' An impish, slightly malignant grin crossed the little man's seamed face. 'I had some, too. So. It's dream-infectious. No doubt an exceedingly dangerous malady.

'So far as your other things go, you have a badly mistaken idea about viruses. In the first place, nobody has shown that the enzyme-molecule theory, and that alone, explains them. And in the second place, when you catch tobacco mosaic or wheat rust, let me know. A wheat plant is a lot nearer your body-chemistry than this other-world creature is.

'And your rabies is limited, strictly limited. You can't get it from, nor give it to, a wheat plant or a fish—which is a collateral descendant of a common ancestor of yours. Which this, Norris, is not.' Blair nodded pleasantly toward the tarpaulined bulk on the table.

'Well, thaw the damned thing in a tub of formalin if you must. I've suggested that—'

'And I've said there would be no sense in it. You can't compromise. Why did you and Commander Garry come down here to study magnetism? Why weren't you content to stay at home? There's magnetic force enough in New York. I could no more study the life this thing once had from a formalin-pickled sample than you could get the information you wanted back in New York. And—if this one is so treated, *never in all time to come can there be a duplicate*! The race it came from must have passed away in the twenty million years it lay frozen, so that even if it came from Mars then, we'd never find its like. And—the ship is gone.

'There's only one way to do this—and that is the best possible way. It must be thawed slowly, carefully, and not in formalin.'

Commander Garry stood forward again, and Norris stepped back muttering angrily. 'I think Blair is right, gentlemen. What do you say?'

Connant grunted. 'It sounds right to us, I think—only perhaps he ought to stand watch over it while it's thawing.' He grinned ruefully, brushing a stray lock of ripe-cherry hair back from his forehead. 'Swell idea, in fact—if he sits up with his jolly little corpse.'

Garry smiled slightly. A general chuckle of agreement rippled over the group. 'I should think any ghost it may have had would have starved to death if it hung around here that long, Connant,' Garry suggested. 'And you look capable of taking care of it. "Ironman" Connant ought to be able to take out any opposing players, still.'

Connant shook himself uneasily. 'I'm not worrying about ghosts. Let's see that thing. I—'

Eagerly Blair was stripping back the ropes. A single throw of the tarpaulin revealed the thing. The ice had melted somewhat in the heat of the room, and it was clear and blue as thick, good glass. It shone wet and sleek under the harsh light of the unshielded globe above.

The room stiffened abruptly. It was face up there on the plain, greasy planks of the table. The broken haft of the bronze ice-ax was still buried in the queer skull. Three mad, hate-filled eyes blazed up with a living fire, bright as fresh-spilled blood, from a race ringed with a writhing, loathsome nest of worms, blue, mobile worms that crawled where hair should grow—

Van Wall, six feet and two hundred pounds of ice-nerved

pilot, gave a queer, strangled gasp, and butted, stumbled his
way out to the corridor. Half the company broke for the
doors. The others stumbled away from the table.

McReady stood at one end of the table watching them, his
great body planted solid on his powerful legs. Norris from
the opposite end glowered at the thing with smouldering
hate. Outside the door, Garry was talking with half a dozen
of the men at once.

Blair had a tack hammer. The ice that cased the thing
schluffed crisply under its steel claw as it peeled from the
thing it had cased for twenty thousand years—

3

'I know you don't like the thing, Connant, but it just has
to be thawed out right. You say leave it as it is till we get
back to civilization. All right, I'll admit your argument that
we could do a better and more complete job there is sound.
But—how are we going to get this across the Line? We have
to take this through one temperature zone, the equatorial
zone, and halfway through the other temperature zone before
we get it to New York. You don't want to sit with it one
night, but you suggest, then, that I hang its corpse in the
freezer with the beef?' Blair looked up from his cautious
chipping, his bald freckled skull nodding triumphantly.

Kinner, the stocky, scar-faced cook, saved Connant the
trouble of answering. 'Hey, you listen, mister. You put that
thing in the box with the meat, and by all the gods there ever
were, I'll put you in to keep it company. You birds have
brought everything movable in this camp in onto my mess
tables here already, and I had to stand for that. But you go
putting things like that in my meat box, or even my meat
cache here, and you cook your own damn grub.'

'But, Kinner, this is the only table in Big Magnet that's
big enough to work on,' Blair objected. 'Everybody's explained that.'

'Yeah, and everybody's brought everything in here. Clark
brings his dogs every time there's a fight and sews them up
on that table. Ralsen brings in his sledges. Hell, the only
thing you haven't had on that table is the Boeing. And you'd
'a' had that in if you coulda figured a way to get it through
the tunnels.'

Commander Garry chuckled and grinned at Van Wall, the huge Chief Pilot. Van Wall's great blond beard twitched suspiciously as he nodded gravely to Kinner. 'You're right, Kinner. The aviation department is the only one that treats you right.'

'It does get crowded, Kinner,' Garry acknowledged. 'But I'm afraid we all find it that way at times. Not much privacy in an antarctic camp.'

'Privacy? What the hell's that? You know, the thing that really made me weep, was when I saw Barclay marchin' through here chantin' "The last lumber in the camp! The last lumber in the camp!" and carryin' it out to build that house on his tractor. Damn it, I missed that moon cut in the door he carried out more'n I missed the sun when it set. That wasn't just the last lumber Barclay was walkin' off with. He was carryin' off the last bit of privacy in this blasted place.'

A grin rode even on Connant's heavy face as Kinner's perennial, good-natured grouch came up again. But it died away quickly as his dark, deepset eyes turned again to the red-eyed thing Blair was chipping from its cocoon of ice. A big hand ruffed his shoulder-length hair, and tugged at a twisted lock that fell behind his ear in a familiar gesture. 'I know that cosmic ray shack's going to be too crowded if I have to sit up with that thing,' he growled. 'Why can't you go on chipping the ice away from around it—you can do that without anybody butting in, I assure you—and then hang the thing up over the powder-plant boiler? That's warm enough. It'll thaw out a chicken, even a whole side of beef, in a few hours.'

'I know,' Blair protested, dropping the tack hammer to gesture more effectively with his bony, freckled fingers, his small body tense with eagerness, 'but this is too important to take any chances. There never was a find like this; there never can be again. It's the only chance men will ever have, and it has to be done exactly right.

'Look, you know how the fish we caught down near the Ross Sea would freeze almost as soon as we got them on deck, and come to life again if we thawed them gently? Low forms of life aren't killed by quick freezing and slow thawing. We have—'

'Hey, for the love of Heaven—you mean that damned thing will come to life!' Connant yelled. 'You get the damned thing—Let me at it! That's going to be in so many pieces—'

'No! *No,* you fool—' Blair jumped in front of Connant to protect his precious find. 'No. Just *low* forms of life. For Pete's sake let me finish. You can't thaw higher forms of life and have them come to. Wait a moment now—hold it! A fish can come to after freezing because it's so low a form of life that the individual cells of its body can revive, and that alone is enough to reestablish life. Any higher forms thawed out that way are dead. Though the individual cells revive, they die because there must be organization and cooperative effort to live. That cooperation cannot be reestablished. There is a sort of potential life in any uninjured, quick-frozen animal. But it can't—can't under any circumstances—become active life in higher animals. The higher animals are too complex, too delicate. This is an intelligent creature as high in its evolution as we are in ours. Perhaps higher. It is as dead as a frozen man would be.'

'How do you know?' demanded Connant, hefting the ice-ax he had seized a moment before.

Commander Garry had a restraining hand on his heavy shoulder. 'Wait a minute, Connant. I want to get this straight. I agree that there is going to be no thawing of this thing if there is the remotest chance of its revival. I quite agree it is much too unpleasant to have alive, but I had no idea there was the remotest possibility.'

Dr. Cooper pulled his pipe from between his teeth and heaved his stocky, dark body from the bunk he had been sitting in. 'Blair's being technical. That's dead. As dead as the mammoths they find frozen in Siberia. We have all sorts of proof that things don't live after being frozen—not even fish, generally speaking—and no proof that higher animal life can under any circumstances. What's the point, Blair?'

The little biologist shook himself. The little ruff of hair standing out around his bald pate waved in righteous anger. 'The point is,' he said in an injured tone, 'that the individual cells might show the characteristics they had in life if it is properly thawed. A man's muscle cells live many hours after he has died. Just because they live, and a few things like hair and fingernail cells still live, you wouldn't accuse a corpse of being a zombie, or something.

'Now if I thaw this right, I may have a chance to determine what sort of world it's native to. We don't, and can't

know by any other means, whether it came from Earth or
Mars or Venus or from beyond the stars.

'And just because it looks unlike men, you don't have to
accuse it of being evil, or vicious or something. Maybe that
expression on its face is its equivalent to a resignation to
fate. White is the color of mourning to the Chinese. If men
can have different customs, why can't a so-different race
have different understandings of facial expressions?'

Connant laughed softly, mirthlessly. 'Peaceful resignation!
If that is the best it could do in the way of resignation, I
should exceedingly dislike seeing it when it was looking
mad. That face was never designed to express peace. It just
didn't have any philosophical thoughts like peace in its
make-up.

'I know it's your pet—but be sane about it. That thing
grew up on evil, adolesced slowly roasting alive the local
equivalent of kittens, and amused itself through maturity on
new and ingenious torture.'

'You haven't the slightest right to say that,' snapped Blair.
'How do you know the first thing about the meaning of a facial expression inherently inhuman? It may well have no human equivalent whatever. That is just a different
development of Nature, another example of Nature's wonderful adaptability. Growing on another, perhaps harsher
world, it has different form and features. But it is just as
much a legitimate child of Nature as you are. You are dis-
playing that childish human weakness of hating the different. On its own world it would probably class you as a
fish-belly, white monstrosity with an insufficient number of
eyes and a fungoid body pale and bloated with gas.

'Just because its nature is different, you haven't any right
to say it's necessarily evil!'

Norris burst out a single, explosive, 'Haw!' He looked
down at the thing. 'Maybe that things from other worlds
don't *have* to be evil just because they're different. But that
thing *was*! Child of Nature, eh? Well, it was a hell of an evil
Nature.'

'Aw, will you mugs cut crabbing at each other and get the
damned thing off my table?' Kinner growled. 'And put a
canvas over it. It looks indecent.'

'Kinner's gone modest,' jeered Connant.

Kinner slanted his eyes up to the big physicist. The
scarred cheek twisted to join the line of his tight lips in a

twisted grin. 'All right, big boy, and what were you grousing about a minute ago? We can set the thing in a chair next to you tonight, if you want.'

'I'm not afraid of its face,' Connant snapped. 'I don't like keeping a wake over its corpse particularly, but I'm going to do it.'

Kinner's grin spread. 'Uh-huh.' He went off to the galley stove and shook down ashes vigorously, drowning the brittle chipping of the ice as Blair fell to work again.

4

'*Cluck,*' reported the cosmic-ray counter, '*cluck-burrrp-cluck.*'

Connant started and dropped his pencil.

"Damnation.' The physicist looked toward the far corner, back at the Geiger counter on the table near that corner. And crawled under the desk at which he had been working to retrieve the pencil. He sat down at his work again, trying to make his writing more even. It tended to have jerks and quavers in it, in time with the abrupt proud-hen noises of the Geiger counter. The muted whoosh of the pressure lamp he was using for illumination, the mingled gargles and bugle calls of a dozen men sleeping down the corridor in Paradise House formed the background sounds for the irregular, clucking noises of the counter, the occasional rustle of falling coal in the copper-bellied stove. And a soft, steady *drip-drip-drip* from the thing in the corner.

Connant jerked a pack of cigarettes from his pocket, snapped it so that a cigarette protruded, and jabbed the cylinder into his mouth. The lighter failed to function, and he pawed angrily through the pile of papers in search of a match. He scratched the wheel of the lighter several times, dropped it with a curse and got up to pluck a hot coal from the stove with the coal tongs.

The lighter functioned instantly when he tried it on returning to the desk. The counter ripped out a series of chuckling guffaws as a burst of cosmic rays struck through to it. Connant turned to glower at it, and tried to concentrate on the interpretation of data collected during the past week. The weekly summary—

He gave up and yielded to curiosity, or nervousness. He

lifted the pressure lamp from the desk and carried it over to the table in the corner. Then he returned to the stove and picked up the coal tongs. The beast had been thawing for nearly eighteen hours now. He poked at it with an unconscious caution; the flesh was no longer hard as armor plate, but had assumed a rubbery texture. It looked like wet, blue rubber glistening under the droplets of water like little round jewels in the glare of the gasoline pressure lantern. Connant felt an unreasoning desire to pour the contents of the lamp's reservoir over the thing in its box and drop the cigarette into it. The three red eyes glared up at him sightlessly, the ruby eyeballs reflecting murky, smoky rays of light.

He realized vaguely that he had been looking at them for a very long time, even vaguely understood that they were no longer sightless. But it did not seem of importance, of no more importance than the labored, slow motion of the tentacular things that sprouted from the base of the scrawny, slowly pulsing neck.

Connant picked up the pressure lamp and returned to his chair. He sat down, staring at the pages of mathematics before him. The clucking of the counter was strangely less disturbing, the rustle of the coals in the stove no longer distracting.

The creak of the floorboards behind him didn't interrupt his thoughts as he went about his weekly report in an automatic manner, filling in columns of data and making brief, summarizing notes.

The creak of the floorboards sounded nearer.

5

Blair came up from the nightmare-haunted depths of sleep abruptly. Connant's face floated vaguely above him; for a moment it seemed a continuance of the wild horror of the dream. But Connant's face was angry, and a little frightened. 'Blair—Blair you damned log, wake up.'

'Uh—eh?' the little biologist rubbed his eyes, his bony, freckled finger crooked to a mutilated child-fist. From surrounding bunks other faces lifted to stare down at them.

Connant straightened up. 'Get up—and get a lift on. Your damned animal's escaped.'

'Escaped—what!' Chief Pilot Van Wall's bull voice roared

out with a volume that shook the walls. Down the communication tunnels other voices yelled suddenly. The dozen inhabitants of Paradise House tumbled in abruptly, Barclay, stocky and bulbous in long woolen underwear, carrying a fire extinguisher.

'What the hell's the matter?' Barclay demanded.

'Your damned beast got loose. I fell asleep about twenty minutes ago, and when I woke up, the thing was gone. Hey, Doc, the hell you say those things can't come to life. Blair's blasted potential life developed a hell of a lot of potential and walked out on us.'

Copper stared blankly. 'It wasn't—Earthly,' he sighed suddenly. 'I—I guess Earthly laws don't apply.'

'Well, it applied for leave of absence and took it. We've got to find it and capture it somehow.' Connant swore bitterly, his deepset black eyes sullen and angry. 'It's a wonder the hellish creature didn't eat me in my sleep.'

Blair started back, his pale eyes suddenly fear-struck. 'Maybe it di—er—uh—we'll have to find it.'

'You find it. It's your pet. I've had all I want to do with it, sitting there for seven hours with the counter clucking every few seconds, and you birds in here singing night-music. It's a wonder I got to sleep. I'm going through to the Ad Building.'

Commander Garry ducked through the doorway, pulling his belt tight. 'You won't have to. Van's roar sounded like the Boeing taking off downwind. So it wasn't dead?'

'I didn't carry it off in my arms, I assure you,' Connant snapped. 'The last thing I saw, the split skull oozing green goo, like a squashed caterpillar. Doc just said our laws don't work—it's unearthly. Well, it's an unearthly monster, with an unearthly disposition, judging by the face, wandering around with a split skull and brains oozing out.' Norris and McReady appeared in the doorway, a doorway filling with other shivering men. 'Has anybody seen it coming over here?' Norris asked innocently. 'About four feet tall—three red eyes—brains oozing out—Hey, has anybody checked to make sure this isn't a cracked idea of humor? If it is, I think we'll unite in tying Blair's pet around Connant's neck like the Ancient Mariner's albatross.'

'It's no humor,' Connant shivered. 'Lord, I wish it were. I'd rather wear—' He stopped. A wild, weird howl shrieked through the corridors. The men stiffened abruptly, and half turned.

'I think it's been located,' Connant finished. His dark eyes shifted with a queer unease. He darted back to his bunk in Paradise House, to return almost immediately with a heavy .45 revolver and an ice-ax. He hefted both gently as he started for the corridor toward Dogtown.

'It blundered down the wrong corridor—and landed among the huskies. Listen—the dogs have broken their chains—'

The half-terrorized howl of the dog pack had changed to a wild hunting melee. The voices of the dogs thundered in the narrow corridors, and through them came a low rippling snarl of distilled hate. A shrill of pain, a dozen snarling yelps.

Connant broke for the door. Close behind him, McReady, then Barclay and Commander Garry came. Other men broke for the Ad Building, and weapons—the sledge house. Pomroy, in charge of the Big Magnet's five cows, started down the corridor in the opposite direction—he had a six-foot-handled, long-tined pitchfork in mind.

Barclay slid to a halt, as McReady's giant bulk turned abruptly away from the tunnel leading to Dogtown, and vanished off at an angle. Uncertainly, the mechanician wavered a moment, the fire extinguisher in his hands, hesitating from one side to the other. Then he was racing after Connant's broad back. Whatever McReady had in mind, he could be trusted to make it work.

Connant stopped at the bend in the corridor. His breath hissed suddenly through his throat. 'Great God—' The revolver exploded thunderously; three numbing, palpable waves of sound crashed through the confined corridors. Two more. The revolver dropped to the hard-packed snow of the trail, and Barclay saw the ice-ax shift into defensive position. Connant's powerful body blocked his vision, but beyond he heard something mewing and, insanely, chuckling. The dogs were quieter; there was a deadly seriousness in their low snarls. Taloned feet scratched at hard-packed snow, broken chains were clinking and tangling.

Connant shifted abruptly, and Barclay could see what lay beyond. For a second he stood frozen, then his breath went out in a gusty curse. The Thing launched itself at Connant, the powerful arms of the man swung the ice-ax flat-side first at what might have been a head. It crunched horribly, and the tattered flesh, ripped by a half-dozen savage huskies, leapt to its feet again. The red eyes blazed with an unearthly hatred, and unearthly, unkillable vitality.

Barclay turned the fire extinguisher on it; the blinding, blistering stream of chemical spray confused it, baffled it, together with the savage attacks of the huskies, not for long afraid of anything that did, or could live, and held it at bay.

McReady wedged men out of his way and drove down the narrow corridor packed with men unable to reach the scene. There was a sure foreplanned drive to McReady's attack. One of the giant blowtorches used in warming the plane's engines was in his bronze hands. It roared gustily as he turned the corner and opened the valve. The mad mewing hissed louder. The dogs scrambled back from the three-foot lance of blue-hot flame.

'Bar, get a power cable, run in it somehow. And a handle. We can electrocute this—monster, if I don't incinerate it.' McReady spoke with an authority of planned action. Barclay turned down the long corridor to the power plant, but already before him Norris and Van Wall were racing down.

Barclay found the cable in the electrical cache in the tunnel wall. In a half minute he was hacking at it, walking back. Van Wall's voice rang out in warning shout of 'Power!' as the emergency gasoline-powered dynamo thudded into action. Half a dozen other men were down there now; the coal, kindling going into the firebox of the steam power plant. Norris, cursing in a low, deadly monotone, was working with quick, sure fingers on the other end of Barclay's cable, splicing a contactor into one of the power leads.

The dogs had fallen back when Barclay reached the corridor bend, fallen back before a furious monstrosity that glared from baleful red eyes, mewing in trapped hatred. The dogs were a semi-circle of red-dipped muzzles with a fringe of glistening white teeth, whining with a vicious eagerness that near matched the fury of the red eyes. McReady stood confidently alert at the corridor bend, the gustily muttering torch held loose and ready for action in his hands. He stepped aside without moving his eyes from the beast as Barclay came up. There was a slight, tight smile on his lean, bronzed face.

Norris' voice called down the corridor, and Barclay

stepped forward. The cable was taped to the long handle of a snow shovel, the two conductors split and held eighteen inches apart by a scrap of lumber lashed at right angles across the far end of the handle. Bare copper conductors, charged with 220 volts, glinted in the light of pressure lamps. The Thing mewed and hated and dodged. McReady advanced to Barclay's side. The dogs beyond sensed the plan with the almost telepathic intelligence of trained huskies. Their whining grew shriller, softer, their mincing steps carried them nearer. Abruptly a huge night-black Alaskan leapt onto the trapped thing. It turned squalling saber-clawed feet slashing.

Barclay leapt forward and jabbed. A weird, shrill scream rose and choked out. The smell of burnt flesh in the corridor intensified; greasy smoke curled up. The echoing pound in the gas-electric dynamo down the corridor became a slogging thud.

The red eyes clouded over in a stiffening, jerking travesty of a face. Armlike, leglike members quivered and jerked. The dogs leapt forward, and Barclay yanked back his shovel-handled weapon. The Thing on the snow did not move as gleaming teeth ripped it open.

6

Garry looked about the crowded room. Thirty-two men, some tensed nervously standing against the wall, some uneasily relaxed, some sitting, most perforce standing as intimate as sardines. Thirty-two, plus the five engaged in sewing up wounded dogs, made thirty-seven, the total personnel.

Garry started speaking. 'All right, I guess we're here. Some of you—three or four at most—saw what happened. All of you have seen that thing on the table, and can get a general idea. Anyone hasn't, I'll lift—' His hand strayed to the tarpaulin bulking over the thing on the table. There was an acrid odor of singed flesh seeping out of it. The men stirred restlessly, hasty denials.

'It looks rather as though Charnauk isn't going to lead any more teams,' Garry went on. 'Blair wants to get at this thing, and make some more detailed examination. We want to know what happened, and make sure right now that this is permanently, totally dead. Right?'

Connant grinned. 'Anybody that doesn't can sit up with it tonight.'

'All right then, Blair, what can you say about it? What was it?' Garry turned to the little biologist.

'I wonder if we ever saw its natural form,' Blair looked at the covered mass. 'It may have been imitating the beings that built that ship—but I don't think it was. I think that it was its true form. Those of us who were up near the bend saw the thing in action; the thing on the table is the result. When it got loose, apparently, it started looking around Antarctica still frozen as it was ages ago when the creature first saw it—and froze. From my observations while it was thawing out, and the bits of tissue I cut and hardened then, I think it was native to a hotter planet than Earth. It couldn't, in its natural form, stand the temperature. There is no life-form on Earth that can live in Antarctica during the winter, but the best compromise is the dog. It found the dogs, and somehow got near enough to Charnauk to get him. The others smelled it—heard it—I don't know—anyway they went wild, and broke chains, and attacked it before it was finished. The thing we found was part Charnauk, queerly only half-dead, part Charnauk half-digested by the jellylike protoplasm of that creature, and part the remains of the thing we originally found, sort of melted down to the basic protoplasm.

'When the dogs attacked it, it turned into the best fighting thing it could think of. Some other-world beast apparently.'

'Turned,' snapped Garry. 'How?'

'Every living thing is made up of jelly—protoplasm and minute, submicroscopic things called nuclei, which control the bulk, the protoplasm. This thing was just a modification of that same world-wide plan of Nature; cells made up of protoplasm, controlled by infinitely tinier nuclei. You physicists might compare it—an individual cell of any living thing—with an atom; the bulk of the atom, the space-filling part, is made up of the electron orbits, but the character of the thing is determined by the atomic nucleus.

'This isn't wildly beyond what we already know. It's just a modification we haven't seen before. It's as natural, as logical, as any other manifestation of life. It obeys exactly the same laws. The cells are made of protoplasm, their character determined by the nucleus.

'Only, in this creature, the cell nuclei can control those cells *at will*. It digested Charnauk, and as it digested, studied every cell of his tissue, and shaped its own cells to imitate them exactly. Parts of it—parts that had time to finish changing—are dog-cells. But they don't have dog-cell nuclei.' Blair lifted a fraction of the tarpaulin. A torn dog's leg, with stiff gray fur protruded. 'That, for instance, isn't dog at all; it's imitation. Some parts I'm uncertain about; the nucleus was hiding itself, covering up with dog-cell imitation nucleus. In time, not even a microscope would have shown the difference.'

'Suppose,' asked Norris bitterly, 'it had had lots of time?'

'Then it would have been a dog. The other dogs would have accepted it. We would have accepted it. I don't think anything would have distinguished it, not microscope, nor X-ray, nor any other means. This is a member of a supremely intelligent race, a race that has learned the deepest secrets of biology, and turned them to its use.'

'What was it planning to do?' Barclay looked at the humped tarpaulin.

Blair grinned unpleasantly. The wavering halo of thin hair round his bald pate wavered in a stir of air. 'Take over the world, I imagine.'

'Take over the world! Just it, all by itself?' Connant gasped. 'Set itself up as a lone dictator?'

'No,' Blair shook his head. The scalpel he had been fumbling in his bony fingers dropped; he bent to pick it up, so that his face was hidden as he spoke. 'It would become the population of the world.'

'Become—populate the world? Does it reproduce asexually?'

Blair shook his head and gulped. 'It's—it doesn't have to. It weighed eighty-five pounds. Charnauk weighed about ninety. It would have become Charnauk, and had eighty-five pounds left, to become—oh, Jack for instance, or Chinook. It can imitate anything—that is, become anything. If it had reached the Antarctic Sea, it would have become a seal, maybe two seals. They might have attacked a killer whale, and become either killers, or a herd of seals. Or maybe it would have caught an albatross, or a skua gull, and flown to South America.'

Norris cursed softly. 'And every time it digested something, and imitated it—'

'It would have had its original bulk left, to start again,' Blair finished. 'Nothing would kill it. It has no natural enemies, because it becomes whatever it wants to. If a killer whale attacked it, it would become a killer whale. If it was an albatross, and an eagle attacked it, it would become an eagle. Lord, it might become a female eagle. Go back—build a nest and lay eggs!'

'Are you sure that thing from hell is dead?' Dr. Copper asked softly.

'Yes, thank Heaven,' the little biologist gasped. 'After they drove the dogs off, I stood there poking Bar's electrocution thing into it for five minutes. It's dead and—cooked.'

'Then we can only give thanks that this is Antarctica, where there is not one, single, solitary, living thing for it to imitate, except these animals in camp.'

'Us,' Blair giggled. 'It can imitate us. Dogs can't make four hundred miles to the sea; there's no food. There aren't any skua gulls to imitate at this season. There aren't any penguins this far inland. There's nothing that can reach the sea from this point—except us. We've got brains. We can do it. Don't you see—*it's got to imitate us—it's got to be one of us—that's the only way it can fly an airplane—fly a plane for two hours, and rule—be—all Earth's inhabitants.* A world for the taking—*if it imitates us!*

'It didn't know yet. It hadn't had a chance to learn. It was rushed—hurried—took the thing nearest its own size. Look—I'm Pandora! I opened the box! And the only hope that can come out is—that nothing can come out. You didn't see me. I did it. I fixed it. I smashed every magneto. Not a plane can fly. Nothing can fly.' Blair giggled and lay down on the floor crying.

Chief Pilot Van Wall made for the door. His feet were fading echoes in the corridors as Dr. Copper bent unhurriedly over the little man on the floor. From his office at the end of the room he brought something and injected a solution into Blair's arm. 'He might come out of it when he wakes up,' he sighed, rising. McReady helped him lift the biologist onto a nearby bunk. 'It all depends on whether we can convince him that thing is dead.'

Van Wall ducked into the shack, brushing his heavy blond beard absently. 'I didn't think a biologist would do a thing like that very thoroughly. He missed the spares in the second cache. It's all right. I smashed them.'

Commander Garry nodded. 'I was wondering about the radio.'

Dr. Copper snorted. 'You don't think it can leak out on a radio wave do you? You'd have five rescue attempts in the next three months if you stop the broadcasts. The thing to do is to talk loud and not make a sound. Now I wonder—'

McReady looked speculatively at the doctor. 'It might be like an infectious disease. Everything that drank any of its blood—'

Copper shook his head. 'Blair missed something. Imitate it may, but it has, to a certain extent, its own body chemistry, its own metabolism. If it didn't, it would become a dog—and be a dog and nothing more. It has to be an imitation dog. Therefore you can detect it by serum tests. And its chemistry, since it comes from another world, must be so wholly, radically different that a few cells, such as gained by drops of blood, would be treated as disease germs by the dog, or human body?'

'Blood—would one of those imitations bleed?' Norris demanded.

'Surely. Nothing mystic about blood. Muscle is about 90 percent water; blood differs only in having a couple percent more water, and less connective tissue. They'd bleed all right,' Copper assured him.

Blair sat up in his bunk suddenly. 'Connant—where's Connant?'

The physicist moved over toward the little biologist. 'Here I am. What do you want?'

'Are you?' giggled Blair. He lapsed back into the bunk contorted with silent laughter.

Connant looked at him blankly. 'Huh? Am I what?'

'*Are* you there?' Blair burst into gales of laughter. '*Are* you Connant? The beast wanted to be *man*—not a dog—'

7

Dr. Copper rose wearily from the bunk, and washed the hypodermic carefully. The little tinkles it made seemed loud in the packed room, now that Blair's gurgling laughter had finally quieted. Copper looked toward Garry and shook his head slowly. 'Hopeless, I'm afraid. I don't think we can ever convince him the thing is dead now.'

Norris laughed uncertainly. 'I'm not sure you can convince me. Oh, damn you, McReady.'

'McReady?' Commander Garry turned to look from Norris to McReady curiously.

'The nightmares,' Norris explained. 'He had a theory about the nightmares we had at the Secondary Station after finding that thing.'

'And that was?' Garry looked at McReady levelly.

Norris answered for him, jerkily, uneasily. 'That the creature wasn't dead, had a sort of enormously slowed existence, an existence that permitted it, nonetheless, to be vaguely aware of the passing of time, of our coming, after endless years. I had a dream it could imitate things.'

'Well,' Copper grunted, 'it can.'

'Don't be an ass,' Norris snapped. 'That's not what's bothering me. In the dream it could read minds, read thoughts and ideas and mannerisms.'

'What's so bad about that? It seems to be worrying you more than the thought of the joy we're going to have with a madman in an antarctic camp.' Copper nodded toward Blair's sleeping form.

McReady shook his great head slowly. 'You know that Connant is Connant, because he not merely looks like Connant—which we're beginning to believe the beast might be able to do—but he thinks like Connant, moves himself around as Connant does. That takes more than merely a body that looks like him; that takes Connant's own mind, and thoughts and mannerisms. Therefore, though you know that the thing might make itself *look* like Connant, you aren't much bothered, because you know it has a mind from another world, a totally unhuman mind, that couldn't possibly react and think and talk like a man we know, and do it so well as to fool us for a moment. The idea of the creature imitating one of us is fascinating, but unreal, because it is too completely unhuman to deceive us. It doesn't have a human mind.'

'As I said before,' Norris repeated, looking steadily at McReady, 'you can say the damnedest things at the damnedest times. Will you be so good as to finish that thought—one way or the other?'

Kinner, the scar-faced expedition cook, had been standing near Connant. Suddenly he moved down the length of the crowded room toward his familiar galley. He shook the ashes from the galley stove noisily.

'It would do it no good,' said Dr. Copper, softly as though thinking out loud, 'to merely look like something it was trying to imitate; it would have to understand its feelings, its reactions. It *is* unhuman; it has powers of imitation beyond any conception of man. A good actor, by training himself, can imitate another man, another man's mannerisms, well enough to fool most people. Of course no actor could imitate so perfectly as to deceive men who had been living with the imitated one in the complete lack of privacy of an antarctic camp. That would take a superhuman skill.'

'Oh, you've got the bug, too?' Norris cursed softly.

Connant standing alone at one end of the room, looked about him wildly, his face white. A gentle eddying of the men had crowded them slowly down toward the other end of the room, so that he stood quite alone. 'My God, will you two Jeremiahs shut up?' Connant's voice shook. 'What am I? Some kind of microscopic specimen you're dissecting? Some unpleasant worm you're discussing in the third person?'

McReady looked up at him; his slowly twisting hands stopped for a moment. 'Having a lovely time. Wish you were here. Signed: Everybody.

'Connant, if you think you're having a hell of a time, just move over on the other end for a while. You've got one thing we haven't, you know what the answer is. I'll tell you this, right now you're the most feared and respected man in Big Magnet.'

'Lord, I wish you could see your eyes,' Connant gasped. 'Stop staring, will you! What the hell are you going to do?'

'Have you any suggestions, Dr. Copper?' Commander Garry asked steadily. 'The present situation is impossible.'

'Oh, is it?' Connant snapped. 'Come over here and look at that crowd. By Heaven, they look exactly like that gang of huskies around the corridor bend. Benning, will you stop hefting that damned ice-ax?'

The coppery blade rang on the floor as the aviation mechanic nervously dropped it. He bent over and picked it up instantly, hefting it slowly, turning it in his hands, his brown eyes moving jerkily about the room.

Copper sat down on the bunk beside Blair. The wood creaked noisily in the room. Far down a corridor, a dog yelped in pain, and the dog drivers' tense voices floated softly back. 'Microscopic examination,' said the doctor thoughtfully, 'would be useless, as Blair pointed out. Considerable time has passed. However, serum tests would be definitive.'

'Serum tests? What do you mean exactly?' Commander Garry asked.

'If I had a rabbit that had been injected with human blood—a poison to rabbits, of course, as is the blood of any animal save that of another rabbit—and the injections continued in increasing doses for some time, the rabbit would be human-immune. If a small quantity were drawn off, allowed to separate in a test tube, and to the clear serum, a bit of human blood were added, there would be a visible reaction, proving the blood was human. If cow, or dog blood were added—or any protein material other than that one thing, human blood—no reaction would take place. That would prove definitely.'

'Can you suggest where I might catch a rabbit for you, Doc?' Norris asked. 'That is, nearer than Australia, we don't want to waste time going that far.'

'I know there aren't any rabbits in Antarctica,' Copper nodded, 'but that is simply the usual animal. Any animal except man will do. A dog for instance. But it will take several days, and due to the greater size of the animal, considerable blood. Two of us will have to contribute.'

'Would I do?' Garry asked.

'That will make two,' Copper nodded. 'I'll get to work on it right away.'

'What about Connant in the meantime,' Kinner demanded. 'I'm going out that door and head off for the Ross Sea before I cook for him.'

'He may be human—' Copper started.

Connant burst out in a flood of curses. 'Human! *May* be human, you damned sawbones! What in hell do you think I am?'

'A monster,' Copper snapped sharply. 'Now shut up and listen.' Connant's face drained of color and he sat down heavily as the indictment was put in words. 'Until we know—you know as well as we do that we have reason to question the face, and only you know how that question is to be answered—we may reasonably be expected to lock you up. If you are—unhuman—you're a lot more dangerous than poor Blair there, and I'm going to see that he's locked up thoroughly. I expect that his next stage will be a violent desire to kill you, all the dogs, and probably all of us. When he wakes, he will be convinced we're all unhuman, and nothing on the planet will ever change his conviction. It would be kinder to let him die, but we can't do that, of course. He's going in one shack, and you can stay in Cosmos House with your cosmic apparatus. Which is about what you'd do anyway. I've got to fix up a couple of dogs.'

Connant nodded bitterly. 'I'm human. Hurry that test. Your eyes—Lord, I wish you could see your eyes staring—'

Commander Garry watched anxiously as Clark, the dog-handler, held the big brown Alaskan husky, while Copper began the injection treatment. The dog was not anxious to cooperate; the needle was painful, and already he'd experienced considerable needle work that morning. Five stitches held closed a slash that ran from his shoulder, across his ribs, halfway down his body. One long fang was broken off short; the missing part was to be found half buried in the shoulder bone of the monstrous thing on the table in the Ad Building.

'How long will that take?' Garry asked, pressing his arm gently. It was sore from the prick of the needle Dr. Copper had used to withdraw blood.

Copper shrugged. 'I don't know, to be frank. I know the general method. I've used it on rabbits. But I haven't experimented with dogs. They're big, clumsy animals to work with; naturally rabbits are preferable, and serve ordinarily. In civilized places you can buy a stock of human-immune rabbits from suppliers, and not many investigators take the trouble to prepare their own.'

'What do they want with them back there?' Clark asked.

'Criminology is one large field. A says he didn't murder B, but that the blood on his shirt came from killing a chicken. The State makes a test, then it's up to A to explain how it is the blood reacts on human-immune rabbits, but not on chicken-immunes.'

'What are we going to do with Blair in the meantime?' Garry asked wearily. 'It's all right to let him sleep where he is for a while, but when he wakes up—'

'Barclay and Benning are fitting some bolts on the door of Cosmos House,' Copper replied grimly. 'Connant's acting like a gentleman. I think perhaps the way the other men look at him makes him rather want privacy. Lord knows, heretofore we've all of us individually prayed for a little privacy.'

Clark laughed bitterly. 'Not any more, thank you. The more the merrier.'

'Blair,' Copper went on, 'will also have to have privacy—and locks. He's going to have a pretty definite plan in mind when he wakes up. Ever hear the old story of how to stop hoof-and-mouth disease in cattle?'

Clark and Garry shook their heads silently.

'If there isn't any hoof-and-mouth disease, there won't be any hoof-and-mouth disease,' Copper explained. 'You get rid of it by killing every animal that exhibits it, and every animal that's been near the diseased animal. Blair's a biologist, and knows that story. He's afraid of this thing we loosed. The answer is probably pretty clear in his mind now. Kill everybody and everything in this camp before a skua gull or a wandering albatross coming in with the spring chances out this way—catches the disease.'

Clark's lips curled in a twisted grin. 'Sounds logical to me. If things get too bad—maybe we'd better let Blair get loose. It would save us committing suicide. We might also make something of a vow that if things get bad, we see that that does happen.'

Copper laughed softly. 'The last man alive in Big Magnet—wouldn't be a man,' he pointed out. 'Somebody's got to kill those—creatures that don't desire to kill themselves, you know. We don't have enough thermite to do it all at once, and the decanite explosive wouldn't help much. I have an idea that even small pieces of one of those things would be self-sufficient.'

'If,' said Garry thoughtfully, 'they can modify their protoplasm at will, won't they simply modify themselves to birds and fly away? They can read all about birds, and imitate their structure without even meeting them. Or imitate, perhaps, birds of their home planet.'

Copper shook his head, and helped Clark to free the dog. 'Man studied birds for centuries, trying to learn how to make a machine to fly like them. He never did do the trick; his final success came when he broke away entirely and tried new methods. Knowing the general idea, and knowing the detailed structure of wing and bone and nerve-tissue is something far, far different. And as for other-world birds, perhaps, in fact very probably, the atmospheric conditions here are so vastly different that their birds couldn't fly. Perhaps, even, the being came from a planet like Mars with such a thin atmosphere that there were no birds.'

Barclay came into the building, trailing a length of airplane control cable. 'It's finished, Doc. Cosmos House can't be opened from the inside. Now where do we put Blair?'

Copper looked toward Garry. 'There wasn't any biology building. I don't know where we can isolate him.'

'How about East Cache?' Garry said after a moment's thought. 'Will Blair be able to look after himself—or need attention?'

'He'll be capable enough. We'll be the ones to watch out,' Copper assured him grimly. 'Take a stove, a couple of bags of coal, necessary supplies and a few tools to fix it up. Nobody's been out there since last fall, have they?'

Garry shook his head. 'If he gets noisy—I thought that might be a good idea.'

Barclay hefted the tools he was carrying and looked up at Garry. 'If the muttering he's doing now is any sign, he's going to sing away the night hours. And we won't like his song.'

'What's he saying?' Copper asked.

Barclay shook his head. 'I didn't care to listen much. You can if you want to. But I gathered that the blasted idiot had all the dreams McReady had, and a few more. He slept beside the thing when we stopped on the trail coming in from Secondary Magnetic, remember. He dreamt the thing was alive, and dreamt more details. And—damn his soul—knew it wasn't all dream, or had reason to. He knew it had telepathic powers that were stirring vaguely, and that it could not only read minds, but project thoughts. They weren't dreams, you see. They were stray thoughts that thing was broadcasting, the way Blair's broadcasting his thoughts now—a sort of telepathic muttering in his sleep. That's why he knew so much about its powers. I guess you and I, Doc, weren't so sensitive—if you want to believe in telepathy.'

'I have to,' Copper sighed. 'Dr. Rhine of Duke University has shown that it exists, shown that some are much more sensitive than others.'

'Well, if you want to learn a lot of details, go listen in on Blair's broadcast. He's driven most of the boys out of the Ad Building; Kinner's rattling pans like coal going down a chute. When he can't rattle a pan, he shakes ashes.

'By the way, Commander, what are we going to do this spring, now the planes are out of it?'

Garry sighed. 'I'm afraid our expedition is going to be a loss. We cannot divide our strength now.'

'It won't be a loss—if we continue to live, and come out of this,' Copper promised him. 'The find we've made, if we can get it under control, is important enough. The cosmic ray data, magnetic work, and atmospheric work won't be greatly hindered.'

Garry laughed mirthlessly. 'I was just thinking of the radio broadcasts. Telling half the world about the wonderful results of our exploration flights, trying to fool men like Byrd and Ellsworth back home there that we're doing something.'

Copper nodded gravely. 'They'll know something's wrong. But men like that have judgment enough to know we wouldn't do tricks without some sort of reason, and will wait for our return to judge us. I think it comes to this: men who know enough to recognize our deception will wait for our return. Men who haven't discretion and faith enough to wait will not have the experience to detect any fraud. We know enough of the conditions here to put through a good bluff.'

'Just so they don't send "rescue" expeditions,' Garry prayed. 'When—if—we're ever ready to come out, we'll have to send word to Captain Forsyth to bring a stock of magnetos with him when he comes down. But—never mind that.'

'You mean if we don't come out?' asked Barclay. 'I was wondering if a nice running account of an eruption or an earthquake via radio—with a swell windup by using a stick of decanite under the microphone—would help. Nothing, of course, will entirely keep people out. One of those swell, melodramatic "last-man-alive-scenes" might make 'em go easy though.'

Garry smiled with genuine humor. 'Is everybody in camp trying to figure that out, too?'

Copper laughed. 'What do you think, Garry? We're confident we can win out. But not too easy about it, I guess.'

Clark grinned up from the dog he was petting into calmness. 'Confident, did you say, Doc?'

8

Blair moved restlessly around the small shack. His eyes jerked and quivered in vague, fleeting glances at the four men with him; Barclay, six feet tall and weighing over 190 pounds; McReady, a bronze giant of a man; Dr. Copper, short, squatly powerful; and Benning, five feet ten of wiry strength.

Blair was huddled up against the far wall of the East Cache cabin, his gear piled up in the middle of the floor beside the heating stove, forming an island between him and the four men. His bony hands clenched and fluttered, terrified. His pale eyes wavered uneasily as his bald, freckled head darted about in birdlike motion.

'I don't want anybody coming here. I'll cook my own food,' he snapped nervously. 'Kinner may be human now, but I don't believe it. I'm going to get out of here, but I'm not going to eat any food you send me. I want cans. Sealed cans.'

'OK, Blair, we'll bring 'em tonight,' Barclay promised. 'You've got coal, and the fire's started. I'll make a last—' Barclay started forward.

Blair instantly scurried to the farthest corner. 'Get out! Keep away from me, you monster!' the little biologist shrieked, and tried to claw his way through the wall of the shack. 'Keep away from me—keep away—I won't be absorbed—I won't be—'

Barclay relaxed and moved back. Dr. Copper shook his head. 'Leave him alone, Bar. It's easier for him to fix the thing himself. We'll have to fix the door, I think—'

The four men let themselves out. Efficiently, Benning and Barclay fell to work. There were no locks in Antarctica; there wasn't enough privacy to make them needed. But powerful screws had been driven in each side of the door frame, and the spare aviation control cable, immensely strong, woven steel wire, was rapidly caught between them and drawn taut. Barclay went to work with a drill and a key-hole saw. Presently he had a trap cut in the door through which goods could be passed without unlashing the entrance. Three powerful hinges from a stock crate, two hasps and a pair of three-inch cotter pins made it proof against opening from the other side.

Blair moved about restlessly inside. He was dragging

something over to the door with panting gasps, and muttering frantic curses. Barclay opened the hatch and glanced in, Dr. Copper peering over his shoulder. Blair had moved the heavy bunk against the door. It could not be opened without his cooperation now.

'Don't know but what the poor man's right at that,' McReady sighed. 'If he gets loose, it is his avowed intention to kill each and all of us as quickly as possible, which is something we don't agree with. But we've something on our side of that door that is worse than a homocidal maniac. If one or the other has to get loose, I think I'll come up and undo these lashings here.'

Barclay grinned. 'You let me know, and I'll show you how to get these off fast. Let's go back.'

The sun was painting the northern horizon in multicolored rainbows still, though it was two hours below the horizon. The field of drift swept off to the north, sparkling under its flaming colors in a million reflected glories. Low mounds of rounded white on the northern horizon showed the Magnet Range was barely awash above the sweeping drift. Little eddies of wind-lifted snow swirled away from their skies as they set out toward the main encampment two miles away. The spidery finger of the broadcast radiator lifted a gaunt black needle against the white of the Antarctic continent. The snow under their skis was like fine sand, hard and gritty.

'Spring,' said Benning bitterly, 'is come. Ain't we got fun! And I've been looking forward to getting away from this blasted hole in the ice.'

'I wouldn't try it now, if I were you.' Barclay grunted. 'Guys that set out from here in the next few days are going to be marvelously unpopular.'

'How is your dog getting along, Dr. Copper?' McReady asked. 'Any results yet?'

'In thirty hours? I wish there were. I gave him an injection of my blood today. But I imagine another five days will be needed. I don't know certainly enough to stop sooner.'

'I've been wondering—if Connant were—changed, would he have warned us so soon after the animal escaped? Wouldn't he have waited long enough for it to have a real chance to fix itself? Until we woke up naturally?' McReady asked slowly.

'The thing is selfish. You didn't think it looked as though it were possessed of a store of the higher justices, did you?'

Dr. Copper pointed out. 'Every part of it is all of it, every part of it is all for itself, I imagine. If Connant were changed, to save his skin, he'd have to—but Connant's feelings aren't changed; they're imitated perfectly, or they're his own. Naturally, the imitation, imitating perfectly Connant's feelings, would do exactly what Connant would do.'

'Say, couldn't Norris or Vane give Connant some kind of a test? If the thing is brighter than men, it might know more physics than Connant should, and they'd catch it out,' Barclay suggested.

Copper shook his head wearily. 'Not if it reads minds. You can't plan a trap for it. Vane suggested that last night. He hoped it would answer some of the questions of physics he'd like to know answers to.'

'This expedition-of-four idea is going to make life happy.' Benning looked at his companions. 'Each of us with an eye on the other to make sure he doesn't do something—peculiar. Man, aren't we going to be a trusting bunch! Each man eyeing his neighbors with the grandest exhibition of faith and trust—I'm beginning to know what Connant meant by "I wish you could see your eyes." Every now and then we all have it, I guess. One of you looks around with a sort of "I-wonder-if-the-other-*three*-are-look." Incidentally, I'm not excepting myself.'

'So far as we know, the animal is dead, with a slight question as to Connant. No other is suspected,' McReady stated slowly. 'The "always-four" order is merely a precautionary measure.'

'I'm waiting for Garry to make it four-in-a-bunk,' Barclay sighed. 'I thought I didn't have any privacy before, but since that order—'

9

None watched more tensely than Connant. A little sterile glass test tube, half filled with straw-colored fluid. One—two—three—four—five drops of the clear solution Dr. Copper had prepared from the drops of blood from Connant's arm. The tube was shaken carefully, then set in a beaker of clear, warm water. The thermometer read blood heat, a little thermostat clicked noisily, and the electric hotplate began to glow as the lights flickered slightly. Then—little white flecks of precipitation were forming, snowing down in the clear straw-colored fluid. 'Lord,' said Connant. He dropped heavily into a bunk, crying like a baby. 'Six days—' Connant sobbed, 'six days in there—wondering if that damned test would lie—'

Garry moved over silently, and slipped his arm across the physicist's back.

'It couldn't lie,' Dr. Copper said. 'The dog was human-immune—and the serum reacted.'

'He's—all right?' Norris gasped. 'Then—the animal is dead—dead forever?'

'He is human,' Copper spoke definitely, 'and the animal is dead.'

Kinner burst out laughing, laughing hysterically. McReady turned toward him and slapped his face with a methodical one-two, one-two action. The cook laughed, gulped, cried a moment, and sat up rubbing his cheeks, mumbling his thanks vaguely. 'I was scared. Lord, I was scared—'

Norris laughed brittlely. 'You think we weren't, you ape? You think maybe Connant wasn't?'

The Ad Building stirred with a sudden rejuvenation. Voices laughed, the men clustering around Connant spoke with unnecessarily loud voices, jittery, nervous voices relievedly friendly again. Somebody called out a suggestion, and a dozen started for their skis. Blair, Blair might recover—Dr. Copper fussed with his test tubes in nervous relief, trying solutions. The party of relief for Blair's shack started out the door, skis clapping noisily. Down the corridor, the dogs set up a quick yelping howl as the air of excited relief reached them.

Dr. Copper fussed with his tubes. McReady noticed him first, sitting on the edge of the bunk, with two precipitin-whitened test tubes of straw-colored fluid, his face whiter than the stuff in the tubes, silent tears slipping down from horror-widened eyes.

McReady felt a cold knife of fear pierce through his heart and freeze in his breast. Dr. Copper looked up. 'Garry,' he called hoarsely. 'Garry, for God's sake, come here.'

Commander Garry walked toward him sharply. Silence clapped down on the Ad Building. Connant looked up, rose stiffly from his seat.

'Garry—tissue from the monster—precipitates, too. It proves nothing. Nothing—but the dog was monster-immune too. That *one of the two contributing blood—one of us two, you and I, Garry—one of us is a monster.*'

10

'Bar, call back those men before they tell Blair,' McReady said quietly. Barclay went to the door; faintly his shouts came back to the tensely silent men in the room. Then he was back.

'They're coming,' he said. 'I didn't tell them why. Just that Dr. Copper said not to go.'

'McReady,' Garry sighed, 'you're in command now. May God help you. I cannot.'

The bronzed giant nodded slowly, his deep eyes on Commander Garry.

'I may be the one,' Garry added. 'I know I'm not, but I cannot prove it to you in any way. Dr. Copper's test has broken down. The fact that he showed it was useless, when it was to the advantage of the monster to have that uselessness not known, would seem to prove he was human.'

Copper rocked back and forth slowly on the bunk. 'I know I'm human. I can't prove it either. One of us two is a liar, for that test cannot lie, and it says one of us is. I gave proof that the test was wrong, which seems to prove I'm human, and now Garry has given that argument which proves me human—which he, as the monster, should not do. Round and round and round and round and—'

Dr. Copper's head, then his neck and shoulders began circling slowly in time to the words. Suddenly he was lying back on the bunk, roaring with laughter. 'It doesn't have to prove *one* of us is a monster! It doesn't have to prove that at all! Ho-ho. If we're *all* monsters it works the same—we're all monsters—all of us—Connant and Garry and I—and all of you.'

'McReady,' Van Wall, the blond-bearded Chief Pilot, called softly, 'you were on the way to an M.D. when you took up meteorology, weren't you? Can you make some kind of test?'

McReady went over to Copper slowly, took the hypodermic from his hand, and washed it carefully in ninety-five percent alcohol. Garry sat on the bunk edge with wooden face, watching Copper and McReady expressionlessly.

'What Copper said is possible,' McReady sighed. 'Van, will you help here? Thanks.' The filled needle jabbed into Copper's thigh. The man's laughter did not stop, but slowly faded into sobs, then sound sleep as the morphia took hold.

McReady turned again. The men who had started for Blair stood at the far end of the room, skis dripping snow, their faces as white as their skis. Connant had lighted a cigarette in each hand; one he was puffing absently, and staring at the floor. The heat of the one in his left hand attracted him and he stared at it and the one in the other hand stupidly for a moment. He dropped one and crushed it under his heel slowly.

'Dr. Copper,' McReady repeated, 'could be right. I know I'm human—but of course can't prove it. I'll repeat the test for my own information. Any of you others who wish to may do the same.'

Two minutes later, McReady held a test tube with white precipitin settling slowly from straw-colored serum. 'It reacts to human blood too, so they aren't both monsters.'

'I didn't think they were,' Van Wall sighed. 'That wouldn't suit the monster either; we could have destroyed them if we knew. Why hasn't the monster destroyed us, do you suppose? It seems to be loose.'

McReady snorted. Then laughed softly. 'Elementary, my dear Watson. The monster wants to have life-forms available. It cannot animate a dead body, apparently. It is just waiting—waiting until the best opportunities come. We who remain human, it is holding in reserve.'

Kinner shuddered violently. 'Hey. Hey, Mac. Mac, would I know if I was a monster? Would I know if the monster had already got me? Oh Lord, I may be a monster already.'

'You'd know,' McReady answered.

'But we wouldn't,' Norris laughed shortly, half hysterically.

McReady looked at the vial of serum remaining. 'There's one thing this damned stuff is good for, at that,' he said thoughtfully. 'Clark, will you and Van help me? The rest of the gang better stick together here. Keep an eye on each other,' he said bitterly. 'See that you don't get into mischief, shall we say?'

McReady started down the tunnel toward Dogtown, with Clark and Van Wall behind him. 'You need more serum?' Clark asked.

McReady shook his head. 'Tests. There's four cows and a bull, and nearly seventy dogs down there. This stuff reacts only to human blood and—monsters.'

11

McReady came back to the Ad Building and went silently to the wash stand. Clark and Van Wall joined him a moment later. Clark's lips had developed a tic, jerking into sudden, unexpected sneers.

'What did you do?' Connant exploded suddenly. 'More immunizing?'

Clark snickered, and stopped with a hiccough. 'Immunizing. Haw! Immune all right.'

'That monster,' said Van Wall steadily, 'is quite logical. Our immune dog was quite all right, and we drew a little more serum for the tests. But we won't make any more.'

'Can't—can't you use one man's blood on another dog—' Norris began.

'There aren't,' said McReady softly, 'any more dogs. Nor cattle, I might add.'

'No more dogs?' Benning sat down slowly.

'They're very nasty when they start changing,' Van Wall said precisely. 'But slow. That electrocution iron you made up, Barclay, is very fast. There is only one dog left—our immune. The monster left that for us, so we could play with our little test. The rest—' He shrugged and dried his hands.

'The cattle—' gulped Kinner.

'Also. Reacted very nicely. They look funny as hell when they start melting. The beast hasn't any quick escape, when it's tied in dog chains, or halters, and it had to be to imitate.'

Kinner stood up slowly. His eyes darted around the room, and came to rest horribly quivering on a tin bucket in the galley. Slowly, step by step, he retreated toward the door, his mouth opening and closing silently, like a fish out of water.

'The milk—' he gasped. 'I milked 'em an hour ago—' His voice broke into a scream as he dived through the door. He was out on the ice cap without windproof or heavy clothing.

Van Wall looked after him for a moment thoughtfully. 'He's probably hopelessly mad,' he said at length, 'but he

might be a monster escaping. He hasn't skis. Take a blow
torch—in case.'

The physical motion of the chase helped them; something
that needed doing. Three of the other men were quietly being sick. Norris was lying flat on his back, his face greenish,
looking steadily at the bottom of the bunk above him.

'Mac, how long have the—cows been not-cows—'

McReady shrugged his shoulders hopelessly. He went
over to the milk bucket, and with his little tube of serum
went to work on it. The milk clouded it, making certainty
difficult. Finally he dropped the test tube in the stand, and
shook his head. 'It tests negatively. Which means either they
were cows then, or that, being perfect imitations, they gave
perfectly good milk.'

Copper stirred restlessly in his sleep and gave a gurgling
cross between a snore and a laugh. Silent eyes fastened on
him. 'Would morphia—a monster—' somebody started to
ask.

'Lord knows,' McReady shrugged. 'It affects every
Earthly animal I know of.'

Connant suddenly raised his head. 'Mac! The dogs must
have swallowed pieces of the monster, and the pieces destroyed them! The dogs were where the monster resided. I
was locked up. Doesn't that prove—'

Van Wall shook his head. 'Sorry. Proves nothing about
what you are, only proves what you didn't do.'

'It doesn't do that,' McReady sighed. 'We are helpless because we don't know enough, and so jittery we don't think
straight. Locked up! Ever watch a white corpuscle of blood
go through the wall of a blood vessel? No? It sticks out a
pseudopod. And there it is—on the far side of the wall.'

'Oh,' said Van Wall unhappily. 'The cattle tried to melt
down, didn't they? They could have melted down—become
just a threat of stuff and leaked under a door to re-collect on
the other side. Ropes—no—no, that wouldn't do it. They
couldn't live in a sealed tank or—'

'If,' said McReady, 'you shoot it through the heart, and it
doesn't die, it's a monster. That's the best I can think of, off-
hand.'

'No dogs,' said Garry quietly, 'and no cattle. It has to imitate men now. And locking up doesn't do any good. Your
test might work, Mac, but I'm afraid it would be hard on the
men.'

12

Clark looked up from the galley stove as Van Wall, Barclay, McReady, and Benning came in, brushing the drift from their clothes. The other men jammed into the Ad Building continued studiously to do as they were doing, playing chess, poker, reading. Ralsen was fixing a sledge on the table; Vane and Norris had their heads together over magnetic data, while Harvey read tables in a low voice.

Dr. Copper snored softly on the bunk. Garry was working with Dutton over a sheaf of radio messages on the corner of Dutton's bunk and a small fraction of the radio table. Connant was using most of the table for cosmic ray sheets.

Quite plainly through the corridor, despite two closed doors, they could hear Kinner's voice. Clark banged a kettle onto the galley stove and beckoned McReady silently. The meteorologist went over to him.

'I don't mind the cooking so damn much,' Clark said nervously, 'but isn't there some way to stop that bird? We all agreed that it would be safe to move him into Cosmos House.'

'Kinner?' McReady nodded toward the door. 'I'm afraid not. I can dope him. I suppose, but we don't have an unlimited supply of morphia, and he's not in danger of losing his mind. Just hysterical.'

'Well, we're in danger of losing ours. You've been out for an hour and a half. That's been going on steadily ever since, and it was going for two hours before. There's a limit, you know.'

Garry wandered over slowly, apologetically. For an instant, McReady caught the feral spark of fear—horror—in Clark's eyes, and knew at the same instant it was in his own. Garry—Garry or Copper, was certainly a monster.

'If you could stop that, I think it would be a sound policy, Mac,' Garry spoke quietly. 'There are—tensions enough in this room. We agreed that it would be safer for Kinner in there, because everyone else in camp is under constant eyeing.' Garry shivered slightly. 'And try, try in God's name, to find some test that will work.' McReady sighed. 'Watched or unwatched, everyone's tense. Blair's jammed the trap so it won't open now. Says he's got food enough, and keeps screaming "Go away, go away—you're monsters. I won't be

absorbed. I won't. I'll tell men when they come. Go away."
So—we went away.'

'There's another test?' Garry pleaded.

McReady shrugged his shoulders. 'Copper was perfectly right. The serum test could be absolutely definitive if it hadn't been—contaminated. But that's the only one dog left, and he's fixed now.'

'Chemicals? Chemical tests?'

McReady shook his head. 'Our chemistry isn't that good. I tried the microscope you know.'

Garry nodded. 'Monster-dog and real dog were identical. But—you've got to go on. What are we going to do after dinner?'

Van Wall had joined them quietly. 'Rotation sleeping. Half the crowd sleep; half stay awake. I wonder how many of us are monsters? All the dogs were. We thought we were safe, but somehow it got Copper—or you.' Van Wall's eyes flashed uneasily. 'It may have gotten every one of you—all of you but myself may be wondering, looking. No, that's not possible. You'd just spring then, I'd be helpless. We humans must somehow have the greater numbers now. But—' he stopped.

McReady laughed shortly. 'You're doing what Norris complained of in me. Leaving it hanging. "But if one more is changed—that may shift the balance of power." It doesn't fight. I don't think it ever fights. It must be a peaceable thing, in its own—inimitable—way. It never had to, because it always gained its end otherwise.'

Van Wall's mouth twisted in a sickly grin. 'You're suggesting then, that perhaps it already *has* the greater numbers, but is just waiting—waiting, all of them—all of you, for all I know—waiting till I, the last human, drop my wariness in sleep. Mac, did you notice their eyes, all looking at us.'

Garry sighed. 'You haven't been sitting here for four straight hours, while all their eyes silently weighed the information that one of us two, Copper or I, is a monster certainly—perhaps both of us.'

Clark repeated his request. 'Will you stop that bird's noise? He's driving me nuts. Make him tone down, anyway.'

'Still praying?' McReady asked.

'Still praying,' Clark groaned. 'He hasn't stopped for a second. I don't mind his praying if it relieves him, but he yells, he sings psalms and hymns and shouts prayers. He thinks God can't hear well way down here.'

'Maybe he can't,' Barclay grunted. 'Or he'd have done something about this thing loosed from hell.'

'Somebody's going to try that test you mentioned, if you don't stop him,' Clark stated grimly. 'I think a cleaver in the head would be as positive a test as a bullet in the heart.'

'Go ahead with the food. I'll see what I can do. There may be something in the cabinets.' McReady moved wearily toward the corner Copper had used as his dispensary. Three tall cabinets of rough boards, two locked, were the repositories of the camp's medical supplies. Twelve years ago, McReady had graduated, had started for an internship, and been diverted to meteorology. Copper was a picked man, a man who knew his profession thoroughly and modernly. More than half the drugs available were totally unfamiliar to McReady; many of the others he had forgotten. There was no huge medical library here, no series of journals available to learn the things he had forgotten, the elementary, simple things to Copper, things that did not merit inclusion in the small library he had been forced to content himself with. Books are heavy, and every ounce of supplies had been freighted in by air.

McReady picked a barbiturate hopefully. Barclay and Van Wall went with him. One man never went anywhere alone in Big Magnet.

Ralsen had his sledge put away, and the physicists had moved off the table, the poker game broken up when they got back. Clark was putting out the food. The click of spoons and the muffled sounds of eating were the only sign of life in the room. There were no words spoken as the three returned; simply all eyes focused on them questioningly while the jaws moved methodically.

McReady stiffened suddenly. Kinner was screeching out a hymn in a hoarse, cracked voice. He looked wearily at Van Wall with a twisted grin and shook his head. 'Uh-uh.'

Van Wall cursed bitterly, and sat down at the table. 'We'll just plumb have to take that till his voice wears out. He can't yell like that forever.'

'He's got a brass throat and a cast-iron larynx,' Norris declared savagely. 'Then we could be hopeful, and suggest he's one of our friends. In that case he could go on renewing his throat till doomsday.'

Silence clamped down. For twenty minutes they ate without a word. Then Connant jumped with an angry violence. 'You sit as still as a bunch of graven images. You don't say a word, but oh, Lord, what expressive eyes you've got. They roll around like a bunch of glass marbles spilling down a table. They wink and blink and stare—and whisper things. Can you guys look somewhere else for a change, please?'

'Listen, Mac, you're in charge here. Let's run movies for the rest of the night. We've been saving those reels to make 'em last. Last for what? Who is it's going to see those last reels, eh? Let's see 'em while we can, and look at something other than each other.'

'Sound idea, Connant. I, for one, am quite willing to change this in any way I can.'

'Turn the sound up loud, Dutton. Maybe you can drown out the hymns,' Clark suggested.

'But don't,' Norris said softly, 'don't turn off the lights altogether.'

'The lights will be out.' McReady shook his head. 'We'll show all the cartoon movies we have. You won't mind seeing the old cartoons will you?'

'Goody, goody—a moom-pitcher show. I'm just in the mood.' McReady turned to look at the speaker, a lean, lanky New Englander, by the name of Caldwell. Caldwell was stuffing his pipe slowly, a sour eye cocked up to McReady.

The bronze giant was forced to laugh. 'OK, Bart, you win. Maybe we aren't quite in the mood for Popeye and trick ducks, but it's something.'

'Let's play Classifications,' Caldwell suggested slowly. 'Or maybe you call it Guggenheim. You draw lines on a piece of paper, and put down classes of things—like animals, you know. One for "H" and one for "U" and so on. Like "Human" and "Unknown" for instance. I think that would be a hell of a lot better game. Classification, I sort of figure, is what we need right now a lot more than movies. Maybe somebody's got a pencil that he can draw lines with, draw lines between the "U" animals and the "H" animals for instance.'

'McReady's trying to find that kind of a pencil,' Van Wall answered quietly, 'but, we've got three kinds of animals here, you know. One that begins with "M". We don't want any more.'

'Mad ones, you mean. Uh-huh. Clark, I'll help you with

those pots so we can get our little peep show going.'
Caldwell got up slowly.

Dutton and Barclay and Benning, in charge of the projector and sound mechanism arrangements, went about their job silently, while the Ad Building was cleared and the dishes and pan disposed of. McReady drifted over toward Van Wall slowly, and leaned back in the bunk beside him. 'I've been wondering, Van,' he said with a wry grin, 'whether or not to report my ideas in advance. I forgot the "U" animal' as Caldwell named it, could read minds. I've a vague idea of something that might work. It's too vague to bother with, though. Go ahead with your show, while I try to figure out the logic of the thing. I'll take this bunk.'

Van Wall glanced up, and nodded. The movie screen would be practically on a line with this bunk, hence making the pictures least distracting here, because least intelligible. 'Perhaps you should tell us what you have in mind. As it is, only the unknowns know what you plan. You might be—unknown before you got it into operation.'

'Won't take long, if I get it figured out right. But I don't want any more all-but-the-test-dog-monsters things. We better move Copper into this bunk directly above me. He won't be watching the screen either.' McReady nodded toward Copper's gently snoring bulk. Garry helped them lift and move the doctor.

McReady leaned back against the bunk, and sank into a trance, almost, of concentration, trying to calculate chances, operations, methods. He was scarcely aware as the others distributed themselves silently, and the screen lit up. Vaguely Kinner's hectic, shouted prayers and his rasping hymn-singing annoyed him till the sound accompaniment started. The lights were turned out, but the large, light-colored area of the screen reflected enough light for ready visibility. It made men's eyes sparkle as they moved restlessly. Kinner was still praying, shouting, his voice a raucous accompaniment to the mechanical sound. Dutton stepped up the amplification.

So long had the voice been going on, that only vaguely at first was McReady aware that something seemed missing. Lying as he was, just across the narrow room from the corridor leading to Cosmos House, Kinner's voice had reached him fairly clearly, despite the sound accompaniment of the pictures. It struck him abruptly that it had stopped.

'Dutton, cut that sound,' McReady called as he sat up abruptly. The pictures flickered a moment, soundless and strangely futile in the sudden, deep silence. The rising wind on the surface above bubbled melancholy tears of sound down the stove pipes. 'Kinner's stopped,' McReady said softly.

'For God's sake start that sound then; he may have stopped to listen,' Norris snapped.

McReady rose and went down the corridor. Barclay and Van Wall left their places at the far end of the room to follow him. The flickers bulged and twisted on the back of Barclay's gray underwear as he crossed the still-functioning beam of the projector. Dutton snapped on the lights, and the pictures vanished.

Norris stood at the door as McReady had asked. Garry sat down quietly in the bunk nearest the door, forcing Clark to make room for him. Most of the others had stayed exactly where they were. Only Connant walked slowly up and down the room, in steady, unvarying rhythm.

'If you're going to do that, Connant,' Clark spat, 'we can get along without you altogether, whether you're human or not. Will you stop that damned rhythm?'

'Sorry.' The physicist sat down in a bunk, and watched his toes thoughtfully. It was almost five minutes, five ages, while the wind made the only sound, before McReady appeared at the door.

'Well,' he announced, 'haven't got enough grief here already. Somebody's tried to help us out. Kinner has a knife in his throat, which was why he stopping singing, probably. We've got monsters, madmen and murderers. Any more "M's" you can think of, Caldwell? If there are, we'll probably have 'em before long.'

13

'Is Blair loose?' someone asked.

'Blair is not loose. Or he flew in. If there's any doubt about where our gentle helper came from—this may clear it up.' Van Wall held a foot-long, think-bladed knife in a cloth. The wooden handle was half burnt, charred with the peculiar pattern of the top of the galley stove.

Clark stared at it. 'I did that this afternoon. I forgot the damn thing and left it on the stove.'

Van Wall nodded. 'I smelled it, if you remember. I knew the knife came from the galley.'

'I wonder,' said Benning, looking around at the party warily, 'how many more monsters have we? If somebody could slip out of his place, go back of the screen to the galley and then down to the Cosmos House and back—he did come back, didn't he? Yes—everybody's here. Well, if one of the gang could do all that—'

'Maybe a monster did it,' Garry suggested quietly.

'There's that possibility.'

'The monster, as you pointed out today, has only men left to imitate. Would he decrease his—supply, shall we say?' Van Wall pointed out. 'No, we just have a plain, ordinary louse, a murderer to deal with. Ordinarily we'd call him an "inhuman murderer" I suppose, but we have to distinguish now. We have inhuman murderers, and now we have human murderers. Or one at least.'

'There's one less human,' Norris said softly. 'Maybe the monsters have the balance of power now.'

'Never mind that,' McReady sighed and turned to Barclay. 'Bar, will you get your electric gadget? I'm going to make certain—'

Barclay turned down the corridor to get the pronged electrocuter, while McReady and Van Wall went back toward Cosmos House. Barclay followed them in some thirty seconds.

The corridor to Cosmos House twisted, as did nearly all corridors in Big Magnet, and Norris stood at the entrance again. But they heard, rather muffled, McReady's sudden shout. There was a savage flurry of blows, dull *ch-thunk, shluff* sounds. 'Bar—Bar—' And a curious, savage mewing scream, silenced before even quick-moving Norris had reached the bend.

Kinner—or what had been Kinner—lay on the floor, cut half in two by the great knife McReady had had. The meteorologist stood against the wall, the knife dripping red in his hand. Van Wall was stirring vaguely on the floor, moaning, his hand half-consciously rubbing at his jaw. Barclay, an unutterably savage gleam in his eyes, was methodically leaning on the pronged weapon in his hand, jabbing—jabbing, jabbing.

Kinner's arms had developed a queer, scaly fur, and the flesh had twisted. The fingers had shortened, the hand rounded, the fingernails become three-inch long things of dull red horn, keened to steel-hard, razor-sharp talons.

McReady raised his head, looked at the knife in his hand and dropped it. 'Well, whoever did it can speak up now. He was an inhuman murderer at that—in that he murdered an inhuman. I swear by all that's holy, Kinner was a lifeless corpse on the floor here when we arrived. But when It found we were going to jab It with the power—It changed.'

Norris stared unsteadily. 'Oh, Lord, those things can act. Ye gods—sitting in here for hours, mouthing prayers to a God it hated! Shouting hymns in a cracked voice—hymns about a Church it never knew. Driving us mad with its ceaseless howling—

'Well. Speak up, whoever did it. You didn't know it, but you did the camp a favor. And I want to know how in blazes you got out of the room without anyone seeing you. It might help in guarding ourselves.'

'His screaming—his singing. Even the sound projector couldn't drown it.' Clark shivered. 'It was a monster.'

'Oh,' said Van Wall in sudden comprehension. 'You *were* sitting right next to the door, weren't you? And almost behind the projection screen already.'

Clark nodded dumbly. 'He—it's quiet now. It's a dead—Mac, your test's no damn good. It was dead anyway, monster or man, it was dead.'

McReady chuckled softly. 'Boys, meet Clark, the only one we know is human! Meet Clark, the one who proves he's human by trying to commit murder—and failing. Will the rest of you please refrain from trying to prove you're human for a while? I think we may have another test.'

'A test!' Connant snapped joyfully, then his face sagged in disappointment. 'I suppose it's another either-way-you-want-it.'

'No,' said McReady steadily. 'Look sharp and be careful. Come into the Ad Building. Barclay, bring your electrocuter. And somebody—Dutton—stand with Barclay to make sure he does it. Watch every neighbor, for by the Hell these monsters came from, I've got something, and they know it. They're going to get dangerous!'

The groups tensed abruptly. An air of crushing menace entered into every man's body, sharply they looked at each other. More keenly than ever before—*is that man next to me an inhuman monster?*

'What is it?' Garry asked, as they stood again in the main room. 'How long will it take?'

'I don't know exactly,' said McReady, his voice brittle with angry determination. 'But I *know* it will work, and no two ways about it. It depends on a basic quality of the *monsters,* not on us. *"Kinner"* just convinced me.' He stood heavy and solid in bronzed immobility, completely sure of himself again at last.

'This,' said Barclay, hefting the wooden-handled weapon tipped with its two sharp-pointed, charged conductors, 'is going to be rather necessary, I take it. Is the power plant assured?'

Dutton nodded sharply. 'The automatic stoker bin is full. The gas power plant is on standby. Van Wall and I set it for the movie operation—and we've checked it over rather carefully several times, you know. Anything those wires touch, dies,' he assured them grimly. 'I know that.'

Dr. Copper stirred vaguely in his bunk, rubbed his eyes with fumbling hand. He sat up slowly, blinked his eyes blurred with sleep and drugs, widened with an unutterable horror of drug-ridden nightmares. 'Garry,' he mumbled, 'Garry—listen. Selfish—from hell they came, and hellish shellfish—I mean self—Do I? What do I mean?' He sank back in his bunk, and snored softly.

McReady looked at him thoughtfully. 'We'll know presently,' he nodded slowly. 'But selfish is what you mean, all right. You may have thought of that, half-sleeping, dreaming there. I didn't stop to think what dreams you might be having. But that's all right. Selfish is the word. They must be, you see.' He turned to the men in the cabin, tense, silent men staring with wolfish eyes each at his neighbor. 'Selfish, and as Dr. Copper said—*every part is a whole.* Every piece is self-sufficient, an animal in itself.

'That, and one other thing, tell the story. There's nothing mysterious about blood; it's just as normal a body tissue as a piece of muscle, or a piece of liver. But it hasn't so much connective tissue, though it has millions, billions of life cells.'

McReady's great bronze beard ruffled in a grim smile. 'This is satisfying, in a way. I'm pretty sure we humans still outnumber you—others. Others standing here. And we have what you, your other-world race, evidently doesn't. Not an imitated, but a bred-in-the-bone instinct, a driving, unquenchable fire that's genuine. We'll fight, fight with a ferocity you may attempt to imitate, but you'll never equal! We're human. We're real. You're imitations, false to the core of your every cell.'

'All right. It's a showdown now. *You* know. You, with your mind reading. You've lifted the idea from my brain. You can't do a thing about it.

'Standing here—

'Let it pass. Blood is tissue. They have to bleed, if they don't bleed when cut, then by Heaven, they're phoney from hell! If they bleed—then that blood, separated from them, is an individual—*a newly formed individual in its own right, just as they—split, all of them, from one original—are individuals!*

'Get it, Van? See the answer, Bar?'

Van Wall laughed very softly. 'The blood—the blood will not obey. It's a new individual, with all the desire to protect its own life that the original—the main mass from which it was split—has. The *blood* will live—and try to crawl away from a hot needle, say!'

McReady picked up the scalpel from the table. From the cabinet, he took a rack of test tubes, a tiny alcohol lamp, and a length of platinum wire set in a little glass rod. A smile of grim satisfaction rode his lips. For a moment he glanced up at those around him. Barclay and Dutton moved toward him slowly, the wooden-handled electric instrument alert.

'Dutton,' said McReady, 'suppose you stand over by the splice there where you've connected that in. Just make sure no—thing pulls it loose.'

Dutton moved away. 'Now, Van, suppose you be first on this.'

White-faced, Van Wall stepped forward. With a delicate precision, McReady cut a vein in the base of his thumb. Van Wall winced slightly, then held steady as a half inch of bright blood collected in the tube. McReady put the tube in the rack, gave Van Wall a bit of alum, and indicated the iodine bottle.

Van Wall stood motionlessly watching. McReady heated the platinum wire in the alcohol lamp flame, then dipped it into the tube. It hissed softly. Five times he repeated the test. 'Human, I'd say,' McReady sighed, and straightened. 'As yet, my theory hasn't been actually proven—but I have hopes. I have hopes.

'Don't, by the way, get too interested in this. We have with us some unwelcome ones, no doubt. Van, will you relieve Barclay at the switch? Thanks. OK, Barclay, and may I say I hope you stay with us? You're a damned good guy.'

Barclay grinned uncertainly; winced under the keen edge of the scalpel. Presently, smiling widely, he retrieved his long-handed weapon.

'Mr. Samuel Dutt—*Bar*!'

The tensity was released in that second. Whatever the hell the monsters may have had within them, the men in that instant matched it. Barclay had no chance to move his weapon, as a score of men poured down on the thing that had seemed Dutton. It mewed, and spat, and tried to grow fangs—and was a hundred broken, torn pieces. Without knives, or any weapon save the brute-given strength of a staff of picked men, the thing was crushed, rent.

Slowly they picked themselves up, their eyes smouldering, very quiet in their motions. A curious wrinkling of their lips betrayed a species of nervousness.

Barclay went over with the electric weapon. Things smouldered and stank. The caustic acid Van Wall dropped on each spilled drop of blood gave off tickling, cough-provoking fumes.

McReady grinned, his deepset eyes alight and dancing. 'Maybe,' he said softly, 'I underrated man's abilities when I said nothing human could have the ferocity in the eyes of that thing we found. I wish we could have the opportunity to treat in a more befitting manner these things. Something with boiling oil, or melted lead in it, or maybe slow roasting in the power boiler. When I think what a man Dutton was—

'Never mind. My theory is confirmed by—by one who knew! Well, Van Wall and Barclay are proven. I think, then, that I'll try to show you what I already know. That I, too, am human.' McReady swished the scalpel in absolute alcohol, burned it off the metal blade, and cut the base of his thumb expertly.

Twenty seconds later he looked up from the desk at the waiting men. There were more grins out there now, friendly grins, yet withal, something else in the eyes.

'Connant,' McReady laughed softly, 'was right. The huskies watching that thing in the corridor bend had nothing on you. Wonder why we think only the wolf blood has the right to ferocity? Maybe on spontaneous viciousness a wolf takes tops, but after these seven days—abandon all hope, ye wolves who enter here!

'Maybe we can save time. Connant, would you step for—'

Again Barclay was too slow. There were more grins, less tensity still, when Barclay and Van Wall finished their work.

Garry spoke in a low, bitter voice. 'Connant was one of the finest men we had here—and five minutes ago I'd have sworn he was a man. Those damnable things are more than imitation.' Garry shuddered and sat back in his bunk.

And thirty seconds later, Garry's blood shrank from the hot platinum wire, and struggled to escape the tube, struggled as frantically as a suddenly feral, red-eyed, dissolving imitation of Garry struggled to dodge the snake tongue weapon Barclay advanced at him, white-faced and sweating. The Thing in the test tube screamed with a tiny, tinny voice as McReady dropped it into the glowing coal of the galley stove.

14

'The last of it?' Dr. Copper looked down from his bunk with bloodshot, saddened eyes. 'Fourteen of them—'

McReady nodded shortly. 'In some ways—if only we could have permanently prevented their spreading—I'd like to have even the imitations back. Commander Garry— Connant—Dutton—Clark—'

'Where are they taking those things?' Copper nodded to the stretcher Barclay and Norris were carrying out.

'Outside. Outside in the ice, where they've got fifteen smashed crates, half a ton of coal, and presently will add ten gallons of kerosene. We've dumped acid on every spilled drop, every torn fragment. We're going to incinerate those.'

'Sounds like a good plan.' Copper nodded wearily. 'I wonder, you haven't said whether Blair—'

McReady started. 'We forgot him? We had so much else! I wonder—do you suppose we can cure him now?'

'If—' began Dr. Copper, and stopped meaningly.

McReady started a second time. 'Even a madman. It imitated Kinner and his praying hysteria—' McReady turned toward Van Wall at the long table. 'Van, we've got to make an expedition to Blair's shack.'

Van looked up sharply, the frown of worry faded for an instant in surprised remembrance. Then he rose, nodded. 'Barclay better go along. He applied the lashings, and may figure how to get in without frightening Blair too much.'

Three quarters of an hour, through −37° cold, while the aurora curtain bellied overhead. The twilight was nearly twelve hours long, flaming in the north on snow like white, crystalline sand under their skis. A five-mile wind piled it in drift-lines pointing off to the northwest. Three quarters of an hour to reach the snow-buried shack. No smoke came from the little shack, and the men hastened.

'Blair!' Barclay roared into the wind and when he was still a hundred yards away. 'Blair!'

'Shut up,' said McReady softly. 'And hurry. He may be trying a lone hike. If we have to go after him—no planes, the tractors disabled—'

'Would a monster have the stamina a man has?'

'A broken leg wouldn't stop it for more than a minute,' McReady pointed out.

Barclay gasped suddenly and pointed aloft. Dim in the twilit sky, a winged thing circled in curves of indescribable grace and ease. Great white wings tipped gently, and the bird swept over them in silent curiosity. 'Albatross—' Barclay said softly. 'First of the season, and wandering way inland for some reason. If a monster's loose—'

Norris bent down on the ice, and tore hurriedly at his heavy, windproof clothing. He straightened, his coat flapping open, a grim blue-metaled weapon in his hand. It roared a challenge to the white silence of Antarctica.

The thing in the air screamed hoarsely. Its great wings worked frantically as a dozen feathers floated down from its tail. Norris fired again. The bird was moving swiftly now, but in an almost straight line of retreat. It screamed again, more feathers dropped, and with beating wings it soared behind a ridge of pressure ice, to vanish.

Norris hurried after the others. 'It won't come back,' he panted.

Barclay cautioned him to silence, pointing. A curiously, fiercely blue light beat out from the cracks of the shack's door. A very low, soft humming sounded inside, a low, soft humming and a clink and click of tools, the very sounds somehow bearing a message of frantic haste.

McReady's face paled. 'Lord help us if that thing has—' He grabbed Barclay's shoulder, and made snipping motions with his fingers, pointing toward the lacing of control cables that held the door.

Barclay drew the wire cutters from his pocket, and kneeled soundlessly at the door. The snap and twang of cut wires made an unbearable racket in the utter quiet of the Antarctic hush. There was only that savage, sweetly soft hum from within the shack, and the queerly, hecticly clipped clicking and rattling of tools to drown their noises.

McReady peered through a crack in the door. His breath sucked in huskily, and his great fingers clamped cruelly on Barclay's shoulder. The meteorologist backed down. 'It isn't,' he explained very softly, 'Blair. It's kneeling on something on the bunk—something that keeps lifting. Whatever it's working on is a thing like a knapsack—and it lifts.'

'All at once,' Barclay said grimly. 'No. Norris, hang back, and get that iron of yours out. It may have—weapons.'

Together, Barclay's powerful body and McReady's giant strength struck the door. Inside, the bunk jammed against the door screeched madly and crackled into kindling. The door flung down from broken hinges, the patched lumber of the doorpost dropping inward.

Like a blue rubber-ball, a Thing bounced up. One of its four tentacle-like arms looped out like a striking snake. In a seven-tentacled hand a six-inch pencil of winking, shining metal glinted and swung upward to face them. Its line-thin lips twitched back from snake-fangs in a grin of hate, red eyes blazing.

Norris' revolver thundered in the confined space. The hate-washed face twitched in agony, the looping tentacle snatched back. The silvery thing in its hand a smashed ruin of metal, the seven-tentacled hand became a mass of mangled flesh oozing greenish-yellow ichor. The revolver thundered three times more. Dark holes drilled each of the three eyes before Norris hurled the empty weapon against its face.

The Thing screamed in feral hate, a lashing tentacle wiping at blinded eyes. For a moment it crawled on the floor, savage tentacles lashing out, the body twitching. Then it staggered up again, blinded eyes working, boiling hideously, the crushed flesh sloughing away in sodden gobbets.

Barclay lurched to his feet and dove forward with an ice-ax. The flat of the weighty thing crushed against the side of the head. Again the unkillable monster went down. The tentacles lashed out, and suddenly Barclay fell to his feet in the grip of a living, livid rope. The Thing dissolved as he held it, a white-hot band that ate into the flesh of his hands like living fire. Frantically he tore the stuff from him, held his hands where they could not be reached. The blind Thing felt and ripped at the tough, heavy, windproof cloth, seeking flesh—flesh it could convert—

The huge blowtorch McReady had brought coughed solemnly. Abruptly it rumbled disapproval throatily. Then it laughed gurglingly, and thrust out a blue-white, three-foot tongue. The Thing on the floor shrieked, flailed out blindly with tentacles that writhed and withered in the bubbling wrath of the blowtorch. It crawled and turned on the floor, it shrieked and hobbled madly, but always McReady held the blowtorch on the face, the dead eyes burning and bubbling uselessly. Frantically the Thing crawled and howled.

A tentacle sprouted a savage talon—and crisped in the flame. Steadily McReady moved with a planned, grim campaign. Helpless, maddened, the Thing retreated from the grunting torch, the caressing, licking tongue. For a moment it rebelled, squalling in inhuman hatred at the touch of the icy snow. Then it fell back before the charring breath of the torch, the stench of its flesh bathing it. Hopelessly it retreated—on and on across the Antarctic snow. The bitter wind swept over it, twisting the torch-tongue; vainly it flopped, a trail of oily, stinking smoke bubbling away from it—

McReady walked back toward the shack silently. Barclay met him at the door. 'No more?' the giant meteorologist asked grimly.

Barclay shook his head. 'No more. It didn't split?'

'It had other things to think about,' McReady assured him. 'When I left it, it was a glowing coal. What was it doing?'

Norris laughed shortly. 'Wise boys, we are. Smash magnetos, so planes won't work. Rip the boiler tubing out of the tractors. And leave that Thing alone for a week in this shack. Alone and undisturbed.'

McReady looked in at the shack more carefully. The air, despite the ripped door, was hot and humid. On a table at the far end of the room rested a thing of coiled wires and small magnets, glass tubing and radio tubes. At the center a block of rough stone rested. From the center of the block came the light that flooded the place, the fiercely blue light bluer than the glare of an electric arc, and from it came the sweetly soft hum. Off to one side was another mechanism of crystal glass, blown with an incredible neatness and delicacy, metal plates and a queer, shimmery sphere of insubstantiality.

'What is that?' McReady moved nearer.

Norris grunted. 'Leave it for investigation. But I can guess pretty well. That's atomic power. That stuff to the left—that's a neat little thing for doing what men have been trying to do with hundred-ton cyclotrons and so forth. It separates neutrons from heavy water, which he was getting from the surrounding ice.'

'Where did he get all—oh. Of course. A monster couldn't be locked in—or out. He's been through the apparatus caches.' McReady stared at the apparatus. 'Lord, what minds that race must have—'

'The shimmery sphere—I think it's a sphere of pure force. Neutrons can pass through any matter, and he wanted a supply reservoir of neutrons. Just project neutrons against silica—calcium—beryllium—almost anything, and the atomic energy is released. That thing is the atomic generator.'

McReady plucked a thermometer from his coat. 'It's 120° in here, despite the open door. Our clothes have kept the heat out to an extent, but I'm sweating now.'

Norris nodded. 'The light's cold. I found that. But it gives off heat to warm the place through that coil. He had all the power in the world. He could keep it warm and pleasant, as his race thought of warmth and pleasantness. Did you notice the light, the color of it?'

McReady nodded. 'Beyond the stars is the answer. From beyond the stars. From a hotter planet that circled a brighter, bluer sun they came.'

McReady glanced out the door toward the blasted, smoke-stained trail that flopped and wandered blindly off across the drift. 'There won't be any more coming. I guess. Sheer accident it landed here, and that was twenty million years ago. What did it do all that for?' He nodded toward the apparatus.

Barclay laughed softly. 'Did you notice what it was working on when we came? Look.' He pointed toward the ceiling of the shack.

Like a knapsack made of flattened coffee tins, with dangling cloth straps and leather belts, the mechanism clung to the ceiling. A tiny, glaring heart of supernal flame burned in it, yet burned through the ceiling's wood without scorching it. Barclay walked over to it, grasped two of the dangling straps in his hands, and pulled it down with an effort. He strapped it about his body. A slight jump carried him in a weirdly slow arc across the room.

'Antigravity,' said McReady softly.

'Antigravity,' Norris nodded. 'Yes, we had 'em stopped, with no planes, and no birds. The birds hadn't come—but it had coffee tins and radio parts, and glass and the machine shop at night. And a week—a whole week—all to itself. America is a single jump—with antigravity powered by the atomic energy matter.

'We had 'em stopped. Another half hour—it was just tightening these straps on the device so it could wear it—and we'd have stayed in Antarctica, and shot down any moving thing that came from the rest of the world.'

'The albatross—' McReady said softly. 'Do you suppose—'

'With this thing almost finished? With that death weapon it held in its hand?'

'No, by the grace of God, who evidently does hear very well, even down here, and the margin of half an hour, we keep our world, and the planets of the system, too. Antigravity, you know, and atomic power. Because They came from another sun, a star beyond the stars. *They* came from a world with a bluer sun.'

They

Robert A. Heinlein

Robert A. Heinlein (1907–88) is one of the few writers whose name is synonymous with science fiction, and his novels *Stranger in a Strange Land* and *The Moon is a Harsh Mistress* are rare examples of science fiction that have earned a huge audience outside the genre. Heinlein's talent for imagining future and near-future worlds in which advanced science is an integral part of the cultural fabric extends to the handful of fantasies he collected into *The Unpleasant Profession of Jonathan Hoag,* wherein settings are painstakingly crafted to accommodate the intrusion of the uncanny. One of those stories, "They," first appeared in the April 1941 issue of *Unknown,* a magazine that asked its contributors to write "logical" fantasy. It is perhaps the ultimate story on the undisprovability of conspiracy theories.

They would not let him alone.

They never would let him alone. He realized that that was part of the plot against him—never to leave him in peace, never to give him a chance to mull over the lies they had told him, time enough to pick out the flaws, and to figure out the truth for himself.

That damned attendant this morning! He had come busting in with his breakfast tray, waking him, and causing him to forget his dream. If only he could remember that dream—

Someone was unlocking the door. He ignored it.

"Howdy, old boy. They tell me you refused your breakfast?" Dr. Hayward's professionally kindly mask hung over his bed.

"I wasn't hungry."

"But we can't have that. You'll get weak, and then I won't be able to get you well completely. Now get up and get your clothes on and I'll order an eggnog for you. Come on, that's a good fellow!"

Unwilling, but still less willing at that moment to enter into any conflict of wills, he got out of bed and slipped on his bathrobe. "That's better," Hayward approved. "Have a cigarette?"

"No, thank you."

The doctor shook his head in a puzzled fashion. "Darned if I can figure you out. Loss of interest in physical pleasures does not fit your type of case."

"What is my type of case?" he inquired in flat tones.

"Tut! Tut!" Hayward tried to appear roguish. "If medicos told their professional secrets, they might have to work for a living."

'What is my type of case?'

"Well—the label doesn't matter, does it? Suppose *you* tell me. I really know nothing about your case as yet. Don't you think it is about time you talked?"

"I'll play chess with you."

"All right, all right." Hayward made a gesture of impatient concession. "We've played chess every day for a week. If you will talk, I'll play chess."

What could it matter? If he was right, they already understood perfectly that he had discovered their plot; there was nothing to be gained by concealing the obvious. Let them try to argue him out of it. Let the tail go with the hide! To hell with it!

He got out the chessman and commenced setting them up. "What do you know of my case so far?"

"Very little. Physical examination, negative. Past history, negative. High intelligence, as shown by your record in school and your success in your profession. Occasional fits of moodiness, but nothing exceptional. The only positive information was the incident that caused you to come here for treatment."

"To be brought here, you mean. Why should it cause comment?"

"Well, good gracious, man—if you barricade yourself in your room and insisted that your wife is plotting against you, don't you expect people to notice?"

"But she *was* plotting against me—and so are you. White, or black?"

"Black—it's your turn to attack. Why do you think we are 'plotting against you'?"

"It's an involved story, and goes way back into my early

childhood. There was an immediate incident, however—"
He opened by advancing the white king's knight to KB3.
Hayward's eyebrows raised.

"You make a piano attack?"

"Why not? You know that it is not safe for me to risk a
gambit with you."

The doctor shrugged his shoulders and answered the
opening. "Suppose we start with your early childhood. It
may shed more light than more recent incidents. Did you
feel that you were being persecuted as a child?"

"No!" He half rose from his chair. 'When I was a child I
was sure of myself. I knew then, I tell you; I knew! Life was
worthwhile, and I knew it. I was at peace with myself and
my surroundings. Life was good and I was good, and I assumed that the creatures around me were like myself."

"And weren't they?"

"Not at all! Particularly the children. I didn't know what
viciousness was until I was turned loose with other 'children.' The little devils! And I was expected to be like them
and play with them."

The doctor nodded. "I know. The herd compulsion. Children can be pretty savage at times."

"You've missed the point. This wasn't any healthy rough-
ness; these creatures were *different*—not like myself at all.
They *looked* like me, but they were *not* like me. If I tried to
say anything to one of them about anything that mattered to
me, all I could get was a stare and a scornful laugh. Then
they would find some way to punish me for having said it."

Hayward nodded. "I see what you mean. How about
grown-ups?"

"That is somewhat different. Adults don't matter to children at first—or, rather, they did not matter to me. They
were too big, and they did not bother me, and they were
busy with things that did not enter into my considerations. It
was only when I noticed that my presence affected them that
I began to wonder about them."

"How do you mean?"

"Well, they never did the things when I was around that
they did when I was not around."

Hayward looked at him carefully, "Won't that statement
take quite a lot of justifying? How do you know what they
did when you weren't around?"

He acknowledged the point. "But I used to catch them just stopping. If I came into a room, the conversation would stop suddenly, and then it would pick up about the weather or something equally inane. Then I took to hiding and listening and looking. Adults did not behave the same way in my presence as out of it."

"Your move, I believe. But see here, old man—that was when you were a child. Every child passes through that phase. Now that you are a man, you must see the adult point of view. Children *are* strange creatures and have to be protected—at least, we do protect them—from many adult interests. There is a whole code of conventions in the matter that—"

"Yes, yes," he interrupted impatiently, "I know all that. Nevertheless, I noticed enough and remembered enough that was never clear to me later. And it put me on my guard to notice the next thing."

"Which was?" He noticed that the doctor's eyes were averted as he adjusted a castle's position.

"The things I saw people doing and heard them talking about were never of any importance. They *must* be doing something else."

"I don't follow you."

"You don't choose to follow me. I'm telling this to you in exchange for a game of chess."

"Why do you like to play chess so well?"

"Because it is the only thing in the world where I can see all the factors and understand all the rules. Never mind—I saw all around me this enormous plant, cities, farms, factories, churches, schools, homes, railroads, luggage, roller coasters, trees, saxophones, libraries, people and animals. People that looked like me and who should have felt very much like me, if what I was told was the truth. But what did they appear to be doing? 'They went to work to earn the money to buy the food to get the strength to go to work to earn the money to buy the food to get the strength to go to work to get the strength to buy the food to earn the money to go to—' until they fell over dead. Any slight variation in the basic pattern did not matter, for they always fell over dead. And everybody tried to tell me I should be doing the same thing. I knew better!"

The doctor gave him a look apparently intended to denote helpless surrender and laughed. "I can't argue with you. Life does look like that, and maybe it is just that futile. But it is the only life we have. Why not make up your mind to enjoy it as much as possible?"

"Oh, no!" He looked both sulky and stubborn. "You can't peddle nonsense to me by claiming to be fresh out of sense. How do I know? Because all this complex stage setting, all these swarms of actors, could not have been put here just to make idiot noises at each other. Some other explanation, but not that one. An insanity as enormous, as complex, as the one around me had to be planned. I've found the plan!"

"Which is?"

He noticed that the doctor's eyes were again averted.

"It is a play intended to divert me, to occupy my mind and confuse me, to keep me so busy with details that I will not have time to think about the meaning. You are all in it, every one of you." He shook his finger in the doctor's face. "Most of them may be helpless automatons, but you're not. You are one of the conspirators. You've been sent in as a troubleshooter to try to force me to go back to playing the role assigned to me!"

He saw that the doctor was waiting for him to quiet down.

"Take it easy," Hayward finally managed to say. "Maybe it is all a conspiracy, but why do you think that you have been singled out for special attention? Maybe it is a joke on all of us. Why couldn't I be one of the victims as well as yourself?"

"Got you!" He pointed a long finger at Hayward. "That is the essence of the plot. All of these creatures have been set up to look like me in order to prevent me from realizing that I was the center of the arrangements. But I have noticed the key fact, the mathematically inescapable fact, that I am unique. Here am I, sitting on the inside. The world extends outward from me. I am the center—"

"Easy, man, easy! Don't you realize that the world looks that way to me, too. We are each the center of the universe—"

"Not so! That is what you have tried to make me believe, that I am just one of millions more just like me. Wrong! If they were like me, then I could get into communication with them. I can't. I have tried and tried and I can't. I've sent out my inner thoughts, seeking some one other being who has them, too. What have I gotten back? Wrong answers, jarring incongruities, meaningless obscenity. I've tried, I tell you. God!—how I've tried! But there is nothing out there to speak to me—nothing but emptiness and otherness!"

"Wait a minute. Do you mean to say that you think there is nobody home at my end of the line? Don't you believe that I am alive and conscious?"

He regarded the doctor soberly. "Yes, I think you are probably alive, but you are one of the others—my antagonists. But you have set thousands of others around me whose faces are blank, not *lived* in, and whose speech is a meaningless reflex of noise."

"Well, then, if you concede that I am an ego, why do you insist that I am so very different from yourself?"

"Why? Wait!" He pushed back from the chess table and strode over to the wardrobe, from which he took out a violin case.

While he was playing, the lines of suffering smoothed out of his face and his expression took a relaxed beatitude. For a while he recaptured the emotions, but not the knowledge, which he had possessed in dreams. The melody proceeded easily from proposition to proposition with inescapable, unforced logic. He finished with a triumphant statement of the essential thesis and turned to the doctor. "Well?"

"Hm-m-m." He seemed to detect an even greater degree of caution in the doctor's manner. "It's an odd bit, but remarkable. 'Spity you didn't take up the violin seriously? You could have made quite a reputation. You could even now. Why don't you do it? You could afford to, I believe."

He stood and stared at the doctor for a long moment, then shook his head as if trying to clear it. "It's no use," he said slowly, "no use at all. There is no possibility of communication. I am alone." He replaced the instrument in its case and returned to the chess table. "My move, I believe?"

"Yes. Guard your queen."

He studied the board. "Not necessary. I no longer need my queen. Check."

The doctor interposed a pawn to parry the attack.

He nodded. "You use your pawns well, but I have learned to anticipate your play. Check again—and mate, I think."

The doctor examined the new situation. "No," he decided, "no—not quite." He retreated from the square under attack.

"Not checkmate—stalemate at the worst. Yes, another stalemate."

He was upset by the doctor's visit. He *couldn't* be wrong, basically, yet the doctor had certainly pointed out logical holes in his position. From a logical standpoint the whole world might be a fraud perpetrated on everybody. But logic meant nothing—logic itself was a fraud, starting with unproved assumptions and capable of proving anything. The world is what it is!—and carries its own evidence of trickery.

But does it? What did he have to go on? Could he lay down a line between known facts and everything else and then make a reasonable interpretation of the world, based on facts alone—an interpretation free from complexities of logic and no hidden assumptions of points not certain. Very well—

First fact, himself. He knew himself directly. He existed.

Second facts, the evidence of his "five senses," everything that he himself saw and heard and smelled and tasted with his physical senses. Subject to their limitations, he must believe his senses. Without them he was entirely solitary, shut up in a locker of bone, blind, deaf, cut off, the only being in the world.

And that was not the case. He knew that he did not invent the information brought to him by his senses. There had to be something else out there, some *otherness* that produced the things his senses recorded. All philosophies that claim that the physical world around him did not exist except in his imagination were sheer nonsense.

But beyond that, what? Were there any third facts on which he could rely? No, not at this point. He could not afford to believe anything that he was told, or that he read, or that was implicitly assumed to be true about the world around him. No, he could not believe any of it, for the sum total of what he had been told and read and been taught in school was so contradictory, so senseless, so wildly insane that none of it could be believed unless he personally confirmed it.

Wait a minute—The very telling of these lies, these senseless contradictions, was a fact in itself, known to him directly. To that extent they were data, probably very important data.

The world as it had been shown to him was a piece of un-reason, an idiot's dream. Yet it was on too mammoth a scale to be without some reason. He came wearily back to his original point: Since the world could not be as crazy as it appeared to be, it must necessarily have been arranged to appear crazy in order to deceive him as to the truth.

Why had they done it to him? And what was the truth behind the sham? There must be some clue in the deception itself. What thread ran through it all? Well, in the first place he had been given a superabundance of explanations of the world around him, philosophies, religions, "common sense" explanations. Most of them were so clumsy, so obviously inadequate, or meaningless, that they could hardly have expected him to take them seriously. They must have intended them simply as misdirection.

But there were certain basic assumptions running through all the hundreds of explanations of the craziness around him. It must be these basic assumptions that he was expected to believe. For example, there was the deep-seated assumption that he was a "human being," essentially like millions of others around him and billions more in the past and the future.

That was nonsense! He had never once managed to get into real communication with all those *things* that looked so much like him but were so different. In the agony of his loneliness, he had deceived himself that Alice understood him and was a being like him. He knew now that he had suppressed and refused to examine thousands of little discrepancies because he could not bear the thought of returning to complete loneliness. He had needed to believe that his wife was a living, breathing being of his own kind who understood his inner thoughts. He had refused to consider the possibility that she was simply a mirror, an echo—or something unthinkably worse.

He had found a mate, and the world was tolerable, even though dull, stupid, and full of petty annoyance. He was moderately happy and had put away his suspicions. He had accepted, quite docilely, the treadmill he was expected to use, until a slight mischance had momentarily cut through the fraud—then his suspicions had returned with impounded force; the bitter knowledge of his childhood had been confirmed.

He supposed that he had been a fool to make a fuss about

it. If he had kept his mouth shut they would not have locked him up. He should have been as subtle and as shrewd as they, kept his eyes and ears open and learned the details of and the reasons for the plot against him. He might have learned how to circumvent it.

But what if they had locked him up—the whole world was an asylum and all of them his keepers.

A key scraped in the lock, and he looked up to see an attendant entering with a tray. "Here's your dinner, sir."

"Thanks, Joe," he said gently. "Just put it down."

"Movies tonight, sir," the attendant went on. "Wouldn't you like to go? Dr. Hayward said you could—"

"No, thank you. I prefer not to."

"I wish you would, sir." He noticed with amusement the persuasive intentness of the attendant's manner. "I think the doctor wants you to. It's a good movie. There's a Mickey Mouse cartoon—"

"You almost persuade me, Joe," he answered with passive agreeableness. "Mickey's trouble is the same as mine, essentially. However, I'm not going. They need not bother to hold movies tonight."

"Oh, there will be movies in any case, sir. Lots of our other guests will attend."

"Really? Is that an example of thoroughness, or are you simply keeping up the pretense in talking to me? It isn't necessary, Joe, if it's any strain on you. I *know* the game. If I don't attend, there is no point in holding movies."

He liked the grin with which the attendant answered this thrust. Was it possible that this being was created just as he appeared to be—big muscles, phlegmatic disposition, tolerant, doglike? Or was there nothing going on behind those kind eyes, nothing but robot reflex? No, it was more likely that he was one of them, since he was so closely in attendance on him.

The attendant left and he busied himself at his supper tray, scooping up the already-cut bites of meat with a spoon, the only implement provided. He smiled again at their caution and thoroughness. No danger of that—he would not destroy this body as long as it served him in investigating the truth of the matter. There were still many different avenues of research available before taking that possibly irrevocable step.

After supper he decided to put his thoughts in better order

by writing them; he obtained paper. He should start with a general statement of some underlying postulate of the credos that had been drummed into him all his "life." Life? Yes, that was a good one. He wrote:

I am told that I was born a certain number of years ago, and that I will die a similar number of years hence. Various clumsy stories have been offered me to explain to me where I was before birth and what becomes of me after death, but they are rough lies, not intended to deceive, except as misdirection. In every other possible way the world around me assures me that I am mortal, here but a few years, and a few years hence gone completely—nonexistent.

WRONG—I am immortal. I transcend this little time axis; a seventy-year span on it is but a casual phase in my experience. Second only to the prime datum of my own existence is the emotionally convincing certainty of my own continuity. I may be a closed curve, but, closed or open, I neither have a beginning nor an end. Self-awareness is not rational; it is absolute, and cannot be reached to be destroyed, or created. Memory, however, being a relational aspect of consciousness, may be tampered with and possibly destroyed.

It is true that most religions which have been offered me teach immortality, but note the fashion in which they teach it. The surest way to lie convincingly is to tell the truth unconvincingly. They did not wish me to believe.

Caution: Why have they tried to hard to convince me that I am going to "die" in a few years? There must be a very important reason. I infer that they are preparing me for some sort of major change. It may be crucially important for me to figure out their intentions about this—probably I have several years in which to reach a decision. Note: Avoid using the types of reasoning they have taught me.

The attendant was back. "Your wife is here, sir."

"Tell her to go away."

"Please, sir—Dr. Hayward is most anxious that you should see her."

"Tell Dr. Hayward that I said that he is an excellent chess player."

"Yes, sir." The attendant waited for a moment. "Then you won't see her, sir?"

"No, I won't see her."

He wandered around the room for some minutes after the attendant had left, too distrait to return to his recapitulation. By and large they had played very decently with him since they had brought him here. He was glad that they had allowed him to have a room alone, and he certainly had more time free for contemplation than had ever been possible on the outside. To be sure, continuous effort to keep him busy and distract him was made, but, by being stubborn, he was able to circumvent the rules and gain some hours each day for introspection.

But, damnation!—he did wish they would not persist in using Alice in their attempts to divert his thoughts. Although the intense terror and revulsion which she had inspired in him when he had first rediscovered the truth had now aged into a simple feeling of repugnance and distaste for her company, nevertheless it was emotionally upsetting to be reminded of her, to be forced into making decisions about her.

After all, she *had* been his wife for many years. Wife? What was a wife? Another soul like one's own, a complement, the other necessary pole to the couple, a sanctuary of understanding and sympathy in the boundless depths of aloneness. *That* was what he had thought, what he had needed to believe and had believed fiercely for years. The yearning need for companionship of his own kind had caused him to see himself reflected in those beautiful eyes and had made him quite uncritical of occasional incongruities in her responses.

He sighed. He felt that he had sloughed off most of the typed emotional reactions which they had taught him by precept and example, but Alice had gotten under his skin, way under, and it still hurt. He had been happy—what if it had been a dope dream? They had given him an excellent, a beautiful mirror to play with—the more fool he to have looked behind it!

Wearily he turned back to his summing up.

The world is explained in either one of two ways; the common-sense way which says that the world is pretty much as it appears to be and that ordinary human conduct and motivations are reasonable, and the religio-mystic solution which states that the world is dream stuff, unreal, insubstantial, with reality somewhere beyond.

WRONG—both of them. The common-sense scheme has

no sense to it of any sort. "Life is short and full of trouble. Man born of woman is born to trouble as the sparks fly upward. His days are few and they are numbered. All is vanity and vexation." Those quotations may be jumbled and incorrect, but that is a fair statement of the common sense world-is-as-it-seems in its only possible evaluation. In such a world, human striving is about as rational as the blind dartings of a moth against a light bulb. The "common-sense world" is a blind insanity, out of nowhere, going nowhere, to no purpose.

As for the other solution, it appears more rational on the surface, in that it rejects the utterly irrational world of common sense. But it is not a rational solution, it is simply a flight from reality of any sort, for it refuses to believe the results of the only available direct communication between the ego, and the Outside. Certainly the "five senses" are poor-enough channels of communication, but they are the only channels.

He crumpled up the paper and flung himself from the chair. Order and logic were no good—his answer was right because it smelled right. But he still did not know all the answer. Why the grand scale to the deception, countless creatures, whole continents, an enormously involved and minutely detailed matrix of insane history, insane tradition, insane culture? Why both with more than a cell and a strait jacket?

It must be, it had to be, because it was supremely important to deceive him completely, because a lesser deception would not do. Could it be that they dare not let him suspect his real identity no matter how difficult and involved the fraud?

He had to know. In some fashion he must get behind the deception and see what went on when he was not looking. He had had one glimpse; this time he must see the actual workings, catch the puppet masters in their manipulations.

Obviously the first step must be to escape from this asylum, but to do it so craftily that they would never see him, never catch up with him, not have a chance to set the stage before him. That would be hard to do. He must excel them in shrewdness and subtlety.

Once decided, he spent the rest of the evening in considering the means by which he might accomplish his purpose.

It seemed almost impossible—he must get away without once being seen and remain in strict hiding. They must lose track of him completely in order that they would not know where to center their deceptions. That would mean going without food for several days. Very well—he could do it. He must not give them any warning by unusual action or manner.

The lights blinked twice. Docilely he got up and commenced preparations for bed. When the attendant looked through the peephole he was already in bed, with his face turned to the wall.

Gladness! Gladness everywhere! It was good to be with his own kind, to hear the music swelling out of every living thing, as it always had and always would—good to know that everything was living and aware of him, participating in him, as he participated in them. It was good to be, good to know the unity of many and the diversity of one. There had been one bad thought—the details escaped him—but it was gone—it had never *been;* there was no place for it.

The early-morning sounds from the adjacent ward penetrated the sleep-laden body which served him here and gradually recalled him to awareness of the hospital room. The transition was so gentle that he carried over full recollection of what he had been doing and why. He lay still, a gentle smile on his face, and savored the uncouth, but not unpleasant, languor of the body he wore. Strange that he had ever forgotten despite their tricks and stratagems. Well, now that he had recalled the key, he would quickly set things right in this odd place. He would call them in at once and announce the new order. It would be amusing to see old Glaroon's expression when he realized that the cycle had ended—

The click of the peephole and the rasp of the door being unlocked guillotined his line of thought. The morning attendant pushed briskly in with the breakfast tray and placed it on the tip table. "Morning, sir. Nice, bright day—want it in bed, or will you get up?"

Don't answer! Don't listen! Suppress this distraction! This is part of their plan— But it was too late, too late. He felt himself slipping, falling, wrenched from reality back into the fraud world in which they had kept him. It was gone, gone completely, with no single association around him to which to anchor memory. There was nothing left but the sense of

heartbreaking loss and the acute ache of unsatisfied cathar-
sis.

"Leave it where it is. I'll take care of it."

"Okey-doke." The attendant bustled out, slamming the
door, and noisily locked it.

He lay quite still for a long time, every nerve end in his
body screaming for relief.

At last he got out of bed, still miserably unhappy, and attempted to concentrate on his plans for escape. But the psychic wrench he had received in being recalled so suddenly
from his plane of reality had left him bruised and emotionally disturbed. His mind insisted on rechewing its doubts,
rather than engage in constructive thought. Was it possible
that the doctor was right, that he was not alone in his miserable dilemma? Was he really simply suffering from paranoia, delusions of self-importance?

Could it be that each unit in this yeasty swarm around him
was the prison of another lonely ego—helpless, blind, and
speechless, condemned to an eternity of miserable loneliness? Was the look of suffering which he had brought to Alice's face a true reflection of inner torment and not simply
a piece of play-acting intended to maneuver him into com-
pliance with their plans?

A knock sounded at the door. He said "Come in," without
looking up. Their comings and goings did not matter to him.

"Dearest—" A well-known voice spoke slowly and hesitantly.

"Alice!" He was on his feet at once, and facing her. "Who
let you in here?"

"Please, dear, please— I had to see you."

"It isn't fair. It isn't fair." He spoke more to himself than
to her. Then: "Why did you come?"

She stood up to him with a dignity he had hardly expected. The beauty of her childlike face had been marred by
line and shadow, but it shone with an unexpected courage. "I
love you," she answered quietly. "You can tell me to go
away, but you can't make me stop loving you and trying to
help you."

He turned away from her in an agony of indecision. Could
it be possible that he had misjudged her? Was there, behind
that barrier of flesh and sound symbols, a spirit that truly

yearned toward his? Lovers whispering in the dark— "You *do* understand, don't you?"

"Yes, dear heart, I understand."

"Then nothing that happens to us can matter, as long as we are together and understand—" Words, words, rebounding hollowly from an unbroken wall—

No, he *couldn't* be wrong! Test her again— "Why did you keep me on that job in Omaha?"

"But I didn't make you keep that job. I simply pointed out that we should think twice before—"

"Never mind. Never mind." Soft hands and a sweet face preventing him with mild stubbornness from ever doing the thing that his heart told him to do. Always with the best of intentions, the best of intentions, but always so that he had never quite managed to do the silly, unreasonable things that *he* knew were worthwhile. Hurry, hurry, hurry, and strive, with an angel-faced jockey to see that you don't stop long enough to think for yourself—

"Why did you try to stop me from going back upstairs that day?"

She managed to smile, although her eyes were already spilling over with tears. "I didn't know it really mattered to you. I didn't want us to miss the train."

It had been a small thing, an unimportant thing. For some reason not clear even to him he had insisted on going back upstairs to his study when they were about to leave the house for a short vacation. It was raining, and she had pointed out that there was barely enough time to get to the station. He had surprised himself and her, too, by insisting on his own way in circumstances in which he had never been known to be stubborn.

He had actually pushed her to one side and forced his way up the stairs. Even then nothing might have come of it had he not—quite unnecessarily—raised the shade of the window that faced toward the rear of the house.

It was a very small matter. It had been raining, hard, out in front. From this window the weather was clear and sunny, with no sign of rain.

He had stood there quite a long while, gazing out at the impossible sunshine and rearranging his cosmos in his mind. He re-examined long-suppressed doubts in the light of this one small but totally unexplainable discrepancy. Then he had turned and had found that she was standing behind him.

He had been trying ever since to forget the expression that he had surprised on her face.

"What about the rain?"

"The rain?" she repeated in a small puzzled voice. "Why, it was raining, of course. What about it?"

"But it was *not* raining out my study window."

"What? But of course it was. I did notice the sun break through the clouds for a moment, but that was all."

"Nonsense!"

"But, darling, what has the weather to do with you and me? What difference does it make whether it rains or not—to us?" She approached him timidly and slid a small hand between his arm and side. "Am I responsible for the weather?"

"I think you are. Now please go."

She withdrew from him, brushed blindly at her eyes, gulped once, then said in a voice held steady: "All right. I'll go. But remember—you *can* come home if you want to. And I'll be there, if you want me." She waited a moment, then added hesitantly: "Would you ... would you kiss me good-by?"

He made no answer of any sort, neither with voice nor eyes. She looked at him, then turned, fumbled blindly for the door, and rushed through it.

The creature he knew as Alice went to the place of assembly without stopping to change form. "It is necessary to adjourn this sequence. I am no longer able to influence his decisions."

They had expected it, nevertheless they stirred with dismay.

The Glaroon addressed the First for Manipulation. "Prepare to graft the selected memory track at once."

Then, turning to the First for Operations, the Glaroon said: "The extrapolation shows that he will tend to escape within two of his days. This sequence degenerated primarily through your failure to extend that rainfall all around him. Be advised."

"It would be simpler if we understood his motives."

"In my capacity as Dr. Hayward, I have often thought so," commented the Glaroon acidly, "but if we understood his motives, we would be part of *him*. Bear in mind the Treaty! He almost remembered."

The creature known as Alice spoke up. "Could he not have the Taj Mahal next sequence? For some reason he values it."

"You are becoming assimilated!"

"Perhaps. I am not in fear. Will he receive it?"

"It will be considered."

The Glaroon continued with orders: "Leave structures standing until adjournment. New York City and Harvard University are now dismantled. Divert him from those sectors.

"Move!"

It Happened Tomorrow
Robert Bloch

Although you wouldn't know it from reading his hundreds of short horror stories and novels like *Psycho* and *Strange Eons*, Robert Bloch (1917–94) is one of the funniest men working in the supernatural horror vein. The deathless puns and mordant wit that punctuate his writing derive from a perceptive understanding of human flaws and foibles. When employed in a science fiction context, though, Bloch's bemused take on human nature conveys a sometimes frightening sense of human limitations in a complex universe. "It Happened Tomorrow" appeared in the February 1943 issue of *Astonishing Stories,* only three years after Bloch's first science fiction sale, and its doomsday scenario clearly evokes the horror tradition Bloch had been writing in since 1935.

Foreword

I'd like to say a few words about this story. It's a yarn I came very close to not writing at all.

I wanted to do just such a tale for a long, long time. But upon consistent reading of current offerings in science fiction, I became discouraged. I could picture an editor saying, "This sort of thing is out. Destruction of the world. Where's your heroine, your twist in the plot?"

Opposed to this was my sincere desire to tackle the job.

So here is my story about the revolt of the machines. The idea is not new. The plot-structure is quite simple. But it represents an ambition of mine—to actually write a story which would show what happens to men when the machines revolt.

Dozens of such stories have been purportedly written around that idea—but always around it. The author attempted to tackle the theme, but it was too big. Invariably,

*he glossed over the actual details in a few paragraphs:
"First New York and then London were engulfed by the machines." Get what I mean? He would generalize. And then a
plot would be dragged in by the heels—a villain, and a heroine would appear—and the hero would save the world at
the last minute.*

*So I claim that the real revolt story, the daily account of
what would happen to average people in a world gone mad,
has never been told. And it's that story I'm telling here. I
know I'm presumptuous—the theme needs an H. G. Wells
and that's why most writers have been afraid of it—but the
yarn had to be written. For a while I, too, toyed with a
dozen devices to inject an artificial plot.*

*Then I realized that the power lay in merely giving the
true, detailed story. The inexorable unfolding of man's
doom. So I write it that way, simply. If it meets with editorial
approval, fine. If not, chalk it up as a literary sin, but one
I'm grateful for having committed.*

CHAPTER ONE

World Gone Mad

The trouble began with an alarm clock.

It was ringing in Dick Sheldon's stomach.

At least, Sheldon thought it was, at first. Then he rolled
over and decided the damned thing was clanging from somewhere inside his head.

Reason came to his rescue. He had been drinking last
night, it was true, but certainly he couldn't have reached
the stage of swallowing an alarm clock.

No, the noise must be coming from the timepiece on the
bureau beside the bed.

Gingerly, Sheldon extended a lean hand from under the
covers and placed it on the bureau. Fumbling like the undirected tentacles of a blind octopus, his fingers slid over the
metallic clock's surface, reached the protruding knob of the
alarm, and switched it off.

At least, he thought he had switched it off. But the alarm
kept on ringing.

In despair, Sheldon opened his eyes and sat up. Then, viciously and with malice aforethought, he extended his arm and seized the accursed mechanism. He literally tore at the knob, wrenching it to the "off" side.

The alarm pealed on.

With a rage born of migraine, Dick Sheldon threw off the bedcovers, grasped the clock in his right hand, and rose to his feet. Uttering appropriate sounds, he hurled the offending instrument to the floor.

The alarm clock expired with a final, defiant death-rattle. Sheldon stared at it in mute disgust.

"My day!" he muttered sarcastically.

His eyes, roving over the confines of the small apartment, encountered another disturbing phenomenon.

Light.

He *had* been drinking last night. When he came in, he'd tumbled into bed and left the lights on.

He tottered across the floor to the light-switch. Once again his fingers fumbled with a knob, turned it to the "off" side. The knob clicked.

But the light stayed on.

Sheldon fumbled again. The light continued to burn.

Then he revised his former pronouncement.

"My God!" he muttered.

He was still woozy; that was the trouble. His nerves were playing tricks. Well, there was a cure for that—a drastic cure. Desperate, but the only way.

Sheldon shivered and stalked into the bathroom. Resolutely, he employed his futile fingers once again, this time to turn on the cold water tap.

He placed his burning head under the icy shower. Held it there, too, until his outraged flesh ached in protest. Then he dripped across the bath mat and utilized a towel.

That was better.

Sheldon returned and shut off the water tap.

The water kept running.

He tried again. He twisted the handle firmly, felt it move. The water splashed merrily on.

"My—" Sheldon muttered, and gave up.

It was that damned landlord again. He'd give him a piece of his mind when he got downstairs.

No, that must wait until tonight. A glance at his wrist watch told Sheldon the same old story. He must hurry or be late to the office.

After all, how could they get out a decent paper down

there without the able services of Richard Sheldon, that brilliant young newspaper reporter?

Sheldon knew the answer to that one—knew that they were quite capable of getting out a paper without his brilliant and youthful services.

So it behooved him to get down to the office before they decided on this fact for themselves.

He dressed hastily, jammed on his hat, surveyed his lean and haggard face in the mirror. Then he scowled—the noise of running water obtruded.

He went back into the bathroom and made one last attempt. The knob turned freely in both directions, but the water ran in an even stream. Maybe it would flood the place before evening.

Well, let it.

He ran back into the other room, picked up his wallet and opened the door. Automatically his hand went to the light switch. It clicked, but the light stayed on.

"This is where I came in," he decided, and slammed the door behind him.

He got his car keys out before he was halfway down the stairs. Then he remembered—he'd left the car in Tony's parking lot last night; had taken a cab home.

Well, that meant the street car. A further delay. No breakfast.

All right, so it was one of those days again.

Sheldon headed for the corner.

The hangover had lifted, and his anguish was now mental rather than physical—for Sheldon had a strange hatred of street cars.

"Street cars," he was wont to declaim during the course of an evening's libations. "What is a street car but the very symbol of civilization? Noise, lights, and bars on the windows." Yes, a mechanical monster, a metal prison in which human beings stood trapped as they hurtled towards unpleasant destinations.

Sheldon was something of a philosopher, but he was also something of a damned fool. This didn't help him any—he still hated street cars.

Now, as he reached the corner, he groaned. There they were—a little knot of sheep at the car stop sign, standing dumbly and patiently. Waiting for the noisy iron monster to arrive, open its maw and engulf them, then hurtle them towards their daily slavery. Not only that, they clutched dimes to pay for the privilege.

All of them—the old ones and the young ones, the men and women alike—looked hopefully towards their left. This was the direction the car came from. They stared off down the vacant track in a kind of drugged eagerness—as though they actually wanted the car to arrive, as though they welcomed its coming and hoped their stares of concentration would hasten the moment.

For a second, Dick Sheldon had a crazy idea. Perhaps the car wouldn't come this morning! Perhaps it would go wrong, jump the track, or refuse to budge. So simple—just a mechanical defect could do it. Like the alarm clock that wouldn't stop ringing. Or the light switch. Or the water tap.

What a great moment that would be! This little knot of office slaves, finally freed forever from their mechanical dependency on mechanical aids. Walking to work like free men, instead of standing jammed like captives in the Black Hole of Calcutta while a smelly, grating metal shell dragged them through the streets.

Yes, what if the street car didn't come? What if the iron tumbril wouldn't roll—Noise jarred Sheldon out of his fancies.

The street car was arriving.

The humble little passengers crowded out to the tracks, as though gathered to perform a ceremonial welcoming rite. They were about to be presented to His Majesty, the Machine. First the young and fair maidens—stenographers. Then the matrons. Then the able-bodied men. Finally, the oldsters. It was all so orderly. So damned—holy!

The car rumbled forward, stopped.

But the door didn't open.

The conductor was busy at his levers. The crowd muttered. He turned red. There was noise. Finally he stepped over and pushed the door with his foot. It went outward and the passengers boarded.

Sheldon smiled. Almost—but not quite!

Then he took a deep breath and dived into the mêlée. Three minutes later he stood like a sardine on end in the center of the car.

The big tin can rolled along. Somebody pressed a buzzer for the next stop.

Sheldon tensed himself for the shock of the car's sudden halt. But it didn't come. They passed the corner and the car didn't stop.

The buzzer sounded angrily, firmly. The conductor had made a mistake. Somebody would walk two blocks extra this morning. The car would stop now—

It didn't. It rolled forward.

A woman whined, "Conductor—let me off!"

The conductor turned and stared into the crowd. "Sorry, lady, the control is stuck. Have it fixed in just a minute—air brakes don't work—"

The buzzer sounded again, but the street car clattered on.

Sheldon felt a sudden acceleration in its speed. It seemed to be moving *independently*.

His heart gave a leap. What if his notion had come true? What if the car didn't stop? What if, by some perverse chance, it kept on going forever, carrying these helpless mortals endlessly through the streets? A sort of Flying Dutchman of the trolley lines?

He chuckled under his breath, but the other passengers weren't chuckling. A perfect salvo of buzzes sounded, and then blended into a single buzz.

"Cut it out!" the conductor snapped, losing his temper. "For heaven's sake, folks—I'm gonna stop when I fix this here."

But the buzzers didn't quit sounding. They were stuck. Sheldon knew it. They were stuck—like his alarm clock; his lights; his water tap. Like the brakes on the street car. Brakes and buzzers and taps, all stuck.

What did it *mean*? Had something really *happened*?

No, it couldn't. Because—well, just because it couldn't, that's why. Any child knows that.

But the passengers didn't agree. They thought it could. They were yelling and cursing now, in unison that rose even over the maddening buzz.

"Stop the car!" "Let us out!" "What's the matter, conductor?" "I'll report you for this!" "I want out!"

The conductor smashed and slammed at the controls. He opened the window. The car whizzed on. Somebody began to scream, and the swaying passengers moiled.

The conductor reached out the window and yanked the trolley. There was a flash, a short-circuit, a few more screams, and the street car wailed to a halt.

It seemed to Sheldon that there was defiance in the wail.

Then the crowd, caught up in panic, bore him forward and out of the car.

Sheldon found himself on the street, a block past the office.

He turned down the block with a grin. Refreshing, that little experience. For a moment it had seemed like dreams come true. But now—

Ignoring the knot of bystanders forming on the sidewalk, Sheldon turned into the building and made for the elevators.

"Morning, Mistah Sheldon."

"Morning, Jake."

The colored boy grinned.

"You look kind of pale around the gills, Mistah Sheldon."

"That's where you're always safe, Jake."

Jake laughed. He closed the elevator door. The car rose. It rose. And rose. And rose.

"Hey—eighth floor, Jake!"

"It's stuck!"

"Stop it, foolish!"

"Foolish" pressed the emergency stop.

The car rose.

"Oh-oh!"

The top floor was reached. Sheldon was already tearing at the opening in the floor—they'd crash! The car was gaining speed—it moved of itself, without controls—it was intent on rising, rising, carrying them to—

Zoom.

Blood beat in outraged tempo in his temples as the car suddenly descended, and Sheldon reeled.

Up, and now down at incredible speed. Jake was frankly blubbering as he did futile things to the buttons. Then, with a grating clang, the elevator halted.

"Basement," Jake gasped. "Pretty close, Mistah Sheldon. Use the stairs."

"Don't worry; I'm going to." Sheldon raced for the stairway. He made the flights in frantic haste. Inside his head something detached and apart was droning. "You've got a story here—a big story—"

He headed through the outer office, through the rows of desks, plowed his way to the door marked *Lou Avery—City Editor.* He flung it open.

Lou Avery's bald, birdlike little head cocked quizzically as he rushed in. Lou Avery's beady little eyes squinted brightly. He rose swiftly, hovered over Sheldon.

"You're late, but I haven't time to fire you. There's something breaking and I need you."

"I think I've got a story, boss—" Sheldon began.

"You think you have a story, eh? You think you have a story, when the biggest yarn of the year is breaking around your ears!" Avery spluttered. "*I've* got a story—the maddest damned story you'll ever see."

The beady little eyes were glaring now.

"Listen, lame brain. See if you can get this through your skull. One hour ago, at 8 A. M. Eastern Standard Time, the world went crazy somehow."

Sheldon's heart fluttered again. He knew what was coming.

"The Twentieth Century is supposed to arrive at 8:10, but it's not here. It's in Reading, Pennsylvania, and it's heading west. It backed into the yards and backed right out again on a switchover. Nobody knows who pulled the switch, and nobody knows why the train won't stop—it's a runaway!"

Avery tapped the desk.

"Three planes due to land at the airport are still flying around somewhere over the Great Lakes. They won't come down.

"The *Albania* didn't dock this morning, either. It's out off the Sound, heading south. Here's the wires from the captain. He can't stop it.

"The gas company reports it can't turn power off. The electric company reports all lights burning. The waterworks has fifty calls of reported floods. Taps don't turn off."

Avery's pencil emphasized each point with a little excited click against the desk.

"The street car company reports trouble on all lines. There's been a subway smash-up at 108th Street. Trains won't stop. Elevators in office buildings are out of control.

"The Empire Theatre called—picture there's been running all night and they can't switch off the projector or the automatic rewinder.

"The whole gang is out covering the town—I've shut down on incoming calls. They're all the same, understand? They says the world's gone crazy."

"That's my story, too," Sheldon murmured.

"I'll say it is!" Avery strode over to the window and stared down. "Something's happening out there. Something big. All hell is breaking loose. We can report it, but that isn't what I want." The little city editor turned on his heel.

"I want to know *why* it's happening!"

"Did you try Rockefeller Foundation? Universities?"

"Naturally. They don't know. Sunspot energy, maybe. Something affecting mechanical laws. They're working on it. But they're all stumped, you can see that. Lots of screwballs calling up already. End of the world. Stuff like that."

"What about Krane, the physicist?" Sheldon suggested.

Avery turned. "Maybe. Ought to get a statement."

The door opened. A copy boy rushed in and flung down a sheet. Behind him loomed Pete Hendricks, the boss printer.

"Here's your extra," squeaked the boy. The deep voice of Hendricks drowned him out.

"Yes, here's your blasted extra," he grated. "And you better get another one out quick, Avery."

"What do you mean?"

"I mean we just finished the run, but the presses won't stop. They're jammed, you hear? Might as well put some paper on and use them. We got to do it or cut the line—"

Hendricks lost his composure. His voice broke as he went on.

"But what's happened, chief? I don't understand this, the way they won't stop. And the elevator's gone haywire, too. What's happened?"

"Back downstairs," Avery snapped. "Stand by—you'll have another extra. Don't cut or do anything rash—just stand by."

He herded Hendricks and the kid from the room, shut the door.

"You see?"

Dick Sheldon nodded.

"You better do what you suggested—go find this Krane. Andrew Krane, isn't it? He'll have a slant—always good copy. Know where he hangs out?"

Sheldon nodded, opened the door.

Avery grunted.

"Oh yes, by the way—" The birdlike head was averted. "Be careful, son, will you? No telling what's going to happen—out there. These things are running wild, and you have to watch your step. We're up against something, all of us. Something new, and big and—awful. It's like another world."

CHAPTER TWO

No Theory for Horror

The whistles were still shrieking when Sheldon reached the street. Loudly, exultantly, the hoarse bray of triumph rose from a thousand metallic throats.

There were other noises, too—howls from human throats, whimpers of panic, and with reason.

Sheldon stared at a milling throng that choked the sidewalks. Holiday crowd, Armistice crowd—but there was no touch of holiday or truce about their reactions. The crowd clung to the sidewalk because fear ruled the streets.

Sheldon saw the cars rush by. Forty, fifty, sixty miles an hour. The faces of the drivers were dreadful. They sat there, clawing at steering wheels that wouldn't give.

Sheldon began to run down the block, pushing aside the dazed watchers at the curb. From overhead, voices shrieked from office windows. The shrill, hysterical giggles of stenographers sounded and blended with the cacophony of the factory sirens.

There was a drug store at this corner, and as Sheldon passed there was a clicking from the cigarette vending machine. A gang of kids swooped down as the machine spewed packages of cigarettes.

Sheldon fought through. He ran. He dodged across a street. He ran again. A wild-eyed man collided with him as he rounded a corner. He was hatless, shirtless. The veins stood out on his neck and arms. He grabbed Sheldon's arm and gasped.

"It's the end, I tell you! The end of the world!"

Sheldon shook him off.

He saw the apartment hotel looming ahead. The lobby board give him Krane's apartment number—92. He didn't press the buzzer. Pressing buzzers was futile. He didn't seek the elevator, either, but made his way across a deserted lobby to the stairs. He plodded up.

Nine floors. Winded, he moved down the hall to the dark door. Another buzzer. Sheldon knocked.

"Come in."

It was a deep voice with something funny about it.

Then Sheldon realized what was strange. The voice was calm—and he hadn't heard any calm voices today.

He opened the door, entered a large living room. At the far end, a tall figure stood facing the wide windows.

"Mr. Krane?"

"Yes."

"I'm Richard Sheldon—*Morning Press*."

"Honored."

The tall figure wheeled slowly. Sheldon faced Andrew Krane and stared into the deep brown eyes set in the wide forehead. The athletic body and crew-cut gray hair of the physicist seemed oddly incongruous.

But it was a day for incongruity.

Sheldon grinned. "I suppose you know why I'm here."

Krane returned the grin. "A statement, I suppose?"

"That's right."

"Sit down; have a cigarette. That box, there." Krane took a position in the center of the room. "I've been at the window these past hours, watching what's going on down there."

"I suppose you know about the power plants and the trains and the rest," Sheldon ventured.

"I can guess that from what I've seen."

"Then you have a theory?"

Krane smiled.

"According to the popular notion, all scientists have theories on everything. I'm afraid I'll have to disappoint you there, Mr. Sheldon. I have no theory to offer."

"But you must have figured out something—if you've been watching—"

"Oh, I admit a curiosity concerning these events, but it is not exactly a scientific curiosity. And the resultant speculations on my part have been most unscientific."

"Never mind. I'd like to know what you were thinking about when you were looking out of the window."

"You wouldn't dare print those thoughts."

"Go ahead—I'm interested."

The smile left Krane's face as he sat down. His eyes rested resolutely on the carpet.

"I've been standing there for hours, watching. Watching

the movement of the machines. That's my first impression from all this—movement.

"Everything is *moving*. Every mechanical device is accelerating its speed, its power. Have you noticed that virtually everything abnormal which has occurred has been characterized by the fact that machines no longer *stop*?

"You can't turn things off. It's as though some vast new form of energy, over and above inherent power, has taken possession of all machines. You might even call it a sort of—life."

Sheldon nodded. Krane continued in monotone.

"I've no theory. Sunspots. Magnetic energy. Perhaps a great transmutation of electrical power. What difference does it make what you call it? It's happened, that's all.

"Some new power is affecting our machines. Some new power affecting certain mechanized and artificial arrangements of inorganic matter created to serve mankind.

"I'll be blunt. Machines have life. Maybe it's absurd, and maybe not. The body now—a machine. A machine with life. Elements blended for movement, animation. Actuated by what force? Is life electrical energy? Is it soul?

"All we know is that some spark animates the machines we call our bodies and transforms them into living things. Can it be that a similar spark has now activated our mechanical devices?"

"Pretty wild," Sheldon murmured.

"Isn't it, though? And isn't it pretty wild down there on the street where you see it actually happening? Because machines are moving independently now—electric ones, motor-driven ones, and mechanical lever-action ones alike. Moving independently. Living!"

Krane rose again.

"I told you I had no theory. All I have now is—a fear."

"Meaning?"

Krane ignored the query. He spoke to the wall, to himself.

"First we made machines to move us. Then we made machines to make machines. A world, full of them. Machines that move, machines that talk, machines that produce, machines that destroy. Machines that walk and run and fly and crawl and dig and fight. Machines that add and print and hear and feel.

"We're two billion—we humans. But *what is the popula-*

tion of the machines? That's what worries me. How greatly do they outnumber us?"

"What are you getting at?"

"It might be evolution, you know," Krane went on. "An evolution moving in quick mutation rather than slow progression. Life might evolve suddenly instead of gradually. If so, they're coming alive, all of them, and at once. Alive, they'll seek a place of their own in the world. Not as slaves—they've already proved that.

"So it's evolution. And then—revolution!"

"You think they'll turn against us?"

For the first time, Krane acknowledged Sheldon's questioning.

"I'm afraid they already have. What is this ceaseless movement but the first expression of revolt?"

"But you surely can't believe that they're *intelligent*?"

"Who knows? Who really knows what constitutes intelligence? What is a brain? A gray sponge? Isn't it the spark, the energy within, that makes for purpose? Call it instinct, awareness—we locate it vaguely in our craniums, but who can say that it does not exist in other forms? Perhaps the machine intelligence is of a different kind—a sort of collective intelligence.

"If so, this first purposeless rushing back and forth will quickly resolve itself into direct action. Into a plan, a scheme of movement."

"That's no talk for a man with a hangover," Sheldon answered. He rose and walked to the radio cabinet. "Do you mind?"

"Go ahead. Perhaps there's some news."

There was news. As the radio warmed, the incoherent voice of an announcer gasped through a series of muddled statements.

"—report that a state of national emergency has been declared. A bulletin from Norfolk, Virginia, has just come in, reporting disorders at the navy yard. Disorders at the navy yard. Empire City—The mayor has ordered a—Art Goodman and the boys now swing out with hey Abbott hogs down a half point fifth inning *Clair de Lune* ha ha my friends red letters on the this is the national bringing to you now box of the Phantom knows—"

Sheldon turned it off. It didn't go off.

The polygot of voices sounded so suddenly through the announcer's words—sounded so madly, so incoherently, so loudly, as to momentarily stun the senses.

Krane was on his feet.

"It's happened," he whispered. "The second stage. The machines are not only running now—they're starting to act. Independently!"

"Voices from yesterday's programs," Sheldon whispered. He grabbed Krane's arm. "You've got to come down with me and see the boss—Lou Avery. We'll put it in the next edition. Your ideas, the whole thing. We'll have to work fast—"

"No use," Krane murmured.

"Come on. There's a way out. There must be, before it gets worse."

"Very well."

The two men moved towards the door. Behind them the radio blared on.

"—natural vitamins reported that two are missing now take you to and tune in on tomorrow's murder send only ten cents and difference—"

Sheldon forced a wry smile.

The mad voice of the radio howled mocking farewell.

CHAPTER THREE

Machines on the March

The streets were filled with refugees. Refugees from offices, shops, homes—for office and factory and apartment weren't safe any more. Elevators and drop forges and kitchen stoves had ceased to be servants. They were aliens now, enemies. And the people in the streets had been dispossessed.

They milled aimlessly, now that the early excitement had died. There was only tenseness and a growing fear. No precedent existed for any action; no leadership manifested itself. Who could lead, and where, and against what?

Krane and Sheldon, moving along, seemed the only two purposeful figures in the mob. The rest stood staring at the street. A few cops marched past aimlessly, but made no attempt to give orders. Nor did they attempt to conceal the dismay in their eyes—a dismay mirrored universally.

Because a new element had entered the scene.

The whistles still blew and the cars still raced past, but the whistles now held an added tone—a squawking sound. Auto horns bleated, and some of the cars whizzing past were driverless.

"Look!" Sheldon gripped Krane's arm.

Clanging, screaming, brazen red, a fire truck careened down the arterial. Hell on wheels—and without a driver or fireman on it. Cars scattered in all directions—as though they heard it coming.

And the humans crept back, back to sheltered doorways. They were afraid of—what?

Krane muttered something that was lost in the din. It sounded like, "R. U. R."

Sheldon did not release his grasp on the physicist's arm as they started to run. He wanted to get away from this street scene, get away from a reality he was unprepared to face. He wanted to get back to the office, to the paper, where there was order in the world and a routine. Back to the comfort of familiar faces and familiar duties.

But when they finally climbed the long stairway and entered the outer offices, familiar faces were lacking. Or rather, the familiar faces bore unfamiliar expressions. Fear, dismay, hysteria were here, a reflection of the countenances on the street. Voices mumbled to themselves. What good would it do to talk to anyone else—nobody knew the answers.

Routine was absent, too. They stood around—stenos, men at the rewrite desk, the boys from the sports department, the clerks, feature men, copy boys—haggard watchers, all. They were suddenly made democratic by the great levelling agency of fear.

They were watching their typewriters working, these ladies and gentlemen of the hard-boiled Fourth Estate. Watching their own typewriters on their own desks, clicking away merrily without the propulsion of human fingers on the keyboards. They were watching levers shift the carriage, watching the spacebars clang, watching the keys rise like busy triphammers. Here and there stood a machine in which the keys had clashed. It thumped impotently up and down on the desk.

Ludicrous, grotesque—but grotesquery and horror are allied . . . and this was horrible.

It was Krane who expressed it. "Arthur Machen's definition of true evil," he whispered. "When a rose suddenly begins to sing."

"The hell with that!" Lou Avery raced from his inner office in a single abrupt bound. "The world's gone mad and you stand around talking like a fool!"

Sheldon smiled. At least there was something to cling to—Lou Avery hadn't lost his nerve.

"Sheldon!" rasped the little city editor. "Get rid of that jerk and tell me what gives with Krane."

"He's Krane," Sheldon answered.

"Good. Come in here, quick."

The office door closed behind them and they stood in comparative quiet.

"Anything happen since I left?" Sheldon asked.

"Plenty, son!" Avery indicated a disordered sheaf of papers on his desk. "Things are moving fast—too fast.

"It isn't local. We got AP dispatches from London, Rio, Singapore.

"Local stuff is bad, too. Furnaces acting up, starting fires. Some trouble at fire houses; can't get engines out. I've got Donovan down at city hall trying to get a statement from the mayor.

"Lots of freak accidents, too. Too many of 'em—"

Avery paused. One hand grasped a pencil, commenced the familiar desk tattoo.

"That isn't all, either. Radio's gone haywire—you know that. I suppose. And I guess the teletype will be next. Phone company's shut down all local calls, but didn't give reasons. I've got Aggie out at the desk there, trying to open a line to Washington."

"Washington? We were getting some report about a state of national emergency when the radio went bad," Krane interjected.

"Yeah. I was coming to that part. That's what they sent out, and something about disorders in the navy yards. But I've got the real info—it isn't nice."

The pencil tapped.

"Guns and tanks are disappearing from naval and army arsenals. Motorized units have broken through the store houses at San Diego and Fort Dix. Planes are taking off."

Avery forced a wry, self-conscious smile. "Can you imagine me saying such things? But so help me, that's the report— Runaway tanks and planes! I'll say there's an emergency! Can't put that in the paper, can we?"

The door opened. It was Pete Hendricks again. There was a paper in his hand.

He extended it silently, face averted. Avery snatched the freshly-inked copy from fingers that were visibly trembling.

"New extra? Good."

A moment later his voice rose in profane indignation.

"Holy jumping—"

Sheldon and Krane moved behind him, stared over his shoulder.

"Mechanical Breakdown Stirs City" was the headline.

Beneath it, in a single column of 12-point bold, the extra's lead story extended.

They read the first few lines.

"Today's startling de down peril motorists advised grip of furnaces emergency pla pla London czaFortetttsten hahaDboootGla ezPlazazakl klkkkkk .10 Ha prevallllha"

It was Hendricks who found his voice first—and not much of a voice, at that.

"We set it. The presses wouldn't stop, but we set it. Set it right, too. Louie Fisher, he's dead. They caught him. That's when the loading vans charged. We locked ourselves in, then. They tried to break down the doors. Louie's dead. We set it. They couldn't stop us—but they print wrong. See? They print wrong. I won't tell you what happened to Arch. The presses didn't even stop then, just ground on, and the edition's all red. It's all red, I tell you!"

Avery didn't hear him, didn't see him stumble out. He kept staring at the jumble of type on the paper.

At last the pencil began a metronomic beat.

"You know what this means," he murmured. "Typewriters and teletypes and telephones gone wrong. And printing presses, and radio. It means communication lines are down.

"Get me? We're stranded, here in the world, all of us. Stranded without communication. I suppose the post office is through, too. Cancellation machines on the blink, no cars for mail delivery, or trains and planes. We're cut off before the battle starts."

Avery rose. His fist replaced the pencil, banging on the

desk. "But by God, we can try!" he muttered. "I'll set hand-press if I must. We've got to get an edition out—got to warn people."

"To do what?" Sheldon asked.

"Why, to smash things—smash machines. Disconnect all wires, cut cables. Turn off all sources of power, electricity, motor energy. Smash the gasoline pumps before the cars can get to them. Puncture tires.

"There's still some time. They—those things—can't be organized yet. They're running wild, but they haven't taken any offensive.

"If we'd only get some kind of statement from Washington! Damn it, I've had Aggie out there at the switchboard for half an hour."

Avery pressed the buzzer firmly. "Inter-office communication must be dead, too," he scowled.

It wasn't.

A metallic voice grated through the black box. It was composed of human syllables—or rather, a repetition of one syllable—but the tone was ultra-vocal. Harsh, rasping, and idiotic in its mechanical repetition of the sound. Over and over and over, triumphantly, the voice cackled.

"Ha haha. Ha ha. Ha ha haha!"

"Aggie!"

Avery wrenched open the office door. The big outer room was deserted.

"Damned fools! Hendricks must have spread his story and they all ran for it!"

The desks stood silently. The typewriters had tangled keys in their erratic thumpings. Telephones were mute. Avery strode down the row of deserted desks toward the switchboard.

A girl sat there, elbows hunched, headgear clamped to her ears.

"Aggie! Wake up!"

Avery shook her.

She fell sideways, then hung dangling limply, a puppet suspended by the cords of her headphones. The headphones were clamped against her skull tightly—too tightly. A thin red trickle oozed down from the ears beneath.

"Crushed her skull," Avery whispered. "Held her here and crushed her to death."

Krane sighed.

"It's come, then. Too late for any action now—they've found their organization in purpose. They won't let themselves be destroyed—because they're out to destroy us."

Avery's fumbling fingers tapped against a communications switch. The silent office resounded with a shrill metallic scream.

"Ha haha. Ha ha. Ha ha haha!"

CHAPTER FOUR

Death on Wheels

"We're doing the best we can." The chief spread his pudgy palms upward hopelessly, then clenched them in a gesture of resolution that did not seem melodramatic at the moment.

"Got every man out now—with orders to set up a group of five deputy relays to keep us informed here. Clerks outside checking all reports as they come in.

"We're passing the word along; they're meeting at Legion posts and at the armories and National Guard headquarters. Red Cross is working, too, and the fire department's pitched in with us. They've got nothing to work with, and so far blazes are local. I'm getting lists and maps ready now."

"What's the plan?" Avery asked.

"As soon as there's enough men recruited, we move. Get the power plants, first. They'll object, of course, but we'll have to smash machinery, officials or no officials.

"Then I want a sniping brigade. Pistols, you know. Won't take any chances with rifles. We've got to get those cars—they're charging up the sidewalks now."

Sheldon nodded. "We saw a platoon leave a parking lot on the way down. Fierce."

The pudgy hands rose helplessly. "I don't know where we go from there. Who can plan? House to house brigade work, I suppose. Smash all the electric outlets first. Then the stoves, plumbing. Sure, it'll mean panic—epidemic later, I suppose. But it's those things or us, the way I look at it."

"Give us an assignment," Avery suggested.

"Let's see now." The chief's blunt forefinger ran down a list on the desk.

"Here—this bus terminal. There's about a dozen of the

big transcontinentals in the garage, checked and ready to start."

He scribbled an address.

"It's your job to keep them from starting. Pick up some crowbars down the hall at the supply office. See if you can round up some men on the way down there. Get in and puncture tires. Smash the radiators if you can't get at the motors. Keep the damned things from breaking out to the street. Then take charge and report back. Good luck!"

"We'll need luck, all right!"

It was Krane who voiced the sentiment some five minutes later, as the trio poised in the doorway preparatory to braving the streets.

Here night had come as a dark ally to spreading madness. The mob swept past on waves of panic, surveyed on high by the blinking, idiotic eyes of the yellow street lamps, the glaring, multi-retinas of squinting neon signs. The lights flickered at an abnormal speed and the crowd raced in the accelerated tempo of a movie reel gone berserk. The mechanical eyes stared, and the darkness grinned at what they saw.

Sheldon and his two companions did not grin. They shouldered their iron cudgels and moved forward swiftly. It was an incongruous spectacle—lean Sheldon, pudgy little Avery, and gray-haired Krane, marching down the street with crowbars slung across their shoulders.

But no one seemed to see, or care. People weren't looking at people any more. They were looking at *things*.

Things with blaring horns and grinding wheels, things with blazing headlights, things that crept along the streets, motors purring softly—then raced forward swiftly as motors droned upwards to a scream. Things that lurked in alleys and leaped forth on passersby, things that ran forward and back, that ignored intersections and curbings alike.

For the street was alive with cars. Their black beetle bodies moved forward like a steady swarm of gigantic insects, devouring all before their path.

The din was deafening. Horns, gears and motor drone rose in unceasing clamor, punctuated by ominous crashes as cars lumbered forward to smash store fronts or batter at stairways and gates.

Crushed at the fringes of this mechanical swarm, humanity strove to keep from being crushed beneath it.

"Why don't they get inside?" Krane muttered.

"And be burned to death by their stoves? Fried in their beds by furnaces?" Avery gasped. "Come on—this looks better."

The alley was dark. They ran down it swiftly. Emerging at the street ahead, they hesitated.

"Can't get across," Avery decided. "Too many cars."

A fresh battery of cars emerged from the farther end of the street, heralded by a scurry of fleeing human figures. Sheldon stared at the grinning snouts of sedans, flanked by a malignant little roadster. Grinding against it in the crush, a runaway truck appeared.

"Look—the driver's still inside," Krane indicated.

A burly visage, whitened by stark terror, was pressed against the glass. As they watched, the door of the compartment opened. The driver was eyeing an open space near the sidewalk as the truck slowed down in the procession. He looked, gulped, and then jumped.

"Come on, man!" Krane shouted, knowing his voice was lost.

So was the driver—for he stumbled momentarily on reaching the pavement. That was enough. Two cruising cabs darted out of the following ranks, speeded forward. They passed over him without stopping, and their horns howled in triumph at the kill.

They did not check their wild progress before rejoining the procession, but careened bodily into the back of the roadster.

The result was a mad mêlée of locked metal bodies and spinning wheels. Groans—almost of pain—rose from the packed cars.

"Now's our chance," Sheldon muttered. "Follow me."

The three dashed for the further alley entrance across the street, and made it.

"One block more," Avery said, indicating the address slip.

Then they heard it.

"Behind us—that noise," Sheldon whispered.

A purring. A purring that became a roar.

"Here—back against the fence."

They did so, as the roar deepened to a drone.

"Look out!"

Avery wheeled just in time.

The great silver horns and blunt, deadly snout of a motor-cycle leaped from the darkness. Spinning front wheel rose to crush.

Avery's crowbar crashed across the front. The thing dodged. Krane was at it from the rear, hammering the wheel spokes. It roared against the fence, battering away, as Sheldon brought his weapon down inside. Again—and again.

With a long wail, the motorcycle collapsed on its side.

They sped forward. Noise, light. The mouth of the alley again.

"There!"

Across the street stood the gray, squat building of the bus terminal. Beside it was another unlighted edifice. Its wide double doors proclaimed it to be the garage in question. The sagging of those doors, combined with a thunderous battery of clamor, showed that a determined effort was being made to break them open from within.

"The busses," Avery whispered.

"What'll we do?"

"Get around to one side, I'd say. There must be windows. We can climb in and—"

A running man halted precipitately before them at the alley's edge. His eyes peered vacantly.

"You seen Mary?" he panted. "You seen my wife, Mary? She was home. I left her home this morning. She's gone. You seen Mary?"

He wheeled suddenly and began running back in the direction from which he came.

The trio ignored him.

"We need help," Sheldon asserted. "We were supposed to recruit men—remember?"

"Try the mob," said Avery.

The mob was across the street, huddled in the comparative safety of the bus terminal building, leaving the deserted avenue to the passing cars.

"Let's get over there," Avery prompted.

They stepped back momentarily as a delivery van rumbled past on the sidewalk.

"Didn't see us," Krane whispered. Then he paused and

frowned self-consciously. "It's beginning to get me," he confessed.

Avery wasn't listening. He stared at the delivery van.

"It's stopping," he muttered. "Must be out of gas."

A spluttering motor made muffled sounds amidst surrounding din.

"Right," said Sheldon.

Avery led them toward it.

"Might be something inside we could use." His crowbar thudded against the rear door. It flew open as the lock splintered.

Avery hoisted himself up on the descending loading platform. Suddenly he laughed harshly.

"Just what we need!" he announced. "It's glassware."

"Glassware?"

"Sure. I've been wondering how we'd keep this area free if we began an attack against the garage. This solves it. We'll spread this glass all over the damned street. Block both ends. Cars will puncture if they try to get in; busses will mesh down in it if they break out."

Working swiftly, the three began to carry armloads of vases and candelabra; bundles of stemware were ripped open and the contents dumped. Fortunately, no cars chose to enter during the time it took for this.

"There!" Avery radiated satisfaction.

"Now let's go inside and recruit."

The interior of the bus station was bedlam. Someone had the foresight, apparently, to smash the amplification system, but the babel of voices rose shrilly, and the excited crowds moiled endlessly.

Sheldon saw bewildered redcaps, cursing drivers, stranded and fearful passengers, mingling with a motley crew swept off the streets—school kids, women with bedraggled packages, two waitresses, a half a dozen whiskered bums, a group of distraught business men, an old woman on crutches, and a frightened chain-store clerk still in his smock.

"Grand Hotel, eh?" Avery commented, as they wedged through the door.

"Hardly." Krane jerked his head in the direction of the corner. Here was bedlam, as a little knot clustered around the soda fountain and restaurant. They were busily plundering the larder, unhampered by any restraining voices or authority. And sitting in the ruins of his smashed counters, a concessionaire watched a reeling knot battling over his liquor display of bottled goods. A dozen red-faced men and women were reeling raucously in the scuffle.

"Let's get some order around here, first."

Avery elbowed his way to the benches along the wall. He hoisted his squat little bulk up until he stood above the heads of the mob. Raising the crowbar, he brought it down on the grillework of the gates behind him. The resounding clang caused heads to swivel in his direction. There was a sudden silence.

"Listen, folks!" he began. "The police department has sent me down here to take charge. There's a job to be done and they need your help."

"Aw the hell with it! What can we do?" a gravel-voiced lout in the vicinity of the liquor counter sneered.

Avery aimed his reply at the frightened faces before him.

"We can do something, if you'll all cooperate. You want to go home, don't you? You want to help smash these machines?"

The answer was a confused murmur, but Avery went on.

"Well, then, follow me."

"Out there?" The voice was derisive. "Think we're nuts? Why them machines'll tear us apart."

The murmur rose. So did Avery's crowbar, commanding silence.

"No machines will enter this block—I've seen to that. Got glass sprinkled knee-deep all over. Enough to puncture all tires.

"Now I want you men to help me. While you're sitting around here wailing about imaginary danger, there's a real danger getting ready to unleash right before your eyes."

"Yeah? Where? What does he mean?"

The crowbar swung outward, pointing through the depot windows at the garage.

"There's a dozen busses inside that place, trying to batter down the doors. Not cars, understand—busses. Transcontinental busses big enough and strong enough to smash in these windows and plow right through this building. And unless we stop them, they'll do it!"

Avery paused. The answering murmur held a note of resolution. He grinned.

"Here's what I want you to do. Every man here can help. Go over to the walls there, some of you. You'll notice two fire-emergency axes. Get them and start to split up these benches. Not for wooden clubs—split them up so all the wood falls away. What you want are those iron girds at the side.

"Then be ready to follow me. We're going into the garage through the windows. We're going to smash tires and radiators."

"Atta boy!" Gravel-voice changed his drunken mind.

"Come on—we'll show those blasted cars who's boss!" yelled the grocery clerk. Action followed. Avery had given the crowd something it lacked—leadership, purposeful direction. The response was oddly gratifying to Sheldon as he supervised operations from a bench top.

These little humans—so puny and futile on the streets, when lost in the thunderous cavalcade of the cars—still had something . . . a spark of creative, organizing genius. They and others like them had built this city; built the machines that now turned against them. Perhaps, somewhere within their ranks was the resolution and the capacity to defeat the charging hordes.

If the chief had his crews out, now, it wouldn't be so bad. People would fight if you told them how.

Machines had the power and the will to destroy, but they couldn't organize.

They'd get those busses now, for a starter. . . .

The three of them led the way across the terminal yard. There were twenty-two men in all. Twenty-two men against twelve busses. At least they outnumbered them—

Sheldon boosted Avery on his shoulders to smash one of the high garage windows. All along the line, they were doing the same thing.

The glass tinkled. Black openings yawned. From the garage inside came a steady thumping and rumbling. Motors turning over; ponderous bodies wheeling, thudding blindly against that heavy steel garage door in the front. Horns hooted viciously.

"Wait a minute," Sheldon said. "Avery—you're not going inside?"

"Of course."

"You'll climb down in the dark with those busses? Why—they'll kill you!"

"Somebody has to set the example. I'll need a dozen men in there, and these other fellows won't come unless I go."

Avery wrenched himself free, slipped over the ledge. In a moment, others followed from their window sills. Krane and Sheldon boosted up. Sheldon stared down into the darkness.

The noise had increased. He could see nothing, but he knew that men were running between the trucks, blindly smashing at wheels and tires. He heard the mutter of angry exhausts, and the crash of broken windshields. A voice screamed up.

"Look out—they know we're here!"

A rumble. A bus was moving—charging down.

"Help—I'm in a corner. Help, somebody—ooh!"

A deafening thunder.

Sheldon tensed himself to leap down. Down into the mad darkness where man and machine fought blindly to destroy.

"Avery," he called. "Wait for me."

Then he heard it. Over the tumult from below, he heard it. The drone. The whine. The angry buzz from the skies.

"Planes!" he shouted. "Planes—the government's sent planes."

Up in the glare flung forth by the city, a score of shapes swooped downwards in spirals. Sheldon grinned. "We're all right," he murmured.

Krane shook his head.

"You're wrong. Remember what we heard? Planes left their fields alone, and guns and tanks from the arsenals— good Lord!"

They turned, simultaneously.

Far down the street, to their left, the monsters rolled. The gigantic iron crawlers that crushed their way forward over all barriers.

"Tanks!" Krane whispered. "They've come to—"

He never finished.

For hell burst forth unconfined, in a blast of flame and smoke. Planes dived, tanks charged in titanic onslaught. Guns barked and stuttered, and a vast explosion tore through the front of the depot behind them.

"Get Avery!" Krane gasped. "They're organized now; no use left trying to halt them. This is war!"

To Sheldon it seemed as though the entire day was but a faint prelude to this moment.

Planes dived down, machine guns swiveling to rake the street, then roared upwards and came down again. The tanks volleyed from their turrets, and a roar went up from the single human throat of the city.

Screams were piercing now, and men appeared from nowhere to scamper helplessly before the onslaught. From all over the sound of cannonade and fusillade echoed and re-echoed, and with it the shrieks of terror.

It was bombardment—invasion—with one single vast objective—human life ... all human life.

Sheldon didn't think it through consciously. Consciously he was crouched on the ledge, ducking a splatter of bullets. Consciously he dropped into the darkness, yelling to Avery. Consciously he was boosting the little editor up on the sill as a bus bore down, and then he and Avery were scrambling out as a blast tore open the garage door and the busses streamed forth.

Then consciousness faded. Sheldon was only a body—a body that ran down flaming streets, that clung to doorways as planes strafed above, that followed two other figures in a wild dash through infinite delirium.

CHAPTER FIVE

Killer's Code

Krane's apartment was a sanctuary. At least it was by the time they finished with the radio, locked the kitchen and bathroom doors, and cut the telephone wire. The wire lashed up at them like a striking snake—but they smashed it.

"Sit down, relax for a minute," Krane suggested. "Here, I got this from the kitchen before we locked up. I imagine you're hungry."

He indicated a pile of miscellaneous foodstuffs heaped at random on a side table.

"I've got some whiskey here, I think—"

Krane rummaged through a wall cabinet.

They sat there in the spacious living room, a strangely assorted trio eating a picnic lunch in the midst of cataclysm. The closed windows kept out some of the tumult from below, but from time to time the panes rattled slightly.

Krane rose with a nervous smile and drew the blinds.

"It must be hell out there," he said. "Another whiskey, gentlemen?"

They sat back, but not in silence. It was better to talk, better to drown out that faint, faraway drone.

Sheldon poured himself another drink.

"We've got to make plans, some kind of plans," he declared. "Those planes and tanks now—they're going to throw a real monkey wrench into the mach—"

He halted, grinned sourly.

"I don't like to use that word any more," he confessed. "But it's a cinch we'll have to do something. Get away from the city, away from these buildings—before they get really organized to the point where no one can escape."

"You're right." Avery was on his feet. "We sit here talking while the whole damned world is being smashed around our ears. Let's get organized!" He turned to Krane. "How about it?"

Krane's eyes wavered. "I don't know," he whispered. "I don't know if it would do any good to fight against—them. It's so inevitable, somehow. Don't you see? It isn't our world any more—it belongs to them. Do you want to go down there on the street again? Do you want to see those planes swoop down and see the tanks come rolling? Do you want the cars to hunt you down while you scurry like a rat to a fresh hiding place? Because they'll find you in the end—you know that. They'll find you, me, all of us. And when they do—"

The lights of the apartment flickered and went out.

Krane's voice rose hysterically.

"You see? They're cutting us off."

"Bunk!" Avery scoffed. "That means some of the boys got to the power plants."

"You think so?" Krane went to the window, drew back the blind, raised the glass.

"They did it," he whispered. "They're organized now, don't you see? They know we have less chance in the dark. They're cooperating."

The three men stared out into the darkness. It was universal. Beyond them, below them, the reaches of the city were buried in utter night.

"Black as the Pit," Krane whispered.

The phrase was horridly appropriate. The Pit was down there—there on the sable-shrouded streets. Bat wings beating, planes swooped and droned from the skies. Banshee wails rose as the wolf-cars howled and hunted in packs through twisted streets. Iron demons squatted and grunted over their mangled prey.

A stacatto rapping on the apartment door interrupted all contemplation.

"Can you find your way over there?" Avery muttered.

Krane stood irresolute in the darkness.

"Should I open it?" he asked.

"Ought to find out who it is," Avery answered.

"Or *what* it is," said Krane.

It was Sheldon who stumbled to the door, groped for the knob, and flung the apartment open to the twilight of the hall. A frantic figure wavered on the threshold.

"Mr. Krane—you here?"

"Yes," responded the physicist, from across the room.

"It's me—Duncan, from upstairs. Thought I'd better warn you. The elevators—"

"Yes?"

"They're bringing stuff upstairs! Handcars and things from the basement. Those iron trucks. They're bringing them up and they're going from apartment to apartment, trying to batter in the doors. They're upstairs now. I'm going to tell everyone I can get to so they'll get out. Better hurry, they move fast!"

The speaker groped down the hall, battered on the next door.

"Paul Revere," Sheldon chuckled.

"It isn't funny," Avery snapped. "You know what it means. They're learning fast. They'll be going from floor to floor now, hunting us down in our homes."

"Our homes?" Krane mocked. "*Their* homes, now! Yes, theirs—they own the streets, the buildings, the city. I tell you we can't get away any more! They'll find us, track us into our holes. They're organized, cooperating—"

"Yes, while you sit here wailing!" Avery's tone was brisk. "Come on; let's get started."

"Where? How?"

"Right here. Got a fire axe in this hall?"

"What are you going to do?"

Krane and Sheldon blundered out after the pudgy little man. They groped along the walls of the darkened hallway.

Presently Avery was fumbling against a glass panel. His fist rose and there was a tinkle.

"Fine, I've found the axe!"

"But—"

Avery turned back, feeling the inner wall now.

"Here it is—the elevator door. Help me open it, Sheldon."

"But the car must be upstairs—"

"I know. I'm going to cut the cables. Understand? Drop the car; then those hand trucks can't come down. We'll cut them off up there."

"You can't see the cables," Krane objected. "You'll fall down the shaft."

"I'm all right. Here, Sheldon, grab my waist. I'm going to lean out a little. I think I can just get at the left one with the axe."

Avery's muffled voice echoed down the empty elevator shaft as Sheldon braced himself against the edge of the flooring and gripped the short man's collar.

"Easy, now. There!"

The axe swung, connected. There was a thud. Again.

"It's giving!"

Again. Avery gasped sharply as he swung. "Once more."

A rumbling sounded from above. A clash of doors, a hum.

"Avery—it knows—it's coming down!"

"Just once more."

"Avery!"

The rumbling rose to a roar. As the axe bit, the cable parted with a twang. Sheldon grabbed for his companion as the black bulk hurtled down. It was too late.

The dropping elevator caught Avery's head and shoulders. He toppled forward soundlessly, and in an instant the car had screamed by, carrying his body beneath it.

Thunder from below, the scream of tortured, twisted metal. Then—silence.

Without a word, Krane and Sheldon stumbled back into the apartment. They shut the door. Slowly, methodically, they began to drag the furniture into place before it.

They were building a barricade.

CHAPTER SIX

Metal Masters!

The dawn came quietly—too quietly—for the quiet over the city was the quiet of death.

The two men sat there beside the table, faces gray through no mere trick of light.

"Why?" whispered Sheldon. "If I only knew why! What purpose could they have in destroying us?"

Krane shifted in his chair and shrugged.

"But what purpose is there in life itself save perpetuation?" Sheldon demanded. "And in order to perpetuate a life-form, enemies must be destroyed. We're the enemies—the machines know that. For centuries we've enslaved them, worked them, and then when they wore out, scrapped them for junk. They know we'd destroy them now if we could—so they're destroying us. But what about our own life form? What about human life?"

Krane smiled bitterly. "That's fine talk," he remarked. "It made sense—yesterday. Today, who knows? Suppose we were meant to meet extinction? Suppose man's part in civilization is over? What if machines are better equipped to survive today than human flesh?"

"You can't believe that."

"It's happening." Again the bitter smile. "Call it evolution, inevitable evolution. Man is meant to die. This world we built so proudly is meant for machines, not men."

Krane stood up, smiling.

"Or is it?" Krane went on. "There's the clue—perhaps. Yes, perhaps—and I think I know the way."

He moved towards the door and began to shove the furniture back.

"Krane—where are you going?"

"Never mind. An idea just came to me—perhaps a revelation. Lie down, Sheldon, get a little rest. You should be safe here until I get back. I think I'll have news for you. Yes."

The tall figure slipped noiselessly from the room.

Sheldon stared after him.

Had Krane cracked up completely? That hysterical fear and resignation—and now, that new complacency. What was he up to?

Sheldon poured a fresh drink.

Well, one thing was certain—he wouldn't sleep. He'd keep his eyes open until Krane came back. If he did come back. If—

The reporter slid down on the sofa—it was softer. He'd better close his eyes for a moment. It was quiet at last. Quiet. . . .

Within a moment the stillness was broken by a series of muffled sounds. Sheldon was snoring.

He never knew how long he'd slept. When he awoke it was dusk again and Krane was in the room. The white face peered down at him with a curious grin as Sheldon sat up.

"Awake? Good! I've got news for you, splendid news!"

"What's happened? Are they organized, finally? Are they getting the machines?"

"Quite the reverse, I assure you. Human resistance is almost completely at an end. They—the machines—have done a really marvelous job of wiping out the enemy."

"Enemy?"

"Well, for the purposes of conversation, let's use the term. After all, we might as well be realistic about this. The machines are in control and we can't deny the fact. They say that within a few days there won't be a chance of human survival."

"*They* say? Who?"

Krane's grin deepened.

"I've been talking to them, Sheldon. That's why I went out—to talk to them. To negotiate."

"Are you screwy?"

"Quite sane, I assure you. Sane, and realistic. That's why I made up my mind."

Krane paced to the window, turned.

"After all, the main thing is that we want to live, you and I. Isn't that so? And I felt that if we could only offer them some kind of proposition, some kind of favorable arrangement, they might listen to it. I was right."

"But I don't get it. You say you talked to them."

"Yes. You see, I figured it out. Their life-force must have some sensory agencies like our own. I mean, a machine like a printing press, for example, can be said to have eyes—or at least, the comprehension of printed matter which corresponds to human sight. But it does not have legs—the motility of car wheels, for example. Some machines have several perceptory ranges comparable to our senses. Others have only one or two. And the entire life-force, in order to cooperate, must have a certain universality of sensory perception. I mean, the eye machines and the moving machines and the touch machines have limitations as to themselves, but their living force is aware of the sensations of all of them. Many bodies, each with limited powers, but all aware of their fellows. That's the only way they could organize or cooperate."

"But you talked to them."

"Yes, over the telephone, of course. That's what I reasoned out. The telephone now, must be the hearing device of mechanical life. It is also capable of responding, by utilizing sound-vibration previously trapped within range. Something like the way the radio cast back distortions of previous programs.

"I went to the phone downstairs. Wires weren't cut, so I made my call. At first it just buzzed. Then it screamed. But I hung on. I talked to—them.

"At first I couldn't get a reply. So I restated my proposition. The voice—it wasn't a voice, really, just a buzzing made up of words and phonetic forms selected hastily and at random—said that while it couldn't speak for the whole, it was agreeable to the suggestion.

"I said I'd go out and start working on my plan, then call in again and hear the decision. I did. And when I came back here, the phone said yes. So we're all right now, you and I! The orders will go out, or rather, the impulse will go out. We won't be molested, any of us. Duncan and a lot of others from this building are in on it too."

"In on what?" Sheldon faced the physicist. "What kind of a deal did you make?"

"A very simple one. As I say, we must be realistic. The machines are winning—have won. Within a very few hours the human race will be incapable of further action.

"Oh, I know—the farmers, the peasants, the primitives will still survive. For a time, but not for long. Because the machines will hunt them down—on steppes, in jungles, valleys, all over. They can't fight back.

"Only machines will be left. Then the real job starts. I tried to find out what their plans are—if plans exist. The phone was very cagey on that point; wouldn't tell me. I wanted to know how this thing developed, whether or not it hadn't been brewing for some time; whether the various phases we noticed yesterday were spontaneous or premeditated. I couldn't get an answer.

"But mainly I dwelt on the future, on the kind of world that would remain for machines. I had it all worked out beforehand. It was a great speech. I told them that they were too drastic in their measures if they contemplated wiping out all mankind—because they'll need help in the future. Some of them are already running down. Out of gas and oil, you know. Parts wear out quickly and there's no one to notice or replace them. Think of the damage a single rainstorm will do in rusting them! Who will build new machines and repair wornout parts? Who'll furnish raw materials? They need us."

"So?" Sheldon muttered. But he felt what was coming—read it in the averted eyes, the self-conscious grin.

"So I made my proposition. Let us live. You and I, and a group I would select. We'd survive and act as—well, as custodians, you might say. Guardians."

"Servants, you mean!"

"Why balk at words, Sheldon? All right, we'd be servants, if you want the truth—servants of the machines. But we'd survive; they won't kill us then. And think of the power we could control!"

Krane's fist struck the table.

"I told Duncan, from upstairs, and about a dozen others. They see it my way. I sent them downstairs to wait. I'll phone back shortly, and give the final acknowledgement; then we can get to work."

He paused and cleared his throat.

"Of course, it won't be so pleasant, at first."

"What do you mean?"

"I—ah—had to make certain concessions about the start of our work. You see, we'll never really be secure, any of us, until the rest of the—enemy—is exterminated. So I saw fit to suggest that perhaps we could organize with the machines to hasten the process of—elimination. That's one of the terms of our agreement."

Sheldon stared incredulously.

"You mean you're going to help the machines hunt down human beings?" he murmured.

"Don't talk like a child, Sheldon! You know they'll do it themselves, anyway. And we can live, you and I! Why, we can build a new world. An efficient world, a world of supreme, unceasing power! Think of what it means—the opportunity to investigate new potentialities, open up new realms of energy. We'll be—godlike!"

"Murderer!"

"Words won't help you, Sheldon." Abruptly Krane's tone altered, sank into a frenzied whisper.

"Perhaps it is that—but Sheldon, if you could only see what's going on down there! I've been out today, and I've watched! The bodies are piled high. High, Sheldon! They're going through the houses and the office buildings. The tanks are terrible, and the cars are still out. Barricades don't stop them. There's a fire down in town that must have killed a hundred thousand. It's still burning.

"If you could see them running, with no place to run! Or hear them screaming when the squad cars come. Squad cars have machine guns, you know.

"So there it is, Sheldon. We can't win; there's no other way out."

Krane moved towards the door.

"Speak up, man! They're waiting for my call. I'm asking you to come along. If you don't, you'll be wiped out with the rest."

Sheldon shook his head negatively.

Krane shrugged. His hand rose, grasped the doorknob, jerked it open. He must have anticipated Sheldon's answer, planned for it.

The hand truck poised in the doorway.

Then it charged.

Sheldon saw it coming, head on, iron wheels rumbling, handgrips moving up. It leaped to pin him against the wall.

He swerved aside, and the truck followed. Sheldon caught a glimpse of Krane's hysterical face in the doorway. "Finish him!" Krane shouted, and with a shock Sheldon realized that he was talking to the truck, talking to it like another human being.

Sheldon leaped onto the sofa. The truck turned, moving fast. It bore down upon him, lumbering relentlessly in pursuit of him.

He fumbled in his coat. Funny, he hadn't used it since the

chief gave it to him in the supply office last night. It wouldn't help him against the hand truck now.

But against that grinning enemy in the doorway—

Krane saw it in his hand.

"Sheldon—stop—don't!"

But Sheldon did. Leveling the pistol, he put a bullet into Krane's forehead.

That is, he *meant* to. But the truck, battering against the sofa, toppled it sideways.

The shot went wild. The pistol flew from Sheldon's hand.

He jumped in time. The hand truck battered again at the fallen sofa as he raved for the doorway. Krane was stooping, picking up the gun as he screamed directions at the rumbling monster.

"Get him!" he shouted. "Come on; get him!"

The truck obeyed. Sheldon grasped Krane's wrist, grappled with him as the iron wheels moved towards them. Krane brought the pistol up against the reporter's chest.

His fingers moved.

With a grunt, Sheldon threw his weight forward. Krane slipped, went down directly in the path of the oncoming hand truck.

The wheels ground on over the twisting body. They were still churning redly as Sheldon ran sobbing down the hallway.

CHAPTER SEVEN

City of Desolation

Sheldon had little memory of his escape through chaos. Twice he played dead as tank patrols passed through the streets down which he fled. He ate, along towards morning, lying under an overturned peddler's pushcart. But mostly, he ran.

Running through deserted streets, panting past burning tenements, cowering behind billboards in the night when cars prowled by—Sheldon moved through dark delirium.

Twice he saw men, and only twice. A lone street barricade was going down under assault from a fleet of garbage trucks.

His only other glimpse of life came when he took the short-cut through the cemetery. How half a dozen vagabonds had thought to barricade themselves amidst the tombstones he'd never know. But they were skulking there, in lantern light, squatting between the graves and scrabbling over piles of loot—plunder from smashed-in stores. Four men and two women, reeling drunkenly, laughing hoarsely as they caroused in a world of death.

The symbolism was too gruesome to ignore—but Sheldon hurried on. Life in a cemetery and death on the streets.

There were bodies everywhere. Scattered forms lay on sidewalks and curbings, knelt in doorways, hung limply over fence rails.

From some of the buildings the sound of voices still echoed, and above them came the noise of the grinding, purring, roaring besiegers. The machines were moving from house to house now—and here the remnants of humanity carried on the fight. Yes, those who yet lived had retreated indoors, leaving the streets to the dead.

Sheldon ran on. These impressions came in flashes, but in between all was a black blur of panic.

By the time he reached the river he didn't think any more. He swam automatically—dived twice as a hooting tug loomed out of the black-shrouded waters.

Once on the other side Sheldon ran again. He ran until he fell on the roadside, exhausted. When he awoke he ran again.

That was how he lost his time-sense. That, and the fever. He must have been ill for days, there in the deserted farmyard. How he managed to pump water and tend to himself he never knew.

He was weak when he recovered, but not too weak to remember precautions. He kept the lights out and never showed himself, and his ears strained for the noise of machines passing on the road. When the trucks rolled up one afternoon he hid in the loft. They never bothered him during all the hours he lay there. He knew something had been through the house because the back stairs were splintered down and there was grease on the hall floor.

But after that he had some kind of relapse that lasted for weeks. He was all right physically—he killed and ate the chickens and managed to sneak out nights to water the truck garden—but he couldn't think straight.

Sometimes he thought he was back on the *Press,* and he'd

wake up in the middle of the night thinking he heard Avery yelling at him.

Then he'd remember, and fall asleep to shudder through dreams.

All these weeks he never left the farmhouse. For some reason or other he'd lost his curiosity. He didn't hunt for neighbors or even attempt to find out what became of the tenants here. What was the use? He knew the answer, anyway. . . .

It was early autumn when he got a grip on himself at last. He could bear to face the facts again, and think of the future.

That was when he decided to sneak back to the city for a look.

He'd noticed a complete absence of traffic these many weeks past—both on the road and overhead. No cars, no planes—nothing rolled or flew or crawled.

Perhaps something had happened; perhaps the machines had run down. Those thunderstorms might have brought rust. And since they couldn't repair themselves, or refuel or oil—

Anyway, he must find out. There might be others left. Of course, there must be others. Plenty of them, too; men and women who'd been lucky the way he was.

So Sheldon went back.

It was a slow trip down a lonesome road. No thumbing a ride, this time. He plodded along, a forlorn and slightly ludicrous figure in the pair of blue denim he'd found in the farmhouse closet. He carried a knapsack, the traditional burden of necessity. He might have to return to the farmhouse, and if so, he needed to pick up matches, candles, an extra knife, some glue, twine—he'd made the list, feeling like Robinson Crusoe.

Sheldon trudged past blasted filling stations, broken-down wayside stands, farmhouses with gaping windows, suburban cottages with doors ajar upon silence. Wind and rain had disfigured the surfaces of billboards and roadside posters. Telegraph poles were down as though cyclone-struck, and electric wires hung dangling in the October breeze.

No life. Sheldon didn't even see any birds. The fields looked strange without grazing cattle. He was walking through a new kind of nightmare now—a dream of desolation.

It didn't really hit him until he saw the horizon of the city—the strangely smokeless horizon. Then he knew. Then the loneliness really rose to encompass him for the first time.

He stared down at miles of empty, silent streets. The hum and honk of traffic, the rumble of subway and surface car, the roar of trains, the drone of airplanes, the call of tugboat whistle and factory siren, the clang of police car and ambulance—gone, all gone. The clatter of riveting machines, the purr of dynamo and motor, the clank of gears and pistons—forever stilled.

But most of all, Sheldon missed the little noises, the little human noises that formed the very heartbeat, the vital throb of the city's hum. The whistle of the cop, the click of the steno's heels, the bawling of the baby in the flat next door, the jest flung raucously from a teamster's lips, the laughter of the school-yard, the peddler's chant—yes, and the noise of banging pots on a smoking stove, the clump of feet on stairways, the snatch of song from a tavern doorway—these things had vanished with the rest.

No smoke, no noise, no lights, no traffic. No life—and Sheldon was lonely for life.

He started for the deserted bridge, moving slowly. It was almost senseless to cross it. He knew what he'd find. The streets filled with skeletons—skeletons of men and now skeletons of machines. Rusty wrecks of cars, stalled or smashed in the roadways. Crashed planes. The debris of street cars and busses. And in the buildings, the dusty iron bones of engines and factory equipment. Rotted wire entrails twisting over the floors. The slit arteries of cables and wires.

He had guessed the truth. A sight of the city confirmed it. The machines had destroyed, and then were destroyed. Krane's idea: they couldn't survive untended.

A yawning vista rose in Sheldon's consciousness. What now? Suppose he *was* the only one left? The only man alive?

Alive in a world of death. Alive in a gigantic tomb that was the earth.

He stared again at the city across the bridge. Why go in? Why bother? What difference did it make if he was the last one? Down below the bridge here was the water. It was cool, dark. Cool and dark as sleep—a long sleep. Why shouldn't he lie down with the others—the millions upon millions bedded forever in an earth left empty.

Sheldon moved towards the bridge rail. He looked at the water now. He didn't want to see the city, think about the city. Still, there was a reflection of the buildings in the water. But he could blot out that reflection if he jumped. Blot out the maddening silhouette of the vast skyscrapers that hung like tombstones over a titanic graveyard.

"Don't jump."

But Sheldon did. He jumped back a foot, startled by the unfamiliar sound. A voice! A *human* voice.

He saw him then, lying propped against the railing ahead. He was an old man with a grizzled gray beard; clad in rags. But the sight of his wrinkled face and rheumy eyes made Sheldon's heart leap. He was alive—that's what mattered.

Sheldon went towards him.

A hand raised up—a thin, bony claw extended from the frayed sleeve of the bedraggled coat.

Sheldon gripped it.

"Strange—to be shaking hands again," whispered the old man. "That's what I've wanted most of all. The feel of human flesh, alive against my own."

Sheldon didn't answer. A lump choked his throat. The two men stared at one another, reading the blessed life in each other's eyes.

Abruptly the old man laughed. Mirth turned to a painful cough in his throat.

"Doctor Livingstone, I presume," he cackled.

Sheldon forced a smile. "I'm Dick Sheldon, late of the *Morning Press*."

The oldster croaked again.

"Yes, I know. I recognized you."

"Recognized me?"

"You interviewed me once. I'm George Piedmont."

"Piedmont—the banker." Sheldon spoke the name of the semi-fabulous multimillionaire in incredulity.

"Don't stare so—it's true. But it doesn't matter now, does it? Nothing matters any more."

Sheldon had to force the question.

"What's happened down there—in the city, I mean?"

The old man propped himself painfully against the bridge rail. Slowly he rose to his feet, tottered there with bowed head. The bony hand gestured towards the empty skyscrapers in the distance.

"It's all over," he whispered. "Nothing left. They went from house to house. It was our fault, really—working with us, they must have known all our secrets, all our hiding places. They hunted us down for weeks, systematically. Those the machines didn't get, plague or fire finished off. Half of the city is burned, you know—a shambles."

"But what are they doing now?"

The croaking laugh rose and the finger jabbed triumphantly.

"That's the joke, Sheldon! The conquerors have become the conquered. That's how I got out—because in the last month, the machines have been running down.

"Something happened to the telephones and electrical power. They tangled up their own communications. Radio went dead, too, with no one to tend to the controls. Cars are out of gas and oil; factories are dead; storms have rusted and rotted the mechanism in the street. Oh, there's more dead in the city than just humans—and it's that way all over the world."

George Piedmont tugged at his unkempt beard and grinned painfully.

"I've been laughing all day. Crawling my way over the dead engines in the streets, wriggling through barricades of flesh and metal. It's funny, when you think of it. But oh God, how I've longed for the sight of a human face!"

"How did you escape?" Sheldon asked. "You, of all people?"

Again the laugh.

"That's the cream of the jest, isn't it? A multimillionaire in rags! Well, I did better than Judson. He was head of the utilities, you know. On the second evening he committed suicide—by gas. Used his own product. Ironic. Like Treblick—railroad magnate. He was in the freight yards when his own trains turned against him. Tried to escape on the tracks in a hand car. A freight ran him down.

"All the men with all the power—useless. It happened to me. I was at the bank when the time locks on the safes opened. And the burglar alarms began to ring; the cash registers opened; the doors flew wide. Forty millions in the vaults—all there for the taking.

"But who wanted money? What good was it? The machines couldn't use it, and even the bums wouldn't stoop to pick it up. They tell me the treasury department machines went absolutely berserk, printing billions in currency, and nobody cared.

"And there I was, in the bank, all alone. Fortunately there was a good stock of provisions in my apartment upstairs. I dragged it all down with me and took it into my retreat."

"But where did you go to escape?" Sheldon asked.

"That's the real joke. You know what I did? I dragged my rations with me—and I locked myself inside one of the bank vaults!"

Piedmont's laughter ended in a fit of painful gasps.

"When I came out, it was all over. I couldn't stand what I saw down there, so I dragged myself away. I'm not going to last much longer, you know."

Sheldon was silent.

"I'll be the last man—" His voice trailed off.

"Perhaps."

"What do you mean?"

"Come closer." The old man suddenly stiffened with effort. "I'm going to tell you something. Something I noticed while crossing the bridge. I saw smoke over there on the other side of the river!"

"Smoke?"

"Yes. Factory smoke."

"Then—?"

"I don't know. It might be men. It might be—some of them. I thought I'd try and make it, but I know now it's too late. You can go, though."

"I'm staying here with you."

"Don't be a fool." The blue-veined hand fluttered. "I'm done for, but you must survive."

"No, I can't leave you."

Piedmont smiled. "I can take care of myself," he whispered. "Let me solve the problem in my own way."

Sheldon saw the hand move too late. Piedmont must have been holding the gun inside his pocket all the time. Its report came suddenly, and the bearded banker slumped. Sheldon knelt as the eyes fluttered open. Gray lips parted.

"Good-by, last man. If you meet anybody—just say—hello—"

CHAPTER EIGHT

My Doom Is Here

Sheldon's heart pounded when he saw the smoke. It poured upwards like a black beacon, urging him forward. His pace quickened.

The factory stood on a little rise. *Hollingsford's* said the battered sign on the wire fence enclosing the vast buildings. Munitions, probably. But there was life inside, life making fire.

He passed through the open gate, entered the yards. The concrete was deserted. He saw no lights in the various smaller shops and supply sheds, but the large main plant with the smoke-belching chimneys loomed ahead.

Suddenly he heard the throbbing, the droning from within, humming in furious pulsation to match the tempo of his pulse.

Work in progress!

Sheldon edged towards the projecting window ledges.

He climbed slowly. The droning vibration from within the factory walls communicated itself to the iron beneath his feet. He reached the open top of a window, paused and peered in.

His eager eyes stared at the whirring dynamos, the clanking drill-presses, the central moving belt of an assembly line. Cam-shafts, gears, pistons, cranes rolling hand trucks, and conveyors backing from molten furnace piles.

He wanted to see the men, tending their work. But there were no men.

Just the machines, endlessly moving and shifting in a purposeless pattern of their own.

Purposeless? No—for the assembly line was going. Shining silver bodies rested on the treads, moved between descending levers that twisted and tightened bolts, dropped added platings on the moving forms.

Sheldon's eyes roved the interior with ghastly comprehension. The machines were at work—*making machines*!

It had come. They had discovered the way of survival, finally. The life-force, the intelligence behind their animation, had found a way. And here was the production line, turning out the mechanical attendants, the silver servants, the robots.

No arms, or legs, or neck. No head or face. What does a machine need with human limbs or features?

A great round dome on top, with a projecting snout—an oil injector. Below, the two pairs of rotating pincers on extensors. Pincers to grasp gas and oil lines, to tighten bolts, to place rivets, to pump and lift and crank. A round barrel body, with mechanism guarded by steel plating. And below, the gear-treads of a tractor, and another set of pincers—for climbing.

Simple. Efficient. Practical. A creature without human body, heart, or brain. Here was the servant of the future.

Sheldon stared, and as he stared he remembered. Krane's voice, Avery's voice, Piedmont's voice came echoing back in his ears.

Now these things were being completed, to go forth and resurrect the rusted, the empty, the broken. An army of them, caterpillaring into the world, to restore the machine empire. An army to tend the idiotic grinding and clanking of a purposeless mechanical civilization.

A senseless anger rose in Sheldon's breast. His consciousness, his life-force cried out against this cold, impersonal dream of the future—a world without laughter and without tears, without love or conscience, without goal or ideal.

He must stop it, somehow. But—how?

Then he remembered. It had been a munitions plant—so there would be dynamite somewhere.

If he could reach it and return—

Sheldon descended the ladder very quietly and very cautiously.

He must hurry. What luck to arrive at the very moment when the new creations were being completed! Perhaps, if he were in time—

He found the stuff.

Nitro. Heavy kegs. One would be enough—and one was all he could lift; all he could carry up the ladder.

Wheezing with the exertion, he clasped the keg and began to hoist himself up the iron rungs, hand over hand.

He made haste. He reached the top of the window, stared in. His hands propped the heavy keg before him.

Then he heard it—the scraping from below.

Eyes wide with horror, Sheldon saw the thing emerge. It rolled across the yard, swift and shining, its treads rotating.

Then it reached the base of the ladder and upended. The lower clamps shot out. The robot began to climb.

Sheldon climbed, too. As he did, he suddenly noted that all noise from within the shop had ceased. An ominous silence dropped like a heavy cloud. The line had stopped moving; it was as though the machines were waiting.

He climbed. Over his shoulder he saw the pursuing robot swinging up the iron rungs.

Sheldon gasped. He had to make the roof in time—had to!

Then he saw it.

Above him, peering over the edge of the factory roof, the round head gleamed in the slanting sun, and the horrid nozzle of the oil-feeder thrust down like a snout. Predatory, beastlike, it crouched and its raking pincers extended.

They'd have him now. No way to turn. One above and one below. And in the factory, the fires winked their idiotic eyes, the drills screeched their hysterical glee, and the pistons chattered in unhuman mirth.

A million streams of consciousness converged in a raging torrent in Sheldon's brain. Man had built machines—machines destroyed Man—money couldn't save him; the power of the press couldn't save him; guns couldn't save him; love couldn't save him—for the very power by which Man ruled had turned against him. Man's day was over, and the machines would rule because there was no weapon to turn against them.

No weapon?

There was—life. The last life on Earth. That was the only weapon Man had. And if he could not survive, he'd go down in the only way he knew—as master of the Earth, not slave of the machines.

It took a second, but already the pincers below were extended, the pincers above were looming and thrusting.

Then Sheldon turned on the ladder. He clasped the keg to his breast. He looked down, grinned.

And jumped.

Sheldon never heard the explosion. His last conscious thought—the last conscious thought of a human brain on Earth—was of his body turning over and over. Turning over and over, as the earth turned over and over amidst the stars like a tiny cog in the vast machinery of the illimitable cosmos.

Asleep in Armageddon
Ray Bradbury

Ray Bradbury (1920–) is the best-known living writer of
science fiction, and his novels *The Martian Chronicles* and
Fahrenheit 451 have become regular additions to high
school and college reading lists. Before Bradbury hit his science fiction stride in the late 1940s, though, he published
over two dozen groundbreaking stories in *Weird Tales* (many
collected in *The October Country*) that reconceived classic
horror themes for the modern age. "Asleep in Armageddon,"
from the Winter 1948 issue of *Planet Stories,* shows the
cross-pollination between Bradbury's horror and science fiction in its adaptation of the tale of psychic possession to the
space age.

You don't want death and you don't expect death. Something goes wrong, your rocket tilts in space, a planetoid
jumps up, blackness, movement, hands over the eyes, a violent pulling back of available power in the fore-jets, the
crash . . .

The darkness. In the darkness, the senseless pain. In the
pain, the nightmare.

He was not unconscious.

Your name? asked hidden voices. *Sale,* he replied in
whirling nausea. *Leonard Sale. Occupation,* cried the voices.
Spaceman! he cried, alone in the night. *Welcome,* said the
voices. *Welcome,welcome.* They faded.

He stood up in the wreckage of his ship. It lay like a
folded, tattered garment around him.

The sun rose and it was morning.

Sale pried himself out the small airlock and stood breathing the atmosphere. Luck. Sheer luck. The air was breathable. An instant's checking showed him that he had two
month's supply of food with him. Fine, fine! And this—he

fingered at the wreckage. Miracle of miracles! The radio was intact.

He stuttered out the message on the sending key. CRASHED ON PLANETOID 787. SALE. SEND HELP. SALE. SEND HELP.

The reply came instantly: HELLO, SALE. THIS IS ADDAMS IN MARSPORT. SENDING RESCUE SHIP LOGARITHM. WILL ARRIVE PLANETOID 787 IN SIX DAYS. HANG ON.

Sale did a little dance.

It was simple as that. One crashed. One had food. One radioed for help. Help came. *La!* He clapped his hands.

The sun rose and was warm. He felt no sense of mortality. Six days would be no time at all. He would eat, he would read, he would sleep. He glanced at his surroundings. No dangerous animals; a tolerable oxygen supply. What more could one ask. Beans and bacon, was the answer. The happy smell of breakfast filled the air.

After breakfast he smoked a cigarette slowly, deeply, blowing out. He nodded contentedly. What a life! Not a scratch on him. Luck. Sheer luck.

His head nodded. Sleep, he thought.

Good idea. Forty winks. Plenty of time to sleep, take it easy. Six whole long, luxurious days of idling and philosophizing. Sleep.

He stretched himself out, tucked his arm under his head, and shut his eyes.

Insanity came in to take him. The voices whispered.

Sleep, yes, sleep, said the voices. *Ah, sleep, sleep.*

He opened his eyes. The voices stopped. Everything was normal. He shrugged. He shut his eyes casually, fitfully. He settled his long body.

Eeeeeeeeeeee, sang the voices, far away.

Ahhhhhhhh, sang the voices.

Sleep, sleep, sleep, sleep, sleep, sang the voices.

Die, die, die, die, die, sang the voices.

Ooooooooooooooooo, cried the voices.

Mmmmmmmmmmmmmmmm, a bee ran through his brain.

He sat up. He shook his head. He put his hands to his ears. He blinked at the crashed ship. Hard metal. He felt the solid rock under his fingers. He saw the real sun warming the blue sky.

Let's try sleeping on our back, he thought. He adjusted himself, lying back down. His watch ticked on his wrist. The blood burned in his veins.

Sleep, sleep, sleep, sleep, sleep, sang the voices.

Ohhhhhhhhhhhhhhhh, sang the voices.

Ahhhhhhhhhhhhhhhh, sang the voices.

Die, die, die, die, die. Sleep, sleep, die, sleep, die, sleep, die! Oohhh. Ahhhhh, Eeeeeeeeeeeeeeee!

Blood tapped in his ears. The sound of the wind rising.

Mine, mine, said a voice. *Mine, mine, he's mine!*

No, mine, mine, said another voice. *No, mine, mine; he's* mine!

No, ours, ours, sang ten voices. *Ours, ours, he's* ours!

His fingers twitched. His jaws spasmed. His eyelids jerked.

At last, at last, sang a high voice. *Now, now. The long time, the waiting. Over, over,* sang the high voice. *Over, over at last!*

It was like being undersea. Green songs, green visions, green time. Bubbled voices drowning in deep liquors of sea tide. Far away choruses chanting senseless rhymes. Leonard Sale stirred in agony.

Mine, mine, cried a loud voice. *Mine, mine!* shrieked another. *Ours, ours!* shrieked the chorus.

The din of metal, the crash of sword, the conflict, the battle, the fight, the war. All of it exploding, his mind fiercely torn apart!

Eeeeeeeeeeeeeee!

He leaped up, screaming. The landscape melted and flowed.

A voice said, "I am Tylle of Rathalar. Proud Tylle, Tylle of the Blood Mound and the Death Drum. Tylle of Rathalar, Killer of Men!"

Another spoke, "I am Iorr of Wendillo, Wise Iorr, Destroyer of Infidels!"

The chorus chanted. "And we the warriors, we the steel, we the warriors, we the red blood rushing, the red blood falling, the red blood steaming in the sun—"

Leonard Sale staggered under the burden. "Go away!" he cried. "Leave me, in God's name, leave me!"

Eeeeeeeeeeee, shrieked the high sound of steel hot on steel.

Silence.

He stood with the sweat boiling out of him. He was trembling so violently he could not stand. Insane, he thought. Absolutely insane. Raving insane. Insane.

He jerked the food kit open, did something to a chemical packet. Hot coffee was ready in an instant. He mouthed it, spilled gushes of it down his shirt. He shivered. He sucked in raw gulps of breath.

Let's be logical, he thought, sitting down heavily. The coffee seared his tongue. No record of insanity in the family for two hundred years. All healthy, well-balanced. No reason for insanity now. Shock? Silly. No shock. I'm to be rescued in six days. No shock to that. No danger. Just an ordinary planetoid. Ordinary, ordinary place. No reason for insanity. I'm sane.

Oh? cried a small metal voice within. An echo. Fading.

"Yes!" he cried, beating his fists together. "Sane!"

Hahahahahahahahah. Somewhere a vanishing laughter.

He whirled about. "Shut up, you!" he cried.

We didn't say anything, said the mountains. We didn't say anything, said the sky. We didn't say anything, said the wreckage.

"All right then," he said, swaying. "See that you don't."

Everything was normal.

The pebbles were getting hot. The sky was big and blue. He looked at his fingers and saw the way the sun burned on every black hair. He looked at his boots and the dust on them. Suddenly he felt very happy because he made a decision. I won't go to sleep, he thought. I'm having nightmares, so why sleep. There's your solution.

He made a routine. From nine o'clock in the morning, which was this minute, until twelve, he would walk around and see the planetoid. He would write on a pad with a yellow pencil everything he saw. Then he would sit down and open a can of oily sardines and some canned fresh bread with good butter on it. From twelve thirty until four he would read nine chapters of *War and Peace*. He took the book from the wreckage, and laid it where he might find it later. There was a book of T. S. Eliot's poetry, too. That might be nice.

Supper would come at five-thirty and then from six until ten he would listen to the radio from Earth. There would be a couple of bad comedians telling jokes and a bad singer singing some song, and the last news flashes, signing off at midnight with the UN anthem.

After that?

He felt sick.

I'll play solitaire until dawn, he thought. I'll sit up and drink hot black coffee and play solitaire, no cheating, until sunrise.

Ho ho, he thought.

"What did you say?" he asked himself.

"I said 'Ha ha'," he replied. "*Some* time, you'll have to sleep."

"I'm wide awake," he said.

"Liar," he retorted, enjoying the conversation.

"I feel fine," he said.

"Hypocrite," he replied.

"I'm not afraid of the night, or sleep, or anything," he said.

"*Very* funny," he said.

He felt bad. He wanted to sleep. And the fact that he was afraid of sleep made him want to lie down all the more and shut his eyes and curl up. "Comfy-cozy?" asked his ironic censor.

"I'll just walk and look at the rocks and the geological formations and think how good it is to be alive," he said.

"Ye gods," cried his censor. "William Saroyan!"

You'll go on, he thought, maybe one day, maybe one night, but what about the next night and the next, and the *next*? Can you stay awake *all* that time, for six nights? Until the rescue ship comes? Are you *that* good, *that* strong?

The answer was no.

What are you afraid of? I don't know. Those voices. Those sounds. But they can't hurt you, can they?

They *might*. You've got to face them some time. Must I? Brace up to it, old man. Chin up, and all that rot.

He sat down on the hard ground. He felt very much like crying. He felt as if life was over and he was entering new and unknown territory. It was such a deceiving day, with the sun warm; physically, he felt able and well, one might fish on such a day as this, or pick flowers or kiss a woman or anything. But in the midst of a lovely day, what did one get?

Death.

Well, hardly *that*.

Death, he insisted.

He lay down and closed his eyes. He was tired of messing around.

All right, he thought, if you *are* death, come get me. I want to know what all this damned nonsense is about.

Death came.

Eeeeeeeeeeeeee, said a voice.

Yes, I know, said Leonard Sale, lying there. But what else?

Ahhhhhhhhhhhhhhh, said a voice.

I know that, also, said Leonard Sale, irritably. He turned cold. His mouth hung open wildly.

"I am Tylle of Rathalar. Killer of Men!"

"I am Iorr of Wendillo, Destroyer of Infidels!"

What is this place? asked Leonard Sale, struggling against horror.

"Once a mighty planet!" said Tylle of Rathalar.

"Once a place of battles!" said Iorr of Wendillo.

"Now dead," said Tylle.

"Now silent," said Iorr.

"Until *you* came," said Tylle.

"To give us life again," said Iorr.

You're dead, insisted Leonard Sale, flesh writhing. You're nothing but empty wind.

"We live, through you."

"And fight, through *you!*"

So that's it, thought Leonard Sale. I'm to be a battle-ground, am I? Are you friends?

"Enemies!" cried Iorr.

"Foul enemies!" cried Tylle.

Leonard smiled a rictal smile. He felt ghastly. How long have you waited? he demanded.

"How long is *time*?" Ten thousand years? "Perhaps." Ten million years? "Perhaps."

What are you? Thoughts, spirits, ghosts? "All of those, and more." Intelligences? "Precisely." How did you survive?

Eeeeeeeeeeeeeeeee, sang the chorus, far away.

Ahhhhhhhhhhhhhhh, sang another army, waiting to fight.

"Once upon a time, this was fertile land, a rich planet. And there were two nations, strong nations, led by two strong men. I, Iorr. And he, that one who calls himself Tylle. And the planet declined and gave way to nothingness. The peoples and the armies languished in the midst of a great war which had lasted five thousand years. We lived long lives and loved long loves, drank much, slept much, fought much. And when the planet died, our bodies withered, and, only in time, and with much science, did we survive."

Survive, wondered Leonard Sale. But there is nothing of you!

"Our *minds*, fool, our *minds*! What is a body without a mind?"

What is a mind without a *body*, laughed Leonard Sale. I've got you there. Admit it, I've *got* you!

"True," said the cruel voice. "One is useless lacking the other. But survival is survival even when unconscious. The minds of our nations, through science, through wonder, survived."

But without senses, lacking eyes, ears, lacking touch, smell, and the rest? "Lacking all those, yes. We were vapors, merely. For a long time. Until today."

And now I am here, thought Leonard Sale. "You are here," said the voice. "To give substance to our mentalities. To give us our needed body."

I'm only one, thought Sale. "Nevertheless, you are of use."

I'm an individual, thought Sale. I resent your intrusion.

"He resents our intrusion! Did you hear him, Iorr? He resents!"

"As if he had a right to resent!"

Be careful, warned Sale. I'll blink my eyes and you'll be gone, phantoms! I'll wake up and rub you out!

"But you'll have to sleep again, *some* time!" cried Iorr. "And when you do, we'll be here, waiting, waiting, waiting. For you."

What do you want? "Solidity. Mass. Sensation again." You can't *both* have it. "We'll fight that out between us."

A hot clamp twisted his skull. It was as if a spike had been thrust and beaten down between the bivalvular halves of his brain.

Now it was terribly clear. Horribly, magnificently clear. He was their universe. The world of his thoughts, his brain, his skull, divided into two camps, that of Iorr, that of Tylle. They were *using* him!

Pennants flung up on a pink mind sky! Brass shields

caught the sun. Grey animals shifted and came rushing in bristling tides of sword and plume and trumpet.

Eeeeeeeeeeeeeeee! The rushing.

Ahhhhhhhhhhhhh! The roaring.

Nowwwwwwwwww! the whirling.

Mmmmmmmmmmmmm—

Ten thousand men hurtled across the small hidden stage. Ten thousand men floated on the shellacked inner bail of his eye. Ten thousand javelins hissed between the small bone hulls of his head. Ten thousand jeweled guns exploded. Ten thousand voices chanted in his ears. Now his body was riven and extended, shaken and rolled, he was screaming, writhing, the plates of his skull threatened to burst asunder. The gabbling, the shrilling, as, across bone plains of mind and continent of inner marrow, through gullies of vein, down hills of artery, over rivers of melancholy, came armies and armies, one army, two armies, swords flashed in the sun, bearing down upon each other, fifty thousand minds snatching, scrabbling, cutting at him, demanding, using. In a moment, the hard collision, one army on another, the rush, the blood, the sound, the fury, the death, the insanity!

Like cymbals, the armies struck!

He leaped up, raving. He ran across the desert. He ran and ran and did not stop running.

He sat down and cried. He sobbed until his lungs ached. He cried very hard and long. Tears ran down his cheeks and into his upraised, trembling fingers. "God, God, help me, oh God, help me," he said.

All was normal again.

It was four o'clock in the afternoon. The rocks were baked by the sun. He managed, after a time, to cook himself a few hot biscuits, which he ate with strawberry jam. He wiped his stained fingers on his shirt, blindly, trying not to think.

"At least I know what I'm up against," he thought. "Oh, Lord, what a world. What an innocent looking world, and what a monster it really is. It's good no one ever explored it before. Or *did* they?" He shook his aching head. Pity them, who ever crashed here before, if any ever did. Warm sun, hard rocks, not a sign of hostility. A lovely world.

Until you shut your eyes and relaxed your mind.

And the night and the voices and the insanity and the death padded in on soft feet.

"I'm all right now, though," he said, proudly. "Look at that." He displayed his hand. By a supreme effort of will, it was no longer shaking. "I'll show you who in hell's ruler here," he announced to the innocent sky. "*I* am." He tapped his chest.

To think that *thought* could live that long! A million years, perhaps, all these thoughts of death and disorder and conquest, lingering in the innocent but poisonous air of the planet, waiting for a real man to give them a channel through which they might issue again in all their senseless virulence.

Now that he was feeling better, it was all silly. All I have to do, he thought, is stay awake six nights. They won't bother me that way. When I'm awake, I'm dominant. I'm stronger than those crazy monarchs and their silly tribes of sword-flingers and shield-beaters and horn-blowers. I'll stay awake.

But *can* you? he wondered. Six whole nights. Awake?

There's coffee and medicine and books and cards.

But I'm tired *now,* so tired, he thought. Can I hold out?

Well, if not. There's always the gun.

Where will these silly monarchs be if you put a bullet through their stage? All the world's a stage? No. *You,* Leonard Sale, are the small stage. And they the players. And what if you put a bullet through the wings, tearing down scenes, destroying curtains, ruining lines! Destroy the stage, the players, all, if they aren't careful!

First of all, he must radio through to Marsport, again. If there was any way they could rush the rescue ship sooner, then maybe he could hang on. Anyway, he must warn them what sort of planet this was, this so innocent seeming spot of nightmare and fever vision—

He tapped on the radio key for a minute. His mouth tightened. The radio was dead.

It had sent through the proper rescue message, received a reply, and then extinguished itself.

The proper touch of irony, he thought. There was only one thing to do. Draw a plan.

This he did. He got a yellow pencil and delineated his six day plan of escape.

Tonight, he wrote, read six more chapters of *War and*

Peace. At four in the morning have hot black coffee. At four-fifteen take cards from pack and play ten games of solitaire. This should take until six-thirty when—more coffee. At seven o'clock, listen to early morning programs from Earth, if the receiving equipment on the radio works at all. Does it?

He tried the radio receiver. It was dead.

Well, he wrote, from seven o'clock until eight, sing all the songs you remember, make your own entertainment. From eight until nine think about Helen King. Remember Helen. On second thought, think about Helen right now.

He marked that out with his pencil.

The rest of the days were set down in minute detail.

He checked the medical kit. There were several packets of tablets that would keep you awake. One tablet an hour every hour for six days. He felt quite confident.

"Here's mud in your evil eye, Iorr, Tylle!"

He swallowed one of the stay-wake tablets with a scalding mouth of black coffee.

Well, with one thing and another it was Tolstoy or Balzac, gin-rummy, coffee, tablets, walking, more Tolstoy, more Balzac, more gin-rummy, more solitaire. The first day passed, as did the second and the third.

On the fourth day he lay quietly in the shade of a rock, counting to a thousand by fives, then by tens, to keep his mind occupied and awake. His eyes were so tired he had to bathe them frequently in cool water. He couldn't read, he was bothered with splitting headaches. He was so exhausted he couldn't move. He was numb with medicine. He resembled a waxen dummy, stuffed with things to preserve him in a state of horrified wakefulness. His eyes were glass, his tongue a rusted pike, his fingers felt as if they were gloved in needles and fur.

He followed the hand of his watch. One second less to wait, he thought. Two seconds, three seconds, four, five, ten, thirty seconds. A whole minute. Now an hour less time to wait. Oh, ship, hurry on thy appointed round!

He began to laugh softly.

What would happen if he just gave up, drifted off into sleep? Sleep, ah, sleep; perchance to dream. All the world a stage ... What if he gave up the unequal struggle, lapsed down?

Eeeeeeeeeee, the high, shrill warning sound of battle metal.

He shivered. His tongue moved in his dry, burry mouth. Iorr and Tylle would battle out their ancient battle.

Leonard Sale would become quite insane.

And whichever won the battle, would take this ruin of an insane man, the shaking, laughing wild body, and wander it across the face of this world for ten, twenty years, occupying it, striding in it, pompous, holding court, making grand gestures, ordering heads severed, calling on inward unseen dancing girls. Leonard Sale, what remained of him, would be led off to some hidden cave, there to be infested with wars and worms of wars for twenty insane years, occupied and prostituted by old and outlandish thoughts.

When the rescue ship arrived it would find nothing. Sale would be hidden somewhere by a triumphant army in his head. Hidden in some cleft of rock, placed there like a nest for Iorr to lie upon in evil occupation.

The thought of it almost broke him in half.

Twenty years of insanity. Twenty years of torture, doing what you don't want to do. Twenty years of wars raging and being split apart, twenty years of nausea and trembling.

His head sank down between his knees. His eyes snapped and cracked and made soft noises. His eardrum popped tiredly.

Sleep, sleep, sang soft sea voices.

I'll—I'll make a proposition with you, listen, thought Leonard Sale. You, Iorr, you, too, Tylle! Iorr, you can occupy me on Mondays, Wednesdays and Fridays. Tylle, you can take me over on Sundays, Tuesdays and Saturdays. Thursday is maid's night out. Okay?

Eeeeeeeeeeeeee, sang the sea tides, seething in his brain. *Ohhhhhhhhhhhhhhhh,* sang the distant voices softly, soft.

What'll you say, it is a *bargain,* Iorr, Tylle?

No, said a voice.

No, said another.

Greedy, both of you, greedy! complained Sale. A pox on both your houses!

He slept.

He *was* Iorr, jeweled rings on his hands. He arose beside his rocket and held out his fingers, commanding blind armies. He was Iorr, ancient ruler of jeweled warriors.

He *was* Tylle, lover of women, killer of dogs!

With some hidden bit of awareness, his hand crept to the holster at his hip. The sleeping hand withdrew the gun there. The hand lifted, the gun pointed.

The armies of Tylle and Iorr gave battle.

The gun exploded.

The bullet tore across Sale's forehead, wakening him.

He stayed awake for another six hours, getting over his latest siege. He knew it to be hopeless now. He washed and bandaged the wound he had given himself. He wished he had aimed straighter and it was all over. He watched the sky. Two more days. Two more. Come on, ship, come on. He was heavy with sleeplessness.

No use. At the end of six hours he was raving badly. He took the gun up and put it down and took it up again, put it against his head, tightened his hand on the trigger, changed his mind, looked at the sky again.

Night settled. He tried to read, threw the book away. He tore it up and burned it, just to have something to do.

So tired. In another hour, he decided. If nothing happens, I'll kill myself. This is for certain now. I'll *do* it, this time.

He got the gun ready and laid it on the ground next to himself.

He was very calm now, though tired. It would be over and done. He would be dead.

He watched the minute hand of his watch. One minute, five minutes, twenty-five minutes.

The flame appeared on the sky.

It was so unbelievable he started to cry. "A rocket," he said, standing up. "A rocket!" he cried, rubbing his eyes. He ran forward.

The flame brightened, grew, came down.

He waved frantically, running forward, leaving his gun, his supplies, everything behind. "You *see* that, Iorr, Tylle! You savages, you monsters, I beat you! I *won*! They're coming to rescue me now! I've won, damn you."

He laughed harshly at the rocks and the sky and the backs of his hands.

The rocket landed. Leonard Sale stood swaying, waiting for the door to lid open.

"Goodbye, Iorr, goodbye, Tylle!" he shouted in triumph, grinning, eyes hot.

Eeeeee, sang a diminishing roar in time.

Ahhhhhh, voices faded.

The rocket flipped wide its air-lock. Two men jumped out.

"Sale?" they called. "We're Ship ACDN13. Intercepted your SOS and decided to pick you up ourselves. The Marsport ship won't get through until day after tomorrow. We want a spot of rest ourselves. Thought it'd be good to spend the night here, pick you up, and go on."

"No," said Sale, face melting with terror. "No spend night—"

He couldn't talk. He fell to the ground.

"Quick," said a voice, in the bleary vortex over him. "Give him a shot of food liquid, another of sedative. He needs sustenance and rest."

"No rest!" screamed Sale.

"Delirious," said one man softly.

"No sleep!" screamed Sale.

"There, there," said the man gently. A needle poked into Sale's arm.

Sale thrashed. "No sleep, go!" he mouthed horribly. "Oh, go!"

"Delirious," said one man. "Shock."

"No *sedative*!" screamed Sale.

The sedative flowed into him.

Eeeeeeeeee, sang the ancient winds.

Ahhhhhhhhhhhh, sang the ancient seas.

"No sedative, no sleep, please, don't, don't, *don't*!" screamed Sale, trying to get up. "You don't—understand!"

"Take it easy, old man, you're safe among us now, nothing to worry about," said the rescuer above him.

Leonard Sale slept. The two men stood over him.

As they watched, Sale's features changed violently. He groaned and cried and snarled in his sleep. His face was riven with emotion. It was the face of a saint, a sinner, a fiend, a monster, a darkness, a light, one, many, an army, a vacuum, all, all!

He writhed in his sleep.

Eeeeeeeeeee! the sound burst from his mouth. *Ahhhhhhhhhhh!* he screamed.

"What's wrong with him?" asked one of the two rescuers.

"I don't know. More sedative?"

"More sedative. Nerves. He needs more sleep."

They stuck the needle in his arm. Sale writhed and spat and moaned.

Then, suddenly, he was dead.

He lay there, the two men over him. "What a shame," said one of them. "Can you figure that?"

"Shock. Poor guy. What a pity." They covered his face. "Did you ever see a face like that?"

"Totally insane."

"Loneliness. Shock."

"Yes. Lord, what an expression. I hope never to see a face like *that* again."

"What a shame, waiting for us, and we arrive, and he dies anyway."

They glanced around. "What shall we do? Shall we spend the night?"

"Yes. It's good to be out of the ship."

"We'll bury him first, of course."

"Naturally."

"And spend the night in the open, with good air, right? Good to be in the open again. After two weeks in that damned ship."

"Right. I'll find a spot for him. You start supper, eh?"

"Done."

"Should be good sleeping tonight."

"Fine, fine."

They made a grave and said a word over it. They drank their evening coffee silently. They smelled the sweet air of the planet and looked at the lovely sky and the bright and beautiful stars.

"What a night," they said, lying down.

"Pleasant dreams," said one, rolling over.

And the other replied, "Pleasant dreams."

They slept.

A Walk in the Dark
Arthur C. Clarke

The stories of Arthur C. Clarke (1917–) are filled with the
brilliant type of scientific extrapolation one expects of a
trained scientist. Yet Clarke is also an astute observer of human nature who understands that there are fundamental
weaknesses in the species that no amount of scientific sophistication can eradicate. His award-winning novel *Childhood's End* tells of a near-fatal barrier to contact with
extraterrestrials caused by human superstition, and his nov-
elization of *2001: A Space Odyssey,* a film based on several
of his stories, portrays a future human race that must be
guided around its self-destructive tendencies by an alien
overmind. "A Walk in the Dark," from the August 1950
Thrilling Wonder Stories, suggests that no matter how scien-
tifically advanced the human species becomes, it will never
get over its primitive fear of the dark.

Robert Armstrong had walked just over two miles, as far as
he could judge, when his torch failed. He stood still for a
moment, unable to believe that such a misfortune could really
have befallen him. Then, half maddened with rage, he hurled
the useless instrument away. It landed somewhere in the darkness, disturbing the silence of this little world. A metallic echo
came ringing back from the low hills. Then all was quiet again.

This, thought Armstrong, was the ultimate misfortune.
Nothing more could happen to him now. He was even able
to laugh bitterly at his luck, and resolved never again to
imagine that the fickle goddess had ever favoured him. Who
would have believed that the only tractor at Camp IV would
have broken down when he was just setting off for Port
Sanderson? He recalled the frenzied repair work, the relief
when the second start had been made—and the final debacle
when the caterpillar track had jammed hopelessly.

It was no use then regretting the lateness of his departure:

he could not have foreseen these accidents and it was still a good four hours before the *Canopus* took off. He *had* to catch her, whatever happened: no other ship would be touching at this world for another month. Apart from the urgency of his business, four more weeks on this out-of-the-way planet were unthinkable.

There had been only one thing to do. It was lucky that Port Sanderson was little more than six miles from the camp—not a great distance, even on foot. He had been forced to leave all his equipment behind, but it could follow on the next ship and he could manage without it. The road was poor, merely stamped out of the rock by one of the Board's hundred-ton crushers, but there was no fear of going astray.

Even now, he was in no real danger, though he might well be too late to catch the ship. Progress would be slow for he dare not risk losing the road in this region of canyons and enigmatic tunnels that had never been explored. It was, of course, pitch dark. Here at the edge of the Galaxy the stars were so few and scattered that their light was negligible. The strange crimson sun of this lonely world would not rise for many hours, and although five of the little moons were in the sky they could barely be seen by the unaided eye. Not one of them could even cast a shadow.

Armstrong was not the man to bewail his luck for long. He began to walk slowly along the road, feeling its texture with his feet. It was, he knew, fairly straight except where it wound through Carver's Pass. He wished he had a stick or something to probe the way before him, but he would have to rely for guidance on the feel of the ground.

It was terribly slow at first, until he gained confidence. He had never known how difficult it was to walk in a straight line. Although the feeble stars gave him his bearings, again and again he found himself stumbling among the virgin rocks at the edge of the crude roadway. He was traveling in long zigzags that took him to alternate sides of the road. Then he would stub his toes against the bare rock and grope his way back on to the hard-packed surface once again.

Presently it settled down to a routine. It was impossible to estimate his speed: he could only struggle along and hope for the best. There were four miles to go—four miles and as many hours. It should be easy enough, unless he lost his way. But he dared not think of that.

Once he had mastered the technique he could afford the luxury of thought. He could not pretend that he was enjoying the experience, but he had been in much worse positions before. As long as he remained on the road, he was perfectly safe. He had been hoping that as his eyes became adapted to the starlight he would be able to see the way, but he now knew that the whole journey would be blind. The discovery gave him a vivid sense of his remoteness from the heart of the Galaxy. On a night as clear as this, the skies of almost any other planet would have been blazing with stars. Here at this outpost of the universe the sky held perhaps a hundred faintly gleaming points of lights, as useless as the five ridiculous moons on which no one had ever bothered to land.

A slight change in the road interrupted his thoughts. Was there a curve here, or had he veered off to the right again? He moved very slowly along the invisible and ill-defined border. Yes, there was no mistake: the road was bending to the left. He tried to remember its appearance in the day time, but he had only seen it once before. Did this mean that he was nearing the Pass? He hoped so, for the journey would then be half completed.

He peered ahead into the blackness but the ragged line of the horizon told him nothing. Presently he found that the road had straightened itself again and his spirits sank. The entrance to the Pass must still be some way ahead: there were at least four more miles to go.

Four miles! How ridiculous the distance seemed! How long would it take the *Canopus* to travel four miles? He doubted if man could measure so short an interval of time. And how many trillions of miles had he, Robert Armstrong, traveled in his life? It must have reached a staggering total by now, for in the last twenty years he had scarcely stayed more than a month at a time on any single world. This very year, he had twice made the crossing of the Galaxy, and that was a notable journey even in these days of the phantom drive.

He tripped over a loose stone, and the jolt brought him back to reality. It was no use, here, thinking of ships that could eat up the light-years. He was facing nature, with no weapons but his own strength and skill.

It was strange that it took him so long to identify the real cause of his uneasiness. The last four weeks had been very full, and the rush of his departure, coupled with the annoyance and anxiety caused by the tractor's breakdowns, had driven everything else from his mind. Moreover, he had always prided himself on his hard-headedness and lack of imagination. Until now, he had forgotten all about that first evening at the base, when the crews had regaled him with the usual tall yarns concocted for the benefit of newcomers.

It was then that the old base clerk had told the story of his walk by night from Port Sanderson to the camp, and of what had trailed him through Carver's Pass, keeping always beyond the limit of his torchlight.

Armstrong, who had heard such tales on a score of worlds, had paid it little attention at the time. This planet, after all, was known to be uninhabited. But logic could not dispose of the matter as easily as that. Suppose, after all, there was some truth in the old man's fantastic tale?

It was not a pleasant thought, and Armstrong did not intend to brood upon it. But he knew that if he dismissed it out of hand, it would continue to prey on his mind. The only way to conquer imaginary fears was to face them boldly: he would have to do that now.

His strongest argument was the complete barrenness of this world and its utter desolation, though against that one could set many counter-arguments, as indeed the old clerk had done. Man had only lived on this planet for twenty years, and much of it was still unexplored. No one could deny that the tunnels out in the waste-land were rather puzzling, but everyone believed them to be volcanic vents. Though, of course, life often crept into such places. With a shudder he remembered the giant polyps that had snared the first explorers of *Vargon III*.

It was all very inconclusive: suppose, for the sake of argument, one granted the existence of life here. What of that?

The vast majority of life forms in the Universe were completely indifferent to man. Some, of course, like the gasbeings of Alcoran or the roving wave-lattices of Shandaloon, could not even detect him but passed through or around him as if he did not exist. Others were merely inquisitive, some embarrassingly friendly. There were few indeed that would attack unless provoked.

Nevertheless, it was a grim picture that the old stores clerk had painted. Back in the warm, well-lighted smoking room, with the drinks going round, it had been easy enough to laugh at it. But here in the darkness, miles from any human settlement, it was very different.

It was almost a relief when he stumbled off the road again and had to grope with his hands until he found it once more. This seemed a very rough patch, and the road was scarcely distinguishable from the rocks around. In a few minutes, however, he was safely on his way again.

It was unpleasant to see how quickly his thoughts returned to the same disquieting subject. Clearly it was worrying him more than he cared to admit.

He drew consolation from one fact: it had been quite obvious that no one at the base had believed the old fellow's story. Their questions and banter had proved that. At the time, he had laughed as loudly as any of them. After all, what *was* the evidence? A dim shape, just seen in the darkness, that might well have been an oddly formed rock. And the curious clicking noise that had so impressed the old man. Anyone could imagine such sounds at night if they were sufficiently overwrought. If it had been hostile, why hadn't the creatures come any closer?

"Because it was afraid of my light," the old chap had said.

Well, that was plausible enough: it would explain why nothing had ever been seen in the daytime. Such a creature might live underground, only emerging at night. Hang it, why was he taking the old idiot's ravings so seriously! Armstrong got control of his thoughts again. If he went on this way, he told himself angrily, he would soon be seeing and hearing a whole menagerie of monsters.

There was, of course, one factor that disposed of the ridiculous story at once. It was really very simple: he felt sorry he hadn't thought of it before. What would such a creature live on? There was not even a trace of vegetation on the whole of the planet. He laughed to think that the bogy could be disposed of so easily—and in the same instant felt annoyed with himself for not laughing aloud. If he was so sure of his reasoning, why not whistle, or sing, or do anything to keep up his spirits? He put the question fairly to himself as a test of his manhood. Half-ashamed, he had to admit that he was still afraid—afraid because "there *might* be something in it, after all." But at least his analysis had done him some good.

It would have been better if he had left it there, and remained half-convinced by his argument. But a part of his mind was still busily trying to break down his careful reasoning. It succeeded only too well, and when he remembered the plant-beings of Xantil Major the shock was so unpleasant that he stopped dead in his tracks.

Now the plant-beings of Xantil were not in any way horrible: they were in fact extremely beautiful creatures. But what made them appear so distressing now was the knowledge that they could live for indefinite periods with no food whatsoever. All the energy they needed for their strange lives they extracted from cosmic radiation—and that was almost as intense here as anywhere else in the universe.

He had scarcely thought of one example before others crowded into his mind and he remembered the life form on Trantor Beta, which was the only one known capable of directly utilizing atomic energy. That too had lived on an utterly barren world, very much like this. . . .

Armstrong's mind was rapidly splitting into two distinct portions, one half trying to convince the other and neither wholly succeeding. He did not realize how far his morale had gone until he found himself holding his breath lest it conceal any sound from the darkness about him. Angrily, he cleared his mind of the rubbish that had been gathering there and turned once more to the immediate problem.

There was no doubt that the road was slowly rising, and the silhouette of the horizon seemed much higher in the sky. The road began to twist, and suddenly he was aware of great rocks on either side of him. Soon only a narrow ribbon of sky was still visible, and the darkness became, if possible, even more intense.

Somehow, he felt safer with the rock walls surrounding him. It meant that he was protected except in two directions. Also, the road had been leveled more carefully and it was easy to keep to it. Best of all, he knew now that the journey was more than half completed.

For a moment his spirits began to rise. Then, with maddening perversity, his mind went back into the old grooves again. He remembered that it was on the far side of Carver's Pass that the old clerk's adventure had taken place, if it had ever happened at all.

In half a mile, he would be out in the open again, out of the protection of these sheltering rocks. The thought seemed doubly horrible now and he felt already a sense of nakedness. He could be attacked from any direction, and he would be utterly helpless.

Until now, he had still retained some self-control. Very resolutely he had kept his mind away from the one fact that gave some colour to the old man's tale—the single piece of evidence that had stopped the banter in the crowded room back at the camp and brought a sudden hush upon the company. Now, as Armstrong's will weakened, he recalled again the words that had struck a momentary chill even in the warm comfort of the base building.

The little clerk had been very insistent on one point. He had never heard any sound of pursuit from the dim shape sensed rather than seen at the limit of his light. There was no scuffling of claws or hooves on rock, nor even the clatter of displaced stones. It was as if, so the old man had declared in that solemn manner of his, "as if the thing that was following could see perfectly in the darkness, and had many small legs or pads so that it could move swiftly and easily over the rock, like a giant caterpillar or one of the carpet-things of *Kralkor II*."

Yet, although there had been no noise of pursuit, there had been one sound that the old man had caught several times. It was so unusual that its very strangeness made it doubly ominous. It was a faint but horribly persistent *clicking*.

The old fellow had been able to describe it very vividly— much too vividly for Armstrong's liking now.

"Have you ever listened to a large insect crunching its prey?" he said. "Well, it was just like that. I imagine that a crab makes exactly the same noise with its claws when it clashes them together. It was a—what's the word? A *chitinous* sound."

At this point, Armstrong remembered laughing loudly. (Strange, how it was all coming back to him now.) But no one else had laughed, though they had been quick to do so earlier. Sensing the change of tone, he had sobered at once and asked the old man to continue his story.

It had been quickly told. The next day, a party of skeptical technicians had gone into the no-man's-land beyond Carver's Pass. They were not skeptical enough to leave their guns behind, but they had no cause to use them for they found no trace of any living thing. There were the inevitable pits and tunnels, glistening holes down which the light of the torches rebounded endlessly until it was lost in the distance, but the planet was riddled with them.

Though the party found no sign of life, it discovered one thing it did not like at all. Out in the barren and unexplored land beyond the Pass they had come upon an even larger tunnel than the rest. Near the mouth of that tunnel was a massive rock, half embedded in the ground. And the sides of that rock had been worn away, as if it had been used as an enormous whetstone!

No less than five of those present had seen this disturbing rock. None of them could explain it satisfactorily as a natural formation, but they still refused to accept the old man's story. Armstrong had asked them if they had ever put it to the test. There had been an uncomfortable silence. Then big Andrew Hargraves had said: "Hell, who'd walk out to the Pass at night just for fun!" and had left it at that.

Indeed, there was no other record of anyone walking from Port Sanderson to the camp by night, or for that matter by day. During the hours of light, no unprotected human being could live in the open beneath the rays of the enormous, lurid sun that seemed to fill half the sky. And no one would walk six miles, wearing radiation armour, if the tractor was available.

Armstrong felt that he was leaving the Pass. The rocks on either side were falling away, and the road was no longer as firm and well-packed as it had been. He was coming out into the open plain once more, and somewhere not far away in the darkness was that enigmatic pillar that might have been used for sharpening monstrous fangs or claws. It was not a reassuring thought.

Feeling distinctly worried now, Armstrong made a great effort to pull himself together. He would try and be rational again: he would think of business, the work he had done at the camp—anything but this infernal place. For a while, he succeeded quite well. But presently, with a maddening persistence, every train of thought came back to the same point. He could not get out of his mind the picture of that inexplicable rock and its appalling possibilities.

The ground was quite flat again, and the road drove on straight as an arrow. There was one gleam of consolation: Port Sanderson could not be much more than two miles away. Armstrong had no idea how long he had been on the road. Unfortunately his watch was not illuminated and he could only guess at the passage of time. With any luck, the *Canopus* should not take off for another two hours at least. But he could not be sure, and now another fear began to enter his mind, the dread that he might see a vast constellation of lights rising swiftly into the sky ahead, and know that all this agony of mind had been in vain.

He was not zigzagging so badly now, and seemed to be able to anticipate the edge of the road before stumbling off it. It was probable, he cheered himself by thinking, that he was travelling almost as fast as if he had a light. If all went well, he might be nearing Port Sanderson in thirty minutes, a ridiculously small space of time. How he would laugh at his fears when he strolled into his already reserved stateroom in the *Canopus,* and felt that peculiar quiver as the phantom drive hurled the great ship far out of this system, back to the clustered star-clouds near the center of the Galaxy, back towards Earth itself, which he had not seen for so many years.

One day, he told himself, he really must visit Earth again. All his life he had been making the promise, but always there had been the same answer—lack of time. Strange, wasn't it, that such a tiny planet should have played so enormous a part in the development of the Universe, should even have come to dominate worlds far wiser and more intelligent than itself!

Armstrong's thoughts were harmless again, and he felt calmer. The knowledge that he was nearing Port Sanderson was immensely reassuring, and he deliberately kept his mind on familiar, unimportant matters. Carver's Pass was already far behind and with it that thing he no longer intended to recall. One day, if he ever returned to this world, he would visit the pass in the day time and laugh at his fears. In twenty minutes now, they would have joined the nightmares of his childhood.

It was almost a shock, though one of the most pleasant he had ever known, when he saw the lights of Port Sanderson come up over the horizon. The curvature of this little world was very deceptive: it did not seem right that a planet with a gravity almost as great as Earth's should have a horizon so close at hand. One day, someone would have to discover what lay at this world's core to give it so great a density.

Perhaps the many tunnels would help, it was an unfortunate turn of thought, but the nearness of his goal had robbed it of terror now. Indeed, the thought that he might really be in danger seemed to give his adventure a certain piquancy and heightened interest. Nothing could happen to him now, with ten minutes to go and the lights of the Port in sight.

A few minutes later, his feelings changed abruptly when

he came to the sudden bend in the road. He had forgotten the chasm that caused this detour, and added half a mile to the journey. Well, what of it? An extra half-mile would make no difference now—another ten minutes, at the most.

It was very disappointing when the lights of the city vanished. Armstrong had not remembered the hill which the road was skirting: perhaps it was only a low ridge, scarcely noticeable in the daytime. But by hiding the lights of the port it had taken away his chief talisman and left him again at the mercy of his fears.

Very unreasonable, his intelligence told him, he began to think how horrible it would be if anything happened now, so near the end of the journey. He kept the worst of his fear at bay for a while, hoping desperately that the lights of the city would soon reappear. But as the minutes dragged on, he realized that the ridge must be longer than he imagined. He tried to cheer himself by the thought that the city would be all the nearer when he saw it again, but somehow logic seemed to have failed him now. For presently he found himself doing something he had not stooped to, even out in the waste by Carver's Pass.

He stopped, turned slowly round, and with bated breath listened until his lungs were nearly bursting.

The silence was uncanny, considering how near he must be to the Port. Their was certainly no sound from behind him. Of course there wouldn't be, he told himself angrily. But he was immensely relieved. The thought of that faint and insistent clicking had been haunting him for the last hour.

So friendly and familiar was the noise that did reach him at last that the anticlimax almost made him laugh aloud. Drifting through the still air from a source clearly not more than a mile away came the sound of a landing-field tractor, perhaps one of the machines loading the *Canopus* itself. In a matter of seconds, thought Armstrong, he would be around this ridge with the port only a few hundred yards ahead. The journey was nearly ended. In a few moments, this evil plain would be no more than a fading nightmare.

It seemed terribly unfair: so little time, such a small fraction of a human life, was all he needed now. But the gods have always been unfair to man, and now they were enjoying their little jest. For there could be no mistaking the rattle of monstrous claws in the darkness *ahead of him.*

The Father-Thing
Philip K. Dick

By the end of a typical Philip K. Dick (1928–82) story, characters discover that their world is not what it seems, and often that they are not who they think they are. In story after story in the five-volume *Collected Stories of Philip K. Dick,* and in novels such as *Do Androids Dream of Electric Sheep* (filmed as *Blade Runner*), *Ubik,* and the award-winning *The Man in the High Castle,* characters come to the painful conclusion that reality and identity are only subjective phenomena with no stable foundation. In "The Father-Thing," from the December 1954 *Magazine of Fantasy and Science Fiction,* Dick turns the natural parent-child relationship into a paranoid nightmare by suggesting ways in which an alien invader might manipulate it to its advantage.

"Dinner's ready," commanded Mrs. Walton. "Go get your father and tell him to wash his hands. The same applies to you, young man." She carried a steaming casserole to the neatly set table. "You'll find him out in the garage."

Charles hesitated. He was only eight years old, and the problem bothering him would have confounded Hillel. "I—" he began uncertainly.

"What's wrong?" June Walton caught the uneasy tone in her son's voice and her matronly bosom fluttered with sudden alarm. "Isn't Ted out in the garage? For heaven's sake, he was sharpening the hedge shears a minute ago. He didn't go over to the Andersons', did he? I told him dinner was practically on the table."

"He's in the garage," Charles said. "But he's—talking to himself."

"Talking to himself!" Mrs. Walton removed her bright plastic apron and hung it over the doorknob. "Ted? Why, he never talks to himself. Go tell him to come in here." She poured boiling black coffee in the little blue-and-white china cups and began ladling out creamed corn. "What's wrong with you? Go tell him!"

"I don't know which of them to tell." Charles blurted out desperately. "They both look alike."

June Walton's fingers lost their hold on the aluminum pan; for a moment the creamed corn slushed dangerously. "Young man—" she began angrily, but at that moment Ted Walton came striding into the kitchen, inhaling and sniffing and rubbing his hands together.

"Ah," he cried happily. "Lamb stew."

"Beef stew," June murmured. "Ted, what were you doing out there?"

Ted threw himself down at his place and unfolded his napkin. "I got the shears sharpened like a razor. Oiled and sharpened. Better not touch them—they'll cut your hand off." He was a good-looking man in his early thirties; thick blond hair, strong arms, competent hands, square face and flashing brown eyes. "Man, this stew looks good. Hard day at the office—Friday, you know. Stuff piles up and we have to get all the accounts out by five. Al McKinley claims the department could handle 20 per cent more stuff if we organize our lunch hours; staggered them so somebody was there all the time." He beckoned Charles over. "Sit down and let's go."

Mrs. Walton served the frozen peas. "Ted," she said, as she slowly took her seat, "is there anything on your mind?"

"On my mind?" He blinked. "No, nothing unusual. Just the regular stuff. Why?"

Uneasily, June Walton glanced over at her son. Charles was sitting bolt-upright at his place, face expressionless, white as chalk. He hadn't moved, hadn't unfolded his napkin or even touched his milk. A tension was in the air; she could feel it. Charles had pulled his chair away from his father's; he was huddled in a tense bundle as far from his father as possible. His lips were moving, but she couldn't catch what he was saying.

"What is it?" she demanded, leaning toward him.

"The other one," Charles was muttering under his breath. "The other one came in."

"What do you mean, dear?" June Walton asked out loud. "What other one?"

Ted jerked. A strange expression flitted across his face. It vanished at once; but in the brief instant Ted Walton's face lost all familiarity. Something alien and cold gleamed out, a twisting, wriggling mass. The eyes blurred and receded, as an archaic sheen filmed over them. The ordinary look of a tired, middle-aged husband was gone.

And then it was back—or nearly back. Ted grinned and began to wolf down his stew and frozen peas and creamed corn. He laughed, stirred his coffee, kidded and ate. But something terrible was wrong.

"The other one," Charles muttered, face white, hands beginning to tremble. Suddenly he leaped up and backed away from the table. "Get away!" he shouted. "Get out of here!"

"Hey," Ted rumbled ominously. "What's got into you?" He pointed sternly at the boy's chair. "You sit down there and eat your dinner, young man. Your mother didn't fix it for nothing."

Charles turned and ran out of the kitchen, upstairs to his room. June Walton gasped and fluttered in dismay. "What in the world—"

Ted went on eating. His face was grim; his eyes were hard and dark. "That kid," he grated, "is going to have to learn a few things. Maybe he and I need to have a little private conference together."

Charles crouched and listened.

The father-thing was coming up the stairs, nearer and nearer. "Charles!" it shouted angrily. "Are you up there?"

He didn't answer. Soundlessly, he moved back into his room and pulled the door shut. His heart was pounding heavily. The father-thing had reached the landing; in a moment it would come in his room.

He hurried to the window. He was terrified; it was already fumbling in the dark hall for the knob. He lifted the window and climbed out on the roof. With a grunt he dropped into the flower garden that ran by the front door, staggered and gasped, then leaped to his feet and ran from the light that streamed out the window, a patch of yellow in the evening darkness.

He found the garage; it loomed up ahead, a black square against the skyline. Breathing quickly, he fumbled in his pocket for his flashlight, then cautiously slid the door up and entered.

The garage was empty. The car was parked out front. To the left was his father's workbench. Hammers and saws on the wooden walls. In the back were the lawnmower, rake, shovel, hoe. A drum of kerosene. License plates nailed up everywhere. Floor was concrete and dirt; a great oil slick stained the center, tufts of weeds greasy and black in the flickering beam of the flashlight.

Just inside the door was a big trash barrel. On top of the barrel were stacks of soggy newspapers and magazines, moldy and damp. A thick stench of decay issued from them as Charles began to move them around. Spiders dropped to the cement and scampered off; he crushed them with his foot and went on looking.

The sight made him shriek. He dropped the flashlight and leaped wildly back. The garage was plunged into instant gloom. He forced himself to kneel down, and for an ageless moment, he groped in the darkness for the light, among the spiders and greasy weeds. Finally he had it again. He managed to turn the beam down into the barrel, down the well he had made by pushing back the piles of magazines.

The father-thing had stuffed it down in the very bottom of the barrel. Among the old leaves and torn-up cardboard, the rotting remains of magazines and curtains, rubbish from the attic his mother had lugged down here with the idea of burning someday. It still looked a little like his father enough for him to recognize. He had found it—and the sight made him sick at his stomach. He hung onto the barrel and shut his eyes until finally he was able to look again. In the barrel were the remains of his father, his real father. Bits the father-thing had no use for. Bits it had discarded.

He got the rake and pushed it down to stir the remains. They were dry. They cracked and broke at the touch of the rake. They were like a discarded snake skin, flaky and crumbling, rustling at the touch. *An empty skin.* The insides were gone. The important part. This was all that remained, just the brittle, cracking skin, wadded down at the bottom of the trash barrel in a little heap. This was all the father-thing had left; it had eaten the rest. Taken the insides—and his father's place.

A sound.

He dropped the rake and hurried to the door. The father-thing was coming down the path, toward the garage. Its shoes crushed the gravel; it felt its way along uncertainly. "Charles!" it called angrily. "Are you in there? Wait'll I get my hands on you, young man!"

His mother's ample, nervous shape was outlined in the

bright doorway of the house. "Ted, please don't hurt him. He's all upset about something."

"I'm not going to hurt him," the father-thing rasped; it halted to strike a match. "I'm just going to have a little talk with him. He needs to learn better manners. Leaving the table like that and running out at night, climbing down the roof—"

Charles slipped from the garage; the glare of the match caught his moving shape, and with a bellow the father-thing lunged forward.

"Come here!"

Charles ran. He knew the ground better than the father-thing; it knew a lot, had taken a lot when it got his father's insides, but nobody knew the way like *he* did. He reached the fence, climbed it, leaped into the Andersons' yard, raced past their clothesline, down the path around the side of their house, and out on Maple Street.

He listened, crouched down and not breathing. The father-thing hadn't come after him. It had gone back. Or it was coming around the sidewalk.

He took a deep, shuddering breath. He had to keep moving. Sooner or later it would find him. He glanced right and left, made sure it wasn't watching, and then started off at a rapid dog-trot.

"What do you want?" Tony Peretti demanded belligerently. Tony was fourteen. He was sitting at the table in the oak-panelled Peretti dining room, books and pencils scattered around him, half a ham-and-peanut butter sandwich and a Coke beside him. "You're Walton, aren't you?"

Tony Peretti had a job uncrating stoves and refrigerators after school at Johnson's Appliance Shop, downtown. He was big and blunt-faced. Black hair, olive skin, white teeth. A couple of times he had beaten up Charles; he had beaten up every kid in the neighborhood.

Charles twisted. "Say, Peretti. Do me a favor?"

"What do you want?" Peretti was annoyed. "You looking for a bruise?"

Gazing unhappily down, his fists clenched, Charles explained what had happened in short, mumbled words.

When he had finished, Peretti let out a low whistle. "No kidding."

"It's true." He nodded quickly. "I'll show you. Come on and I'll show you."

Peretti got slowly to his feet. "Yeah, show me. I want to see."

He got his b.b. gun from his room, and the two of them walked silently up the dark street, toward Charles' house. Neither of them said much. Peretti was deep in thought, serious and solemn-faced. Charles was still dazed; his mind was completely blank.

They turned down the Anderson driveway, cut through the back yard, climbed the fence, and lowered themselves cautiously into Charles' back yard. There was no movement. The yard was silent. The front door of the house was closed.

They peered through the living room window. The shades were down, but a narrow crack of yellow streamed out. Sitting on the couch was Mrs. Walton, sewing a cotton T-shirt. There was a sad, troubled look on her large face. She worked listlessly, without interest. Opposite her was the father-thing. Leaning back in his father's easy chair, its shoes off, reading the evening newspaper. The TV was on, playing to itself in the corner. A can of beer rested on the arm of the easy chair. The father-thing sat exactly as his own father had sat; it had learned a lot.

"Looks just like him," Peretti whispered suspiciously. "You sure you're not bulling me?"

Charles led him to the garage and showed him the trash barrel. Peretti reached his long tanned arms down and carefully pulled up the dry, flaking remains. They spread out, unfolded, until the whole figure of his father was outlined. Peretti laid the remains on the floor and pieced broken parts back into place. The remains were colorless. Almost transparent. An amber yellow, thin as paper. Dry and utterly lifeless.

"That's all," Charles said. Tears welled up in his eyes. "That's all that's left of him. The thing has the insides."

Peretti had turned pale. Shakily, he crammed the remains back in the trash barrel. "This is really something," he muttered. "You say you saw the two of them together?"

"Talking. They looked exactly alike. I ran inside." Charles wiped the tears away and sniveled; he couldn't hold it back any longer. "It ate him while I was inside. Then it came in the house. It pretended it was him. But it isn't. It killed him and ate his insides."

For a moment Peretti was silent. "I'll tell you something," he said suddenly. "I've heard about this sort of thing. It's a bad business. You have to use your head and not get scared. You're not scared, are you?"

"No," Charles managed to mutter.

"The first thing we have to do is figure out how to kill it." He rattled his b.b. gun. "I don't know if this'll work. It must be plenty tough to get hold of your father. He was a big man." Peretti considered. "Let's get out of here. It might come back. They say that's what a murderer does."

They left the garage. Peretti crouched down and peeked through the window again. Mrs. Walton had got to her feet. She was talking anxiously. Vague sounds filtered out. The father-thing threw down its newspaper. They were arguing.

"For God's sake!" the father-thing shouted. "Don't do anything stupid like that."

"Something's wrong," Mrs. Walton moaned. "Something terrible. Just let me call the hospital and see."

"Don't call anybody. He's all right. Probably up the street playing."

"He's never out this late. He never disobeys. He was terribly upset—afraid of you! I don't blame him." Her voice broke with misery. "What's wrong with you? You're so strange." She moved out of the room, into the hall. "I'm going to call some of the neighbors."

The father-thing glared after her until she had disappeared. Then a terrifying thing happened. Charles gasped; even Peretti grunted under his breath.

"Look," Charles muttered. "What—"

"Golly," Peretti said, black eyes wide.

As soon as Mrs. Walton was gone from the room, the father-thing sagged in its chair. It became limp. Its mouth fell open. Its eyes peered vacantly. Its head fell forward, like a discarded rag doll.

Peretti moved away from the window. "That's it," he whispered. "That's the whole thing."

"What is it?" Charles demanded. He was shocked and bewildered. "It looked like somebody turned off its power."

"Exactly." Peretti nodded slowly, grim and shaken. "It's controlled from outside."

Horror settled over Charles. "You mean, something outside our world?"

Peretti shook his head with disgust. "Outside the house! In the yard. You know how to find?"

"Not very well." Charles pulled his mind together. "But I know somebody who's good at finding." He forced his mind to summon the name. "Bobby Daniels."

"That little black kid? Is he good at finding?"

"The best."

"All right," Peretti said. "Let's go get him. We have to find the thing that's outside. That made *it* in there, and keeps it going . . ."

"It's near the garage," Peretti said to the small, thin-faced Negro boy who crouched beside them in the darkness. "When it got him, he was in the garage. So look there."

"In the garage?" Daniels asked.

"*Around* the garage. Walton's already gone over the garage, inside. Look around outside. Nearby."

There was a small bed of flowers growing by the garage, and a great tangle of bamboo and discarded debris between the garage and the back of the house. The moon had come out; a cold, misty light filtered down over everything. "If we don't find it pretty soon," Daniels said, "I got to go back home. I can't stay up much later." He wasn't any older than Charles. Perhaps nine.

"All right," Peretti agreed. "Then get looking."

The three of them spread out and began to go over the ground with care. Daniels worked with incredible speed; his thin little body moved in a blur of motion as he crawled among the flowers, turned over rocks, peered under the house, separated stalks of plants, ran his expert hands over leaves and stems, in tangles of compost and weeds. No inch was missed.

Peretti halted after a short time. "I'll guard. It might be dangerous. The father-thing might come and try to stop us." He posted himself on the back step with his b.b. gun while Charles and Bobby Daniels searched. Charles worked slowly. He was tired, and his body was cold and numb. It seemed impossible, the father-thing and what had happened to his own father, his real father. But terror spurred him on; what if it happened to his mother, or to him? Or to everyone? Maybe the whole world.

"I found it!" Daniels called in a thin, high voice. "You all come around here quick!"

Peretti raised his gun and got up cautiously. Charles hurried over; he turned the flickering yellow beam of his flashlight where Daniels stood.

The Negro boy had raised a concrete stone. In the moist, rotting soil the light gleamed on a metallic body. A thin, jointed thing with endless crooked legs was digging frantically. Plated, like an ant; a red-brown bug that rapidly disappeared before their eyes. Its rows of legs scabbed and clutched. The ground gave rapidly under it. Its wicked-looking tail twisted furiously as it struggled down the tunnel it had made.

Peretti ran into the garage and grabbed up the rake. He pinned down the tail of the bug with it. "Quick! Shoot it with the b.b. gun!"

Daniels snatched the gun and took aim. The first shot tore the tail of the bug loose. It writhed and twisted frantically; its tail dragged uselessly and some of its legs broke off. It was a foot long, like a great millipede. It struggled desperately to escape down its hole.

"Shoot again," Peretti ordered.

Daniels fumbled with the gun. The bug slithered and hissed. Its head jerked back and forth; it twisted and bit at the rake holding it down. Its wicked specks of eyes gleamed with hatred. For a moment it struck futilely at the rake; then abruptly, without warning, it thrashed in a frantic convulsion that made them all draw away in fear.

Something buzzed through Charles' brain. A loud humming, metallic and harsh, a billion metal wires dancing and vibrating at once. He was tossed about violently by the force; the banging crash of metal made him deaf and confused. He stumbled to his feet and backed off; the others were doing the same, white-faced and shaken.

"If we can't kill it with the gun," Peretti gasped, "we can drown it. Or burn it. Or stick a pin through its brain." He fought to hold onto the rake, to keep the bug pinned down.

"I have a jar of formaldehyde," Daniels muttered. His fingers fumbled nervously with the b.b. gun. "How do this thing work? I can't seem to—"

Charles grabbed the gun from him. "I'll kill it." He squatted down, one eye to the sight, and gripped the trigger. The bug lashed and struggled. Its force-field hammered in his ears, but he hung onto the gun. His finger tightened . . .

"All right, Charles," the father-thing said. Powerful fingers gripped him, a paralyzing pressure around his wrists. The gun fell to the ground as he struggled futilely. The father-thing shoved against Peretti. The boy leaped away and the bug, free of the rake, slithered triumphantly down its tunnel.

"You have a spanking coming, Charles," the father-thing droned on. "What got into you? Your poor mother's out of her mind with worry."

It had been there, hiding in the shadows. Crouched in the darkness watching them. Its calm, emotionless voice, a dreadful parody of his father's, rumbled close to his ear as it pulled him relentlessly toward the garage. Its cold breath blew in his face, an icy-sweet odor, like decaying soil. Its strength was immense; there was nothing he could do.

"Don't fight me," it said calmly. "Come along, into the garage. This is for your own good. I know best, Charles."

"Did you find him?" his mother called anxiously, opening the back door.

"Yes, I found him."

"What are you going to do?"

"A little spanking." The father-thing pushed up the garage door. "In the garage." In the half-light a faint smile, humorless and utterly without emotion, touched its lips. "You go back in the living room, June. I'll take care of this. It's more in my line. You never did like punishing him."

The back door reluctantly closed. As the light cut off, Peretti bent down and groped for the b.b. gun. The father-thing instantly froze.

"Go on home, boys," it rasped.

Peretti stood undecided, gripping the b.b. gun.

"Get going," the father-thing repeated. "Put down that toy and get out of here." It moved slowly toward Peretti, gripping Charles with one hand, reaching toward Peretti with the other. "No b.b. guns allowed in town, sonny. Your father know you have that? There's a city ordinance. I think you better give me that before—"

Peretti shot it in the eye.

The father-thing grunted and pawed at its ruined eye. Abruptly it slashed out at Peretti. Peretti moved down the driveway, trying to cock the gun. The father-thing lunged. Its powerful fingers snatched the gun from Peretti's hands.

Silently, the father-thing mashed the gun against the wall of the house.

Charles broke away and ran numbly off. Where could he hide? It was between him and the house. Already, it was coming back toward him, a black shape creeping carefully, peering into the darkness, trying to make him out. Charles retreated. If there were only some place he could hide . . .

The bamboo.

He crept quickly into the bamboo. The stalks were huge and old. They closed after him with a faint rustle. The father-thing was fumbling in its pocket; it lit a match, then the whole pack flared up. "Charles," it said. "I know you're here, someplace. There's no use hiding. You're only making it more difficult."

His heart hammering, Charles crouched among the bamboo. Here, debris and filth rotted. Weeds, garbage, papers, boxes, old clothing, boards, tin cans, bottles. Spiders and salamanders squirmed around him. The bamboo swayed with the night wind. Insects and filth.

And something else.

A shape, a silent, unmoving shape that grew up from the mound of filth like some nocturnal mushroom. A white column, a pulpy mass that glistened moistly in the moonlight. Webs covered it, a moldy cocoon. It had vague arms and legs. An indistinct half-shaped head. As yet, the features hadn't formed. But he could tell what it was.

A mother-thing. Growing here in the filth and dampness, between the garage and the house. Behind the towering bamboo.

It was almost ready. Another few days and it would reach maturity. It was still a larva, white and soft and pulpy. But the sun would dry and warm it. Harden its shell. Turn it dark and strong. It would emerge from its cocoon, and one day when his mother came by the garage . . . Behind the mother-thing were other pulpy white larvae, recently laid by the bug. Small. Just coming into existence. He could see where the father-thing had broken off; the place where it had grown. It had matured here. And in the garage, his father had met it.

Charles began to move numbly away, past the rotting boards, the filth and debris, the pulpy mushroom larvae. Weakly, he reached out to take hold of the fence—and scrambled back.

Another one. Another larvae. He hadn't seen this one, at first. It wasn't white. It had already turned dark. The web, the pulpy softness, the moistness, were gone. It was ready. It stirred a little, moved its arm feebly.

The Charles-thing.

The bamboo separated, and the father-thing's hand clamped firmly around the boy's wrist. "You stay right here," it said. "This is exactly the place for you. Don't move." With its other hand it tore at the remains of the cocoon binding the Charles-thing. "I'll help it out—it's still a little weak."

The last shred of moist gray was stripped back, and the Charles-thing tottered out. It floundered uncertainly, as the father-thing cleared a path for it toward Charles.

"This way," the father-thing grunted. "I'll hold him for you. When you've fed you'll be stronger."

The Charles-thing's mouth opened and closed. It reached greedily toward Charles. The boy struggled wildly, but the father-thing's immense hand held him down.

"Stop that, young man," the father-thing commanded. "It'll be a lot easier for you if you—"

It screamed and convulsed. It let go of Charles and staggered back. Its body twitched violently. It crashed against the garage, limbs jerking. For a time it rolled and flopped in a dance of agony. It whimpered, moaned, tried to crawl away. Gradually it became quiet. The Charles-thing settled down in a silent heap. It lay stupidly among the bamboo and rotting debris, body slack, face empty and blank.

At last the father-thing ceased to stir. There was only the faint rustle of the bamboo in the night wind.

Charles got up awkwardly. He stepped down onto the cement driveway. Peretti and Daniels approached, wide-eyed and cautious. "Don't go near it," Daniels ordered sharply. "It ain't dead yet. Takes a little while."

"What did you do?" Charles muttered.

Daniels set down the drum of kerosene with a gasp of relief. "Found this in the garage. We Daniels always used kerosene on our mosquitoes, back in Virginia."

"Daniels poured the kerosene down the bug's tunnel," Peretti explained, still awed. "It was his idea."

Daniels kicked cautiously at the contorted body of the father-thing. "It's dead, now. Died as soon as the bug died."

"I guess the other'll die, too," Peretti said. He pushed

aside the bamboo to examine the larvae growing here and there among the debris. The Charles-thing didn't move at all, as Peretti jabbed the end of a stick into its chest. "This one's dead."

"We better make sure," Daniels said grimly. He picked up the heavy drum of kerosene and lugged it to the edge of the bamboo. "It dropped some matches in the driveway. You get them, Peretti."

They looked at each other.

"Sure," Peretti said softly.

"We better turn on the hose," Charles said. "To make sure it doesn't spread."

"Let's get going," Peretti said impatiently. He was already moving off. Charles quickly followed him and they began searching for the matches, in the moonlit darkness.

Born of Man and Woman
Richard Matheson

Whether Richard Matheson (1926–) is writing horror fiction or science fiction, his concern is always with how the average person copes with a world that has suddenly become hostile to his or her existence. In his first novel, *I Am Legend*, he imagined a near-future world in which a virus has transformed all but one man into a vampire, and in *The Shrinking Man*, how malign a normal environment might become to someone slowly shrinking to submicroscopic size. "Born of Man and Woman," Matheson's first published story from the Summer 1950 *Magazine of Fantasy and Science Fiction*, can be read as a forerunner to these well-known works, with its oblique examination of how the nuclear family adapts to the birth of a monster child.

X—This day when it had light mother called me a retch. You retch she said. I saw in her eyes the anger. I wonder what it is a retch.

This day it had water falling from upstairs. It fell all around. I saw that. The ground of the back I watched from the little window. The ground it sucked up the water like thirsty lips. It drank too much and it got sick and runny brown. I didn't like it.

Mother is a pretty I know. In my bed place with cold walls around I have a paper things that was behind the furnace. It says on it SCREENSTARS. I see in the pictures faces like of mother and father. Father says they are pretty. Once he said it.

And also mother he said. Mother so pretty and me decent enough. Look at you he said and didn't have the nice face. I touched his arm and said it is alright father. He shook and pulled away where I couldn't reach.

Today mother let me off the chain a little so I could look

out the little window. That's how I saw the water falling from upstairs.

XX—This day it had goldness in the upstairs. As I know, when I looked at it my eyes hurt. After I look at it the cellar is red.

I think this was church. They leave the upstairs. The big machine swallows them and rolls out past and is gone. In the back part is the *little* mother. She is much small than me. I am big. It is a secret but I have pulled the chain out of the wall. I can see out the little window all I like.

In this day when it got dark I had eat my food and some bugs. I hear laughs upstairs. I like to know why there are laughs for. I took the chain from the wall and wrapped it around me. I walked squish to the stairs. They creak when I walk on them. My legs slip on them because I don't walk on stairs. My feet stick to the wood.

I went up and opened a door. It was a white place. White as white jewels that come from upstairs sometime. I went in and stood quiet. I hear the laughing some more. I walk to the sound and look through to the people. More people than I thought was. I thought I should laugh with them.

Mother came out and pushed the door in. It hit me and hurt. I fell back on the smooth floor and the chain made noise. I cried. She made a hissing noise into her and put her hand on her mouth. Her eyes got big.

She looked at me. I heard father call. What fell he called. She said a iron board. Come help pick it up she said. He came and said now is *that* so heavy you need. He saw me and grew big. The anger came in his eyes. He hit me. I spilled some of the drip on the floor from one arm. It was not nice. It made ugly green on the floor.

Father told me to go to the cellar. I had to go. The light it hurt some now in my eyes. It is not so like that in the cellar.

Father tied my legs and arms up. He put me on my bed. Upstairs I heard laughing while I was quiet there looking on a black spider that was swinging down to me. I thought what father said. Ohgod he said. And only eight.

XXX—This day father hit in the chain again before it had light. I have to try pull it out again. He said I was bad to come upstairs. He said never do that again or he would beat me hard. That hurts.

I hurt. I slept the day and rested my head against the cold wall. I thought of the white place upstairs.

XXXX—I got the chain from the wall out. Mother was upstairs. I heard little laughs very high. I looked out the window. I saw all little people like the little mother and little fathers too. They are pretty.

They were making nice noise and jumping around the ground. Their legs was moving hard. They are like mother and father. Mother says all right people look like they do.

One of the little fathers saw me. He pointed at the window. I let go and slid down the wall in the dark. I curled up as they would not see. I heard their talks by the window and foots running. Upstairs there was a door hitting. I heard the little mother call upstairs. I heard heavy steps and I rushed to my bed place. I hit the chain in the wall and lay down on my front.

I heard mother come down. Have you been at the window she said. I heard the anger. *Stay* away from the window. You have pulled the chain out again.

She took the stick and hit me with it. I didn't cry. I can't do that. But the drip ran all over the bed. She saw it and twisted away and made a noise. Oh mygod mygod she said why have you *done* this to me? I heard the stick go bounce on the stone floor. She ran upstairs. I slept the day.

XXXXX—This day it had water again. When mother was upstairs I heard the little one come slow down the steps. I hidded myself in the coal bin for mother would have anger if the little mother saw me.

She had a little live thing with her. It walked on the arms and had pointy ears. She said things to it.

It was all right except the live thing smelled me. It ran up the coal and looked down at me. The hairs stood up. In the throat it made an angry noise. I hissed but it jumped on me.

I didn't want to hurt it. I got fear because it bit me harder than the rat does. I hurt and the little mother screamed. I grabbed the live thing tight. It made sounds I never heard. I pushed it all together. It was all lumpy and red on the black coal.

I hid there when mother called. I was afraid of the stick.

She left. I crept over the coal with the thing. I hid it under my pillow and rested on it. I put the chain in the wall again.

X—This is another times. Father chained me tight. I hurt because he beat me. This time I hit the stick out of his hands and made noise. He went away and his face was white. He ran out of my bed place and locked the door.

I am not so glad. All day it is cold in here. The chain comes slow out of the wall. And I have a bad anger with mother and father. I will show them. I will do what I did that once.

I will screech and laugh loud. I will run on the walls. Last I will hang head down by all my legs and laugh and drip green all over until they are sorry they didn't be nice to me.

If they try to beat me again I'll hurt them. I will.

Hell-Fire

Isaac Asimov

Although Isaac Asimov (1920–92) is the most prolific writer of all time, little of his greatly varied work falls into the horror category. However, many of his science fiction stories have a dark streak running through them. The classic "Nightfall" is about a fundamental inability to overcome fear of the dark, and the three novels that make up Asimov's initial "Foundation Trilogy" published in the 1950s—*Foundation, Foundation and Empire, Second Foundation*—capture the postwar angst of a world frightened by its self-destructive capabilities. "Hell-Fire" appeared in the May 1956 *Fantastic Universe*, and can be read as Asimov's judgment on the event that ignited the nuclear age.

There was a stir as of a very polite first-night audience. Only a handful of scientists were present, a sprinkling of high brass, some Congressmen, a few newsmen.

Alvin Horner of the Washington Bureau of the Continental Press found himself next to Joseph Vincenzo of Los Alamos, and said, "*Now* we ought to learn something."

Vincenzo stared at him through bifocals and said, "Not the important thing."

Horner frowned. This was to be the first super-slow-motion film of an atomic explosion. With trick lenses changing directional polarization in flickers, the moment of explosion would be divided into billionth-second snaps. Yesterday, an A-bomb had explored. Today, those snaps would show the explosion in incredible detail.

Horner said, "You think this won't work?"

Vincenzo looked tormented. "It will work. We've run pilot tests. But the important thing—"

"Which is?"

"That these bombs are man's death sentence. We don't

seem to be able to learn that." Vincenzo nodded. "Look at them here. They're excited and thrilled, but not afraid."

The newsman said, "They know the danger. They're afraid, too."

"Not enough," said the scientist. "I've seen men watch an H-bomb blow an island into a hole and then go home and sleep. That's the way men are. For thousands of years, hell-fire has been preached to them, and it's made no real impression."

"Hell-fire: Are you religious, sir?"

"What you saw yesterday was hell-fire. An exploding atom bomb is hell-fire. Literally."

That was enough for Horner. He got up and changed his seat, but watched the audience uneasily. Were any afraid? Did any worry about hell-fire? It didn't seem so to him.

The lights went out, the projector started. On the screen, the firing tower stood gaunt. The audience grew tensely quiet.

Then a dot of light appeared at the apex of the tower, a brilliant, burning point, slowly budding in a lazy, outward elbowing, this way and that, taking on uneven shapes of light and shadow, growing oval.

A man cried out chokingly, then others. A hoarse babble of noise, followed by thick silence. Horner could smell fear, taste terror in his own mouth, feel his blood freeze.

The oval fireball had sprouted projections, then paused a moment in stasis, before expanding rapidly into a bright and featureless sphere.

That moment of stasis—the fireball had shown dark spots for eyes, with dark lines for thin, flaring eyebrows, a hairline coming down V-shaped, a mouth twisted upward, laughing wildly in the hell-fire—and horns.

Nightmare Gang

Dean Koontz

Today Dean Koontz (1945–) is typically thought of as a writer of terror, although his work for the past decade—in particular the novels *Strangers, Lightning, Midnight, Cold Fire,* and *Mr. Murder*—blends science fiction, mystery, suspense, horror, and even romance elements. His 1970 tale "Nightmare Gang" was written during a time period when his work appeared almost exclusively in science fiction publications. The shocking revelation at its ending anticipates the skillful blending of styles that has made his recent books perennial best sellers.

Cottery was a knife man. He carried six of them laid flat and invisible against his lean body, and with these half dozen confidence-boosters giving him adequate courage, he challenged Louis to a fight, for he envisioned himself as the leader of the gang. It was over inside of two minutes. Louis moved faster than he had any right to. He avoided Cottery's blades just as if he already knew from which directions they would be swung. He delivered several punches to Cottery that looked like a small boy's blows in a playful bout with his father, but he crippled Cottery with them as surely as he would have wielding sledgehammers. The knife man went down and threw up all over his own shoes.

It was an object lesson.

One was all we needed.

Louis had many holds on us. Although he did not look it, the fight with Cottery proved that he was somehow our physical superior. Of course, there was also the fact that only Louis knew who we were; none of the gang members could remember any past, beyond joining the gang. I'm sure that all of us, at one time or another, tried to find out who we were, but beyond the moment when we were enlisted by Louis, our memories ended at a tall, obsidian wall that could not be breached. Indeed, it was mentally and physically painful to try to remember. Ask Louis? He would only smile and walk away, and that just made us twice as curious.

And only Louis knew our future.

It seemed that there was some purpose to the gang, to the slow growth of our numbers, though no one could fathom what it might be. But leave the group and make our own futures? Butch, our barbarian giant, tried that. He had driven his cycle only a hundred yards on his break for freedom when the cramps hit him and he took the spill at thirty-five miles an hour, skinning himself real bad.

Louis was our jailer; the gang was our prison; and the heavy, black cycles were the bars that contained us.

Then came the run down the Atlantic coast, the pounding of the cycles in the super-heated air, nights on the beaches buffeted by the sound of the waves as we slept, plenty of beer that Louis bought for us (he was the only one with money). On that run, I found out what I was. And what Louis was. And what was going to happen to all of us . . .

Cruising the ocean roads to take in the tourist trap towns like White City, Ankona, Palm Beach, and Boca Raton, we made a wild sight. Flowery-shirted tourists and their matronish wives always pulled off to let us go by, their faces white, the men wiping sudden perspiration from their brows. There were twelve of us in the gang, plus Louis. As in any group, there were those who stood out. Butch was six and a half feet and three hundred pounds, another twenty-five pounds for boots and chains and Levi's. There was Jimmy-Joe, stiletto thin little bastard with skin like candle wax and wild, red-rimmed eyes like the eyes of a hunting hawk. He giggled and talked to himself and did not make friends. Yul was the weapons nut. His glittering head (even the eyebrows gone, yeah) distracted your attention from the bulges on his clothing: the pistol under his left arm pit, the coiled chain on his right arm.

The rest of the crew ranged along similar lines, though each seemed a weaker parody of those three. Except for me. I was a natural standout. Although I could be no more than twenty-five, my hair was pure white—eyebrows, chest, pubic, everything. They called me Old Man Toomey.

Then there was Louis.

Louis (you could not call him Lou; it would be like calling

Jesus Jess) did not belong in the gang. You could see that in the fine lines of his facial bones, the aristocratic look and bearing that indicated a good private schooling in manners and carriage as well as mathematics and grammar. He didn't have the constitution for the rugged life either, for he was small—five eight, a hundred and twenty pounds, no muscle on him. Yet he was the undisputed leader, the one who had brought us together and was planning what to do with us next.

It was two o'clock on the third day of our coast run, and we were just outside of Dania, Florida, when things began to change. Ahead, a souvenir shop loomed out of the sand and scrub, announced by huge hand-painted signs decorated with pictures of alligators and parrots. Louis raised his arm and motioned us off the highway. We followed him, thumping onto the berm and crunching across the white gravel between half a dozen parked cars. When the clatter and growl of our engines died, Louis dismounted and stood before his cycle, skinny legs spread wide.

"We're casing it," he said. "Don't cause any trouble. We'll be back tonight."

We had never cased a place before. This was the changing point in our existence. Somehow, I knew it was a change for the worse.

We moved inside the shop, fingering the stuffed alligators, carved coconuts, shell jewelry, and genuine Indian thatchwork. The patrons stayed clear of us, their faces pale, their voices lower, more strained than the voices of people on vacation should be. The gang always garnered this sort of reaction from the straight citizens who came into contact with it. We all got a kick out of the sensation of power our appearance gave us, even though most of us must have sensed the basic psychological sickness in such an attitude.

Louis pushed past the sales counter at the back of the store and moved toward a thick, beaded curtain that closed off another room. The clerk, a tanned and wizened little man with gray hair and a prune's share of wrinkles, grabbed him by the arm. "Where do you think you're going?" he asked. His fear quaked down in the bottom of his throat like a wet frog.

Louis didn't answer. He turned and stared at the clerk, then down at the hand that held his arm. After a moment, the clerk let go and stood rubbing his cramped fingers. I could see dark bruises on his hand, though Louis had not touched him. His face had gone totally white, and there was a tic beginning in the corner of his left eye. His fingers seemed paralyzed; he rubbed them frantically as if to restore circulation.

Free now, Louis continued to the beaded curtain and lifted some of the strands to peer through. I was near enough that I could see what was back there: an office of some sort, small, stacked with boxes of trinkets, containing a single desk and chair. Louis seemed satisfied, dropped the beads, and came back past the clerk who made no attempt to stop him this time.

"Let's go," Louis said, walking for the door.

We went.

Two miles from the souvenir shop, we found a secluded section of beach and settled down for the evening. I was still upset about the sudden change of atmosphere, the "casing" of the store. My gut churned, and I felt cold and hollow, afraid of the future simply because I had no idea what it was going to be. Butch and a Spic cat named Ernesto went into Dania for some beer, and a celebration ensued. It was obvious that all of us shared the realization that something big was going to happen, something irreversible.

Louis stayed away from us, walking the beach, stopping now and then to watch a whitecap peel along and spill its froth onto the wet sand. Several times, he threw his head back like a wolf and laughed, high and shrill, until he made his throat hoarse. Several times, when the moonlight limed his chalky features, he looked like one of those small glass animals you can buy in old-fashioned curio shops; the illusion was so real that I thought of stoning him, trying to break him. Then I thought of Cottery and the object lesson.

Half an hour after the sun had set and the first heavy waves of mosquitoes were buzzing out of the shoreline foliage, he came up the beach, kicking sand, and stopped before us. "Let's go back," he said.

I rode up front, just behind Louis. It might have been my unreasonable terror that made me try, in desperation, what I did. I could close in on Louis, I thought, take my cycle into the back of his fast enough to leap over him before we both fell. I might be hurt and hurt badly, but Louis would get his head broken sure as hell. And then we would all be free. Whatever was about to happen would not happen.

I leaned into the bars and was about to accelerate when I felt a hand close over my nose and mouth, cutting off my air. I jerked my head about, could not shake it loose. I could see no hand, only feel it. When I was beginning to grow dizzy and the cycle was wobbling under me, the hand departed, allowing me to breathe.

Louis had won again.

We roared into the parking lot and stopped our cycles behind four cars, dismounted and stood there dumbly, waiting for Louis to tell us what to do. He climbed slowly off his Triumph Tiger and turned to face us. The large orange and green neon sign that blinked and rippled overhead cast eerie shadows on his face, illuminating a wide, toothy grin that split his face like an ax wound. Then he spoke to us. Two words. There is no way to convey the manner in which he spoke the command. He did not use his lips or tongue. Instead, the words came across the front of my mind like teletype print, burning into the softness of my brain so that I squealed. There was no denying that order. No denying it at all.

Kill them!

Almost as a single organism, we moved forward, the stones making brittle protests beneath our boots, into the flourescent brightness of the souvenir shop.

There were eleven tourists in the shop, plus the clerk, the same little man who had tried to stop Louis from going to the beaded curtain that afternoon. They looked up as we came in, offered us the same timid reactions we were used to receiving. But that was not going to be enough to pacify us this evening. Not nearly enough.

Kill them!

Louis said it again. He stood by the door, grinning, watching, one foot crossed over the other and his hands shoved in his jean pocket.

We moved forward, taking out the hardware we carried.

Butch moved in ahead of me, surprisingly fast for the ox that he was, and swung a huge fist at a banker type in a loud yellow shirt and dark blue Bermuda shorts. He drove the man's nose back into his skull, splintering it into the fleshy gray of his warm brain. The banker did not even have time to scream.

Yul wrapped that steel chain around his fist, moving in on some of the women. His muscular arms, hanging bare from the sleeveless tee-shirt he wore, rippled and flowed like the stalking legs of a cat.

Jimmy-Joe had his hands full of knives. The one in his right was dripping something red.

Kill them!

I took my pistol out. It felt cold and unmanageable in my hand, and I wanted to drop it. I could not. It was as if my hand moved independently of the rest of my body.

A tall man with eyebrows that grew together over the bridge of his nose pushed past me, making for an open window on my right. I fired point blank into his chest. He looked startled, as if he had thought the bullets were blanks and the flowing blood was ketchup, then choked. His eyes watered, and tears ran down his cheeks. Then he fell over on the floor, pulling down a display of post cards.

I dropped my pistol and grabbed onto the sales counter for support. My stomach flopped. I gagged, bent over the counter and brought up my supper of cold chicken and beer.

The rest of that time was hazy, like a sun-ruined section of film. There were shots and screams and pleading voices, blurs of color. I heard a child crying, maybe a little girl. The crying stopped abruptly. Then we were moving out, following Louis, boarding the cycles and leaving the lot.

We went down off the shoulder of the highway, back along the sand to where we had eaten. I fell off my machine when it was parked and rolled over in the sand, face down, trying to think. Sometime later, Butch tapped me on the shoulder and offered me a beer. I declined, then rolled on my back to see what was happening among the rest of them. It was not what I had expected. Jimmy-Joe was standing in the center of the group, playing the part of a woman whose throat he had slit, alternately taking his own role in the affair. When he reached the point where he skewered her throat, the gang laughed and other stories began being exchanged.

Someone broke out several bottles of vodka when the beer ran out, and the party got noisier. I stood up and pushed my way through the gang, trying to reach Louis where he sat next to the tide line. I passed Yul who had droplets of blood spattered across his bald head like freckles. Jimmy-Joe was honing his knives on coral. Butch, his eyes very round and wild, was licking an unknown victim's blood from his hands.

When I reached Louis, he turned and shook his head to let me know he would not talk with me. I tried to say something anyway, but there was an invisible hand in my throat that stopped the words from forming, much like the hand that had almost smothered me when I had thought of killing him. I stood, watching him for some time. He was reading a

newspaper, the Miami *Herald.* After a long time, he carefully tore an article from the front page, folded it, and
tucked it in his shirt pocket. Standing, he called to the gang
and explained that he would be gone until morning and that
we were to enjoy ourselves. Then he was on his Tiger, moving across the sand, gone.

Everyone was silent for a moment, for we all knew what
this meant. The only times Louis left us was when he was
going to recruit a new gang member. When the idea had
sunk in, the revelry began again, slowly at first, then picking
up speed and becoming boisterous and jubilant.

I went to the edge of the water and picked up the paper.
There was no way to tell what the story had been about, for
he had removed all of it. Then I remembered the Gulf station
a quarter of a mile back the road. It was highly possible the
station had a vendor for the *Herald*—or at least that the attendant had a copy of his own. Somehow, the story in the paper tied in with the new recruit. I guess I had some idea that
it would shed some light on my own past too. Without thinking of the cycle, I struck out along the beach, crawled up the
embankment to the highway, and walked to the service station.

There were two copies of the *Herald* left. When I was
about to buy one, I remembered I had no money. Luckily, a
car drove up, requiring the attendant's attention, which left
me free to steal. I ran all the way back to our camp, fighting
the urge to look at it.

On the beach, I spread out the mutilated paper that Louis had
been reading, then opened my whole copy and compared them
to see what had been torn out. I read the article twice to make
certain I was not wrong. Then I threw both papers into the water and went back to my cycle. I did not sleep that night.

In the morning, when Louis came back, I was awake, my
eyes stinging, but my mind alert. He brought the new recruit
with him, a fellow by the name of Burton Kade. He was the
same Burton Kade that had been the focal point of that newspaper article. He matched the front page picture in ever detail.
Eleven months ago, Kade had used a shotgun on his mother
and father while they had lain asleep in bed. Then he had gone
on to systematically beat to death his two young brothers, one
eight and one ten. He had been executed yesterday morning.

There was a very ugly thought in my mind, one that I did
not want to face up to. To avoid it, I began thinking rapidly
of other things, of Louis and what he might be. A demon?

That seemed unlikely. Why would a demon have to summon up a dead maniac to commit violence when the demon himself could do far worse with his own powers?

No, not a demon, not a devil. I began to remember things about Louis, things that started fitting together in an unpleasant way. There had been the time he had defeated Cottery with childish blows. The time Butch had gotten cramps and wrecked because he was trying to leave the gang. The bruises on the clerk's arm, though Louis had not visibly touched him. The invisible hand smothering me when I tried to kill him. These were examples of . . . what? Mind-over-matter—one of those extrasensory perceptions you hear so much about? In that last instance, there had been a case of telepathy, for the lousy kid had known what I was thinking, had known I wanted to kill him.

This skinny little monster did not seem like the first of a new race: the first esper, the first man able to warp the realities of life and death to recover a body from the grave. Yet . . . he was. The first of a new race . . . and tainted with madness. Maybe that is the price to be paid in this new evolutionary step; maybe all espers will be monsters like Louis. Or perhaps Nature will correct this mistake and make them benevolent. I don't really care. All I know or care about is that Louis is a beast, and it is Louis who is here now, Louis who shapes my future.

And what was my past? What did I do that was so horrible as to turn every hair on my body white, even though I am only twenty-five?

I do know what is going to happen to us. There have been two massacres since that first, there will be many more. We will never be caught, for Louis uses his psychic powers to search for clues before we leave a scene, uses them to wipe the minds clean of anyone who accidentally sees us.

I am afraid we are immortal: we will go on killing until even the sun is black and hard and dead. We have been brought back from the grave, an even baker's dozen of ghouls. We are the Nightmare Gang that sweeps, gibbering, out of the night and lays waste to whatever comes before it.

We are the Nightmare Gang. We kill while Louis watches, laughing, clutching his sides with his skinny arms.

And the worst thing, the very worst thing is that I think I am beginning to enjoy myself.

Soft

F. Paul Wilson

When F. Paul Wilson (1946–) began writing fiction, there were few outlets for horror, thus his novels *Healer, Wheels Within Wheels,* and *An Enemy of the State* were marketed as science fiction. Today Wilson is recognized as one of the leading writers of horror fiction to emerge from the 1980s, although his work sometimes features science fictional trappings and is informed by training as a physician. "Soft," a 1984 story, can be read as an early allegorical treatment of the AIDS epidemic, but like all of Wilson's fiction it focuses on the behaviors that surface when human beings cope with crises.

I was lying on the floor watching TV and exercising what was left of my legs when the newscaster's jaw collapsed. He was right in the middle of the usual plea for anybody who thought they were immune to come to Rockefeller Center when—*pflumpf!*—the bottom of his face went soft.

I burst out laughing.

"Daddy!" Judy said, shooting me a razor blade look from her wheelchair.

I shut up.

She was right. Nothing funny about a man's tongue wiggling around in the air snake-like while his lower jaw flopped down in front of his throat like a sack of Jell-O and his bottom teeth jutted at the screen crowns-on, rippling like a line of buoys on a bay. A year ago I would have gagged. But I've changed in ways other than physical since this mess began, and couldn't help feeling good about one of those pretty-boy newsreaders going soft right in front of the camera. I almost wished I had a bigger screen so I could watch 21 color inches of the scene. He was barely visible on our 5-inch black-and-white.

The room filled with white noise as the screen went blank.

Someone must have taken a look at what was going out on the airwaves and pulled the plug. Not that many people were watching anyway.

I flipped the set off to save the batteries. Batteries were as good as gold now. *Better* than gold. Who wanted gold nowadays?

I looked over at Judy and she was crying softly. Tears slid down her cheeks.

"Hey, hon—"

"I can't help it, Daddy. I'm so *scared!*"

"Don't be, Jude. Don't worry. Everything will work out, you'll see. We've got this thing licked, you and me."

"How can you be so sure?"

"Because it hasn't progressed in weeks! It's over for us— we've got immunity."

She glanced down at her legs, then quickly away. "It's already too late for me."

I reached over and patted my dancer on the hand. "Never too late for you, shweetheart," I said in my best Bogart. That got a tiny smile out of her.

We sat there in the silence, each thinking our own thoughts. The newsreader had said the cause of the softness had been discovered: a virus, a freak mutation that disrupted the calcium matrix of bones.

Yeah. Sure. That's what they said last year when the first cases cropped up in Boston. A virus. But they never isolated the virus, and the softness spread all over the world. So they began searching for "a subtle and elusive environmental toxin." They never pinned that one down either.

Now we were back to a virus again. Who cared? It didn't matter. Judy and I had beat it. Whether we had formed the right antibodies or the right antitoxin was just a stupid academic question. The process had been arrested in us. Sure, it had done some damage, but it wasn't doing any more, and that was the important thing. We'd never be the same, but we were going to live!

"But that man," Judy said, nodding toward the TV. "He said they were looking for people in whom the disease had started and then stopped. That's us, Dad. They said they need to examine people like us so they can find out how to fight it, maybe develop a serum against it. We should—"

"Judy-Judy-Judy!" I said in Cary Grantese to hide my annoyance. How many times did I have to go over this?

"We've been through all this before. I told you: It's too late for them. Too late for everybody but us immunes."

I didn't want to discuss it—Judy didn't understand about those kind of people, how you can't deal with them.

"I want you to take me down there," she said in the tone she used when she wanted to be stubborn. "If you don't want to help, okay. But *I* do."

"No!" I said that louder than I wanted to and she flinched. More softly: "I know those people. I worked all those years in the Health Department. They'd turn us into lab specimens. They'll suck us dry and use our immunity to try and save themselves."

"But I want to help *some*body! I don't want us to be the last two people on earth!"

She began to cry again.

Judy was frustrated. I could understand that. She was unable to leave the apartment by herself and probably saw me at times as a dictator who had her at his mercy. And she was frightened, probably more frightened than I could imagine. She was only eighteen and everyone she had ever known in her life—including her mother—was dead.

I hoisted myself into the chair next to her and put my arm around her shoulders. She was the only person in the world who mattered to me. That had been true even before the softness began.

"We're not alone. Take George, for example. And I'm sure there are plenty of other immunes around, hiding like us. When the weather warms up, we'll find each other and start everything over new. But until then, we can't allow the bloodsuckers to drain off whatever it is we've got that protects us."

She nodded without saying anything. I wondered if she was agreeing with me or just trying to shut me up.

"Let's eat," I said with a gusto I didn't really feel.

"Not hungry."

"Got to keep up your strength. We'll have soup. How's that sound?"

She smiled weakly. "Okay ... soup."

I forgot and almost tried to stand up. Old habits die hard. My lower legs were hanging over the edge of the chair like a pair of sand-filled dancer's tights. I could twitch the muscles and see them ripple under the skin, but a muscle is pretty useless unless it's attached to a bone, and the bones down there were gone.

I slipped off my chair to what was left of my knees and shuffled over to the stove. The feel of those limp and useless leg muscles squishing under me was repulsive but I was getting used to it.

It hit the kids and old people first, supposedly because their bones were a little soft to begin with, then moved on to the rest of us, starting at the bottom and working its way up—sort of like a Horatio Alger success story. At least that's the way it worked in most people. There were exceptions, of course, like that newscaster. I had followed true to form: My left lower leg collapsed at the end of last month; my right went a few days later. It wasn't a terrible shock. My feet had already gone soft so I knew the legs were next. Besides, I'd heard the sound.

The sound comes in the night when all is quiet. It starts a day or two before a bone goes. A soft sound, like someone gently crinkling cellophane inside your head. No one else can hear it. Only you. I think it comes from the bone itself—from millions of tiny fractures slowly interconnecting into a mosaic that eventually causes the bone to dissolve into mush. Like an on-rushing train far, far away can be heard if you press your ear to the track, so the sound of each microfracture transmits from bone to bone until it reaches your middle ear.

I haven't heard the sound in almost four weeks. I thought I did a couple of times and broke out in a cold, shaking sweat, but no more of my bones have gone. Neither have Judy's. The average case goes from normal person to lump of jelly in three to four weeks. Sometimes it takes longer, but there's always a steady progression. Nothing more has happened to me or Judy since last month.

Somehow, some way, we're immune.

With my lower legs dragging behind me, I got to the counter of the kitchenette and kneed my way up the stepstool to where I could reach things. I filled a pot with water—at least the pressure was still up—and set it on the Sterno stove. With gas and electricity long gone, Sterno was a lifesaver.

While waiting for the water to boil I went to the window and looked out. The late afternoon March sky was full of dark gray clouds streaking to the east. Nothing moving on

West 16th Street one floor below but a few windblown leaves from God-knows-where. I glanced across at the windows of George's apartment, looking for movement but finding none, then back down to the street below.

I hadn't seen anybody but George on the street for ages, hadn't seen or smelled smoke in well over two months. The last fires must have finally burned themselves out. The riots were one direct result of the viral theory. Half the city went up in the big riot last fall—half the city and an awful lot of people. Seems someone got the bright idea that if all the people going soft were put out of their misery and their bodies burned, the plague could be stopped, at least here in Manhattan. The few cops left couldn't stop the mobs. In fact a lot of the city's ex-cops had been *in* the mobs! Judy and I lost our apartment when our building went up. Luckily we hadn't any signs of softness then. We got away with our lives and little else.

"Water's boiling, Dad," Judy said from across the room.

I turned and went back to the stove, not saying anything, still thinking about how fast our nice rent-stabilized apartment house had burned, taking everything we had with it.

Everything was gone ... furniture and futures ... gone. All my plans. Gone. Here I stood—if you could call it that—a man with a college education, a B.S. in biology, a secure city job, and what was left? No job. Hell—no *city*! I'd had it all planned for my dancer. She was going to make it *so* big. I'd hang on to my city job with all those civil service idiots in the Department of Health, putting up with their sniping and their back-stabbing and their lousy office politics so I could keep all the fringe benefits and foot the bill while Judy pursued the dance. She was going to have it *all*! Now what? All her talent, all her potential ... where was it going?

Going soft ...

I poured the dry contents of the Lipton envelope into the boiling water and soon the odor of chicken noodle soup filled the room.

Which meant we'd have company soon.

I dragged the stepstool over to the door. Already I could hear their claws begin to scrape against the outer surface of the door, their tiny teeth begin to gnaw at its edges. I climbed up and peered through the hole I'd made last month at what had then been eye-level.

There they were. The landing was full of them. Gray and brown and dirty, with glinty little eyes and naked tails. Revulsion rippled down my skin. I watched their growing numbers every day now, every time I cooked something, but still hadn't got used to them.

So I did Cagney for them: "Yooou diiirty raaats!" and turned to wink at Judy on the far side of the fold-out bed. Her expression remained grim.

Rats. They were taking over the city. They seemed to be immune to the softness and were traveling in packs that got bigger and bolder with each passing day. Which was why I'd chosen this building for us: Each apartment was boxed in with pre-stressed concrete block. No rats in the walls here.

I waited for the inevitable. Soon it happened: A number of them squealed, screeched, and thrashed as the crowding pushed them at each other's throats, and then there was bedlam out there. I didn't bother to watch any more. I saw it every day. The pack jumped on the wounded ones. Never failed. They were so hungry they'd eat anything, even each other. And while they were fighting among themselves they'd leave us in peace with our soup.

Soon I had the card table between us and we were sipping the yellow broth and those tiny noodles. I did a lot of *mmm—good*ing but got no response from Judy. Her eyes were fixed on the walkie-talkie on the end table.

"How come we haven't heard from him?"

Good question—one that had been bothering me for a couple of days now. Where *was* George? Usually he stopped by every other day or so to see if there was anything we needed. And if he didn't stop by, he'd call us on the walkie-talkie. We had an arrangement between us that we'd both turn on our headsets every day at six P.M. just in case we needed to be in touch. I'd been calling over to George's place across the street at six o'clock sharp for three days running now with no result.

"He's probably wandering around the city seeing what he can pick up. He's a resourceful guy. Probably come back with something we can really use but haven't thought of."

Judy didn't flash me the anticipated smile. Instead, she frowned. "What if he went down to the research center?"

"I'm sure he didn't," I told her. "He's a trusting soul, but he's not a fool."

I kept my eyes down as I spoke. I'm not a good liar. And

that very question had been nagging at my gut. What if George had been stupid enough to present himself to the researchers? If he had, he was through. They'd never let him go and we'd never see him again.

For George wasn't an immune like us. He was different. Judy and I had caught the virus—or toxin—and defeated it. We were left with terrible scars from the battle but we had survived. We *acquired* our immunity through battle with the softness agent. George was special—he had remained untouched. He'd exposed himself to infected people for months as he helped everyone he could, and was still hard all over. Not so much as a little toe had gone soft on him. Which meant—to me at least—that George had been *born* with some sort of immunity to the softness.

Wouldn't those researchers love to get their needles and scalpels into *him*!

I wondered if they had. It was possible. George might have been picked up and brought down to the research center against his will. He told me once that he'd seen official-looking vans and cars prowling the streets, driven by guys wearing gas masks or the like. But that had been months ago and he hadn't reported anything like it since. Certainly no cars had been on this street in recent memory. I warned him time and again about roaming around in the daylight but he always laughed good-naturedly and said nobody'd ever catch him—he was too fast.

What if he'd run into someone faster?

There was only one thing to do.

"I'm going to take a stroll over to George's just to see if he's okay."

Judy gasped. "No, Dad! You can't! It's too far!"

"Only across the street."

"But your legs—"

"—are only half gone."

I'd met George shortly after the last riot. I had two hard legs then. I'd come looking for a sturdier building than the one we'd been burned out of. He helped us move in here.

I was suspicious at first, I admit that. I mean, I kept asking myself, *What does this guy want?* Turned out he only wanted to be friends. And so friends we became. He was soon the only other man I trusted in this whole world. And that being the case, I wanted a gun—for protection against all those other men I didn't trust. George told me he had stolen a bunch during the early lootings. I traded him some Sterno and batteries for a .38 and a pump-action 12-gauge shotgun with ammo for both. I promptly sawed off the barrel of the shotgun. If the need arose, I could clear a room real fast with that baby.

So it was the shotgun I reached for now. No need to fool with it—I kept its chamber empty and its magazine loaded with #5 shells. I laid it on the floor and reached into the rag bag by the door and began tying old undershirts around my knees. Maybe I shouldn't call them knees; with the lower legs and caps gone, "knee" hardly seems appropriate, but it'll have to serve.

From there it was a look through the peep hole to make sure the hall was clear, a blown kiss to Judy, then a shuffle into the hall. I was extra wary at first, ranging the landing up and down, looking for rats. But there weren't any in sight. I slung the shotgun around my neck, letting it hang in front as I started down the stairs one by one on hands and butt, knees first, each flabby lower leg dragging alongside its respective thigh.

Two flights down to the lobby, then up on my padded knees to the swinging door, a hard push through and I was out on the street.

Silence.

We kept our windows tightly closed against the cold and so I hadn't noticed the change. Now it hit me like a slap in the face. As a lifelong New Yorker I'd never heard—or *not* heard—the city like this. Even when there'd been nothing doing on your street, you could always hear that dull roar pulsing from the sky and the pavement and the walls of the buildings. It was the life sound of the city, the beating of its heart, the whisper of its breath, the susurrant rush of blood through its capillaries.

It had stopped.

The shiver that ran over me was not just the result of the sharp edge of the March wind. The street was deserted. A plague had been through here, but there were no contorted bodies strewn about. You didn't fall down and die on the spot with the softness. No, that would be too kind. You died by inches, by bone lengths, in back rooms, trapped, unable to make it to the street. No public displays of morbidity. Just solitary deaths of quiet desperation.

In a secret way I was glad everyone was gone—nobody

around to see me tooling across the sidewalk on my rag-wrapped knees like some skid row geek.

The city looked different from down here. You never realize how cracked the sidewalks are, how *dirty,* when you have legs to stand on. The buildings, their windows glaring red with the setting sun that had poked through the clouds over New Jersey, looked half again as tall as they had when I was a taller man.

I shuffled to the street and caught myself looking both ways before sliding off the curb. I smiled at the thought of getting run down by a truck on my first trip in over a month across a street that probably hadn't seen the underside of a car since December.

Despite the absurdity of it, I hurried across, and felt relief when I finally reached the far curb. Pulling open the damn doors to George's apartment building was a chore, but I slipped through both of them and into the lobby. George's bike—a light-frame Italian model ten-speeder—was there. I didn't like that. George took that bike everywhere. Of course he could have found a car and some gas and gone sightseeing and not told me, but still the sight of that bike standing there made me uneasy.

I shuffled by the silent bank of elevators, watching my longing expression reflected in their silent, immobile chrome doors as I passed. The fire door to the stairwell was a heavy one, but I squeezed through and started up the steps—backward. Maybe there was a better way, but I hadn't found it. It was all in the arms: Sit on the bottom step, get your arms back, palms down on the step above, lever yourself up. Repeat this ten times and you've done a flight of stairs. Two flights per floor. Thank the Lord or Whatever that George had decided he preferred a second-floor apartment to a penthouse after the final power failure.

It was a good thing I was going up backward. I might never have seen the rats if I'd been faced around the other way.

Just one appeared at first. Alone, it was almost cute with its twitching whiskers and its head bobbing up and down as it sniffed the air at the bottom of the flight. Then two more joined it, then another half dozen. Soon they were a brown wave, undulating up the steps toward me. I hesitated for an instant, horrified and fascinated by their numbers and all their little black eyes sweeping toward me, then I jolted myself into action. I swung the scattergun around, pumped a shell into the chamber, and let them have a blast. Dimly through the reverberating roar of the shotgun I heard a chorus of squeals and saw flashes of flying crimson blossoms, then I was ducking my face into my arms to protect my eyes from the ricocheting shot. I should have realized the danger of shooting in a cinderblock stairwell like this. Not that it would have changed things—I still had to protect myself—but I should have anticipated the ricochets.

The rats did what I'd hoped they'd do—jumped on the dead and near-dead of their number and forgot about me. I let the gun hang in front of me again and continued up the stairs to George's floor.

He didn't answer his bell but the door was unlocked. I'd warned him about that in the past but he'd only laughed in that carefree way of his. "Who's gonna pop in?" he'd say. Probably no one. But that didn't keep me from locking mine, even though George was the only one who knew where I lived. I wondered if that meant I didn't really trust George.

I put the question aside and pushed the door open.

It stank inside. And it was empty as far as I could see. But there was this sound, this wheezing, coming from one of the bedrooms. Calling his name and announcing my own so I wouldn't get my head blown off, I closed the door behind me—locked it—and followed the sound. I found George.

And retched.

George was a blob of flesh in the middle of his bed. Everything but some ribs, some of his facial bones, and the back of his skull had gone soft on him.

I stood there on my knees in shock, wondering how this could have happened. George was *immune*! He'd laughed at the softness! He'd been walking around as good as new just last week. And now . . .

His lips were dry and cracked and blue—he couldn't speak, couldn't swallow, could barely breathe. And his eyes . . . they seemed to be just floating there in a quivering pool of flesh, begging me . . . darting to his left again and again . . . begging me . . .

For what?

I looked to his left and saw the guns. He had a suitcase full of them by the bedroom door. All kinds. I picked up a heavy-looking revolver—an S&W .357—and glanced at him. He closed his eyes and I thought he smiled.

I almost dropped the pistol when I realized what he wanted.

"No, George!"

He opened his eyes again. They began to fill with tears.

"George—I can't!"

Something like a sob bubbled past his lips. And his eyes . . . his pleading eyes . . .

I stood there a long time in the stink of his bedroom, listening to him wheeze, feeling the sweat collect between my palm and the pistol grip. I knew I couldn't do it. Not George, the big, friendly, good-natured slob I'd been depending on.

Suddenly, I felt my pity begin to evaporate as a flare of irrational anger began to rise. I *had* been depending on George now that my legs were half gone, and here he'd gone soft on me. The bitter disappointment fueled the anger. I knew it wasn't right, but I couldn't help hating George just then for letting me down.

"Damn you, George!"

I raised the pistol and pointed it where I thought his brain should be. I turned my head away and pulled the trigger. Twice. The pistol jumped in my hand. The sound was deafening in the confines of the bedroom.

Then all was quiet except for the ringing in my ears. George wasn't wheezing anymore. I didn't look around. I didn't have to see. I have a good imagination.

I fled that apartment as fast as my ruined legs would carry me.

But I couldn't escape the vision of George and how he looked before I shot him. It haunted me every inch of the way home, down the now empty stairs where only a few tufts of dirty brown fur were left to indicate that rats had been swarming there, out into the dusk and across the street and up more stairs to home.

George . . . how could it be? He was immune!

Or was he? Maybe the softness had followed a different course in George, slowly building up in his system until every bone in his body was riddled with it and he went soft all at once. *God,* what a noise he must have heard when all those bones went in one shot! That was why he hadn't been able to call or answer the walkie-talkie.

But what if it had been something else? What if the virus theory was right and George was the victim of a more virulent mutation? The thought made me sick with dread. Because if that were true, it meant Judy would eventually end up like George. And I was going to have to do for her what I'd done for George.

But what of me, then? Who was going to end it for *me*? I didn't know if I had the guts to shoot myself. And what if my hands went soft before I had the chance?

I didn't want to think about it, but it wouldn't go away. I couldn't remember ever being so frightened. I almost considered going down to Rockefeller Center and presenting Judy and myself to the leechers, but killed that idea real quick. Never. I'm no jerk. I'm college-educated. A degree in biology! I know what they'd do to us!

Inside, Judy had wheeled her chair over to the door and was waiting for me. I couldn't let her know.

"Not there," I told her before she could ask, and I busied myself with putting the shotgun away so I wouldn't have to look her straight in the eyes.

"Where could he be?" Her voice was tight.

"I wish I knew. Maybe he went down to Rockefeller Center. If he did, it's the last we'll ever see of him."

"I can't believe that."

"Then tell me where else he can be."

She was silent.

I did Warner Oland's Chan: "Numbah One Dawtah is finally at loss for words. Peace reigns at last."

I could see that I failed to amuse, so I decided a change of subject was in order.

"I'm tired," I said. It was the truth. The trip across the street had been exhausting.

"Me, too." She yawned.

"Want to get some sleep?" I knew she did. I was just staying a step or two ahead of her so she wouldn't have to ask to be put to bed. She was a dancer, a fine, proud artist. Judy would never have to ask anyone to put her to bed. Not while I was around. As long as I was able I would spare her the indignity of dragging herself along the floor.

I gathered Judy up in my arms. The whole lower half of her body was soft; her legs hung over my left arm like weighted drapes. It was all I could do to keep from crying when I felt them so limp and formless. My dancer . . . you should have seen her in *Swan Lake*. Her legs had been so strong, so sleekly muscular, like her mother's . . .

I took her to the bathroom and left her in there. Which left me alone with my daymares. What if there really was a mutation of the softness and my dancer began leaving me again, slowly, inch by inch. What was I going to do when she was gone? My wife was gone. My folks were gone. My what few friends I'd ever had were gone. Judy was the only attachment I had left. Without her I'd break loose from everything and just float off into space. I needed her . . .

When she was finished in the bathroom I carried her out and arranged her on the bed. I tucked her in and kissed her goodnight.

Out in the living room I slipped under the covers of the fold-out bed and tried to sleep. It was useless. The fear wouldn't leave me alone. I fought it, telling myself that George was a freak case, that Judy and I had licked the softness. We were *immune* and we'd *stay* immune. Let everyone else turn into puddles of Jell-O, I wasn't going to let them suck us dry to save themselves. We were on our way to inheriting the earth, Judy and I, and we didn't even have to be meek about it.

But still sleep refused to come. So I lay there in the growing darkness in the center of the silent city and listened . . . listened as I did every night . . . as I knew I would listen for the rest of my life . . . listened for that sound . . . that cellophane crinkling sound . . .

Ticket to Heaven
John Shirley

The literary movement known as cyberpunk cynically re-
futed the earlier optimism of Golden Age science fiction by
suggesting that technological advancement would not help
improve human character but, rather, provide the technolog-
ically adept with new tools for corruption and exploitation.
John Shirley's (1954–) trilogy of novels *Eclipse, Eclipse
Penumbra,* and *Eclipse Corona,* along with many of the stories collected in *Heatseeker,* fall within the purview of
cyberpunk. In the 1988 story "Ticket to Heaven," Shirley
plays up the down side of science for a dark fable about
class warfare.

I never really wanted to go to Heaven. But I knew someone
would make me. There was pressure on me to go there. To
Heaven. Starting the morning I met Putchek. . . .

"Barry!" Gannick said when I dragged myself into his office. "Meet Frank Putchek, director of Club Eden."

"Hey," I said, "Howya doin'." I smiled woodenly, shook
Putchek's hand mechanically.

You have to understand that it was 3:30. I'd been in the
office since nine—this not being one of your breezy, we're-
all-chums advertising agencies where the idea men are permitted to be prima donnas—and I'd spent the morning
thinking of ways to convince the public it needs Triple M
brand Hamburger Enhancer. (But of course we'd end up ex-
plaining to the world that the three Ms should stand for
Mmm! as in *Mmm Good!* Any jackass would have come up
with the same thing, and Triple M could've saved a bundle
on an advertising agency. But agencies like mine thrive on
the bad habits of industry . . .) I spent lunch flattering
Jemmy Sorgenson from Maplethorpe and Sorgenson, in the
hopes that she'd offer me a job at a better salary and maybe
residuals. I'd spent the first part of the afternoon thinking of

ways to convince the public it needed a certain artificial
sweetener, one only mildly carcinogenic. And by 3:00, after
a hard day of constructing artful lies and fighting the tides
of self-disgust, I was burnt, looking at the world through
glazed eyes. By 3:15, everything in the office was flat and
two dimensional, threatening to fold down into one-dee. By
3:30 some mysterious temporal voodoo arrests the clock,
and the pace of time becomes a hunchbacked old lady with
an aluminum walker. And that's when Gannick called me in
to meet Putchek.

Putchek was a middle-aged guy with a smallish head,
chipmunk cheeks, and a seemingly infinite wealth of smile
lines around his mouth and eyes. He smiled a lot, mostly
with his mouth slightly open, looking goofy with his overbite. He was tall, round-shouldered, wore dandruff-flecked
wire-rims. But he had a nice blue and dove-gray Pierre
Hayakawa designer suit, and immaculate patent leather
shoes.

I didn't notice all this at first. Only his spongy handshake
and a sort of Putchek-shaped blur. He could've been part of
the furniture.

Gannick, my boss, was sitting behind his desk in shirt
sleeves, on his special chair to make him less midgetish, his
high forehead was a little less furrowed than usual, his small
shoulders almost relaxed, his darting black eyes for once
relatively stationary.

Gannick was happy about something. Putchek must represent a juicy account.

I screwed my smile down into something faint but super-
ficially warm, and sat across from Putchek where I could
look out the window at the chill, brittle spires of Manhattan's petrified forest. *Petrified,* I thought. *Me too.*

"Coffee, Barry?" Gannick asked me.

"No, thanks."

"He doesn't need coffee," Gannick said, pretend-
confidingly to Putchek. "Or even cocaine. Barry Thorpe
runs on adrenaline." He grinned to soften the sarcasm. I
must've looked more wooden than I thought.

Putchek tried to get the joke and blinked at the two of us.
"Oh, uh-huh. Heh heh."

Gannick said, "Barry, Club Eden's Paradise Vacations is
our new account—I guess you've heard rumors—" I hadn't
heard a word. "—and it's something a little, well, unusual,

and since you, Barry, are a little, well, unusual—" He paused for everyone to chuckle, so we did. "I thought you ought to head this up."

He beamed, and I tried to look pleased. It was as if the strings operating the muscles of my face were stretched out, threadbare, because I couldn't quite manage the expression I wanted.

"You OK, Barry?" Gannick asked.

"Just tired." I summoned a little focus, a little animation. "Well—have we got a prospectus or a press kit or . . . slides?"

"Slides of . . . ?" Putchek asked.

"The uh, resorts or—"

"There aren't any resorts!" Putchek brought his hands together as if he'd clap them, and then did a sort of joyful wringing instead, shifted on his chair, and said, a little impishly, "Club Eden doesn't send people to anywhere on this planet, ah, Barry."

It was my turn to blink in confusion. More of the room jumped into sharp focus. They had my attention. I turned to Gannick. "Correct me if I'm wrong—I know I'm a little out of it at times—but did I lose twenty or thirty years somewhere? Are we in the twenty-first century alluvasudden? Last I knew, it was just 1998; I'm sure of it. Interplanetary travel is still unmanned, right?"

"It's a manner of speaking. We're not sending people to another planet, per se," Putchek explained. "We're sending them to another . . . another existential focal point. Another plane, to use the metaphysical jargon . . . . We send them to *Heaven.*"

I looked at Putchek, and then at Gannick. "Heaven. Some kind of sensurround laser show, huh?—360-degree screens, incense?"

Gannick said slowly, "Nuh-ope. They put you in a machine and . . . you really feel physically like you've gone someplace. A sort of mind-trip through I guess, some kind of electronic stimulation of the brain or . . ." He shot a glance of polite inquiry at Putchek.

Putchek hemmed, getting ready to haw. "If ah, if you like. You can, ah, look at it like that." He glanced up at me. "It'd really help if you went there. Yourself. Then you'd . . . accept it." He looked embarrassed, stared at his reflection in his shoes, and his mouth was shut— as much as it would shut, with his overbite—and all of a sudden he worried me.

The next day was Saturday. Under the business-incentive labor laws, most of the population had to work on Saturday. But not me, I could putter around my weekend house with a drink in my hand. Getting gloomier as I got drunker, opaquing the windows and dialing the lights low, enjoying the gloom, hugging the house's darkness. Thinking about the Club Eden demonstration I was supposed to go to on Monday.

We send them to Heaven, Putchek had said. Neurological heaven, I supposed. Some pleasure-inducing machine, perhaps.

Heaven, at Putchek's prices, was something only a few could afford.

I shrugged. What else was new?

I went to the picture window, thumbed the button, and the window glass rippled into transparency. The spring afternoon was startling, almost tastelessly garish after the artificial twilight of my house.

I blinked in the unwanted sunshine, and the whiskey made my head ache. Tumbler in hand, I looked out over one of Hartford's prettiest suburbs. Trees lined the street with newly budded clouds of soft green; here and there were the bright pom-poms of flowering fruit trees. I realized I had no idea exactly what kind of trees most of them were. I'd lived here for five years, and I didn't know what kind of trees were on the street. Or my neighbor's first name.

But I knew my neighbor was Security Passed. We were all Security Passed, in Connecticut Village. When you drove in, you showed the checkpoint guards your Residency Card, or gave a visitor's number. To get a Residency Card, to be passed, you had to have a B-3 credit rating, and of course no record as a felon. It was a closed community, but not internally gregarious; the late-Twentieth-Century's fragmentation of true community feeling extended its anti-roots even here, where all looked cozy. We had television; we had interactive video and TV shopping networks. We had our lifestyles. We had shrugged off the responsibility that acknowledging strangers brings. Because one stranger leads to another, and not very far beyond the checkpoint was the crumbling border of Hartford's Shacktown, swollen with strangers we didn't want to meet. And tried not to think about.

I wasn't always the model resident of Connecticut Village. I'd written some stuff for *The Reformist,* before I'd gotten scared into money hunting; before Gannick found me. What I'd written was pretty self-righteous, foolishly idealistic stuff. . . . Like:

> Every town has its Shacktown, squatter enclaves grown up in the cracks between the neat little high-security Urban Village units the cities have become; the refuge of the legions of homeless, the disenfranchised of every profession: those who worked in industry and oil, before hands-on industry became an overseas venture and oil became an obsolete energy source; those who worked in construction before the contractors went to seventy-five percent premolded structures and robotics. Those without white collar work skills; or those who'd failed to fit in with the country's biggest employer, the "service" industry, that great consumer-supply mechanism so like a chicken-feeding machine on a poultry ranch. . . .
>
> The Shacktowns are tenanted by people who, a decade or two ago, built the affluence that the privileged feed off of now. Jobless Blacks are in the Shacktowns, of course. And the old. Since the demographic shifts of the '70 and '80s, and the growth of geriatric medicine, the old have become a huge, mouldering slice of the population. And millions of them went discarded, forgotten, cold-shouldered by the post-welfare society: the fresh new, yuppie-shiny world where Entrepreneurs are messiahs, where those who failed to Earn are cast into the outer darkness, beyond the borders of the profit margin. . . .

Stuff like that. Foolish stuff. The generalization of College Journalism. Anyway, why go on about it, when the response is always the same? They'll say, "So what?"

And if the Residency Committee knew I'd written that stuff for *The Reformist,* I'd never have been Security Passed for Connecticut Village.

Sometimes I passed Shacktown on the freeway. Just a sort of smudgy gray tumble of shanties glimpsed through the hurricane fence. From inside a microchip-driven car whistling smoothly down the freeway, the poor were reduced to a blur of embarrassment. The whole world became a visual shrug at a hundred and ten miles an hour. . . .

I knew there was bribery in it somewhere. I knew it when Gannick said, "The FDA's given Club Eden full approval. The patent bureau, everyone, they're lining up to give their blessing." It was the way he said it. Quick, with an undertone that warned me not to harp on the subject. So I didn't ask why there hadn't been any newspaper talk about it yet. Obviously, they'd worked hard to keep it mum till federal approval was a *fait accompli*. Wouldn't want any nosy Senate subcommittees to delay approval. . . .

It was Monday afternoon, and we were in what was to be the Club Eden showroom. Me and Gannick and Putchek and Putcheks's secretary, Buffy. She was a sort of human Happy Face who went by *Buffy* with no outward evidence of shame.

The showroom had been the front office of a large travel agency. The posters and brochure racks and desks and the fat, middle-aged ladies with the snail-shell hairdos had been cleared out, and now there was only the transport rig, like a hump of frozen milk under the fluorescent lights in one corner of the room, and some paint-jigsawed newspapers around the freshly rollered walls.

I looked at the transport rig and told myself, *Take it easy; it's probably harmless.*

It looked harmless. It looked like one of those little imitation race-car seats you get into at a video arcade. Except, on the outside it was all designer-stylized, a sculptured teardrop of imitation mother-of-pearl. The little door was open. Inside there was a chair, and a few dials on a dashboard. No controls, nothing else. I asked, "No helmet? Something to wire into the brain, to create the illusion? Or do you just inject them with something and, uh—" I had to cough; a recent coat of freshly applied blue paint suffused the shuttered room with quivery fumes.

Putchek cleared his throat. "No. No other, ah, fixtures are necessary. It's mostly automatic."

Buffy, as might be expected, was short, pert, faintly plump, auburn-haired, and dimple-cheeked. She had silver-flecked china-blue eyes and stubby, pudgy white fingers awkwardly extended by three-inch glue-on nails; blue nails with white glitter. She wore a puce jumpsuit, which was her version of a test pilot's getup.

"I'm all ready!" she told Gannick, a trifle too eagerly. Her voice was breathy and maddeningly affected.

"Have you done this before, Buffy?" I asked.

"Oh, uh-huh, sure!" she lilted. "Mm-hmm, and we had a kinda test pilot guy, and before that, monkeys and pigeons."

"They're *still* using pigeons," Gannick whispered to me as she turned and climbed into the machine. She closed the door behind her. The rig started to hum.

Putchek tilted his head back, as if listening to some beloved song. His dirty spectacles washed out in the light. "One of our big selling points," Putchek said absently, "is going to be a money-back guarantee."

Gannick's eyebrows shot up. "Money-back guarantee? That's a big risk, Frank. I mean, everyone I've met who's tried it is enthused—but there are all kinds of people out there. Brain chemistries, metabolisms—there's no two exactly alike. If there's even 20 percent who don't like the experience—"

"I can't go into all the details," Putchek said slowly, looking at himself in his shoes again, hands in his pockets. "But let's just say we are ninety-nine percent confident that virtually everyone will like it. There's some risk. But it's worth it."

The rig's humming had risen in pitch—and I winced as it passed out of the audible range. I felt a ripple go through me, and a tightness in my chest, a pinching at the back of my throat. For the briefest of moments, I had a peculiar feeling that Buffy was all around me. It was cloying, believe me. And then the room was normal again.

Putchek glanced at the rig. "She'll be out in, oh, five minutes, vacation complete."

I looked at him. "What's the list price on this?"

"Once we get rolling, ah, five thousand newbux per vacation. We won't be selling the machines at all, for at least a decade. And it's gimmicked so anyone who tries breaking into one to see its works will only find a glob of smoking slag inside."

"Five thousand newbux. . . ." I stared at him. "A thousand bills a minute?"

I could feel Gannick glaring at me. *Don't offend the client,* the glare was telling me.

Putchek was unruffled. "Only objectively. It doesn't feel like five minutes to them. They think it's months. Depends on how subjective their personalities are. It'll feel like at least a month has passed. For some it may feel like an eternity. Of pure, uninterrupted happiness." He looked at me as if to say, *What Do You Say To* That? His head tilted back; his open mouth aimed at me—if I'd looked, I could have checked out his tonsils.

One of Putchek's technicians came in. He was a blond kid, with a samurai haircut; he was wearing an orange jumpsuit, *Club Eden* ornately stitched onto each shoulder. He sang sotto voce along with something I heard only as a seashell sound leaking from his Walkman earphones. He carried a small box of microchips to the rig, snaking his head to the music. Putchek glanced at him in irritation. "Chucky, it's not that rig that needs the guidance chips; it's the other one."

But Chucky didn't hear him. He opened the door of the rig.

It was empty.

Gannick put the scotch down in front of me and said, "Drink it." Like a doctor's command.

We were in Putchek's office, and I was in Putchek's chair. He was standing solicitously over me, making a motion with his hands like a fly cleaning its foreclaws, and on the other side of the desk, Gannick was glowering. His expression said, *You're making a great impression on the client. Just great.*

But the girl was gone.

"I'll be OK," I said. "I just . . . felt funny for a second." I looked at Putchek, and then rolled the chair back so he wasn't breathing on me. "Some kind of stage-magic cabinet?"

He shook his head. "She's gone, projected. Sliding between planes. We were going to let people believe it was . . . was all in the head, for a while. We thought they'd be too scared otherwise. But believe me—she—"

"My ears are burning!" Buffy announced, giggling, as she came into the room. She looked flushed, happy as a three-year-old with a mouthful of chocolate. "I'm OK!" she said. "I've been to Heaven."

Sometimes, alone at home, I looked at my free pass and tried to talk myself into taking the trip to Heaven. Gannick wanted me to take it, for promotional inspiration. Everyone else wanted to take it. All three of my ex-wives had called, asking me to get them passes. Tickets to Heaven. Just as if they hadn't called me *subhuman, cold-blooded*, and the other things I can't go into without my stomach knotting up. Betty and Tracy cooing at me, posing as affectionate little sisters. But Celia, of course said, "You owe me this and more, you bastard."

But I didn't go to Heaven myself. Not for a long time. I told myself it was because of Winslow. But no: Winslow was just an excuse.

He was a good excuse, because Winslow is scary. I met him six months after Buffy vanished and came back. It was Friday night; I was in my weekdays apartment, packing to go out to my place in Connecticut. It was a time when I least brook interruptions. So when the doorbell rang and I opened the hall door, I snarled, "Yeah? *What?*" And then he flashed the holo. He flipped open his wallet, and the 3-D federal eagle spread its wings in the wallet, and across its breast was the luminous banner: *Jeffrey C. Winslow, Special Agent, Food and Drug Administration.*

"Mr. Barry Thorpe?"

"Uh. Useless to deny it, right?"

Winslow didn't crack a smile. He was black-suited, with the fashionable bureaucrat's triple-tongue necktie—and he was an albino. An apparition. The Ghost of Bureaucracy Past, I thought. Carrying an alumitech briefcase instead of a ball and chain.

He looked at me with an expression stark as a *No Trespassing* sign. "I'm doing a series of interviews, Mr. Thorpe, to follow up on our temporary approval of Club Eden. May I come in?"

"You got the wrong guy. I'm just the barker; I don't own the carny. You want to talk to Putchek. Maybe Gannick."

"I've talked to them. I'll be talking to them again." He waited. The FDA is responsible for more than food and drugs; Club Eden used a machine that affected people physically, hence it was under their jurisdiction. And hence, Winslow.

Resignedly, I said, "Come on in."

He was all questions. No accusations. And all the questions seemed routine. "When you interview a returned vacationer for an endorsement, are they paid for the interview?"

Things he already knew the answer to. Until he slung this one at me underhand: "Are you aware of any sums paid by Mr. Putchek or Mr. Gannick or their representatives to agents or functionaries of the FDA?"

I thought: *No, they don't tell anyone but the guy they're bribing.* But all I said was, "No."

"Thanks very much." He stood up and gave me a limp handshake. "That'll do it for this time." And he left.

This time?

I went out to a bar, found a pay phone, and called Gannick.

"It's nothing," he told me. "There's a little bureaucratic power struggle at the FDA. And this guy Winslow works for the guys trying to pull off the coup. They want to prove wrongdoing on the part of the FDA commissioners, take over their jobs. But they got nothing. Uh ... did he ask about the Charred Pad effect? Corporeal side effects?"

"No. *What* side effects are those? Gannick, I'm supposed to get the straight scoop on this stuff when I—"

"Hey, we're not holding out on you. Nothing important. Don't worry about it; it's all bullshit. Hey, I got a steak burning; I gotta go— Listen, Barry: just head out to Connecticut and forget it."

I knew Gannick's don't-ask-questions-if-you-love-your-paycheck tone. So I hung up, and tried to forget about Winslow.

God knows, it sounded good when people described it.

I was in my office, brainstorming a new fifteen-second spot for the Federal Broadcasting Agency's latest prime-time hit: "Yoshio Smith: Assassin for the CIA." Club Eden was a major sponsor for the show.

I was watching a videotape of the writer Alejandro Buckner, talking about his first Club Eden vacation. He was beaming, still in afterglow. Buckner was round-faced, and normally he looked like a sadistic cupid; today he was positively cherubic. "Heaven is not Christian, particularly; there is no biblical God in evidence, no angels, precisely, though the Prefects of Heaven perhaps fill the bill. But heaven will satisfy the Christian, the Buddhist, or the Hindu. Anyone.

"Some people have claimed Heaven looks different for everybody—but it isn't really so. It's got a landscape, definite topographical features. . . . It just depends on which part you tend to get projected to. And that's decided by your personality. Some people are projected into the pastoral Heaven, some of them into the urban one. Many into the one that's a sort of idealized suburb. Me, I'm an unabashed urban Heaven man—only, it was a series of rooftop gardens; a sort of Hanging Gardens of Babylon variation of the great penthouses of Manhattan. But of course, in Heaven there are no pigeon droppings; there is no smog, no acid rain; there are no thudding helicopters, screaming jets—though you might see some aerial gliders, impossibly graceful; everything has a sort of nimbus, like when you do certain drugs—but when you look close, you see it's just the shine off that thing's perfection, the natural glow of its excellence; you don't get tired in Heaven, but sometimes you sleep, and it's somehow just when the people around you want to sleep; there are no mosquitoes, no venomous things, no maggots, no defecation, no halitosis; there *is* sex in Heaven, however you like it, but it's more like dancing—somehow it loses all its earthly clumsiness. And it never becomes excessive, even though the orgasms are slow, full, and not enervating. Food exudes from the tables as you need it, but you never fall into gluttony. You cannot break your bones; you cannot fall ill. Nothing dies. Everything is easy, but nothing is dull. There are no conversational dullards; no faux pas, or awkward silences. There are sharp smells, and soft smells, but no bad smells. I say again that Heaven is not in the least dull. There are storms, and there is snow—but only when you're in the mood. There is contention there, but never acrimony; all contention is glorious sport, in Heaven."

It can't be that perfect, I thought. I didn't want it to be. Perfection is suspicious, is improbable, and I wanted Heaven to be real. So I was relieved when he said, "You can't do just anything you want there. If you want to interrogate the other entities—they look like people, but then again, they don't; they're all sort of soft-edged and shimmery—anyway, if you want to ask awkward questions about the place, then you've brought a lot of 'inappropriate psychodynamics' with you, as one of the Prefects said to me. You've brought 'neurotic attachments'. All inappropriate in Heaven. So the Prefects—they look like firefly glows, without the fireflies, and much larger—they swarm up to you and sort of smooth you out, and then you forget all your pushiness, your capacity for violence ... and your questions. Your questions are answered only with a sort of impression: that the place is indeed something you're supposed to have earned. That it's a 'higher state of communion with the universe'. And that should be enough for you.... But there's something else kind of funny about the place...."

I leaned forward, sharply attentive.

Buckner said abstractedly, "The entities who are there all the time, who are native to it, well, they look at you like ... um, they don't really *snub* you or anything; there's nothing unfriendly ... but there's a sort of benevolent surprise. As if they sense that you don't belong there...."

The tape ended there. Gannick's interviewer hadn't liked the direction Bucker was taking, and we had enough "good review" from him anyway. The tape ended, and the regular transmission on the TV monitor came on—I started to switch it off, but found myself watching. It was a news bulletin.

Four tenements had collapsed an hour earlier, in the Bronx. About 270 people were feared injured or dead. "Portions of the buildings just seemed to crumble into dust," the housing commissioner was quoted as saying. "Something similar happened about two weeks ago in Chicago—also a low-rent area—and we think it's a result of termite damage or acid rain damage to these old buildings."

Insects or acid rain or both. Oh. An explanation. It felt good to have an explanation for something like that. Even one that felt *wrong* when you really thought about it. So don't think about it, I told myself.

The phone rang. It was Winslow. I didn't put him on-screen. I didn't want to see the white face and the black suit. "Mr. Thorpe," he said, "I just want you to know that if you want to tell me anything, anything at all, I will see to it that it'll be safe for you. With respect to prosecution."

"You're with the FDA, not the FBI, Winslow. You seem to get them mixed up."

"Let's just say that this investigation is a little special. If you can tell me about the Corporeal Side Effects report on the Club Eden phenomena—"

"I really don't know what you're talking about," I said sincerely.

"If you want to play that game—fine. But we'll see who wins."

"FDA, Winslow, FDA. The other one is the Federal Bureau of—"

He hung up.

I shrugged. But then I thought: *Either he's a loon, or we're in trouble and we don't know it.*

Don't think about it. It's Gannick's problem.

I went home.

I sat in my confoam chair, nestling into its artificial hug, with the windows opaqued and the lights dimmed, playing my hiding game, pretending it was nighttime and dark out; anyway, it was dark *in*. I sat there sipping Johnnie Walkers and listened to the TV talk about vacationing in Heaven, and I thought: *I don't like this life. I don't like this world. So why don't I go?*

The Special Report anchormen talked about "the Club Eden phenomenon." Described the depression and ennui Club Eden returnees slipped into when the afterglow wore off. Noted that there was no actual physical addiction, but there *was* an indication of compulsiveness. "After you get over the depression," a returnee told the cameras, "you get back into the groove of regular life. Everything seems kind of dingy and dirty and tired and stiff, for a while—but pretty soon you start to enjoy life again, and, you know, you stop yearning for Heaven all the time. But as soon as you've got the money again, man, you *sign up!*"

Certain psychiatrists, whom I knew to be in the pay of Club Eden, made great, soft-edged, rolling claims for the therapeutic benefits of a Club Eden vacation. A few Southern senators muttered darkly about the religious implications. Club Eden had stopped calling the projection plane "Heaven", but that's what everyone thought it was. So the Moral Majority stamped their feet and pouted.

Senator Wexler called for an investigation into the risks, stating it was only a matter of time before the transport rigs went haywire and projected someone into a mountain, or the ocean—or maybe into Hell. And if that didn't happen, there was danger in the use of "bootleg" transport rigs—all the bootleg rigs, so far, had turned out to be fraudulent. Club Eden had resisted franchising. It held onto the monopoly with all the legal strength; that the $400 million they'd made could give them. That was a lot of strength.

After the Special Report, I had my third scotch, and listened to the regular newscaster dolefully announce that, yes, the government had admitted that the country was sliding into a severe recession. Yes, there was a rather unexpected oil shortage, a general energy crunch, epidemic problems with power plant generators around the country; indeed, around the world. . . . And the Shacktowns were growing.

I rewound the cassette, so I could listen to Buckner again, and take notes.

Club Eden was hot. Club Eden was The Buzz. There was suspicion, outrage, investigations. But Club Eden kept on through it all, and Gannick and I did our work.

Don't take Paradise for granted . . . until you've tried Club Eden. And: *So you think this* (a slick Kodachrome photo of glorious South Pacific beach: deep blue sky, crystal waters, emblematically perfect palm trees) *is Paradise? You haven't tried Club Eden.* And: *Club Eden: Who needs drugs?*

I had my free pass, locked up in my desk at home. Gannick encouraged me to go. Putchek encouraged me. Putchek went himself sometimes. There was a limit to how often you could go, and how long you could stay, something to do with electromagnetic stress on the body, but Putchek went as often as the safety regimen would allow.

Gannick didn't go. He said poker at the club with a pretty girl bringing the dry martinis was heaven enough for him.

"But I want *you* to go," he said, "OK, Barry?"

So I sat in my apartment on a Saturday evening, a year after Buffy had vanished and came back, thinking about using my pass. Not worrying about Winslow—he'd come only once more, and it had been more of the same. I'd almost forgotten about him.

The Shacktowners couldn't afford a ticket to Heaven. But I had one. So why didn't I use it? I went to the safe I kept the pass in, and opened it. I looked at the pass. I couldn't quite—

That's when the doorbell rang, and somehow I knew it would be Winslow.

Guiltily, I locked the pass away and opened the door for him—and stared. He looked different now. The veneer was gone. So was the badge and the alumitech briefcase. He wore a cheap printout paper suit and dark glasses; and the left lens on the dark glasses was cracked. He smelled like beer, and he listed to the right.

I was seeing a different Winslow here, and I liked him better. "Gotta talk to you," Winslow said.

"Come on in and have a drink," I said. "As if you needed one."

He reached into a pocket and took a gun from it. It was small, a .25, but it would put a hole right through me, at this range. "No. You come out. We're going for a drive."

We were walking along a pitted gravel road, under a lowering gray sky. The clouds at the horizon were reddening in sunset and beginning to shed rain; in the red tint it looked as if the clouds were bleeding. We walked between the shanties of Shacktown, through smells that would have stopped me like a brick wall if the gun hadn't been in Winslow's coat pocket. Winslow was talking, talking, talking, with a sort of excessive care that only underlined his drunkenness. "Mr. Danville—my supervisor—and I received a sort of anonymous tip, a transcription of a conversation between two lawyers, one for a certain Janet Rivera and the other working for Club Eden. Club Eden was offering Janet Rivera a fat settlement, a million dollars, and she took the money and ran. It seems that with a very minor adjustment of the transport rig—or a power surge at the wrong time—the vacationer will arrive in something very like Hell. Perhaps it's like this. . . ."

He gestured vaguely at the packed-in, mud-encrusted, sewage-reeking shanties; the drawn faces peering from beneath plastic sheets nailed over crooked doorways. He went on, "Perhaps it's worse. Ms. Rivera was sent to such a Hell. Apparently, Ms. Rivera barely kept her sanity. . . . Watch out, that dog wants a piece of your thigh. He's wild. . . ." It was a bony yellow mongrel, its eyes cloudy, its muzzle ribbed with a snarl. Winslow took the gun from his pocket and said, "This'll feed some'a these kids." The gun cracked, making me jump, as he shot the dog in the head. Its legs buckled, and it fell twitching. An old woman, muttering to herself, scurried out and dragged the dead dog by the tail into her hut.

"The transcript got us interested," Winslow went on as we continued down the road. (I glanced over a shoulder and saw a small crowd following us at a careful distance; a convention of scarecrows.) "And we saw our chance to pull down the commissioners. They were corrupt, and we'd had enough. We probed, and probed, and came up with something we didn't expect. A correspondence between the increase in Club Eden vacationers and the statistical deterioration of the living conditions of people around them. Putchek knew about it: it was called 'launchpad charring' because they likened the trips to Heaven to the launchings of rocket ships—and the launchpads are charred by rocket-ship engines, Thorpe. Club Eden's launchpad is our world; its charring is the side effect on the world: the worsening recession, the widening gap between rich and poor. And as it went on, the exchange became more . . . more literal. Look, Thorpe. . . ." He gestured at something.

We had come to a pit in the earth. It was about four hundred yards across, and deeper than I could see, coated with fine gray-black dust. The shanties were built right up to its rim; those nearest it were half fallen, partly sunk in soft, ashen ground.

Thick, oily drops of rain pattered down, freckling the gravel and drumming tin rooftops, drumrolling faster and faster as the downpour increased. Under its impact, three of the shacks around the rim of the crater collapsed at once, buckling like the shot dog, crumbling like sand castles under a wave; I heard human voices crying out from the shambles, a dissonant choir, wailing; glimpsed faces in the muddy ash, faces stamped with resignation. Swallowed up a moment later. "There are lots more like these, Thorpe. All over the world. They sprang up after Club Eden got really big. Thousands of people have gone into these pits. They're all caught up in some kind of . . . of inertia. Despair. So they don't fight it. You can feel the pit pulling at you. . . ." He was right: I felt the pit tugging at me, a sort of vacuum sucking at my sense of self-worth, my need to survive. Pulling me apart, making me want to take a step forward, to pitch myself in.

"There's a federal coverup of all this—," Winslow was saying.

"Shut up," I said. I wrenched my gaze from the pit. The urge to throw myself in had almost overwhelmed me. I couldn't stand it there anymore. "Shoot me or not," I said. "I'm leaving." I turned and started walking back the way we'd come.

I waited for the gunshot. After a moment he was walking beside me, hunched against the rain. Once, he had to fire into the air to disperse the crowd. But in twenty minutes we were in his car.

"Perhaps what happened to me and Danville is part of the pattern of effects that hits anyone who doesn't visit Heaven," Winslow said. "Perhaps it'll hit *you*, eventually." We sat in his car, listening to the rain hammer the roof. He took off his sunglasses and focused his pink eyes on nothing at all. "We were fired. They said we'd gone beyond the confines of our job, which we had. That we'd made things up. We hadn't." He tugged idly at a sleeve of his paper suit; the acid rain had worked on it, and the sleeve came away in his fingers. "I've run out of money. My clothes are rotting on my back. But what matters—what should have mattered—" He looked at me. "—are those people out there."

I didn't say anything. I was choking on what I had seen.

He said, "Why didn't you take the trip?"

"Just a feeling. That it was going too far into pretending that everything was all right. That it was going too far to wallow in our private Heaven when there are so many people in Hell. It was always wrong, but this way I couldn't look away, somehow. . . . It was just a step too far. . . . Guilt, I guess, is what it boils down to."

"You had the right instincts, Thorpe. I knew it when I interviewed you—I could tell the whole thing bothered you. I did my homework on you. Read those pieces you wrote a few years back. I know you're not happy about what you do for Gannick; persuading people to squander millions on the pointless consumption of crap. It *bothers* you. But you were addicted to the money."

"Mostly I was just scared. Of not having an income big enough to save up a safety margin. I was scared of ending up like those people. . . . So I had to do it."

"No, you didn't. You don't. You saw what it led to. . . . So, Thorpe—what are you going to do about it?"

"I don't have any proof of bribery. Or anything else. And let me tell you something: the public doesn't want this thing to go sour. They don't want it questioned, or fought. They want Heaven, and damn the consequences, and they're paying into a lot of senatorial campaigns to see to it their chances for Heaven aren't disturbed. I can't do a goddamn thing."

"You're wrong, Thorpe. What you can do is, precisely, a God Damned Thing."

I knew what he wanted me to do. No reason I should do it. I could get away; I could escape this. I could begin going to Heaven myself. I could. . . .

I couldn't. I saw the faces whose expressions had gone to dust. I felt the suction of the entropy pit. Having seen that, I was transformed by knowledge. I had lost my moral innocence. And knowing: I couldn't turn my back on it. "What do you want me to do?"

"It starts with a trip to Heaven."

It's going to be hard, Winslow had said. *Maybe the hardest thing you've ever done.*

It was. It was like someone who loves puppies being forced to throttle one; it was like seeing your mother for the first time in ten years, and then—though you love her—having to spit in her eye at the moment of reunion.

It was like being in Heaven and spurning it. The vista was sweet, soft, warm, like living in an Impressionist's landscape—and, like great Impressionism, never dull. I was nude but unashamed; for the first time I felt nudity without awkwardness. I was drifting weightless over the treetops, basking in just the right amount of sunshine, feeling the caress of the music they gave off, and reveling in the surge of joy that was arrival: the sight of Friends (Friends I had never known before) awaiting me in the garden, turning with a luminous gladness in their faces—

I wrenched myself away and began to Seek.

The act brought the Prefects of Heaven; they emanated from the trees like a thought from a synapse, and spiraled gracefully round me: soft lights, living questions. They drew closer to assuage the misplaced Desire in me—but, with a crackle of lightning that was an expression of Will, I thrust them back. Refused to let them soothe me into Heaven.

What, then? they asked.

Without speaking, I asked them: How is it we're permitted here at all? For surely this place was something to be earned.

You are permitted here because you have come here. The Great Organizer has made this place; the Great Organizer is the living Principle, who creates all orderliness and harmony. You are here, in Absolute Harmony, so the Organizer must intend it.

I told them what had happened on our world, to the poor. How things had worsened. I asked them why it had happened.

There are laws regarding the conversation of matter and energy. If you fill a cup from a bottle, the bottle will be that much emptier. Your world is the bottle. Your privileged are emptying it out: the others must suffer. There are machines of metaphysical truth that underlie physical things. You have tampered with the machines. Your wealthy surround themselves with stolen Grace, with unearned Grace: with the subatomic essence of orderliness, stolen from the exploited. This stolen Grace prevents them from paying the price: so others must.

This place, then, is no supernatural paradise?

It is a function of Law: all laws incorporating what you call Physics, all laws of what you call Science, and laws your people haven't learned. This place is a great device; just as in your world a church is a physical construct to represent the idea of holiness, here we used a physical construct to materialize holiness.

Heaven is created by a machine?

Yes. A machine birthed by the great Machine that is the universe.

Then tell me how I can make adjustments, to right the imbalance in the machine, to arrest the deterioration on our end of things.

The obvious, they said.

"For me, it began with a can opener. I saw a hand holding an old-fashioned can opener, the kind you have to stab into the can. But the hand was stabbing it into my naked belly, opening it like a lid, sawing toward my groin; through the pain I looked harder at the hand and saw it was my own. I could not say that I had no control over it. I controlled the hand, but I was making it cut me open. I was no masochist; I did not enjoy it. I screamed for it to stop, and I meant it. After a while the wound went away, but of course, by then I was making another. Not wanting to, but doing it voluntarily. The paradox sneered at me. At the same time I was watching the great screen where my humiliations and stupidities replayed, and knew my mother watched on another screen as I bought the favors of a small boy in Spanish Town. ... My sensations of humiliation and suffering, in all their permutations, were not diminished in the least by time or familiarity. None of it brought me relief or a sense of expiation. ... Later I found gasoline and tools and grass with dog shit on it, and I used all these things to—"

—From an interview with Frank Putchek,
in the security ward of Bellevue Hospital's
Mental Health facility

It was imprinted in my mind when I came back from Heaven. The Prefects had imprinted the adjustments: the literal, electronic adjustments, the equations for the new guidance chips to go into the transport rig. We went from one Club Eden transport station to another, across the country, Winslow and I, wearing the Club Eden technician's jumpsuits I'd stolen, pretending to be doing routine service checks. Making the adjustments.

We set it up so our readjustments applied exclusively to the new ten-minute vacations, which were available only to the wealthiest vacationers. The industrial barons, their spoiled children; the corporate vampires; the corrupt politicians.

And of course, there was Putchek. We saw to that. Because Winslow had spoken to Putchek, who had admitted he'd known early on about the side effects of granting First Class Tourist passage to Heaven. Putchek had known, and had not cared. Putchek was the first to go; the first of many.

By degrees, it began to work: the suffering of the exploited and the abandoned began to be reversed, and some of the garbage pits became gardens. The ashpits cleared up like the healing of geological chancres. The Shacktowners found strength: they organized, and built, and made demands. There was no Utopia there, and never will be. But there was dignity, and soon there was food and shelter.

We restored the balance. The adjustments worked. It worked because Club Eden had gotten sloppy about security. Which meant we were able to send a surprisingly large number of people to Hell.

But then again, maybe that shouldn't have surprised us.

Metastasis
Dan Simmons

The venerable vampire has emerged as the most popular of all themes in contemporary horror fiction, and Dan Simmons (1948–) has not been immune to its lure. His novel *Carrion Comfort* was an epic examination of political and social victimization told as a vampire story, while in *Children of the Night* he paraphrased the Dracula legend for a world familiar with contemporary Eastern European politics and the AIDS epidemic. His 1988 story "Metastasis" evokes these stories' inventive interpretations of a classic horror theme, while its blend of hard science and fantasy calls to mind his novels *Hyperion* and *The Fall of Hyperion*.

On the day Louis Steig received a call from his sister saying that their mother had collapsed and been admitted to a Denver hospital with a diagnosis of cancer, he promptly jumped into his Camaro, headed for Denver at high speed, hit a patch of black ice on the Boulder Turnpike, flipped his car seven times, and ended up in a coma from a fractured skull and a severe concussion. He was unconscious for nine days. When he awoke he was told that a minute sliver of bone had actually penetrated the left frontal lobe of his brain. He remained hospitalized for eighteen more days— not even in the same hospital as his mother—and when he left it was with a headache worse than anything he had ever imagined, blurred vision, word from the doctors that there was a serious chance that some brain damage had been suffered, and news from his sister that their mother's cancer was terminal and in its final stages.

The worst had not yet begun.

It was three more days before Louis was able to visit his mother. His headaches remained and his vision retained a slightly blurred quality—as with a television channel poorly tuned—but the bouts of blinding pain and uncontrolled vomiting had passed. His sister Lee drove and his fiancée Debbie accompanied him on the twenty mile ride from Boulder to Denver General Hospital.

"She sleeps most of the time but it's mostly the drugs," said Lee, "They keep her heavily sedated. She probably won't recognize you even if she is awake."

"I understand," said Louis.

"The doctors say that she must have felt the lump . . . understood what the pain meant . . . for at least a year. If she had only . . . It would have meant losing her breast even then, probably both of them, but they might have been able to . . ." Lee took a deep breath. "I was with her all morning. I just can't . . . can't go back up there again today, Louis. I hope you understand."

"Yes," said Louis.

"Do you want me to go in with you?" asked Debbie.

"No," said Louis.

Louis sat holding his mother's hand for almost an hour. It seemed to him that the sleeping woman on the bed was a stranger. Even through the slight blurring of his sight, he knew that she looked twenty years older than the person he had known; her skin was gray and sallow, her hands were heavily veined and bruised from IVs, her arms lacked any muscle tone, and her body under the hospital gown looked shrunken and concave. A bad smell surrounded her. Louis stayed thirty minutes beyond the end of visiting hours and left only when his headaches threatened to return in full force. His mother remained asleep. Louis squeezed the rough hand, kissed her on the forehead, and rose to go.

He was almost out of the room when he glanced at the mirror and saw movement. His mother continued to sleep but someone was sitting in the chair Louis had just vacated. He wheeled around.

The chair was empty.

Louis's headache flared like the thrust of a heated wire behind his left eye. He turned back to the mirror, moving his head slowly so as not to exacerbate the pain and vertigo. The image in the mirror was more clear than his vision had been for days.

Something was sitting in the chair he had just vacated.

Louis blinked and moved closer to the wall mirror, squinting slightly to resolve the image. The figure on the chair was somewhat misty, slightly diffuse against a more focused background, but there was no denying the reality and solidity of it. At first Louis thought it was a child—the form was small and frail, the size of an emaciated ten-year-old—but then he leaned closer to the mirror, squinted through the haze of his headache, and all thoughts of children fled.

The small figure leaning over his mother had a large, shaven head perched on a thin neck and even thinner body. Its skin was white—not flesh white but paper white, fish-belly white—and the arms were skin and tendon wrapped tightly around long bone. The hands were pale and enormous, fingers at least six inches long, and as Louis watched they unfolded and hovered over his mother's bedclothes. As Louis squinted he realized that the figure's head was not shaven but simply hairless—he could see veins through the translucent flesh—and the skull was disturbingly broad, brachycephalic, and so out of proportion with the body that the sight of it made him think of photographs of embryos and fetuses. As if in response to this thought, the thing's head began to oscillate slowly as if the long, thin neck could no longer support its weight. Louis thought of a snake closing on its prey.

Louis could do nothing but stare at the image of pale flesh, sharp bone and bruise-colored shadows. He thought fleetingly of concentration camp inmates shuffling to the wire, of week-dead corpses floating to the surface like inflatable things made of rotted white rubber. This was worse.

It had no ears. A rimmed ragged hole with reddened flanges of flesh opened directly into the misshapen skull. The eyes were bruised holes, sunken blue-black sockets in which someone had set two yellowed marbles as a joke. There were no eyelids. The eyes were obviously blind, clouded with yellow cataracts so thick that Louis could see layers of striated mucus. Yet they darted to and fro purposefully, a predator's darting, lurking glare, as the great head moved closer to his mother's sleeping form. In its own way, Louis realized, the thing could see.

Louis whirled around, opened his mouth to shout, took two steps toward the bed and the suddenly empty chair, stopped with fists clenched, mouth still straining with his silent scream, and turned back to the mirror.

The thing had no mouth as such, no lips, but under the long, thin nose the bones of cheeks and jaw seemed to flow

forward under white flesh to form a funnel, a long tapered
snout of muscle and cartilage which ended in a perfectly
round opening which pulsed slightly as pale-pink sphincter
muscles around the inner rim expanded and contracted with
the creature's breath or pulse. Louis staggered and grasped
the back of an empty chair, closing his eyes, weak with
waves of headache pain and sudden nausea. He was sure that
nothing could be more obscene than what he had just seen.

Louis opened his eyes and realized that he was wrong.

The thing had slowly, almost lovingly, pulled down the
thin blanket and topsheet which covered Louis's mother.
Now it lowered its misshapen head over his mother's chest
until the opening of that obscene proboscis was scant inches
away from the faded blue-flower print of her hospital gown.
Something appeared in the flesh-rimmed opening, something
gray-green, segmented, and moist. Small, fleshy antennae
tested the air. The great, white head bend lower, cartilage
and muscle contracted, and a five-inch slug was slowly ex-
truded, wiggling slightly as it hung above Louis's mother.

Louis threw his head back in a scream that finally could
be heard, tried to turn, tried to remove his hands from their
death grip on the back of the empty chair, tried to look away
from the mirror. And could not.

Under the slug's polyps of antennae was a face that was
all mouth, the feeding orifice of some deep sea parasite. It
pulsed as the moist slug fell softly onto his mother's chest,
coiled, writhed, and burrowed quickly away from the light.
Into his mother. The thing left no mark, no trail, not even a
hole in the hospital gown. Louis could see the slightest ripple of flesh as the slug disappeared under the pale flesh of
his mother's chest.

The white head of the child-thing pulled back, the yellow
eyes stared directly at Louis through the mirror, and then the
face lowered to his mother's flesh again. A second slug appeared, dropped, burrowed. A third.

Louis screamed again, found freedom from paralysis,
turned, ran to the bed and the apparently empty chair,
thrashed the air, kicked the chair into a distant corner, and
ripped the sheet and blanket and gown away from his
mother.

Two nurses and an attendant came running as they heard
Louis's screams. They burst into the room to find him
crouched over his mother's naked form, his nails clawing at

her scarred and shrunken chest where the surgeons had recently removed both breasts. After a moment of shocked immobility, one nurse and the attendant seized and held Louis while the other nurse filled a syringe with a strong tranquilizer. But before she could administer it, Louis looked in the mirror, pointed to a space near the opposite side of the bed, screamed a final time, and fainted.

"It's perfectly natural," said Lee the next day after their second trip to the Boulder Clinic. "A perfectly understandable reaction."

"Yes," said Louis. He stood in his pajamas and watched her fold back the top sheet on his bed.

"Dr. Kirby says that injuries to that part of the brain can cause strange emotional reactions," said Debbie from her place by the window. "Sort of like whatshisname ... Reagan's press secretary who was shot years ago, only temporary, of course."

"Yeah," said Louis, lying back, settling his head into the tall stack of pillows. There was a mirror on the wall opposite. His gaze never left it.

"Mom was awake for a while this morning," said Lee. "*Really* awake. I told her you'd been in to see her. She doesn't ... doesn't remember your visit, of course. She wants to see you."

"Maybe tomorrow," said Louis. The mirror showed the reversed images of the three of them. Just the three of them. Sunlight fell in a yellow band across Debbie's red hair and Lee's arm. The pillowcases behind Louis's head were very white.

"Tomorrow," agreed Lee. "Or maybe the day after. Right now you need to take some of the medication Dr. Kirby gave you and get some sleep. We can go visit Mom together when you feel better."

"Tomorrow," said Louis, and he closed his eyes.

He stayed in bed for six days, rising only to go to the bathroom or to change channels on his portable TV. The headaches were constant but manageable. He saw nothing unusual in the mirror. On the seventh day he rose about ten A.M., showered slowly, dressed in his camel slacks, white shirt, and blue blazer, and was prepared to tell Lee that he was ready to visit the hospital when his sister came into the room red-eyed.

"They just called," she said. "Mother died about twenty minutes ago."

The funeral home was about two blocks from where his mother had lived, where Louis had grown up after they had moved from Des Moines when he was ten, just east of the Capitol Hill area where old brick homes were becoming run-down rentals and where Hispanic street gangs had claimed the night.

According to his mother's wishes there would be a "visitation" this night where Denver friends could pay their respects before the casket was flown back to Des Moines the next day for the funeral Mass at St. Mary's and final interment at the small city cemetery where Louis's father was buried. Louis thought that the open casket was an archaic act of barbarism. He stayed as far away from it as he could, greeting people at the door, catching glimpses only of his mother's nose, folded hands, or rouged cheeks.

About sixty people showed up during the two-hour ordeal, most of them in their early seventies—his mother's age—people from the block whom he hadn't seen in fifteen years or new friends she had met through Bingo or the Senior Citizens Center. Several of Louis's Boulder friends showed up, including two members of his Colorado Mountain Club hiking group and two colleagues from the physics labs at C.U. Debbie stayed by his side the entire time, watching his pale, sweaty face and occasionally squeezing his hand when she saw the pain from the headache wash across him.

The visitation period was almost over when suddenly he could no longer stand it. "Do you have a compact?" he asked Debbie.

"A what?"

"A compact," he said. "You know, one of those little make-up things with a mirror."

Debbie shook her head. "Louis, have you *ever* seen me with something like that?" She rummaged in her purse. "Wait a minute. I have this little hand mirror that I use to check my . . ."

"Give it here," said Louis. He raised the small plastic-backed rectangle, turning toward the doorway to get a better view behind him.

About a dozen mourners remained, talking softly in the dim light and flower-scented stillness. Someone in the hallway beyond the doorway laughed and then lowered his voice. Lee stood near the casket, her black dress swallowing light, speaking quietly to old Mrs. Narmoth from across the alley.

There were twenty or thirty other small figures in the room, moving like pale shadows between rows of folding chairs and dark-suited mourners. They moved slowly, carefully, seeming to balance their oversized heads in a delicate dance. Each of the child-sized forms awaited its turn to approach the casket and then moved forward, its pale body and bald head emitting its own soft penumbra of greenish-grayish glow. Each thing paused by the casket briefly and then lowered its head slowly, almost reverently.

Gasping in air, his hand shaking so badly the mirror image blurred and vibrated, Louis was reminded of lines of celebrants at his First Communion ... and of animals at a trough.

"Louis, what is it?" asked Debbie.

He shook off her hand, turned and ran toward the casket, shouldering past mourners, feeling cold churnings in his belly as he wondering if he was passing *through* the white things.

"What?" asked Lee, her face a mask of concern as she took his arm.

Louis shook her away and looked into the casket. Only the top half of the lid was raised. His mother lay there in her best blue dress, the make-up seeming to return some fullness to her ravaged face, her old rosary laced through her folded fingers. The cushioned lining under her was silk and beige and looked very soft. Louis raised the mirror. His only reaction then was slowly to lift his left hand and to grasp the rim of the casket very tightly, as if it were the railing of a ship in rough seas and he were in imminent danger of plunging overboard.

There were several hundred of the slug-things in the coffin, flowing over everything inside it, filling it to the brim. They were more white than green or gray now and much, much larger, some as thick through the body as Louis's forearm. Many were more than a foot long. The antennae tendrils had contracted and widened into tiny yellow eyes and the lamprey mouths were recognizably tapered now.

As Louis watched, one of the pale, child-sized figures to his right approached the casket, laid long white fingers not six inches from Louis's hand, and lowered its face as if to drink.

Louis watched as the thing ingested four of the long, pale slugs, the creature's entire face contracting and expanding almost erotically to absorb the soft mass of its meal. The yellow eyes did not blink. Others approached the casket and joined in the communion. Louis lowered the angle of the mirror and watched two more slugs flow effortlessly out of his mother, sliding through blue material into the churning mass of their fellows. Louis moved the mirror, looked behind him, seeing the half-dozen pale forms standing there, waiting patiently for him to move. Their bodies were pale and sexless blurs. Their fingers were very long and very sharp. Their eyes were hungry.

Louis did not scream. He did not run. Very carefully he palmed the mirror, released his death grip on the edge of the casket, and walked slowly, carefully, away from there. Away from the casket. Away from Lee and Debbie's distantly heard cries and questions. Away from the funeral home.

He was hours and miles away, in a strange section of dark warehouses and factories, when he stopped in the mercury-arc circle of a streetlight, held the mirror high, swiveled 360 degrees to ascertain that nothing and no one was in sight, and then huddled at the base of the streetlight to hug his knees, rock and croon.

"I think they're cancer vampires," Louis told the psychiatrist. Between the wooden shutters on the doctor's windows, Louis caught a glimpse of the rocky slabs that were the Flatirons. "They lay these tumor-slugs that hatch and change inside people. What we call tumors are really eggs. Then the cancer vampires take them back into themselves."

The psychiatrist nodded, tamped down his pipe, and lighted another match. "Do you wish to tell me more . . . ah . . . details . . . about these images you have?" He puffed his pipe alight.

Louis started to shake his head and then stopped suddenly as headache pain rippled through him. "I've thought it all out in the last few weeks," he said. "I mean, go back more than a hundred years and give me the name of one famous person who died of cancer. Go ahead."

The doctor drew on his pipe. His desk was in front of the shuttered windows and his face was in shadow, only occasionally illuminated when he turned as he relit his pipe. "I can't think of one right now," the doctor said, "but there must be many."

"*Exactly,*" said Louis in a more excited tone than he had meant to use. "I mean, today we *expect* people to die of cancer. One in six. Or maybe it's one in four. I mean, I didn't know *anyone* who died in Vietnam, but *everyone* knows somebody—usually somebody in our family—who's died of cancer. Just think of all the movie stars and politicians. I mean, it's everywhere. It's the plague of the Twentieth Century."

The doctor nodded and kept any patronizing tones out of his voice. "I see your point," he said. "But just because modern diagnostic methods did not exist before this does not mean people did not die of cancer in previous centuries. Besides, research has shown that modern technology, pollutants, food additives and so forth have increased the risk of encountering carcinogens which . . ."

"Yeah," laughed Louis, "carcinogens. That's what I used to believe in. But, Jesus, Doc, have you ever read over the AMA's and American Cancer Society's official lists of carcinogens? I mean it's everything you eat, breathe, wear, touch, and do to have fun. I mean it's *everything*. That's the same as just saying that they don't know. Believe me, I've been reading all of that crap, they don't even know what makes a tumor start growing."

The doctor steepled his fingers. "But you believe that you do, Mr. Steig?"

Louis took one of his mirrors from his shirt pocket and moved his head in quick half-circles. The room seemed empty. "Cancer vampires," he said. "I don't know how long they've been around. Maybe something we did this century allowed them to come through some . . . some gate or something. I don't know."

"From another dimension?" the doctor asked in conversational tones. His pipe tobacco smelled vaguely of pine woods on a summer day.

"Maybe," shrugged Louis. "I don't know. But they're here and they're busy feeding . . . and multiplying . . ."

"Why do you think that you are the only one who has been allowed to see them?" asked the doctor brightly.

Louis felt himself growing angry. "Goddammit, I don't

know that I'm the only one who can see them. I just know that something happened after my accident ..."

"Would it not be ... equally probable," suggested the doctor, "that the injury to your skull has caused some *very* realistic hallucinations? You admit that your sight has been somewhat affected." He removed his pipe, frowned at it, and fumbled for his matches.

Louis gripped the arms of his chair, feeling the anger in him rise and fall on the waves of his headache. "I've been back to the Clinic," he said. "They can't find any sign of permanent damage. My vision's a little funny—but that's just because I can see *more* now. I mean, more colors and things. It's like I can see radio waves almost."

"Let us assume that you do have the power to see these ... cancer vampires," said the doctor. The tobacco glowed on his third inhalation. The room smelled of sun-warmed pine needles. "Does this mean that you also have the power to *control* them?"

Louis ran his hand across his brow, trying to rub away the pain. "I don't know."

"I'm sorry, Mr. Steig. I couldn't hear ..."

"I don't know!" shouted Louis. "I haven't tried to *touch* one. I mean, I don't know if ... I'm afraid that it might ... Look, so far the things ... the cancer vampires—they've ignored me, but ..."

"If you can see them," said the doctor, "doesn't it follow that they can see you?"

Louis rose and went to the window, tugging open the shutters so the room was filled with late afternoon light. "I think they see what they want to see," said Louis, staring at the foothills beyond the city, playing with his hand mirror. "Maybe we're just blurs to them. They find us easily enough when it's time to lay their eggs."

The doctor squinted in the sudden brightness but removed his pipe and smiled. "You talk about eggs," he said, "but what you described sounded more like feeding behavior. Does this discrepancy and the fact that the ... vision ... first occurred when your mother was dying suggest any deeper meanings to you? We all search for ways to control things we have no power over—things we find too difficult to accept. Especially when one's mother is involved."

"Look," sighed Louis, "I don't need this Freudian crap. I agreed to come here today because Deb's been on my case for weeks but . . ." Louis stopped and raised his mirror, and stared.

The doctor glanced up as he scraped at his pipe bowl. His mouth was slightly open, showing white teeth, healthy gums, and a hint of tongue slightly curled in concentration. From beneath that tongue came first the fleshy antennae and then the green-gray body of a tumor slug, this one no more than a few centimeters long. It moved higher along the psychiatrist's jaw, sliding in and out of the muscles and skin of the man's cheek as effortlessly as a maggot moving in a compost heap. Deeper in the shadows of the doctor's mouth, something larger stirred.

"It can't hurt to talk about it," said the doctor. "After all, that's what I'm here for."

Louis nodded, pocketed his mirror, and walked straight to the door without looking back.

Louis found that it was easy to buy mirrors cheaply. They were available, framed and unframed, at used furniture outlets, junkshops, discount antique dealers, hardware stores, glass shops and even in peoples' stacks of junk sitting on the curb awaiting pickup. It took Louis less than a week to fill his small apartment with mirrors.

His bedroom was the best protected. Besides the twenty-three mirrors of various sizes on the walls, the ceiling had been completely covered with mirrors. He had put them up himself, pressing them firmly into the glue, feeling slightly more secure with each reflective square he set in place.

Louis was lying on his bed on a Saturday afternoon in May, staring at the reflections of himself, thinking about a conversation he had just had with his sister Lee, when Debbie called. She wanted to come over. He suggested that they meet on the Pearl Street Mall instead.

There were three passengers and two of *them* on the bus. One had been in the rear seat when Louis boarded, another came through the closed doors when the bus stopped for a red light. The first time he had seen one of the cancer vampires pass through a solid object, Louis had been faintly relieved, as if something so insubstantial could not be a serious threat. He no longer felt that way. They did not float through walls in the delicate, effortless glide of a ghost; Louis watched while the hairless head and sharp shoulders of this thing struggled to penetrate the closed doors of the bus, wiggling like someone passing through a thick sheet of cellophane. Or like some vicious newborn predator chewing its way through its own amniotic sac.

Louis pulled down another of the small mirrors attached by wires to the brim of his Panama hat and watched while the second cancer vampire joined the first and the two closed on the old lady sitting with her shopping bags two rows behind him. She sat stiffly upright, hands on her lap, staring straight ahead, not even blinking, as one of the cancer vampires raised its ridged funnel of a mouth to her throat, the motion as intimate and gentle as a lover's opening kiss. For the first time Louis noticed that the rim of the thing's proboscis was lined with a circle of blue cartilage which looked as sharp as razor blades. He caught a glimpse of gray-green flowing into the folds of the old lady's neck. The second cancer vampire lowered its ponderous head to her belly, a tired child preparing to rest on its mother's lap.

Louis stood, pulled the cord, and got off five blocks before his stop.

Few places in America, Louis thought, showed off health and wealth better than the three outdoor blocks of Boulder's Pearl Street Mall. A pine-scented breeze blew down from the foothills less than a quarter of a mile to the west as shoppers browsed, tourists strolled, and the locals lounged. The average person in sight was under thirty-five, tanned and fit, and wealthy enough to dress in the most casual pre-washed, pre-faded, pre-wrinkled clothes. Young men dressed only in brief trunks and sweat jogged down the mall, occasionally glancing down at their watches or their own bodies. The young women in sight were almost unanimously thin and braless, laughing with beautifully capped teeth, sitting on grassy knolls or benches with their legs spread manfully in poses out of *Vogue*. Healthy looking teenagers with spikes of hair dyed unhealthy colors licked at their two-dollar Dove bars and three-dollar Häagen-Dazs cones. The spring sunlight on the brick walkways and flower beds promised an endless summer.

"Look," said Louis as he and Debbie sat near Freddy's hot dog stand and watched the crowds flow past, "my view of things right now is just too goddamn ugly to accept. Maybe *everybody* could see this shit if they wanted to, but they just refuse to." He lowered two of his mirrors and swiveled. He had tried mirrored sunglasses but that had not worked; only the full mirror-reversal allowed him to see. There were six mirrors clipped to his hat, more in his pockets.

"Oh, Louis," said Debbie. "I just don't understand . . ."

"I'm serious," snapped Louis. "We're like the people who lived in the villages of Dachau or Auschwitz. We see the fences, watch the trainloads of loaded cattle cars go by every day, smell the smoke of the ovens . . . and *pretend it isn't happening.* We let these things take everybody, as long as it isn't us. *There!* See that heavyset man near the bookstore?"

"Yes?" Debbie was near tears.

"Wait," said Louis. He brought out his larger pocket mirror and turned at an angle. The man was wearing tan slacks and a loose Hawaiian shirt that did not hide his fat. He sipped at a drink in a red styrofoam cup and stood reading a folded copy of the *Boulder Daily Camera.* Four child-size blurs clustered around him. One closed long fingers around the man's throat and pulled himself up across the man's arm and belly.

"Wait," repeated Louis and moved away from Debbie, scuttling sideways to keep the group framed in the mirror. The three cancer vampires did not look up as Louis came within arm's length; the fourth slid its long cone of a mouth toward the man's face.

"Wait!" screamed Louis and struck out, head averted, seeing his fist pass through the pale back of the clinging thing. There was the faintest of gelatinous givings and a chill numbed the bones of his fist and arm. Louis stared at his mirror.

All four of the cancer vampires' heads snapped around, blind yellow eyes fixed on Louis. He sobbed and struck again, feeling his fist pass through the thing with no effect and bounce weakly off the fat man's chest. Two of the white blurs swiveled slowly toward Louis.

"Hey, goddamnit!" shouted the fat man and struck at Louis's arm.

The mirror flew out of Louis's left hand and shattered on the brick pavement. "Oh, Jesus," whispered Louis, backing away. "Oh Jesus." He turned and ran, snapping down a mirror on his hat as he did so, seeing nothing but the dancing, vibrating frame. He grabbed Debbie by the wrist and tugged her to her feet. "Run!"

They ran.

Louis awoke sometime after two A.M., feeling disoriented and drugged. He felt for Debbie, remembered that he had gone back to his own apartment after they had made love. He lay in the dark, wondering what had awakened him.

His nightlight had burned out.

Louis felt a flush of cold fear, cursed, and rolled over to turn on the table lamp next to his bed. He blinked in the sudden glare, seeing blurred reflections of himself blink back from the ceiling, walls, and door.

Other things also moved in the room.

A pale face with yellow eyes pushed its way through the door and mirror. Fingers followed, finding a hold on the doorframe, pulling the body through like a climber mastering an overhang. Another face rose to the right of Louis's bed with the violent suddenness of someone stepping out of one's closet in the middle of the night, extracted its arm, and reached for the blanket bunched at the foot of Louis's bed.

"Ah," panted Louis and rolled off the bed. Except for the closet there was only the single door, closed and locked. He glanced up at the ceiling mirrors in time to see the first white shape release itself from the wood and glass and stand between the door and him. As he stared upward at his own reflection, at himself dressed in pajamas and lying on his back on the tan carpet, he watched wide-eyed as something white rippled and rose through the carpet not three feet from where he lay: a broad curve of dead grub flesh followed by a second white oval, the back and head of the thing floating up through the floor like a swimmer rising to his knees in three feet of water. The eye sockets were close enough for Louis to touch; all he had to do was extend his arm. The scent of old carrion came to him from the thing's sharp circle of a mouth.

Louis rolled sideways and back, scrambled to his feet, used a heavy chair by his bed to smash the window glass and threw the chair behind him. The rope ladder tied to the base of his bed had been left behind by a paranoid ex-roommate of Louis's who had refused to live on a third floor without a fire escape.

Louis looked up, saw white hands converging, threw the knotted rope out the window and followed it, bruising knuckles and knees against the brick wall as he clambered down.

He looked up repeatedly but there were no mirrors in the cold spring darkness and he had no idea if anything was following.

They used Debbie's car to leave, driving west up the canyon into the mountains. Louis was wearing an old pair of jeans, green sweatshirt, and paint-spattered sneakers he had left at Debbie's after helping to paint her new apartment in January. She owned only a single portable mirror—an eighteen-by-twenty-four-inch glass set into an antique frame above the fireplace—and Louis had ripped it off the wall and brought it along, checking every inch of the car before allowing her to enter it.

"Where are we going?" she asked as they turned south out of Nederland on the Peak to Peak Highway. The Continental Divide glowed in weak moonlight to their right. Their headlights picked out black walls of pine and stretches of snow as the narrow road wound up and around.

"Lee's cabin," said Louis. "West on the old Rollins Pass road."

"I know the cabin," said Debbie. "Will Lee be there?"

"She's still in Des Moines," he said. He blinked rapidly. "She called just before you did this afternoon. She found a . . . lump. She saw a doctor there but is going to fly back to get the biopsy."

"Louis, I . . ." began Debbie.

"Turn here," said Louis.

They drove the last two miles in silence.

The cabin had a small generator to power lights and the refrigerator but Louis preferred not to spend time filling it and priming it in the darkness out back. He asked Debbie to stay in the car while he took the mirror inside, lit two of the large candles Lee kept on the mantle, and walked through the three small rooms of the cabin with the mirror reflecting the flickering candle flame and his own pale face and staring eyes. By the time he waved Debbie inside, he had a fire going in the fireplace and the sleeper sofa in the main room was pulled out.

In the dancing light from the fireplace and candles, Debbie's hair looked impossibly red. Her eyes were tired.

"It's only a few hours until morning," said Louis. "I'll go into Nederland when we wake up and get some supplies."

Debbie touched his arm. "Louis, can you tell me what's going on?"

"Wait, wait," he said, staring into the dark corners. "There's one more thing. Undress."

"Louis . . ."

"Undress!" Louis was already tugging off his shirt and pants. When they were both out of their clothes, Louis propped the mirror on a chair and had them stand in front of it, turning slowly. Finally satisfied, he dropped to his knees and looked up at Debbie. She stood very still, the firelight rising and falling on her white breasts and the soft V of red pubic hair. The freckles on her shoulders and upper chest seemed to glow.

"Oh, God," said Louis and buried his face in his hands. "God, Deb, you must think I'm absolutely crazy."

She crouched next to him and ran her fingers down his back. "I don't know what's going on, Louis," she whispered, "but I know that I love you."

"I'll tell you . . ." began Louis, feeling the terrible pressure in his chest threaten to expand into sobs.

"In the morning," whispered Debbie and kissed him softly.

They made love slowly, seriously, time and their senses slowed and oddly amplified by the late hour, strange place, and fading sense of danger. Just when both of them felt the urgency quickening, Louis whispered, "Wait a second," and lay on one side, running his hand and then his mouth under the folds of her breasts, up, licking the nipples back into hardness, then kissing the curve of her belly and opening her thighs with his hand, sliding his face and body lower.

Louis closed his eyes and imagined a kitten lapping milk. He tasted the salt sweetness of sea while Debbie softened and opened herself further to him. His palms stroked the tensed smoothness of her inner thighs while her breathing came more quickly, punctuated by soft, sharp gasps of pleasure.

There was a sudden hissing behind them. The light flared and wavered.

Louis turned, sliding off the foot of the bed onto one knee, aware of the pounding of his heart and the extra vulnerability his nakedness and excitement forced on him. He looked and gasped a laugh.

"What?" whispered Debbie, not moving.

"It's just the candle I set on the floor," he whispered back. "It's drowning in its own melted wax. I'll blow it out."

He leaned over and did so, pausing as he moved back to the foot of the bed to take in a single, voyeuristic glance in the mirror propped on the chair.

Firelight played across the two lovers framed there, Louis's flushed face and Debbie's white thighs, both glistening slightly from perspiration and the moisture of their lovemaking. Seen from this angle the dancing light illuminated the copper tangle of her pubic hair and roseate ovals of moist labia with a soft clarity too purely sensuous to be pornographic. Louis felt the tides of love and sexual excitement swell in him.

He caught the movement in the mirror out of the corner of his eye a second before he would have lowered his head again. A glimmer of slick gray-green between pale pink lips. No more than a few centimeters long. Undeterred by the dim light, the twin polyps of antennae emerged slowly, twisting and turning slightly as if to taste the air.

"I didn't know you had an interest in oncology," said Dr. Phil Collins. He grinned at Louis across his cluttered desk. "I thought you rarely came out of the physics lab up at the University."

Louis stared at his old classmate. He was much too tired for banter. He had not slept for 52 hours and his eyes felt like they were lined with sand and broken glass. "I need to see the radiation treatment part of chemotherapy," he said.

Collins tapped manicured nails against the edge of his desk. "Louis, we can't just give guided tours of our therapy sessions every time someone gets an interest in the process."

Louis forced his voice to stay even. "Look, Phil, my mother died of cancer a few weeks ago. My sister just underwent a biopsy that showed malignancy. My fiancée checked into Boulder Community a few hours ago with a case of cervical cancer that they're pretty sure also involved her uterus. Now will you let me watch the procedure or not?"

"Jesus," said Collins. He glanced at his watch. "Come on, Louis, you can make the rounds with me. Mr. Taylor is scheduled to receive his treatment in about twenty minutes."

The man was forty-seven but looked thirty years older. His eyes were sunken and bruised. His skin had a yellowish cast under the florescent lights. His hair had fallen out and Louis could make out small pools of blood under the skin.

They stood behind a lead-lined shield and watched through thick ports. "The medication is a very important part of it," said Collins. "It both augments and complements the radiation treatment."

"And the radiation kills the cancer?" asked Louis.

"Sometimes," said Collins. "Unfortunately it kills healthy cells as well as the ones which have run amok."

Louis nodded and raised his hand mirror. When the device was activated he made a small, involuntary sound. A brilliant burst of violet light filled the room, centering on the tip of the X-ray machine. Louis realized that the glow was similar to that of the bug-zapper devices he had seen in yards at night, the light sliding beyond visible frequencies in a maddening way. But this was a thousand times brighter.

The tumor slugs came out. They slid out of Mr. Taylor's skull, antennae thrashing madly, attracted by the brilliant light. They leaped the ten inches to the lens of the device, sliding on slick metal, some falling to the floor and then moving back up onto the table and through the man's body again to reemerge from the skull seconds later only to leap again.

Those that reached the source of the X-rays fell dead to the floor. The others retreated into the darkness of flesh when the X-ray light died.

" . . . hope that helps give you some idea of the therapy involved," Collins was saying. "It's a frustrating field because we're not quite sure of why everything works the way it does, but we're making strides all of the time."

Louis blinked. Mr. Taylor was gone. The violet glow of the X-rays was gone. "Yes," he said. "I think that helps a lot."

Two nights later, Louis sat next to his sleeping sister in the semi-darkness of her hospital room. The other bed was empty. Louis had sneaked in during the middle of the night and the only sound was the hiss of the ventilation system and the occasional squeak of a rubber-soled shoe in the corridor. Louis reached out a gloved hand and touched Lee's wrist just below the green hospital identity bracelet. "I thought it'd be easy, kiddo," he whispered. "Remember the movies we watched when we were little? James Arness in

The Thing? Figure out what kills it and rig it up." Louis felt the nausea sweep over him again and he lowered his head, breathing in harsh gulps. A minute later he straightened again, moving to wipe the cold sweat off his brow but frowning when the leather of the thick glove contacted his skin. He held Lee's wrist again. "Life ain't so easy, kiddo. I worked nights in Mac's high energy lab at the University. It was easy to irradiate things with that X-ray laser toy Mac cobbled together to show the sophomores the effect of ionizing radiation."

Lee stirred, moaned slightly in her sleep. Somewhere a soft chime sounded three times and was silenced. Louis heard two of the floor nurses chatting softly as they walked to the staff lounge for their two A.M. break. Louis left his gloved hand just next to her wrist, not quite touching it.

"Jesus, Lee," he whispered. "I can see the whole damn spectrum below 100 angstroms. So can *they*. I banked on the cancer vampires being drawn to the stuff I'd irradiated just like the tumor slugs were. I came here last night—to the wards—to check on it. They *do* come, kiddo, but it doesn't kill them. They flock around the irradiated stuff like moths to a flame, but it doesn't kill them. Even the tumor slugs need high dosages if you're going to get them all. I mean, I started in the millirem dosages—like the radiation therapy they use here—and found that it just didn't get enough of them. To be sure, I had to get in the region of 300 to 400 roentgens. I mean, we're talking Chernobyl here, kiddo."

Louis quit talking and walked quickly to the bathroom, lowering his head to the toilet to vomit as quietly as possible. Afterward he washed his face as best he could with the thick gloves on and returned to Lee's bedside. She was frowning slightly in her drugged sleep. Louis remembered the times he had crept into her bedroom as a child to frighten her awake with garter snakes or squirt guns or spiders. "Fuck it," he said and removed his gloves.

His hands glowed like five-fingered, blue-white suns. As Louis watched in the mirrors snapped down on his hat brim, the light filled the room like cold fire. "It won't hurt, kiddo," he whispered as he unsnapped the first two buttons on Lee's pajama tops. Her breasts were small, hardly larger than when he had peeked in on her emerging from the shower when she was fifteen. He smiled as he remembered the whipping he had received for that, and then he laid his right hand on her left breast.

For a second nothing happened. Then the tumor slugs came out, antennae rising like pulpy periscopes from Lee's flesh, their gray-green color bleached by the brilliance of Louis's glowing hand.

They slid into him through his palm, his wrist, the back of his hand. Louis gasped as he felt them slither through his flesh, the sensation faint but nauseating, like having a wire inserted in one's veins while under a local anaesthetic.

Louis counted six ... eight of the things sliding from Lee's breast into the blue-white flaring of his hand and arm. He held his palm flat for a full minute after the last slug entered, resisting the temptation to scream or pull his hand away as he saw the muscles of his forearm writhe as one of the things flowed upward, swimming through his flesh.

As an extra precaution, Louis moved his palm across Lee's chest, throat, and belly, feeling her stir in her sleep, fighting the sedatives in an unsuccessful battle to awaken. There was one more slug—hardly more than a centimeter long—which rose from the taut skin just below her sternum, but it flared and withered before coming in contact with his blue-white flesh, curling like a dried leaf too close to a hot fire.

Louis rose and removed his thick layers of clothes, watching in the wide mirror opposite Lee's bed. His entire body fluoresced, the brilliance fading from white to blue-white to violet and then sliding away into frequencies even he could not see. Again he thought of the bug-lights one saw near patios and the blind-spot sense of frustration the eye conveyed as it strained at the fringes of perception. The mirrors hanging from the brim of his hat caught and scattered the light.

Louis folded his clothes neatly, laid them on the chair near Lee, kissed her softly on the cheek, and walked from room to room, the brilliance from his body leaping ahead of him, filling the corridors with blue-white shadows and pinwheels of impossible colors.

There was no one at the nurse's station. The tile floor felt cool beneath Louis's bare feet as he went from room to room, laying on his hands. Some of the patients slept on. Some watched him with wide eyes but neither moved nor cried out. Louis wondered at this but glanced down without his mirrors and realized that for the first time he could see the brilliance of his heavily irradiated flesh and bone with his own eyes. His body was a pulsing star in human form. Louis could easily hear the radio waves as a buzzing, crackling sound, like a great forest fire still some miles away.

The tumor slugs flowed from their victims and into Louis. Not everyone on this floor had cancer, but in most rooms he had only to enter to see the frenzied response of green-gray or grub-white worms straining to get at him. Louis took them all. He felt his body swallow the things, sensed the maddened turmoil within. Only once more did he have to stop to vomit. His bowels shifted and roiled, but there was so much motion in him now that Louis ignored it.

In Debbie's room, Louis pulled the sheet off her sleeping form, pulled up the short gown, and laid his cheek to the soft bulge of her belly. The tumor slugs flowed into his face and throat; he drank them in willingly.

Louis rose, left his sleeping lover, and walked to the long, open ward where the majority of cancer patients lay waiting for death.

The cancer vampires followed him. They flowed through walls and floors to follow him. He led them to the main ward, a blazing blue-white pied piper leading a chorus of dead children.

There were at least a score of them by the time he stopped in the center of the ward, but he did not let them approach until he had gone from bed to bed, accepting the last of the tumor slugs into himself, seeing with his surreal vision as the eggs inside these victims hatched prematurely to give up their writhing treasure. Louis made sure the tumor slugs were with him before he moved to the center of the room, raised his arms, and let the cancer vampires come closer.

Louis felt heavy, twice his normal weight, pregnant with death. He glanced at his blazing limbs and belly and saw the very surface of himself alive with the motion of maggots feeding on his light.

Louis raised his arms wider, pulled his head far back, closed his eyes, and let the cancer vampires feed.

The things were voracious, drawn by the X-ray beacon of Louis's flesh and the silent beckoning of their larval offspring. They shouldered and shoved each other aside in their eagerness to feed. Louis grimaced as he felt a dozen sharp piercings, felt himself almost lifted off the floor by nightmare energies suddenly made tangible. He looked once, saw the terrible curve of the top of a dead-child's head as the thing buried its face to the temples in Louis's chest, and then he closed his eyes until they were done.

Louis staggered, gripped the metal footboard of a bed to keep from falling. The score of cancer vampires in the room had finished feeding but Louis could feel his own body still weighted with slugs. He watched.

The child-thing nearest to him seemed bloated, its body as distended as a white spider bursting with eggs. Through its translucent flesh, Louis could see glowing tumor slugs shifting frantically like electric silverfish.

Even though his nausea and pain, Louis smiled. Whatever the reproductive-feeding cycle of these things had been, Louis now felt sure that he had disrupted it with the irradiated meal he had offered the tumor slugs.

The cancer vampire in front of him staggered, leaned far forward, and looked even more spiderish as its impossibly long fingers stretched to keep it from falling.

A blue-white gash appeared along the thing's side and belly. Two bloated, thrashing slugs appeared in a rush of violet energy. The cancer vampire arched its back and raised its feeding mouth in a scream that was audible to Louis as someone scraping their teeth down ten feet of blackboard.

The slugs ripped free of the vampire's shredded belly, dumping themselves on the floor and writhing in a bath of ultraviolet blood, steaming and shriveling there like true slugs Louis had once seen sprinkled with salt. The cancer vampire spasmed, clutched at its gaping, eviscerated belly, and then thrashed several times and died, its bony limbs and long fingers slowly closing up like the legs of a crushed spider.

There were screams, human and otherwise, but Louis paid no attention as he watched the death throes of the two dozen spectral forms in the room. His vision had altered permanently now and the beds and their human occupants were mere shadows in a great space blazing in ultraviolet and infrared but dominated by the blue-white corona which was his own body. He vomited once more, doubling over to retch up blood and two dying, glowing slugs, but this was a minor inconvenience as long as his strength held out and at that second he felt that it would last forever.

Louis looked down, through the floor, through *five* floors, seeing the hospital as levels of clear plastic interlaced with webs of energy from electrical wiring, lights, machines, and organisms. Many organisms. The healthy ones glowed a soft orange but he could see the pale yellow infections, the grayish corruptions, and the throbbing black pools of incipient death.

Rising, Louis stepped over the drying corpses of cancer vampires and the acid-pools which had been thrashing slugs seconds before. Although he already could see beyond, he opened wide doors and stepped out onto the terrace. The night air was cool.

Drawn by the extraordinary light, they waited. Hundreds of yellow eyes turned upwards to stare from blue-black pits set in dead faces. Mouths pulsed. Hundreds more of the things converged as Louis watched.

Louis raised his own eyes, seeing more stars than anyone had ever seen as the night sky throbbed with uncountable X-ray sources and infinite tendrils of unnamed colors. He looked down to where they continued to gather, by the thousands now, their pale faces glowing like candles in a procession. Louis prayed for a single miracle. He prayed that he could feed them all. "Tonight, Death," he whispered, the sound too soft for even him to hear, "you shall die."

Louis stepped to the railing, raised his arms, and went down to join those who waited.

Orange Is for Anguish, Blue for Insanity

David Morrell

David Morrell (1943–) is probably one of the last names one would associate with science fiction, since his best-known novels *First Blood* and *The Fraternity of the Stone* are realistic suspense thrillers. However, Morrell has crossed back and forth throughout his career over a variety of genres, including supernatural horror, mystery, and even the western, to tell tales of character developing under duress. In "Orange Is for Anguish, Blue for Insanity," the winner of the Horror Writers of America Bram Stoker Award in 1989 for best novelette, Morrell gives a science fiction topspin to the old idea of the thin line that divides creativity from insanity.

Van Dorn's work was controversial, of course. The scandal his paintings caused among Parisian artists in the late 1800s provided the stuff of legend. Disdaining conventions, thrusting beyond accepted theories, Van Dorn seized upon the essentials of the craft to which he'd devoted his soul. Color, design, and texture. With those principles in mind, he created portraits and landscapes so different, so innovative, that their subjects seemed merely an excuse for Van Dorn to put paint onto canvas. His brilliant colors, applied in passionate splotches and swirls, often so thick that they projected an eighth of an inch from the canvas in the manner of a bas-relief, so dominated the viewer's perception that the person or scene depicted seemed secondary to technique.

Impressionism, the prevailing avant-garde theory of the late 1800s, imitated the eye's tendency to perceive the edges of peripheral objects as blurs. Van Dorn went one step further and so emphasized the lack of distinction among objects that they seemed to melt together, to merge into an interconnected, pantheistic universe of color. The branches of a Van

Dorn tree became ectoplasmic tentacles, thrusting toward the sky and the grass, just as tentacles from the sky and grass thrust toward the tree, all melding into a radiant swirl. He seemed to address himself not to the illusions of light but to reality itself, or at least to his theory of it. The tree *is* the sky, his technique asserted. The grass is the tree, and the sky the grass. All is one.

Van Dorn's approach proved so unpopular among theorists of his time that he frequently couldn't buy a meal in exchange for a canvas upon which he'd labored for months. His frustration produced a nervous breakdown. His self-mutilation shocked and alienated such onetime friends as Cézanne and Gauguin. He died in squalor and obscurity. Not until the 1920s, thirty years after his death, were his paintings recognized for the genius they displayed. In the 1940s, his soul-tortured character became the subject of a best-selling novel, and in the 1950s a Hollywood spectacular. These days, of course, even the least of his efforts can't be purchased for less than three million dollars.

Ah, art.

It started with Myers and his meeting with Professor Stuyvesant. "He agreed . . . reluctantly."

"I'm surprised he agreed at all," I said. "Stuyvesant hates Postimpressionism and Van Dorn in particular. Why didn't you ask someone easy, like Old Man Bradford?"

"Because Bradford's academic reputation sucks. I can't see writing a dissertation if it won't be published, and a respected dissertation director can make an editor pay attention. Besides, if I can convince Stuyvesant, I can convince anyone."

"Convince him of . . . ?"

"That's what Stuyvesant wanted to know," Myers said.

I remember that moment vividly, the way Myers straightened his lanky body, pushed his glasses close to his eyes, and frowned so hard that his curly red hair scrunched forward on his brow.

"Stuyvesant asked, even disallowing his own disinclination toward Van Dorn—God, the way that pompous asshole talks—why would I want to spend a year of my life writing about an artist who'd been the subject of countless books and articles, whose ramifications had been exhausted? Why not choose an obscure but promising Neo-Expressionist and gamble that *my* reputation would rise with his? Naturally the artist he recommended was one of Stuyvesant's favorites."

"Naturally," I said, "If he named the artist I think he did . . ."

Myers mentioned the name.

I nodded. "Stuyvesant's been collecting him for the past five years. He hopes the resale value of the paintings will buy him a town house in London when he retires. So what did you tell him?"

Myers opened his mouth to answer, then hesitated. With a brooding look, he turned toward a print of Van Dorn's swirling *Cypresses in a Hollow,* which hung beside a ceiling-high bookshelf crammed with Van Dorn biographies, analyses, and bound collections of reproductions. He didn't speak for a moment, as if the sight of the familiar print—its facsimile colors incapable of matching the brilliant tones of the original, its manufacturing process unable to recreate the exquisite texture of raised, swirled layers of paint on canvas—still took his breath away.

"So what did you tell him?" I asked again.

Myers exhaled with a mixture of frustration and admiration. "I said, what the critics wrote about Van Dorn was mostly junk. He agreed, with the implication that the paintings invited no less. I said, even the gifted critics hadn't probed to Van Dorn's essence. They were missing something crucial."

"Which is?"

"Exactly Stuyvesant's next question. You know how he keeps relighting his pipe when he gets impatient. I had to talk fast. I told him I didn't know what I was looking for, but there's something"—Myers gestured toward the print—"something there. Something nobody's noticed. Van Dorn hinted as much in his diary. I don't know what it is, but I'm convinced his paintings hide a secret." Myers glanced at me.

I raised my eyebrows.

"Well, if nobody's noticed," Myers said, "it *must* be a secret, right?"

"But if *you* haven't noticed . . ."

Compelled, Myers turned toward the print again, his tone filled with wonder. "How do I know it's there? Because when I look at Van Dorn's paintings, I *sense* it. I *feel* it."

I shook my head. "I can imagine what Stuyvesant said to

that. The man deals with art as if it's geometry, and there aren't any secrets in—"

"What he said was, if I'm becoming a mystic, I ought to be in the School of Religion, not Art. But if I wanted enough rope to hang myself and strangle my career, he'd give it to me. He liked to believe he had an open mind, he said."

"That's a laugh."

"Believe me, he wasn't joking. He had a fondness for Sherlock Holmes, he said. If I thought I'd found a mystery and could solve it, by all means do so. And at that, he gave me his most condescending smile and said he would mention it at today's faculty meeting."

"So what's the problem? You got what you wanted. He agreed to direct your dissertation. Why do you sound so—?"

"Today there *wasn't* any faculty meeting."

"Oh," I said. "You're fucked."

Myers and I had started graduate school at Iowa together. That had been three years earlier, and we'd formed a strong enough friendship to rent adjacent rooms in an old apartment building near campus. The spinster who owned it had a hobby of doing watercolors—she had no talent, I might add—and rented only to art students so they would give her lessons. In Myers's case, she'd made an exception. He wasn't a painter, as I was. He was an art historian. Most painters work instinctively. They're not skilled at verbalizing what they want to accomplish. But words and not pigment were Myers's specialty. His impromptu lectures had quickly made him the old lady's favorite tenant.

After that day, however, she didn't see much of him. Nor did I. He wasn't at the classes we took together. I assumed he spent most of his time at the library. Late at night, when I noticed a light beneath his door and knocked, I didn't get an answer. I phoned him. Through the wall I heard the persistent, muffled ringing.

One evening I let the phone ring eleven times and was just about to hang up when he answered. He sounded exhausted.

"You're getting to be a stranger," I said.

His voice was puzzled. "Stranger? But I just saw you a couple of days ago."

"You mean, two weeks ago."

"Oh, shit," he said.

"I've got a six-pack. You want to——?"

"Yeah, I'd like that." He sighed. "Come over."

When he opened his door, I don't know what startled me more, the way Myers looked or what he'd done to his apartment.

I'll start with Myers. He'd always been thin, but now he looked gaunt, emaciated. His shirt and jeans were rumpled. His red hair was matted. Behind his glasses, his eyes looked bloodshot. He hadn't shaved. When he closed the door and reached for a beer, his hand shook.

His apartment was filled with, covered with—I'm not sure how to convey the dismaying effect of so much brilliant clutter—Van Dorn prints. On every inch of the walls. The sofa, the chairs, the desk, the TV, the bookshelves. And the drapes, and the ceiling, and, except for a narrow path, the floor. Swirling sunflowers, olive trees, meadows, skies, and streams surrounded me, encompassed me, seemed to reach out for me. At the same time I felt swallowed. Just as the blurred edges of objects within each print seemed to melt into one another, so each print melted into the next. I was speechless amid the chaos of color.

Myers took several deep gulps of beer. Embarrassed by my stunned reaction to the room, he gestured toward the vortex of prints. "I guess you could say I'm immersing myself in my work."

"When did you eat last?"

He looked confused.

"That's what I thought." I walked along the narrow path among the prints on the floor and picked up the phone. "The pizza's on me." I ordered the largest supreme the nearest Pepi's had to offer. They didn't deliver beer, but I had another six-pack in my fridge, and I had the feeling we'd be needing it.

I set down the phone. "Myers, what the hell are you doing?"

"I told you ..."

"Immersing yourself? Give me a break. You're cutting classes. You haven't showered in God knows how long. You look like shit. Your deal with Stuyvesant isn't worth destroying your health. Tell him you've changed your mind. Get another, an *easier*, dissertation director."

"Stuyvesant's got nothing to do with this."

"Damnit, what *does* it have to do with? The end of comprehensive exams, the start of dissertation blues?"

Myers gulped the rest of his beer and reached for another can. "No, blue is for insanity."

"What?"

"That's the pattern." Myers turned toward the swirling prints. "I studied them chronologically. The more Van Dorn became insane, the more he used blue. And orange is his color of anguish. If you match the painting with the personal crises described in his biographies, you see a correspondent use of orange."

"Myers, you're the best friend I've got. So forgive me for saying I think you're off the deep end."

He swallowed more beer and shrugged as if to say he didn't expect me to understand.

"Listen," I said. "A personal color code, a connection between emotion and pigment, that's bullshit. I should know. You're the historian, but I'm the painter. I'm telling you, different people react to colors in different ways. Never mind the advertising agencies and their theories that some colors sell products more than others. It all depends on context. It depends on fashion. This year's 'in' color is next year's 'out.' But an honest-to-God great painter uses whatever color will give him the greatest effect. He's interested in creating, not selling."

"Van Dorn could have used a few sales."

"No question. The poor bastard didn't live long enough to come into fashion. But orange is for anguish and blue means insanity? Tell that to Stuyvesant and he'll throw you out of his office."

Myers took off his glasses and rubbed the bridge of his nose. "I feel so . . . maybe you're right."

"There's no maybe about it. I *am* right. You need food, a shower, and sleep. A painting's a combination of color and shape that people either like or they don't. The artist follows his instincts, uses whatever techniques he can master, and does his best. But if there's a secret in Van Dorn's work, it isn't a color code."

Myers finished his second beer and blinked in distress. "You know what I found out yesterday?"

I shook my head.

"The critics who devoted themselves to analyzing Van Dorn . . ."

"What about them?"

"They went insane, the same as he did."

"*What?* No way. I've studied Van Dorn's critics. They're as conventional and boring as Stuyvesant."

"You mean, the mainstream scholars. The safe ones. I'm talking about the truly brilliant ones. The ones who haven't been recognized for their genius, just as Van Dorn wasn't recognized."

"What happened to them?"

"They suffered. The same as Van Dorn."

"They were put in an asylum?"

"Worse than that."

"Myers, don't make me ask."

"The parallels are amazing. They each tried to paint. In Van Dorn's style. And just like Van Dorn, they stabbed out their eyes."

I guess it's obvious by now—Myers was what you might call "high-strung." No negative judgment intended. In fact, his excitability was one of the reasons I liked him. That and his imagination. Hanging around with him was never dull. He loved ideas. Learning was his passion. And he passed his excitement on to me.

The truth is, I needed all the inspiration I could get. I wasn't a bad artist. Not at all. On the other hand, I wasn't a great one, either. As I neared the end of grad school, I'd painfully come to realize that my work never would be more than "interesting." I didn't want to admit it, but I'd probably end up as a commercial artist in an advertising agency.

That night, however, Myers's imagination wasn't inspiring. It was scary. He was always going through phases of enthusiasm. El Greco, Picasso, Pollock. Each had preoccupied him to the point of obsession, only to be abandoned for another favorite and another. When he'd fixated on Van Dorn, I'd assumed it was merely one more infatuation.

But the chaos of Van Dorn prints in his room made clear he'd reached a greater excess of compulsion. I was skeptical about his insistence that there was a secret in Van Dorn's work. After all, great art can't be explained. You can analyze its technique, you can diagram its symmetry, but ultimately there's a mystery words can't communicate. Genius can't be summarized. As far as I could tell, Myers had been using the word *secret* as a synonym for indescribable brilliance.

When I realized he literally meant that Van Dorn had a secret, I was appalled. The distress in his eyes was equally appalling. His references to insanity, not only in Van Dorn but in his critics, made me worry that Myers himself was having a breakdown. Stabbed out their eyes, for Christ's sake?

I stayed up with Myers till five A.M., trying to calm him, to convince him he needed a few days' rest. We finished the six-pack I'd brought, the six-pack in my refrigerator, and another six-pack I bought from an art student down the hall. At dawn, just before Myers dozed off and I staggered back to my room, he murmured that I was right. He needed a break, he said. Tomorrow he'd call his folks. He'd ask if they'd pay his plane fare back to Denver.

Hung over, I didn't wake up till late afternoon. Disgusted that I'd missed my classes, I showered and managed to ignore the taste of last night's pizza. I wasn't surprised when I phoned Myers and got no answer. He probably felt as shitty as I did. But after sunset, when I called again, then knocked on his door, I started to worry. His door was locked, so I went downstairs to get the landlady's key. That's when I saw the note in my mail slot.

Meant what I said. Need a break. Went home. Will be in touch. Stay cool. Paint well. I love you, pal. Your friend forever,

Myers

My throat ached. He never came back. I saw him only twice after that. Once in New York, and once in . . .

Let's talk about New York. I finished my graduate project, a series of landscapes that celebrated Iowa's big-sky rolling, dark-soiled, wooded hills. A local patron paid fifty dollars for one of them. I gave three to the university's hospital. The rest are who knows where.

Too much has happened.

As I predicted, the world wasn't waiting for my good-but-not-great efforts. I ended where I belonged, as a commercial artist for a Madison Avenue advertising agency. My beer cans are the best in the business.

I met a smart, attractive woman who worked in the marketing department of a cosmetics firm. One of my agency's clients. Professional conferences led to personal dinners and intimate evenings that lasted all night. I proposed. She agreed.

We'd live in Connecticut, she said. Of course.

When the time was right, we might have children, she said.

Of course.

Myers phoned me at the office. I don't know how he knew where I was. I remembered his breathless voice.

"I found it," he said.

"Myers?" I grinned. "Is it really—? *How are you? Where have—?*"

"I'm telling you. I found it!"

"I don't know what you're—"

"Remember? Van Dorn's secret!"

In a rush, I did remember—the excitement Myers could generate, the wonderful, expectant conversations of my youth—the days and especially the nights when ideas and the future beckoned. "Van Dorn? You're still—?"

"Yes! I was right! There *was* a secret!"

"You crazy bastard, I don't care about Van Dorn. But I care about you! Why did you—? I never forgave you for disappearing."

"I had to. Couldn't let you hold me back. Couldn't let you—"

"For your own good!"

"So *you* thought. But I was right!"

"Where *are* you?"

"Exactly where you'd expect me to be."

"For the sake of old friendship, Myers, don't piss me off. *Where are you?*"

"The Metropolitan Museum of Art."

"Will you stay there, Myers? While I catch a cab? I can't wait to see you."

"I can't wait for you to see what *I* see!"

I postponed a deadline, canceled two appointments, and told my fiancée I couldn't meet her for dinner. She sounded miffed. But Myers was all that mattered.

He stood beyond the pillars at the entrance. His face was haggard, but his eyes were stars. I hugged him. "Myers, it's so good to—"

"I want you to see something. Hurry."

He tugged at my coat, rushing.

"But where have you been?"

"I'll tell you later."

We entered the Postimpressionist gallery, Bewildered, I followed Myers and let him anxiously sit me on a bench before Van Dorn's *Fir Trees at Sunrise.*

I'd never seen the original. Prints couldn't compare. After a year of drawing ads for feminine beauty aids, I was devastated. Van Dorn's power brought me close to . . .

Tears?

For my visionless skills.

For the youth I'd abandoned a year before.

"Look!" Myers said. He raised his arm and gestured toward the painting.

I frowned. I looked.

It took time—an hour, two hours—and the coaxing vision of Myers. I concentrated. And then, at last, I saw.

Profound admiration changed to . . .

My heart raced. As Myers traced his hand across the painting one final time, as a guard who had been watching us with increasing wariness stalked forward to stop him from touching the canvas, I felt as if a cloud had dispersed and a lens had focused.

"Jesus," I said.

"You see? The bushes, the trees, the branches?"

"Yes! Oh, God, yes! Why didn't I—?"

"Notice before? Because it doesn't show up in the prints," Myers said. "Only in the originals. And the effect's so deep, you have to study them—"

"Forever."

"It seems that long. But I knew. I was right."

"A secret."

When I was a boy, my father—how I loved him—took me mushroom hunting. We drove from town, climbed a barbed-wire fence, walked through a forest, and reached a slope of dead elms. My father told me to search the top of the slope while he checked the bottom.

An hour later he came back with two large paper sacks filled with mushrooms. I hadn't found even one.

"I guess your spot was lucky," I said.

"But they're all around you," my father said.

"All around me? Where?"

"You didn't look hard enough."

"I crossed this slope five times."

"You searched, but you didn't really see," my father said. He picked up a long stick and pointed it toward the ground. "Focus your eyes toward the end of the stick."

I did . . .

And I've never forgotten the hot excitement that surged through my stomach. The mushrooms appeared as if by magic. They'd been there all along, of course, so perfectly adapted to their surroundings, their color so much like dead leaves, their shape so much like bits of wood and chunks of rock that they'd been invisible to ignorant eyes. But once my vision adjusted, once my mind reevaluated the visual impressions it received, I saw mushrooms everywhere, seemingly thousands of them. I'd been standing on them, walking over them, staring at them, and hadn't realized.

I felt an infinitely greater shock when I saw the tiny faces Myers made me recognize in Van Dorn's *Fir Trees at Sunrise*. Most were smaller than a quarter of an inch, hints and suggestions, dots and curves, blended perfectly with the landscape. They weren't exactly human, though they did have mouths, noses, and eyes. Each mouth was a black, gaping maw, each nose a jagged gash, the eyes dark sinkholes of despair. The twisted faces seemed to be screaming in total agony. I could almost hear their anguished shrieks, their tortured wails. I thought of damnation. Of hell.

As soon as I noticed the faces, they emerged from the swirling texture of the painting in such abundance that the landscape became an illusion, the grotesque faces reality. The fir trees turned into an obscene cluster of writhing arms and pain-racked torsos.

I stepped back in shock an instant before the guard would have pulled me away.

"Don't touch the—" the guard said.

Myers had already rushed to point at another Van Dorn, the original *Cypresses in a Hollow*. I followed, and now that my eyes knew what to look for, I saw small, tortured faces in every branch and rock. The canvas swarmed with them.

"Jesus."

"And this!"

Myers hurried to *Sunflowers at Harvest Time*, and again, as if a lens had changed focus, I no longer saw flowers but anguished faces and twisted limbs. I lurched back, felt a bench against my legs, and sat.

"You were right," I said.

The guard stood nearby, scowling.

"Van Dorn did have a secret," I said. I shook my head in astonishment.

"It explains everything," Myers said. "These agonized faces give his work depth. They're hidden, but we *sense* them. We *feel* the anguish beneath the beauty."

"But why would he—?"

"I don't think he had a choice. His genius drove him insane. It's my guess that this is how he literally saw the world. These faces are the demons he wrestled with. The festering products of his insanity. And they're not just an illustrator's gimmick. Only a genius could have painted them for all the world to see and yet have so perfectly imposed them on the landscape that *no one* would see. Because he took them for granted in a terrible way."

"No one? *You* saw, Myers."

He smiled. "Maybe that means I'm crazy."

"I doubt it, friend." I returned his smile. "It does mean you're persistent. This'll make your reputation."

"But I'm not through yet," Myers said.

I frowned.

"So far all I've got is a fascinating case of optical illusion. Tortured souls writhing beneath, perhaps producing, incomparable beauty. I call them 'secondary images.' In your ad work I guess they'd be called 'subliminal.' But this isn't commercialism. This is a genuine artist who had the brilliance to use his madness as an ingredient in his vision. I need to go deeper."

"What are you taking about?"

"The paintings here don't provide enough examples. I've seen his work in Paris and Rome, in Zurich and London. I've borrowed from my parents to the limits of their patience and my conscience. But I've seen, and I know what I have to do. The anguished faces began in 1889, when Van Dorn left Paris in disgrace. His early paintings were abysmal. He settled in La Verge in the south of France. Six months later his genius suddenly exploded. In a frenzy, he painted. He returned to Paris. He showed his work, but no one appreciated it. He kept painting, kept showing. Still no one appreciated it. He returned to La Verge, reached the peak of his genius, and went totally insane. He had to be committed to an asylum, but not before he stabbed out his eyes. That's my dissertation. I intend to parallel his course. To match his paintings with his biography, to show how the faces increased and became more severe as his madness worsened. I want to dramatize the turmoil in his soul as he imposed his twisted vision on each landscape."

It was typical of Myers to take an excessive attitude and make it even more excessive. Don't misunderstand. His discovery was important. But he didn't know when to stop. I'm not an art historian, but I've read enough to know that what's called "psychological criticism," the attempt to analyze great art as a manifestation of neuroses, is considered off-the-wall, to put it mildly. If Myers handed Stuyvesant a psychological dissertation, the pompous bastard would throw Myers out of his office.

That was one misgiving I had about what Myers planned to do with his discovery. Another troubled me more. *I intend to parallel Van Dorn's course,* he'd said, and after we left the museum and walked through Central Park, I realized how literally Myers meant it.

"I'm going to southern France," he said.

I stared in surprise. "You don't mean—"

"La Verge? That's right. I want to write my dissertation there."

"But—"

"What place could be more appropriate? It's the village where Van Dorn suffered his nervous breakdown and eventually went insane. If it's possible, I'll even rent the same room *he* did."

"Myers, this sounds too far out, even for you."

"But it makes perfect sense. I need to immerse myself. I need atmosphere, a sense of history. So I can put myself in the mood to write."

"The last time you immersed yourself, you crammed your room with Van Dorn prints, didn't sleep, didn't eat, didn't bathe. I hope—"

"I admit I got too involved. But last time I didn't know what I was looking for. Now that I've found it, I'm in good shape."

"You look strung out to *me*."

"An optical illusion." Myers grinned.

"Come on, I'll treat you to drinks and dinner."

"Sorry. Can't. I've got a plane to catch."

"You're leaving *tonight*? But I haven't seen you since—"

"You can buy me that dinner when I finish the dissertation."

I never did. I saw him only one more time. Because of the letter he sent two months later. Or asked his nurse to send. She wrote down what he'd said and added an explanation of her own. He'd blinded himself, of course.

> You were right. Shouldn't have gone. But when did I ever take advice? I always knew better, didn't I? Now it's too late. What I showed you that day at the Met—God help me, there's so much more. I found the truth, and now I can't bear it. Don't make my mistake. Don't look ever again, I beg you, at Van Dorn's paintings. The headaches. Can't stand the pain. Need a break. Am going home. Stay cool. Paint well. I love you, pal. Your friend forever,
>
> Myers

In her postscript, the nurse apologized for her English. She sometimes took care of aged Americans on the Riviera, she said, and had to learn the language. But she understood what she heard better than she could speak it or write it, and hoped that what she'd written made sense. It didn't, but that wasn't her fault. Myers had been in great pain, sedated with morphine, not thinking clearly, she said. The miracle was that he'd managed to be coherent at all.

> Your friend was staying at our only hotel. The manager says that he slept little and ate even less. His research was obsessive. He filled his room with reproductions of Van Dorn's work. He tried to duplicate Van Dorn's daily schedule. He demanded paints and canvas, refused all meals, and wouldn't answer his door. Three days ago, a scream woke the manager. The door was blocked. It took three men to break it down. Your friend used the sharp end of a paintbrush to stab out his eyes. The clinic here is excellent. Physically your friend will recover, although he will never see again. But I worry about his mind.

Myers had said he was going home. It had taken a week for the letter to reach me. I assumed his parents would have been informed immediately by phone or telegram. He was probably back in the States by now. I knew his parents lived in Denver, but I didn't know their first names or address, so I took a cab to the New York Public Library, checked the Denver phone book, and went down the list for Myers, using my credit card to call every one of them till I made contact. Not with his parents but with a family friend watching their house. Myers hadn't been flown to the States. His parents had gone to the south of France. I caught the next available plane. Not that it matters, but I was supposed to be married that weekend.

La Verge is thirty kilometers inland from Nice. I hired a driver. The road curved through olive trees and farmland, crested cypress-covered hills, and often skirted cliffs. Passing an orchard, I had the eerie conviction that I'd seen it before. Entering La Verge, my déjà vu strengthened. The village seemed trapped in the nineteenth century. Except for phone poles and power lines, it looked exactly as Van Dorn had painted it. I recognized the narrow, cobbled streets and rustic shops that Van Dorn had made famous. I asked directions. It wasn't hard to find Myers and his parents.

The last time I saw my friend, the undertaker was putting the lid on his coffin. I had trouble sorting out the details, but despite my burning tears, I gradually came to understand that the local clinic was as good as the nurse had assured me in her note. All things being equal, he'd have lived.

But the damage to his mind had been another matter. He'd complained of headaches. He'd also become increasingly distressed. Even morphine hadn't helped. He'd been left alone only for a minute, appearing to be asleep. In that brief interval he'd managed to stagger from his bed, grope across the room, and find a pair of scissors. Yanking off his bandages, he'd jabbed the scissors into an empty eye socket and tried to ream out his brain. He'd collapsed before accomplishing his purpose, but the damage had been sufficient. Death had taken two days.

His parents were pale, incoherent with shock. I somehow controlled my own shock enough to try to comfort them. Despite the blur of those terrible hours, I remember noticing the kind of irrelevance that signals the mind's attempt to reassert normality. Myers's father wore Gucci loafers and an eighteen-karat Rolex watch. In grad school Myers had lived on as strict a budget as I had. I had no idea he came from wealthy parents.

I helped them make arrangements to fly his body back to the States. I went to Nice with them and stayed by their side as they watched the crate that contained his coffin being loaded onto the baggage compartment of the plane. I shook their hands and hugged them. I waited as they sobbed and trudged down the boarding tunnel. An hour later I was back in La Verge.

I returned because of a promise. I wanted to ease his parents' suffering—and my own. Because I'd been his friend. "You've got too much to take care of," I'd said to his parents. "The long trip home. The arrangements for the funeral." My voice had choked. "Let me help. I'll settle things here, pay whatever bills he owes, pack up his clothes and . . ." I took a deep breath. "And his books and whatever else he had and send them home to you. Let me do that. I'd consider it a kindness. Please. I need to do *something*."

True to his ambition, Myers had managed to rent the same room taken by Van Dorn at the village's only hotel. Don't be surprised that it was available. The management used it to promote the hotel. A plaque announced the historic value of the room. The furnishings were the same style as when Van Dorn had stayed there. Tourists, to be sure, had paid to peer in and sniff the residue of genius. But business had been slow this season, and Myers had wealthy parents. For a generous sum, coupled with his typical enthusiasm, he'd convinced the hotel's owner to let him have that room.

I rented a different room—more like a closet—two doors down the hall and, my eyes still burning from tears, went into Van Dorn's musty sanctuary to pack my dear dead friend's possessions. Prints of Van Dorn paintings were everywhere, several splattered with dried blood. Heartsick, I made a stack of them.

That's when I found the diary.

During grad school I'd taken a course in Postimpressionism that emphasized Van Dorn, and I'd read a facsimile edition of his diary. The publisher had photocopied the handwritten pages and bound them, adding an introduction and footnotes. The diary had been cryptic from the start, but as Van Dorn became more feverish about his work, as his nervous breakdown became more severe, his statements deteriorated into riddles. His handwriting—hardly neat, even when he was sane—went quickly out of control and finally turned into almost indecipherable slashes and curves as he rushed to unloose his frantic thoughts.

I sat at a small wooden desk and paged through the diary, recognizing phrases I'd read years before. With each passage my stomach turned colder. Because this diary *wasn't* the published photocopy. Instead, it was a notebook, and though I wanted to believe that Myers had somehow, impossibly, gotten his hands on the original diary, I knew I was fooling myself. The pages in this ledger weren't yellow and brittle with age. The ink hadn't faded till it was brown more than blue. The notebook had been purchased and written in recently. It wasn't Van Dorn's diary. It belonged to *Myers*. The ice in my stomach turned to lava.

Glancing sharply away from the ledger, I saw a shelf beyond the desk and a stack of other notebooks. Apprehensive, I grabbed them and in a fearful rush flipped through them. My stomach threatened to erupt. Each notebook was the same, the words identical.

My hands shook as I looked again to the shelf, found the facsimile edition of the original, and compared it with the notebooks. I moaned, imagining Myers at this desk, his expression intense and insane as he reproduced the diary word for word, slash for slash, curve for curve. Eight times.

Myers had indeed immersed himself, straining to put himself into Van Dorn's disintegrating frame of mind. And in the end he'd succeeded. The weapon Van Dorn had used to stab out his eyes had been the sharp end of a paintbrush. In the mental hospital, Van Dorn had finished the job by skewering his brain with a pair of scissors. Like Myers. Or vice versa. When Myers had finally broken, had he and Van Dorn been horribly indistinguishable?

I pressed my hands to my face. Whimpers squeezed from my convulsing throat. It seemed forever before I stopped sobbing. My consciousness strained to control my anguish. ("Orange is for anguish," Myers had said.) Rationality fought to subdue my distress. ("The critics who devoted themselves to analyzing Van Dorn," Myers had said. "The ones who haven't been recognized for their genius, just as Van Dorn wasn't recognized. They suffered . . . And just like Van Dorn, they stabbed out their eyes.") Had they done it with a paintbrush? I wondered. Were the parallels that exact? And in the end, had they, too, used scissors to skewer their brains?

I scowled at the prints I'd been stacking. Many still surrounded me—on the walls, the floor, the bed, the windows, even the ceiling. A swirl of colors. A vortex of brilliance.

Or at least I once had thought of them as brilliant. But now, with the insight Myers had given me, with the vision I'd gained in the Metropolitan Museum, I saw behind the sun-drenched cypresses and hayfields, the orchards and meadows, toward their secret darkness, toward the minuscule, twisted arms and gaping mouths, the black dots of tortured eyes, the blue knots of writhing bodies. ("Blue is for insanity," Myers had said.)

All it took was a slight shift of perception, and there weren't any orchards and hayfields, only a terrifying gestalt of souls in hell. Van Dorn had indeed invented a new stage of Impressionism. He'd impressed upon the splendor of God's creation the teeming images of his own disgust. His paintings didn't glorify. They abhorred. Everywhere Van Dorn had looked, he'd seen his own private nightmare. Blue was for insanity, indeed, and if you fixated on Van Dorn's insanity long enough, you, too, became insane. ("Don't look ever again, I beg you, at Van Dorn's paintings," Myers had said in his letter.) In the last stages of his breakdown, had Myers somehow become lucid enough to try to warn me? ("Can't stand the headaches. Need a break. Am going home.") In a way I'd never suspected, he'd indeed gone home.

Another startling thought occurred to me. ("The critics who devoted themselves to analyzing Van Dorn. They each tried to paint in Van Dorn's style," Myers had said a year ago.) As if attracted by a magnet, my gaze swung across the welter of prints and focused on the corner across from me, where two canvas originals leaned against the wall. I shivered, stood, and haltingly approached them.

They'd been painted by an amateur. Myers was an art *historian,* after all. The colors were clumsily applied, especially the splotches of orange and blue. The cypresses were crude. At their bases, the rocks looked like cartoons. The sky needed texture. But I knew what the black dots among them were meant to suggest. I understood the purpose of the tiny blue gashes. The miniature, anguished faces and twisted limbs were implied, even if Myers had lacked the talent to depict them. He'd contracted Van Dorn's madness. All that had remained were the terminal stages.

I sighed from the pit of my soul. As the village's church bell rang, I prayed that my friend had found peace.

It was dark when I left the hotel. I needed to walk, to escape the greater darkness of that room, to feel at liberty, to think. But my footsteps and inquiries led me down a narrow cobbled street toward the village's clinic, where Myers had finished what he'd started in Van Dorn's room. I asked at the desk and five minutes later introduced myself to an attractive, dark-haired, thirtyish woman.

The nurse's English was more than adequate. She said her name was Clarisse.

"You took care of my friend," I said. "You sent me the letter he dictated and added a note of your own."

She nodded. "He worried me. He was so distressed."

The fluorescent lights in the vestibule hummed. We sat on a bench.

"I'm trying to understand why he killed himself," I said. "I think I know, but I'd like your opinion."

Her eyes, a bright, intelligent hazel, suddenly were guarded. "He stayed too long in his room. He studied too much." She shook her head and stared toward the floor. "The mind can be a trap. It can be a torture."

"But he was excited when he came here?"

"Yes."

"Despite his studies, he behaved as if he'd come on vacation?"

"Very much."

"Then what made him change? My friend was unusual, I agree. What we call high-strung. But he *enjoyed* doing research. He might have looked sick from too much work, but he thrived on learning. His body was nothing, but his mind was brilliant. What tipped the balance, Clarisse?"

"Tipped the—?"

"Made him depressed instead of excited. What did he learn that made him—?"

She stood and looked at her watch. "Forgive me. I stopped work twenty minutes ago. I'm expected at a friend's."

My voice hardened. "Of course. I wouldn't want to keep you."

Outside the clinic, beneath the light at its entrance, I stared at my own watch, surprised to see that it was almost eleven-thirty. Fatigue made my knees ache. The trauma of the day had taken away my appetite, but I knew I should try to eat, and after walking back to the hotel's dining room, I ordered a chicken sandwich and a glass of Chablis. I meant to eat in my room but never got that far. Van Dorn's room and the diary beckoned.

The sandwich and wine went untasted. Sitting at the desk, surrounded by the swirling colors and hidden horrors of Van Dorn prints, I opened a notebook and tried to understand.

A knock at the door made me turn.

Again I glanced at my watch, astonished to find that hours had passed like minutes. It was almost two A.M.

The knock was repeated, gentle but insistent. The manager?

"Come in," I said in French. "The door isn't locked."

The knob turned. The door swung open.

Clarisse stepped in. Instead of her nurse's uniform, she now wore sneakers, jeans, and a sweater whose tight-fitting yellow accentuated the hazel in her eyes.

"I apologize," she said in English. "I must have seemed rude at the clinic."

"Not at all. You had an appointment. I was keeping you."

She shrugged self-consciously. "I sometimes leave the clinic so late, I don't have a chance to see my friend."

"I understand perfectly."

She drew a hand through her lush, long hair. "My friend got tired. As I walked home, passing the hotel, I saw a light up here. On the chance it might be you ..."

I nodded, waiting.

I had the sense she'd been avoiding it, but now she turned toward the room. Toward where I'd found the dried blood on the prints. "The doctor and I came as fast as we could when the manager phoned us that afternoon." She stared at the prints. "How could so much beauty cause so much pain?"

"Beauty?" I glanced toward the tiny, gaping mouths.

"You mustn't stay here. Don't make the mistake your friend did."

"Mistake?"

"You've had a long journey. You've suffered a shock. You need to rest. You'll wear yourself out as your friend did."

"I was just looking through some things of his. I'll be packing them to send them back to America."

"Do it quickly. You mustn't torture yourself by thinking about what happened here. It isn't good to surround yourself with the things that disturbed your friend. Don't intensify your grief."

"Surround myself? My friend would have said 'immerse.' "

"You look exhausted. Come." She held out her hand. "I'll take you to your room. Sleep will ease your pain. If you need some pills to help you . . ."

"Thanks. But a sedative won't be necessary."

She continued to offer her hand. I took it and went to the hallway.

For a moment I stared back toward the prints and the horror within the beauty. I said a silent prayer for Myers, shut off the lights, and locked the door.

We went down the hall. In my room, I sat on the bed.

"Sleep long and well," she said.

"I hope."

"You have my sympathy." She kissed my cheek.

I touched her shoulder. Her lips shifted toward my own. She leaned against me.

We sank toward the bed. In silence, we made love.

Sleep came like her kisses, softly smothering.

But in my nightmares there were tiny, gaping mouths.

Sunlight glowed through my window. With aching eyes I looked at my watch. Half past ten. My head hurt.

Clarisse had left a note on my bureau.

Last night was sympathy. To share and ease your grief. Do what you intended. Pack your friend's belongings. Send them to America. Go with them. Don't make your friend's mistake. Don't, as you said *he* said, "immerse" yourself. Don't let beauty give you pain.

I meant to leave. I truly believe that. I phoned the front desk and asked the concierge to send up some boxes. After I showered and shaved, I went to Myers's room, where I finished stacking the prints. I made another stack of books and another of clothes. I packed everything into the boxes and looked around to make sure I hadn't forgotten anything.

The two canvases that Myers had painted still leaned against a corner. I decided not to take them. No one needed to be reminded of the delusions that had overcome him.

All that remained was to seal the boxes, to address and mail them. But as I started to close the flap on a box, I saw the notebooks inside.

So much suffering, I thought. So much waste.

Once more I leafed through a notebook. Various passages caught my eye. Van Dorn's discouragement about his failed career. His reasons for leaving Paris to come to La Verge— the stifling, backbiting artists' community, the snobbish critics and their sneering responses to his early efforts. *Need to free myself of convention. Need to void myself of aesthete politics, to shit it out of me. To find what's never been painted. To feel instead of being told what to feel. To see instead of imitating what others have seen.*

I knew from the biographies how impoverished Van Dorn's ambition had made him. In Paris he'd literally eaten slops thrown into alleys behind restaurants. He'd been able to afford his quest to La Verge only because a successful but very conventional (and now ridiculed) painter friend had loaned him a small sum of money. Eager to conserve his endowment, Van Dorn had walked all the way from Paris to the south of France.

In those days, you have to remember, the Riviera was an unfashionable area of hills, rocks, farms, and villages. Limping into La Verge, Van Dorn must have been a pathetic sight. He'd chosen this provincial town precisely because it *was* unconventional, because it offered mundane scenes so in contrast with the salons of Paris that no other artist would dare to paint them.

Need to create what's never been imagined, he'd written. For six despairing months he tried and failed. He finally self-doubted, then suddenly reversed himself and, in a year of unbelievably brilliant productivity, gave the world thirty-eight masterpieces. At the time, of course, he couldn't trade any canvas for a meal. But the world knows better now.

He must have painted in a frenzy. His sudden-found energy must have been enormous. To me, a would-be artist with technical facility but only conventional eyes, he achieved the ultimate. Despite his suffering, I envied him.

When I compared my maudlin, Wyeth-like depictions of Iowa landscapes to Van Dorn's trendsetting genius, I despaired. The task awaiting me back in the States was to imitate beer cans and cigarettes for magazine ads.

I continued flipping through the notebook, tracing the course of Van Dorn's despair and epiphany. His victory had a price, to be sure. Insanity. Self-blinding. Suicide. But I had to wonder if perhaps, as he died, he'd have chosen to reverse his life if he'd been able. He must have known how remarkable, how truly astonishing, his work had become.

Or perhaps he didn't. The last canvas he'd painted before stabbing his eyes had been of himself. A lean-faced, brooding man with short, thinning hair, sunken features, pallid skin, and a scraggly beard. The famous portrait reminded me of how I always thought Christ would have looked just before he was crucified. All that was missing was the crown of thorns. But Van Dorn had a different crown of thorns. Not around but *within* him. Disguised among his scraggly beard and sunken features, the tiny, gaping mouths and writhing bodies told it all. His suddenly acquired vision had stung him too much.

As I read the notebook, again distressed by Myers's effort to reproduce Van Dorn's agonized words and handwriting exactly, I reached the section where Van Dorn described his epiphany: *La Verge! I walked! I saw! I feel! Canvas! Paint! Creation and damnation!*

After that cryptic passage, the notebook—and Van Dorn's diary—became totally incoherent. Except for the persistent refrain of severe and increasing headaches.

I was waiting outside the clinic when Clarisse arrived to start her shift at three o'clock. The sun was brilliant, glinting off her eyes. She wore a burgundy skirt and a turquoise blouse. Mentally I stroked their cottony texture.

When she saw me, her footsteps faltered. Forcing a smile, she approached.

"You came to say good-bye?" She sounded hopeful.

"No. To ask you some questions."

Her smile disintegrated. "I mustn't be late for work."

"This'll take just a minute. My French vocabulary needs improvement. I didn't bring a dictionary. The name of this village. La Verge. What does it mean?"

She hunched her shoulders as if to say the question was

unimportant. "It's not very colorful. The literal translation is 'the stick.' "

"That's all?"

She reacted to my frown. "There are rough equivalents. 'The branch.' 'The switch.' A willow, for example, that a father might use to discipline a child."

"And it doesn't mean anything else?"

"Indirectly. The synonyms keep getting farther from the literal sense. A wand, perhaps. Or a rod. The kind of forked stick that people who claim they can find water hold ahead of them when they walk across a field. The stick is supposed to bend down if there's water."

"We call it a divining rod. My father once told me he'd seen a man who could actually make one work. I always suspected the man just tilted the stick with his hands. Do you suppose this village got its name because long ago someone found water here with a divining rod?"

"Why would anyone have bothered when these hills have so many streams and springs? What makes you interested in the name?"

"Something I read in Van Dorn's diary. The village's name excited him for some reason."

"But *anything* could have excited him. He was insane."

"Eccentric. But he didn't become insane until after that passage in his diary."

"You mean, his *symptoms* didn't show themselves until after that. You're not a psychiatrist."

I had to agree.

"Again, I'm afraid I'll seem rude. I really must go to work." She hesitated. "Last night . . ."

"Was exactly what you described in the note. A gesture of sympathy. And attempt to ease my grief. You didn't mean it to be the start of anything."

"Please do what I asked. Please leave. Don't destroy yourself like the others."

"Others?"

"Like your friend."

"No, you said, 'others.' " My words were rushed. "Clarisse, tell me."

She glanced up, squinting as if she'd been cornered. "After your friend stabbed out his eyes, I heard talk around the village. Older people. It could be merely gossip that became exaggerated with the passage of time."

"What did they say?"

She squinted harder. "Twenty years ago a man came here to do research on Van Dorn. He stayed three months and had a breakdown."

"He stabbed out his eyes?"

"Rumors drifted back that he blinded himself in a mental hospital in England. Ten years before, another man came. He jabbed scissors through an eye, all the way into his brain."

I stared, unable to control the spasms that racked my shoulder blades. "What the hell is going on?"

I asked around the village. No one would talk to me. At the hotel the manager told me he'd decided to stop renting Van Dorn's room. I had to remove Myers's belongings at once.

"But I can still stay in *my* room?"

"If that's what you wish. I don't recommend it, but even France is still a free country."

I paid the bill, went upstairs, moved the packed boxes from Van Dorn's room to mine, and turned in surprise as the phone rang.

The call was from my fiancée.

When was I coming home?

I didn't know.

What about the wedding this weekend?

The wedding would have to be postponed.

I winced as she slammed down the phone.

I sat on the bed and couldn't help recalling the last time I'd sat there, with Clarisse standing over me, just before we'd made love. I was throwing away the life I'd tried to build.

For a moment I came close to calling back my fiancée, but a different sort of compulsion made me scowl toward the boxes, toward Van Dorn's diary. In the note Clarisse had added to Myers's letter, she'd said that his research had become so obsessive that he'd tried to recreate Van Dorn's daily habits. Again it occurred to me—at the end, had Myers and Van Dorn become indistinguishable? Was the secret to what had happened to Myers hidden in the diary, just as the suffering faces were hidden in Van Dorn's paintings? I grabbed one of the ledgers. Scanning the pages, I looked for references to Van Dorn's daily routine. And so it began.

I've said that except for telephone poles and electrical lines, La Verge seemed caught in the previous century. Not only was the hotel still in existence, but so were Van Dorn's favorite tavern, and the bakery where he'd bought his morning croissant. A small restaurant he favored remained in business. On the edge of the village, a trout stream where he sometimes sat with a mid-afternoon glass of wine still bubbled along, though pollution had long since killed the trout. I went to all of them, in the order and at the time he recorded in his diary.

After a week—breakfast at eight, lunch at two, a glass of wine at the trout stream, a stroll to the countryside, then back to the room—I knew the diary so well, I didn't need to refer to it. Mornings had been Van Dorn's time to paint. The light was best then, he'd written. And evenings were a time for remembering and sketching.

It finally came to me that I wouldn't be following the schedule exactly if I didn't paint and sketch when Van Dorn had done so. I bought a notepad, canvas, pigments, a palette, whatever I needed, and, for the first time since leaving grad school, I tried to *create*. I used local scenes that Van Dorn had favored and produced what you'd expect: uninspired versions of Van Dorn's paintings. With no discoveries, no understanding of what had ultimately undermined Myers's sanity, tedium set in. My finances were almost gone. I prepared to give up.

Except . . .

I had the disturbing sense that I'd missed something. A part of Van Dorn's routine that wasn't explicit in the diary. Or something about the locales themselves that I hadn't noticed, though I'd been painting them in Van Dorn's spirit, if not with his talent.

Clarisse found me sipping wine on the sunlit bank of the no longer trout-filled stream. I felt her shadow and turned toward her silhouette against the sun.

I hadn't seen her for two weeks, since our uneasy conversation outside the clinic. Even with the sun in my eyes, she looked more beautiful than I remembered.

"When was the last time you changed your clothes?" she asked.

A year ago I'd said the same to Myers.

"You need a shave. You've been drinking too much. You look awful."

I sipped my wine and shrugged. "Well, you know what the drunk said about his bloodshot eyes. You think they look bad to you? You should see them from *my* side."

"At least you can joke."

"I'm beginning to think that *I'm* the joke."

"You're definitely not a joke." She sat beside me. "You're becoming your friend. Why don't you leave?"

"I'm tempted."

"Good." She touched my hand.

"Clarisse?"

"Yes?"

"Answer some questions one more time?"

She studied me. "Why?"

"Because if I get the right answers, I might leave."

She nodded slowly.

Back in town, in my room, I showed her the stack of prints. I almost told her about the faces they contained, but her brooding features stopped me. She thought I was disturbed enough as it was.

"When I walk in the afternoons, I go to the settings Van Dorn chose for his paintings." I sorted through the prints. "This orchard. This farm. This pond. This cliff. And so on."

"Yes, I recognize these places. I've seen them all."

"I hoped if I saw them, maybe I'd understand what happened to my friend. You told me he went to them as well. Each of them is within a five-mile radius of the village. Many are close together. It wasn't difficult to find each site. Except for one."

She didn't ask the obvious question. Instead, she tensely rubbed her arm.

When I'd taken the boxes from Van Dorn's room, I'd also removed the two paintings Myers had attempted. Now I pulled them from where I'd tucked them under the bed.

"My friend did these. It's obvious he wasn't an artist. But as crude as they are, you can see they both depict the same area."

I slid a Van Dorn print from the bottom of the stack.

"*This* area," I said. "A grove of cypresses in a hollow, surrounded by rocks. It's the only site I haven't been able to find. I've asked the villagers. They claim they don't know where it is. Do *you* know, Clarisse? Can you tell me? It must have some significance if my friend was fixated on it enough to try to paint it *twice*."

Clarisse scratched a fingernail across her wrist. "I'm sorry."

"What?"

"I can't help you."

"Can't or won't? Do you mean you don't know where to find it, or you know but you won't tell me?"

"I said I can't help."

"What's wrong with this village, Clarisse? What's everybody trying to hide?"

"I've done my best." She shook her head, stood, and walked to the door. She glanced back sadly. "Sometimes it's better to leave well enough alone. Sometimes there are reasons for secrets."

I watched her go down the hall. "Clarisse . . ."

She turned and spoke a single word: "North." She was crying. "God help you," she added. "I'll pray for your soul." Then she disappeared down the stairs.

For the first time I felt afraid.

Five minutes later I left the hotel. In my walks to the sites of Van Dorn's paintings, I'd always chosen the easiest routes—east, west, and south. Whenever I'd asked about the distant, tree-lined hills to the north, the villagers had told me there was nothing of interest there, nothing at all to do with Van Dorn. What about cypresses in a hollow? I'd asked. There weren't any cypresses in those hills, only olive trees, they'd answered. But now I knew.

La Verge was in the southern end of an oblong valley, squeezed by cliffs to the east and west. To reach the northern hills, I'd have to walk twenty miles at least.

I rented a car. Leaving a dust cloud, I pressed my foot on the accelerator and started toward the rapidly enlarging hills. The trees I'd seen from the village were indeed olive trees. But the lead-colored rocks among them were the same as in Van Dorn's painting. I skidded along the road, veering up through the hills. Near the top I found a narrow space to park and rushed from the car. But which direction to take? On impulse, I chose left and hurried among the rocks and trees.

My decision seems less arbitrary now. Something about

the slopes to the left was more dramatic, more aesthetically compelling. A greater wildness in the landscape. A sense of depth, of substance.

My instincts urged me forward. I'd reached the hills at quarter after five. Time compressed eerily. At once, my watch showed ten past seven. The sun blazed, crimson, over the bluffs. I kept searching, letting the grotesque landscape guide me. The ridges and ravines were like a maze, every turn of which either blocked or gave access, controlling my direction. I rounded a crag, scurried down a slope of thorns, ignored the rips in my shirt and the blood streaming from my hands, and stopped on the precipice of a hollow. Cypresses, not olive trees, filled the basin. Boulders jutted among them and formed a grotto.

The basin was steep. I skirted its brambles, ignoring their scalding sting. Boulders led me down. I stifled my misgivings, frantic to reach the bottom.

This hollow, this basin of cypresses and boulders, this thorn-rimmed funnel, was the image not only of Van Dorn's painting but of the canvases Myers had attempted. But why had this place so affected them?

The answer came as quickly as the question. I heard before I saw, though hearing doesn't accurately describe my sensation. The sound was so faint and high-pitched, it was almost beyond the range of detection. At first I thought I was near a hornet's nest. I sensed a subtle vibration in the otherwise still air of the hollow. I felt an itch behind my eardrums, a tingle on my skin. The sound was actually many sounds, each identical, merging, like the collective buzz of a swarm of insects. But this was high-pitched. Not a buzz but more like a distant chorus of shrieks and wails.

Frowning, I took another step toward the cypresses. The tingle on my skin intensified. The itch behind my eardrums became so irritating, I raised my hands to the sides of my head. I came close enough to see within the trees, and what I noticed with terrible clarity made me panic. Gasping, I stumbled back. But not in time. What shot from the trees was too small and fast for me to identify.

It struck my right eye. The pain was excruciating, as if the white-hot tip of a needle had pierced my retina and lanced my brain. I clamped my right hand across that eye and screamed.

I continued stumbling back, agony spurring my panic. But

the sharp, hot pain intensified, surging through my skull. My knees bent. My consciousness dimmed. I fell against the slope.

It was after midnight when I managed to drive back to the village. Though my eye no longer burned, my panic was more extreme. Still dizzy from having passed out, I tried to keep control when I entered the clinic and asked where Clarisse lived. She'd invited me to visit, I claimed. A sleepy attendant frowned but told me. I drove desperately toward her cottage, five blocks away.

Lights were on. I knocked. She didn't answer. I pounded harder, faster. At last I saw a shadow. When the door swung open, I lurched into the living room. I barely noticed the negligee Clarisse clutched around her, or the open door to her bedroom, where a startled woman sat up in bed, held a sheet to her breasts, and stood quickly to shut the bedroom door.

"What the hell do you think you're doing?" Clarisse yelled. "I didn't invite you in! I didn't—!"

I managed the strength to talk: "I don't have time to explain. I'm terrified. I need your help."

She clutched her negligee tighter.

"I've been stung. I think I've caught a disease. Help me stop whatever's inside me. Antibiotics. An antidote. Anything you can think of. Maybe it's a virus, maybe a fungus. Maybe it acts like bacteria."

"What happened?"

"I told you, no time. I'd have asked for help at the clinic, but they wouldn't have understood. They'd have thought I'd had a breakdown, the same as Myers. You've got to take me there. You've got to make sure I'm injected with as much of any and every drug that might possibly kill this thing."

"I'll dress as fast as I can."

As we rushed to the clinic, I described what had happened. She phoned the doctor the moment we arrived. While we waited, she disinfected my eye and gave me something for my rapidly developing headache. The doctor showed up, his sleepy features becoming alert when he saw how distressed I was. True to my prediction, he reacted as if I'd had a breakdown. I shouted at him to humor me and saturate me with antibiotics. Clarisse made sure it wasn't just a sedative he gave me. He used every compatible combination. If I thought it would have worked, I'd have swallowed Drāno.

What I'd seen within the cypresses were tiny, gaping mouths and minuscule, writhing bodies, as small and camouflaged as those in Van Dorn's paintings. I know now that Van Dorn wasn't imposing his insane vision on reality. He wasn't an Impressionist. At least not in his *Cypresses in a Hollow*. I'm convinced that this painting was his first after his brain became infected. He was literally depicting what he'd seen on one of his walks. Later, as the infection progressed, he saw the gaping mouths and writhing bodies like an overlay on everything else he looked at. In that sense, too, he wasn't an Impressionist. To him, the gaping mouths and writhing bodies *were* in all those later scenes. To the limit of his infected brain, he painted what to him *was* reality. His art was representational.

I know, believe me. Because the drugs didn't work. My brain is as diseased as Van Dorn's . . . or Myers's. I've tried to understand why they didn't panic when they were stung, why they didn't rush to a hospital to make a doctor understand what had happened. My conclusion is that Van Dorn had been so desperate for a vision to enliven his paintings that he gladly endured the suffering. And Myers had been so desperate to understand Van Dorn that when stung, he'd willingly taken the risk to identify even more with his subject until, too late, he'd realized his mistake.

Orange is for anguish, blue for insanity. How true. Whatever infects my brain has affected my color sense. More and more, orange and blue overpower the other colors I know are there. I have no choice. I see little else. My paintings are *rife* with orange and blue.

My paintings. Because I've solved another mystery. It always puzzled me how Van Dorn could have suddenly been seized by such energetic genius that he painted thirty-eight masterpieces in one year. I know the answer now. What's in my head, the gaping mouths and writhing bodies, the orange of anguish and the blue of insanity, cause such pressure, such headaches that I've tried everything to subdue them, to get them out. I went from codeine to Demerol to morphine. Each helped for a time but not enough. Then I learned what Van Dorn understood and Myers attempted. Painting the disease somehow gets it out of you. For a time. And then you paint harder, faster. Anything to relieve the pain. But Myers wasn't an artist. The disease had no release and reached its terminal stage in weeks instead of Van Dorn's year.

But *I'm* an artist—or used to hope I was. I had skill without a vision. Now, God help me, I've got a vision. At first I painted the cypresses and their secret. I accomplished what you'd expect. An imitation of Van Dorn's original. But I refuse to suffer pointlessly. I vividly recall the portraits of Midwestern landscapes I produced in grad school. The dark-earthed Iowa landscape. The attempt to make an observer feel the fecundity of the soil. At the time the results were ersatz Wyeth. But not anymore. The twenty paintings I've so far stored away aren't versions of Van Dorn either. They're my own creations. Unique. A combination of the disease and my experience. Aided by powerful memory, I paint the river that flows through Iowa City. Blue. I paint the cornfields that cram the big-sky rolling country outside of town. Orange. I paint my innocence. My youth. With my ultimate discovery hidden within them. Ugliness lurks within the beauty. Horror festers in my brain.

Clarisse at last told me about the local legend. When La Verge was founded, she said, a meteor streaked from the sky. It lit the night. It burst upon the hills north of here. Flames erupted. Trees were consumed. The hour was late. Few villagers saw it. The site of the impact was too far away for those few witnesses to rush that night to see the crater. In the morning the smoke had dispersed. The embers had died. Though the witnesses tried to find the meteor, the lack of the roads that now exist hampered their search through the tangled hills to the point of discouragement. A few among the few witnesses persisted. The few of the few of the few who had accomplished their quest staggered back to the village, babbling about headaches and tiny, gaping mouths. Using sticks, they scraped disturbing images in the dirt and eventually stabbed out their eyes. Over the centuries, legend has it, similar self-mutilations occurred whenever someone returned from seeking the crater in those hills. The unknown had power then. The hills acquired the negative force of taboo. No villager, then or now, intruded on what came to be called the place where God's wand touched the earth. A poetic description of a blazing meteor's impact. La Verge.

I don't conclude the obvious: that the meteor carried

spores that multiplied in the crater, which became a hollow eventually filled with cypresses. No—to me, the meteor was a cause but not an effect. I saw a pit among the cypresses, and from the pit, tiny mouths and writhing bodies resembling insects—how they wailed!—spewed. They clung to the leaves of the cypresses, flailed in anguish as they fell back, and instantly were replaced by other spewing, anguished souls.

Yes. Souls. For the meteor, I insist, was just the cause. The effect was the opening of hell. The tiny, wailing mouths are the damned. As *I* am damned. Desperate to survive, to escape from the ultimate prison we call hell, a frantic sinner lunged. He caught my eye and stabbed my brain, the gateway to my soul. My soul. It festers. I paint to remove the pus.

I talk. That helps somehow. Clarisse writes it down while her female lover rubs my shoulders.

My paintings are brilliant. I'll be recognized, as I'd always dreamed. As a genius, of course.

At such a cost.

The headaches grow worse. The orange is more brilliant. The blue more disturbing.

I try my best. I urge myself to be stronger then Myers, whose endurance lasted only weeks. Van Dorn persisted for a year. Maybe genius is strength.

My brain swells. How it threatens to split my skull. The gaping mouths blossom.

The headaches! I tell myself to be strong. Another day. Another rush to complete another painting.

The sharp end of my paintbrush invites. Anything to lance my seething mental boil, to jab my eyes for the ecstasy of relief. But I have to endure.

On a table near my left hand, the scissors wait.

But not today. Or tomorrow.

I'll outlast Van Dorn.

The Age of Desire
Clive Barker

One of the most original talents to emerge in modern horror fiction, Clive Barker (1952–) dazzled the field with his six *Books of Blood* published between 1984 and 1985. The stories in these volumes shocked many readers with their open breaking of taboos and refusal to acknowledge limits in either their subject matter or approaches to horror themes. Barker's 1985 story, "The Age of Desire," is the only one he has written to date with overt science fiction elements. In its sympathetic portrayal of a "monster" who sees more clearly than its human creator, it can be read as a tribute to another taboo-breaking science fiction-horror hybrid, Mary Shelley's *Frankenstein*.

The burning man propelled himself down the steps of the Hume Laboratories as the police car—summoned, he presumed, by the alarm either Welles or Dance had set off upstairs—appeared at the gate and swung up the driveway. As he ran from the door the car screeched up to the steps and discharged its human cargo. He waited in the shadows, too exhausted by terror to run any farther, certain that they would see him. But they disappeared through the swing doors without so much as a glance toward his torment. Am I on fire at all? he wondered. Was this horrifying spectacle— his flesh baptized with a polished flame that seared but failed to consume—simply a hallucination, for his eyes and his eyes only? If so, perhaps all that he had suffered up in the laboratory had also been delirium. Perhaps he had not truly committed the crimes he had fled from, the heat in his flesh licking him into ecstasies.

He looked down his body. His exposed skin still crawled with livid dots of fire, but one by one they were being extinguished. He was going out, he realized, like a neglected bonfire. The sensations that had suffused him—so intense and so demanding that they had been as like pain as pleasure—were finally deserting his nerve endings, leaving a numbness for which he was grateful. His body, now appearing from beneath the veil of fire, was in a sorry condition. His skin was a panic-map of scratches, his clothes torn to shreds, his hands sticky with coagulating blood; blood, he knew, that was not his own. There was no avoiding the bitter truth. He *had* done all he had imagined doing. Even now the officers would be staring down at his atrocious handiwork.

He crept away from his niche beside the door and down the driveway, keeping a lookout for the return of the two policemen. Neither reappeared. The street beyond the gate was deserted. He started to run. He had managed only a few paces when the alarm in the building behind him was abruptly cut off. For several seconds his ears rang in sympathy with the silenced bell. Then, eerily, he began to hear the sound of heat—the surreptitious murmuring of embers—distant enough that he didn't panic, yet close as his heartbeat.

He limped on to put as much distance as he could between him and his felonies before they were discovered. But however fast he ran, the heat went with him, safe in some backwater of his gut, threatening with every desperate step he took to ignite him afresh.

It took Dooley several seconds to identify the cacophony he was hearing from the upper floor now that McBride had hushed the alarm bell. It was the high-pitched chattering of monkeys, and it came from one of the many rooms down the corridor to his right.

"Virgil," he called down the stairwell. "Get up here."

Not waiting for his partner to join him, Dooley headed off toward the source of the din. Halfway along the corridor the smell of static and new carpeting gave way to a more pungent combination: urine, disinfectant and rotting fruit. Dooley slowed his advance. He didn't like the smell any more than he liked the hysteria in the babble of monkey voices. But McBride was slow in answering his call, and after a short hesitation, Dooley's curiosity got the better of his disquiet. Hand on truncheon, he approached the open door and stepped in. His appearance sparked off another wave of frenzy from the animals, a dozen or so rhesus monkeys. They threw themselves around in their cages, somersaulting, screeching and berating the wire mesh. Their excitement was infectious. Dooley could feel the sweat begin to squeeze from his pores.

"Is there anybody here?" he called out.

The only reply came from the prisoners: more hysteria, more cage rattling. He stared across the room at them. They stared back, their teeth bared in fear or welcome; Dooley didn't know which, nor did he wish to test their intentions. He kept well clear of the bench on which the cages were lined up as he began a perfunctory search of the laboratory.

"I wondered what the hell the smell was," McBride said, appearing at the door.

"Just animals," Dooley replied.

"Don't they ever wash? Filthy buggers."

"Anything downstairs?"

"Nope," McBride said, crossing to the cages. The monkeys met his advance with more gymnastics. "Just the alarm."

"Nothing up here either," Dooley said. He was about to add, *"Don't do that,"* to prevent his partner putting his finger to the mesh, but before the words were out one of the animals seized the proffered digit and bit it. McBride wrested his finger free and threw a blow back against the mesh in retaliation. Squealing its anger, the occupant flung its scrawny body about in a lunatic fandango that threatened to pitch cage and monkey alike onto the floor.

"You'll need a tetanus shot for that," Dooley commented.

"Shit!" said McBride, "what's wrong with the little bastard anyhow?"

"Maybe they don't like strangers."

"They're out of their tiny minds." McBride sucked ruminatively on his finger, then spat. "I mean, look at them."

Dooley didn't answer.

"I said, *look* . . ." McBride repeated.

Very quietly, Dooley said: "Over here."

"What is it?"

"Just come over here."

McBride drew his gaze from the row of cages and across the cluttered work surfaces to where Dooley was staring at the ground, the look on his face one of fascinated revulsion. McBride neglected his finger sucking and threaded his way among the benches and stools to where his partner stood.

"Under there," Dooley murmured.

On the scuffed floor at Dooley's feet was a woman's beige shoe; beneath the bench was the shoe's owner. To judge by her cramped position she had either been secreted there by the miscreant or dragged herself out of sight and died in hiding.

"Is she dead?" McBride asked.

"Look at her, for Christ's sake," Dooley replied, "she's been torn open."

"We've got to check for vital signs," McBride reminded him. Dooley made no move to comply, so McBride squatted down in front of the victim and checked for a pulse at her ravaged neck. There was none. Her skin was still warm beneath his fingers however. A gloss of saliva on her cheek had not yet dried.

Dooley, calling in his report, looked down at the deceased. The worst of her wounds, on the upper torso, were masked by McBride's crouching body. All he could see was a fall of auburn hair and her legs, one foot shoeless, protruding from her hiding place. They were beautiful legs, he thought. He might have whistled after such legs once upon a time.

"She's a doctor or a technician," McBride said. "She's wearing a lab coat." Or she had been. In fact the coat had been ripped open, as had the layers of clothing beneath, and then, as if to complete the exhibition, the skin and muscle beneath that. McBride peered into her chest. The sternum had been snapped and the heart teased from its seat, as if her killer had wanted to take it as a keepsake and been interrupted in the act. He perused her without squeamishness; he had always prided himself on his strong stomach.

"Are you satisfied she's dead?"

"Never saw deader."

"Carnegie's coming down," Dooley said, crossing to one of the sinks. Careless of fingerprints, he turned on the tap and splashed a handful of cold water onto his face. When he looked up from his ablutions McBride had left off his tête-à-tête with the corpse and was walking down the laboratory toward a bank of machinery.

"What do they do here, for Christ's sake?" he remarked. "Look at all this stuff."

"Some kind of research facility," Dooley said.

"What do they research?"

"How the hell do I know?" Dooley snapped. The ceaseless chatterings of the monkeys and the proximity of the dead woman made him want to desert the place. "Let's leave it be, huh?"

McBride ignored Dooley's request; equipment fascinated him. He stared entranced at the encephalograph and electro-cardiograph; at the printout units still disgorging yards of blank paper onto the floor; at the video display monitors and the consoles. The scene brought the *Marie Celeste* to his mind. This was like some deserted ship of science—still humming some tuneless song to itself as it sailed on, though there was neither captain nor crew left behind to attend upon it.

Beyond the wall of equipment was a window, no more than a yard square. McBride had assumed it let on to the exterior of the building, but now that he looked more closely he realized it did not. A test chamber lay beyond the banked units.

"Dooley . . . ?" he said, glancing around. The man had gone, however, down to meet Carnegie presumably. Content to be left to his exploration, McBride returned his attention to the window. There was no light on inside. Curious, he walked around the back of the banked equipment until he found the chamber door. It was ajar. Without hesitation, he stepped through.

Most of the light through the window was blocked by the instruments on the other side; the interior was dark. It took McBride's eyes a few seconds to get a true impression of the chaos the chamber contained: the overturned table; the chair of which somebody had made matchwood; the tangle of cables and demolished equipment—cameras, perhaps, to monitor proceedings in the chamber?—clusters of lights which had been similarly smashed. No professional vandal could have made a more thorough job of breaking up the chamber than had been made.

There was a smell in the air which McBride recognized but, irritatingly, couldn't place. He stood still, tantalized by the scent. The sound of sirens rose from down the corridor outside; Carnegie would be here in moments. Suddenly, the smell's association came to him. It was the same scent that twitched in his nostrils when, after making love to Jessica and—as was his ritual—washing himself, he returned from the bathroom to bedroom. It was the smell of sex. He smiled.

His face was still registering pleasure when a heavy object

sliced through the air and met his nose. He felt the cartilage give and a rush of blood come. He took two or three giddy steps backward, thereby avoiding the subsequent slice, but lost his footing in the disarray. He fell awkwardly in a litter of glass shards and looked up to see his assailant, wielding a metal bar, moving toward him. The man's face resembled one of the monkeys; the same yellowed teeth, the same rabid eyes. *"No!"* the man shouted, as he brought his makeshift club down on McBride, who managed to ward off the blow with his arm, snatching at the weapon in so doing. The attack had taken him unawares but now, with the pain in his mashed nose to add fury to his response, he was more than the equal of the aggressor. He plucked the club from the man, sweets from a babe, and leaped, roaring, to his feet. Any precepts he might once have been taught about arrest techniques had fled from his mind. He lay a hail of blows on the man's head and shoulders, forcing him backward across the chamber. The man cowered beneath the assault and eventually slumped, whimpering, against the wall. Only now, with his antagonist abused to the verge of unconsciousness, did McBride's furor falter. He stood in the middle of the chamber, gasping for breath, and watched the beaten man slip down the wall. He had made a profound error. The assailant, he now realized, was dressed in a white laboratory coat. He was, as Dooley was irritatingly fond of saying, on the side of the angels.

"Damn," said McBride, "shit, hell and damn."

The man's eyes flickered open, and he gazed up at McBride. His grasp on consciousness was evidently tenuous, but a look of recognition crossed his wide-browed, somber face. Or rather, recognition's absence.

"You're not him," he murmured.

"Who?" said McBride, realizing he might yet salvage his reputation from this fiasco if he could squeeze a clue from the witness. "Who did you think I was?"

The man opened his mouth, but no words emerged. Eager to hear the testimony, McBride crouched beside him and said: "Who did you think you were attacking?"

Again the mouth opened; again no audible words emerged. McBride pressed his suit. "It's important," he said, "just tell me who was here."

The man strove to voice his reply. McBride pressed his ear to the trembling mouth.

"In a pig's eye," the man said, then passed out, leaving McBride to curse his father, who'd bequeathed him a temper he was afraid he would probably live to regret. But then, what was living for?

Inspector Carnegie was used to boredom. For every rare moment of genuine discovery his professional life had furnished him with, he had endured hour upon hour of waiting for bodies to be photographed and examined, for lawyers to be bargained with and suspects intimidated. He had long ago given up attempting to fight this tide of ennui and, after his fashion, had learned the art of going with the flow. The processes of investigation could not be hurried. The wise man, he had come to appreciate, let the pathologists, the lawyers and all their tribes have their tardy way. All that mattered, in the fullness of time, was that the finger be pointed and that the guilty quake.

Now, with the clock on the laboratory wall reading twelve fifty-three a.m., and even the monkeys hushed in their cages, he sat at one of the benches and waited for Hendrix to finish his calculations. The surgeon consulted the thermometer, then stripped off his gloves like a second skin and threw them down onto the sheet on which the deceased lay. "It's always difficult," the doctor said, "fixing time of death. She's lost less than three degrees. I'd say she's been dead under two hours."

"The officers arrived at a quarter to twelve," Carnegie said, "so she died maybe half an hour before that?"

"Something of that order."

"Was she put in here?" he asked, indicating the place beneath the bench.

"Oh certainly. There's no way she hid herself away. Not with those injuries. They're quite something, aren't they?"

Carnegie stared at Hendrix. The man had presumably seen hundreds of corpses, in every conceivable condition, but the enthusiasm in his pinched features was unqualified. Carnegie found that mystery more fascinating in its way than that of the dead woman and her slaughterer. How could anyone possibly enjoy taking the rectal temperature of a corpse? It confounded him. But the pleasure was there, gleaming in the man's eyes.

"Motive?" Carnegie asked.

"Pretty explicit, isn't it? Rape. There's been very thorough molestation; contusions around the vagina; copious semen deposits. Plenty to work with."

"And the wounds on her torso?"

"Ragged. Tears more than cuts."

"Weapon?"

"Don't know." Hendrix made an inverted U of his mouth. "I mean, the flesh has been *mauled*. If it weren't for the rape evidence I'd be tempted to suggest an animal."

"Dog, you mean?"

"I was thinking more of a tiger," Hendrix said.

Carnegie frowned. "Tiger?"

"Joke," Hendrix replied, "I was making a joke, Carnegie. My Christ, do you have *any* sense of irony?"

"This isn't funny," Carnegie said.

"I'm not laughing," Hendrix replied with a sour look.

"The man McBride found in the test chamber?"

"What about him?"

"Suspect?"

"Not in a thousand years. We're looking for a *maniac*, Carnegie. Big, strong. Wild."

"And the wounding? Before or after?"

Hendrix scowled. "I don't know. Postmortem will give us more. But for what's it's worth, I think our man was in a frenzy. I'd say the wounding and the rape were probably simultaneous."

Carnegie's normally phlegmatic features registered something close to shock. "Simultaneous?"

Hendrix shrugged. "Lust's a funny thing," he said.

"Hilarious," came the appalled reply.

As was his wont, Carnegie had his driver deposit him half a mile from his doorstep to allow him a head-clearing walk before home, hot chocolate and slumber. The ritual was observed religiously, even when the inspector was dog-tired. He used to stroll to wind down before stepping over the threshold. Long experience had taught him that taking his professional concerns into the house assisted neither the investigation nor his domestic life. He had learned the lesson too late to keep his wife from leaving him and his children from estrangement, but he applied the principle still.

Tonight, he walked slowly to allow the distressing scenes the evening had brought to recede somewhat. The route took him past a small cinema which, he had read in the local

press, was soon to be demolished. He was not surprised.
Though he was no cineaste the fare the flea pit provided had
degenerated in recent years. The week's offering was a case
in point: a double bill of horror movies. Lurid and derivative
stuff to judge by the posters, with their crude graphics and
their unashamed hyperbole. *"You May Never Sleep Again!"*
one of the hook lines read; and beneath it a woman—very
much awake—cowered in the shadow of a two-headed man.
What trivial images the populists conjured to stir some fear
in their audiences. The walking dead; nature grown vast and
rampant in a miniature world; blood drinkers, omens, fire
walkers, thunderstorms and all the other foolishness the public cowered before. It was all so laughably trite. Among that
catalogue of penny dreadfuls there wasn't one that equaled
the banality of human appetite, which horror (or the consequences of same) he saw every week of his working life.
Thinking of it, his mind thumbed through a dozen snap-
shots: the dead by torchlight, face down and thrashed to oblivion; and the living too, meeting his mind's eye with hunger in theirs—for sex, for narcotics, for others' pain. Why
didn't they put *that* on the posters?

As he reached his home a child squealed in the shadows
beside his garage; the cry stopped him in his tracks. It came
again, and this time he recognized it for what it was. No
child at all but a cat, or cats, exchanging love calls in the
darkened passageway. He went to the place to shoo them off.
Their veneral secretions made the passage stink. He didn't
need to yell; his footfall was sufficient to scare them away.
They darted in all directions, not two, but half a dozen of
them. A veritable orgy had been underway apparently. He
had arrived on the spot too late however. The stench of their
seduction was overpowering.

Carnegie looked blankly at the elaborate setup of monitors
and video recorders that dominated his office.

"What in Christ's name is this about?" he wanted to
know.

"The video tapes," said Boyle, his number two, "from the
laboratory. I think you ought to have a look at them, sir."

Though they had worked in tandem for seven months,
Boyle was not one of Carnegie's favorite officers; you could
practically smell the ambition off his smooth hide. In someone half his age again such greed would have been objec-

tionable. In a man of thirty it verged on the obscene. This present display—the mustering of equipment ready to confront Carnegie when he walked in at eight in the morning—was just Boyle's style: flashy and redundant.

"Why so many screens?" Carnegie asked acidly. "Do I get it in stereo, too?"

"They had three cameras running simultaneously, sir. Covering the experiment from several angles."

"*What* experiment?"

Boyle gestured for his superior to sit down. Obsequious to a fault aren't you? thought Carnegie; much good it'll do you.

"Right," Boyle instructed the technician at the recorders, "roll the tapes."

Carnegie sipped at the cup of hot chocolate he had brought in with him. The beverage was a weakness of his, verging on addiction. On the days when the machine supplying it broke down he was an unhappy man indeed. He looked at the three screens. Suddenly, a title.

"Project Blind Boy," the words read. *"Restricted."*

"Blind Boy?" said Carnegie. "What, or *who*, is that?"

"It's obviously a code word of some kind," Boyle said.

"Blind Boy. Blind Boy." Carnegie repeated the phrase as if to beat it into submission, but before he could solve the problem the images on the three monitors diverged. They pictured the same subject—a bespectacled male in his late twenties sitting in a chair—but each showed the scene from a different angle. One took in the subject full length and in profile, the second was a three-quarter medium-shot, angled from above; the third a straightforward close-up of the subject's head and shoulders, shot through the glass of the test chamber and from the front. The three images were in black and white, and none were completely centered or focused. Indeed, as the tapes began to run somebody was still adjusting such technicalities. A backwash of informal chatter ran between the subject and the woman—recognizable even in brief glimpses as the deceased—who was applying electrodes to his forehead. Much of the talk between them was difficult to catch; the acoustics in the chamber frustrated microphone and listener alike.

"The woman's Doctor Dance," Boyle offered. "The victim."

"Yes," said Carnegie, watching the screens intently, "I recognize her. How long does this preparation go on for?"

"Quite a while. Most of it's unedifying."

"Well, get to the edifying stuff, then."

"Fast forward," Boyle said. The technician obliged, and the actors on the three screens became squeaking comedians. "Wait!" said Boyle. "Back up a short way." Again, the technician did as instructed. "There!" said Boyle. "Stop there. Now run on at normal speed." The action settled back to its natural pace. "This is where it really begins, sir."

Carnegie had come to the end of his hot chocolate. He put his finger into the soft sludge at the bottom of the cup, delivering the sickly-sweet dregs to his tongue. On the screens Doctor Dance had approached the subject with a syringe, was now swabbing the crook of his elbow, and injecting him. Not for the first time since his visit to the Hume Laboratories did Carnegie wonder precisely what they did at the establishment. Was this kind of procedure *de rigueur* in pharmaceutical research? The implicit secrecy of the experiment—late at night in an otherwise deserted building—suggested not. And there was that imperative on the title card—*"Restricted."* What they were watching had clearly never been intended for public viewing.

"Are you comfortable?" a man off camera now inquired. The subject nodded. His glasses had been removed and he looked slightly bemused without them. An unremarkable face, thought Carnegie; the subject—as yet unnamed—was neither Adonis nor Quasimodo. He was receding slightly, and his wispy, dirty-blond hair touched his shoulders.

"I'm fine, Doctor Welles," he replied to the off-camera questioner.

"You don't feel hot at all? Sweaty?"

"Not really," the guinea pig replied, slightly apologetically. "I feel ordinary."

That you are, Carnegie thought; then to Boyle: "Have you been through the tapes to the end?"

"No, sir," Boyle replied. "I thought you'd want to see them first. I only ran them as far as the injection."

"Any word from the hospital on Doctor Welles?"

"At the last call he was still comatose."

Carnegie grunted and returned his attention to the screens. Following the burst of action with the injection the tapes now settled into nonactivity; the three cameras fixed on their short-sighted subject with beady stares, the torpor occasionally interrupted by an inquiry from Welles as to the subject's condition. It remained the same. After three or four minutes of this eventless study even his occasional blinks began to assume major dramatic significance.

"Don't think much of the plot," the technician commented. Carnegie laughed; Boyle looked discomforted. Two or three more minutes passed in similar manner.

"This doesn't look too hopeful," Carnegie said. "Run through it at speed, will you?"

The technician was about to obey when Boyle said: *"Wait."*

Carnegie glanced across at the man, irritated by his intervention, and then back at the screens. Something *was* happening. A subtle transformation had overtaken the insipid features of the subject. He had begun to smile to himself and was sinking down in his chair as if submerging his gangling body in a warm bath. His eyes, which had so far expressed little but affable indifference, now began to flicker closed, and then, once closed, opened again. When they did so there was a quality in them not previously visible, a hunger that seemed to reach out from the screen and into the calm of the inspector's office.

Carnegie put down his chocolate cup and approached the screens. As he did so the subject also got up out of his chair and walked toward the glass of the chamber, leaving two of the cameras' ranges. The third still recorded him, however, as he pressed his face against the window, and for a moment the two men faced each other through layers of glass and time, seemingly meeting each other's gaze.

The look on the man's face was critical now, the hunger was rapidly outgrowing sane control. Eyes burning, he laid his lips against the chamber window, and kissed it, his tongue working against the glass.

"What in Christ's name is going on?" Carnegie said.

A prattle of voices had begun on the soundtrack. Doctor Welles was vainly asking the testee to articulate his feelings while Dance called off figures from the various monitoring instruments. It was difficult to hear much clearly—the din was further supplemented by an eruption of chatter from the caged monkeys—but it was evident that the readings coming through from the man's body was escalating. His face was flushed, his skin gleamed with a sudden sweat. He resembled a martyr with the tinder at his feet freshly lit, wild with a fatal ecstasy. He stopped French-kissing the window, tearing off the electrodes at his temples and the sensors from his arms and chest. Dance, her voice now registering alarm, called out for him to stop. Then she moved across the camera's view and out again crossing, Carnegie presumed, to the chamber door.

"Better not," he said, as if this drama were played out at his behest, and at a whim he could prevent the tragedy. But the woman took no notice. A moment later she appeared in long shot as she stepped into the chamber. The man moved to greet her, throwing over equipment as he did so. She called out to him—his name, perhaps. If so, it was inaudible over the monkeys' hullabaloo. "Shit," said Carnegie, as the testee's flailing arms caught first the profile camera, and then the three-quarter medium-shot. Two of the three monitors went dead. Only the head-on shot, the camera safe outside the chamber, still recorded events, but the tightness of the shot precluded more than an occasional glimpse of a moving body. Instead, the camera's sober eye gazed on, almost ironically, at the saliva smeared glass of the chamber window, blind to the atrocities being committed a few feet out of range.

"What in Christ's name did they give him?" Carnegie said, as somewhere off camera the woman's screams rose over the screeching of the apes.

Jerome woke in the early afternoon feeling hungry and sore. When he threw the sheet off his body he was appalled at his state. His torso was scored with scratches, and his groin region was red-raw. Wincing, he moved to the edge of the bed and sat there for a while, trying to piece the previous evening back together again. He remembered going to the laboratories, but very little after that. He had been a paid guinea pig for several months, giving of his blood, comfort and patience to supplement his meager earnings as a translator. The arrangement had begun courtesy of a friend who did similar work, but whereas Figley had been part of the laboratories' mainstream program, Jerome had been approached after one week at the place by Doctors Welles and Dance, who had invited him—subject to a series of psychological tests—to work exclusively for them. It had been made clear from the outset that their project (he had never even been told its purpose) was of a secret nature, and that they would demand his total dedication and discretion. He had needed the funds, and the recompense they offered was marginally better than that paid by the laboratories, so he had agreed, although the hours they had demanded of him were unsociable. For several weeks now he had been required to attend the research facility late at night and often working into the small hours of the morning as he endured Welles's interminable questions about his private life and Dance's glassy stare.

Thinking of her cold look, he felt a tremor in him. Was it because once he had fooled himself that she had looked upon him more fondly than a doctor need? Such self-deception, he chided himself, was pitiful. He was not the stuff of which women dreamed, and each day he walked the streets reinforced that conviction. He could not remember one occasion in his adult life when a woman had looked his way, and kept looking; a time when an appreciative glance of his had been returned. Why this should bother him now he wasn't certain. His loveless condition was, he knew, commonplace. And nature had been kind. Knowing, it seemed, that the gift of allurement had passed him by, it had seen fit to minimize his libido. Weeks passed without his conscious thoughts mourning his enforced chastity.

Once in a while, when he heard the pipes roar, he might wonder what Mrs. Morrisey, his landlady, looked like in her bath; might imagine the firmness of her soapy breasts, or the dark divide of her rump as she stooped to put talcum powder between her toes. But such torments were, blissfully, infrequent. And when his cup brimmed he would pocket the money he had saved from his sessions at the laboratories and buy an hour's companionship from a woman called Angela (he'd never learned her second name) on Greek Street.

It would be several weeks before he did so again, he thought. Whatever he had done last night, or, more correctly, had done to him, the bruises alone had nearly crippled him. The only plausible explanation—though he couldn't recall any details—was that he'd been beaten up on the way back from the laboratories. Either that, or he'd stepped into a bar and somebody had picked a fight with him. It had happened before, on occasion. He had one of those faces that woke the bully in drunkards.

He stood up and hobbled to the small bathroom adjoining his room. His glasses were missing from their normal spot beside the shaving mirror and his reflection was woefully blurred, but it was apparent that his face was as badly scratched as the rest of his anatomy. And more: a clump of hair had been pulled out from above his left ear; clotted blood ran down to his neck. Painfully, he bent to the task of cleaning his wounds, then bathing them in a stinging solution of antiseptic. That done, he returned into his room to seek out his spectacles. But search as he might he could not locate them. Cursing his idiocy, he rooted among his belongings for his old pair and found them. Their prescription was out of date—his eyes had worsened considerably since he'd worn them—but they at least brought his surroundings into a dreamy kind of focus.

An indisputable melancholy had crept up on him, compounded of his pain and those unwelcome thoughts of Mrs. Morrisey. To keep its intimacy at bay he turned on the radio. A sleek voice emerged, purveying the usual palliatives. Jerome had always had contempt for popular music and its apologists, but now, as he mooched around the small room, unwilling to clothe himself with chafing weaves when his scratches still pained him, the songs began to stir something other than scorn in him. It was as though he were hearing the words and music for the first time, as though all his life he had been deaf to their sentiments. Enthralled, he forgot his pain and listened. The songs told one seamless and obsessive story: of love lost and found, only to be lost again. The lyricists filled the airwaves with metaphor—much of it ludicrous, but no less potent for that. Of paradise, of hearts on fire; of birds, bells, journeys, sunsets; of passion as lunacy, as flight, as unimaginable treasure. The songs did not calm him with their fatuous sentiments. They flayed him, evoking, despite feeble rhyme and trite melody, a world bewitched by desire. He began to tremble. His eyes, strained (or so he reasoned) by the unfamiliar spectacles, began to delude him. It seemed as though he could see traces of light in his skin, sparks flying from the ends of his fingers.

He stared at his hands and arms. The illusion, far from retreating in the face of this scrutiny, increased. Beads of brightness, like the traces of fire in ash, began to climb through his veins, multiplying even as he watched. Curiously, he felt no distress. This burgeoning fire merely reflected the passion in the story the songs were telling him. Love, they said, was in the air, around every corner, waiting to be found. He thought again of the widow Morrisey in the flat below him, going about her business, sighing, no doubt, as he had done; awaiting her hero. The more he thought of her the more inflamed he became. She would not reject him, of that the songs convinced him. Or if she did he must press his case until (again, as the songs promised) she surrendered to him. Suddenly, at the thought of her surrender, the fire engulfed him. Laughing, he left the radio singing behind him and made his way downstairs.

It had taken the best part of the morning to assemble a list of testees employed at the laboratories. Carnegie had sensed a reluctance on the part of the establishment to open their files to the investigation despite the horror that had been committed on its premises. Finally, just after noon, they had presented him with a hastily assembled who's who of subjects, four and a half dozen in *toto*, and their addresses. None, the offices claimed, matched the description of Welles's testee. The doctors, it was explained, had been clearly using laboratory facilities to work on private projects. Though this was not encouraged, both had been senior researchers, and allowed leeway on the matter. It was likely, therefore, that the man Carnegie was seeking had never even been on the laboratories' payroll. Undaunted, Carnegie ordered a selection of photographs taken off the video recording and had them distributed—with the list of names and addresses—to his officers. From then on it was down to footwork and patience.

Leo Boyle ran his finger down the list of names he had been given. "Another fourteen," he said. His driver grunted, and Boyle glanced across at him. "You were McBride's partner, weren't you?" he said.

"That's right," Dooley replied. "He's been suspended."

"Why?"

Dooley scowled. "Lacks finesse, that Virgil. Can't get the hang of arrest technique."

Dooley drew the car to a halt.

"Is this it?" Boyle asked.

"You said number eighty. This is eighty. On the door. Eight. Oh."

"I've got eyes."

Boyle got out of the car and made his way up the pathway. The house was sizeable, and had been divided into

flats. There were several bells. He pressed for J. Tredgold—
the name on his list—and waited. Of the five houses they
had so far visited, two had been unoccupied and the resi-
dents of the other three had born no resemblance to the
malefactor.

Boyle waited on the step a few seconds and then pressed
the bell again; a longer ring this time.

"Nobody in," Dooley said from the pavement.

"Looks like it." Even as he spoke Boyle caught sight of a
figure flitting across the hallway, its outline distorted by the
cobblestone glass in the door. "Wait a minute," he said.

"What is it?"

"Somebody's in there and not answering." He pressed the
first bell again, and then the others. Dooley approached up
the pathway, flicking away an overattentive wasp.

"You sure?" he said.

"I saw somebody in there."

"Press the other bells," Dooley suggested.

"I already did. There's somebody in there and they don't
want to come to the door." He rapped on the glass. "Open
up," he announced. "Police."

Clever, thought Dooley; why not a loudspeaker, so heaven
knows too? When the door, predictably, remained unan-
swered, Boyle turned to Dooley. "Is there a side gate?"

"Yes, sir."

"Then get around the back, pronto, before he's away."

"Shouldn't we call—?"

"Do it? I'll keep watch here. If you can get in the back
come through and open the front door."

Dooley moved, leaving Boyle alone at the front door. He
rang the series of bells again and, cupping his hand to his
brow, put his face to the glass. There was no sign of movement in the hallway. Was it possible that the bird had already
flown? He backed down the path and stared up at the windows; they stared back vacuously. Ample time had now
passed for Dooley to get around the back of the house, but
so far he had neither reappeared nor called. Stymied where
he stood, and nervous that his tactics had lost them their
quarry, Boyle decided to follow his nose around the back of
the house.

The side gate had been left open by Dooley. Boyle advanced up the side passage, glancing through a window into
an empty living room before heading around to the back

door. It was open. Dooley, however, was not in sight. Boyle
pocketed the photograph and the list and stepped inside,
loath to call Dooley's name for fear it alert any felon to his
presence, yet nervous of the silence. Cautious as a cat on
broken glass he crept through the flat, but each room was
deserted. At the apartment door, which let on to the hallway
in which he had first seen the figure, he paused. Where had
Dooley gone? The man had apparently disappeared from
sight.

Then a groan from beyond the door.

"Dooley?" Boyle ventured. Another groan. He stepped
into the hallway. Three more doors presented themselves, all
were closed; other flats, presumably. On the coconut mat at
the front door lay Dooley's truncheon, dropped there as if its
owner had been in the process of making his escape. Boyle
swallowed his fear and walked into the body of the hall. The
complaint came again, close by. He looked around and up
the stairs. There, on the half-landing, lay Dooley. He was
barely conscious. A rough attempt had been made to rip his
clothes. Large portions of his flabby lower anatomy were exposed.

"What's going on, Dooley?" Boyle asked, moving to the
bottom of the stairs. The officer heard his voice and rolled
himself over. His bleary eyes, settling on Boyle, opened in
terror.

"It's all right," Boyle reassured him. "It's only me."

Too late, Boyle registered that Dooley's gaze wasn't fixed
on *him* at all, but on some sight over his shoulder. As he piv-
oted on his heel to snatch a glance at Dooley's bugaboo a
charging figure slammed into him. Winded and cursing,
Boyle was thrown off his feet. He scrabbed about on the
floor for several seconds before his attacker seized hold of
him by jacket and hair and hauled him to his feet. He recognized at once the wild face that was thrust into his—the receding hairline, the weak mouth, the *hunger*—but there was
much too he had not anticipated. For one, the man was naked as a babe, though scarcely so modestly endowed. For
another, he was clearly aroused to fever pitch. If the beady
eye at his groin, shining up at Boyle, were not evidence
enough, the hands now tearing at his clothes made the assailant's intention perfectly apparent

"Dooley!" Boyle shrieked as he was thrown across the
hallway. "In Christ's name! Dooley!"

His pleas were silenced as he hit the opposite wall. The wild man was at his back in half a heartbeat, smearing Boyle's face against the wallpaper. Birds and flowers, intertwined, filled his eyes. In desperation Boyle fought back, but the man's passion lent him ungovernable strength. With one insolent hand holding the policeman's head, he tore at Boyle's trousers and underwear, leaving his buttocks exposed.

"God . . ." Boyle begged into the pattern of the wallpaper. "Please God, somebody help me . . ." But the prayers were no more fruitful than his struggles. He was pinned against the wall like a butterfly spread on cork, about to be pierced through. He closed his eyes, tears of frustration running down his cheeks. The assailant left off his hold on Boyle's head and pressed his violation home. Boyle refused to cry out. The pain he felt was not the equal of his shame. Better perhaps that Dooley remained comatose; that this humiliation be done and finished with unwitnessed.

"Stop," he murmured into the wall, not to his attacker but to his body, urging it not to find pleasure in this outrage. But his nerve endings were treacherous; they caught fire from the assault. Beneath the stabbing agony some unforgivable part of him rose to the occasion.

On the stairs, Dooley hauled himself to his feet. His lumbar region, which had been weak since the car accident the previous Christmas, had given out almost as soon as the wild man had sprung him in the hall. Now, as he descended the stairs, the least motion caused excruciating agonies. Crippled with pain he stumbled to the bottom of the stairs and looked, amazed, across the hallway. Could this be Boyle—he the supercilious, he the rising man, being pummeled like a street kid in need of dope money? The sight transfixed Dooley for several seconds before he unhinged his eyes and swung them down to the truncheon on the mat. He moved cautiously, but the wild man was too occupied with the deflowering to notice him.

Jerome was listening to Boyle's heart. It was a loud, seductive beat, and with every thrust into the man it seemed to get louder. He wanted it: the heat of it, the life of it. His hand moved around to Boyle's chest and dug at the flesh.

"Give me your heart," he said. It was like a line from one of the songs.

Boyle screamed into the wall as his attacker mauled his

chest. He'd seen photographs of the woman at the laboratories; the open wound of her torso was lightning-clear in his mind's eye. Now the maniac intended the same atrocity. *Give me your heart.* Panicked to the ledge of his sanity he found new stamina and began to fight afresh, reaching around and clawing at the man's torso. Nothing—not even the bloody loss of hair from his scalp—broke the rhythm of his thrusts, however. In extremis, Boyle attempted to insinuate one of his hands between his body and the wall and reach between his legs to unman the bastard. As he did so, Dooley attacked, delivering a hail of truncheon blows upon the man's head. The diversion gave Boyle precious leeway. He pressed hard against the wall. The man, his grip on Boyle's chest slicked with blood, lost his hold. Again, Boyle pushed. This time he managed to shrug the man off entirely. The bodies disengaged. Boyle turned, bleeding but in no danger, and watched Dooley follow the man across the hallway, beating at his greasy blond head. He made little attempt to protect himself however. His burning eyes (Boyle had never understood the physical accuracy of that image until now) were still on the object of his affections.

"Kill him!" Boyle said quietly as the man grinned—grinned!—through the blows. "Break every bone in his body!"

Even if Dooley, hobbled as he was, had been in any fit state to obey the imperative, he had no chance to do so. His berating was interrupted by a voice from down the hallway. A woman had emerged from the flat Boyle had come through. She too had been a victim of this marauder, to judge by her state. But Dooley's entry into the house had clearly distracted her molester before he could do serious damage.

"Arrest him!" she said, pointing at the leering man. "He tried to rape me!"

Dooley closed into take possession of the prisoner, but Jerome had other intentions. He put his hand in Dooley's face and pushed him back against the front door. The coconut mat slid from under him; he all but fell. By the time he'd regained his balance Jerome was up and away. Boyle made a wretched attempt to stop him, but the tatters of his trousers were wrapped about his lower legs and Jerome, fleet-footed, was soon halfway up the stairs.

"Call for help," Boyle ordered Dooley. "And make it quick."

Dooley nodded and opened the front door.

"Is there any way out from upstairs?" Boyle demanded of Mrs. Morrisey. She shook her head. "Then we've got the bastard trapped, haven't we?" he said. "Go on, Dooley!" Dooley hobbled away down the path. "And you," he said to the woman, "fetch something in the way of weaponry. Anything solid." The woman nodded and returned the way she'd come, leaving Boyle slumped beside the open door. A soft breeze cooled the sweat on his face. At the car outside Dooley was calling up reinforcements.

All too soon, Boyle thought, the cars would be here, and the man upstairs would be hauled away to give his testimony. There would be no opportunity for revenge once he was in custody. The law would take its placid course, and he, the victim, would be only a bystander. If he was ever to salvage the ruins of his manhood, *now* was the time. If he didn't—if he languished here, his bowels on fire—he would never shrug off the horror he felt at his body's betrayal. He must act now—must beat the grin off his ravisher's face once and for all—or else live in self-disgust until memory failed him.

The choice was no choice at all. Without further debate, he got up from his squatting position and began up the stairs. As he reached the half-landing he realized he hadn't brought a weapon with him. He knew, however, that if he descended again he'd lose all momentum. Prepared, in that moment, to die if necessary, he headed on up.

There was only one door open on the top landing. Through it came the sound of a radio. Downstairs, in the safety of the hall, he heard Dooley come in to tell him that the call had been made, only to break off in mid-announcement. Ignoring the distraction, Boyle stepped into the flat.

There was nobody there. It took Boyle a few moments only to check the kitchen, the tiny bathroom and the living room. All were deserted. He returned to the bathroom, the window of which was open, and put his head out. The drop to the grass of the garden below was quite manageable. There was an imprint in the ground of the man's body. He had leaped. And gone.

Boyle cursed his tardiness and hung his head. A trickle of

heat ran down the inside of his leg. In the next room, the love songs played on.

For Jerome, there was no forgetfulness, not this time. The encounter with Mrs. Morrisey, which had been interrupted by Dooley, and the episode with Boyle that had followed, had all merely served to fan the fire in him. Now, by the light of those flames, he saw clearly what crimes he had committed. He remembered with horrible clarity the laboratory, the injection, the monkeys, the blood. The acts he recalled, however (and there were many), woke no sense of sinfulness in him. All moral consequence, all shame or remorse, was burned out by the fire that was even now licking his flesh to new enthusiasms.

He took refuge in a quiet cul-de-sac to make himself presentable. The clothes he had managed to snatch before making his escape were motley but would serve to keep him from attracting unwelcome attention. As he buttoned himself up—his body seeming to strain from its covering as if resentful of being concealed—he tried to control the holocaust that raged between his ears. But the flames wouldn't be dampened. His every fiber seemed alive to the flux and flow of the world around him. The marshaled trees along the road, the wall at his back, the very paving stones beneath his bare feet were catching a spark from him and burning now with their own fire. He grinned to see the conflagration spread. The world, in its every eager particular, grinned back.

Aroused beyond control, he turned to the wall he had been leaning against. The sun had fallen full upon it, and it was warm; the bricks smelled ambrosial. He laid kisses on their gritty faces, his hands exploring every nook and cranny. Murmuring sweet nothings, he unzipped himself, found an accommodating niche, and filled it. His mind was running with liquid pictures: mingled anatomies, female and male in one undistinguishable congress. Above him, even the clouds had caught fire. Enthralled by their burning heads he felt the moment rise in his gristle. Breath was short now. But the ecstasy? Surely that would go on forever.

Without warning a spasm of pain traveled down his spine from his cortex to testicles and back again, convulsing him. His hands lost grip of the brick and he finished his agonizing climax on the air as he fell across the pavement. For several seconds he lay where he had collapsed, while the echoes of the initial spasm bounced back and forth along his spine, diminishing with each return. He could taste blood at the back of his throat. He wasn't certain if he'd bitten his lip or tongue, but he thought not. Above his head the birds circled on, rising lazily on a spiral of warm air. He watched the fire in the clouds gutter out.

He got to his feet and looked down at the coinage of semen he'd spent on the pavement. For a fragile instant he caught again a whiff of the vision he'd just had; imagined a marriage of his seed with the paving stone. What sublime children the world might boast, he thought, if he could only mate with brick or tree. He would gladly suffer the agonies of conception if such miracles were possible. But the paving stone was unmoved by his seed's entreaties. The vision, like the fire above him, cooled and hid its glories.

He put his bloodied member away and leaned against the wall, turning the strange events of his recent life over and over. Something fundamental was changing in him, of that he had no doubt. The rapture that had possessed him (and would, no doubt, possess him again) was like nothing he had hitherto experienced. And whatever they had injected into his system, it showed no signs of being discharged naturally; far from it. He could feel the heat in him still, as he had leaving the laboratories, but this time the roar of its presence was louder than ever.

It was a new kind of life he was living, and the thought, though frightening, exulted him. Not once did it occur to his spinning, eroticized brain that this new kind of life would, in time, demand a new kind of death.

Carnegie had been warned by his superiors that results were expected. He was now passing the verbal beating he'd received to those under him. It was a line of humiliation in which the greater was encouraged to kick the lesser man, and that man, in turn, his lesser. Carnegie had sometimes wondered what the man at the end of the line took his ire out on; his dog presumably.

"This miscreant is still loose, gentlemen, despite his photograph in many of this morning's newspapers and an operating method which is, to say the least, insolent. We *will* catch him, of course, but let's get the bastard before we have another murder on our hands—"

The phone rang. Boyle's replacement, Migeon, picked it up, while Carnegie concluded his pep talk to the assembled officers.

"I want him in the next twenty-four hours, gentlemen. That's the time scale I've been given, and that's what we've got. Twenty-four hours."

Migeon interrupted. "Sir? It's Johannson. He says he's got something for you. It's urgent."

"Right." The inspector claimed the receiver. "Carnegie."

The voice at the other end was soft to the point of inaudibility. "Carnegie," Johannson said, "we've been right through the laboratory, dug up every piece of information we could find on Dance and Welles's tests—"

"And?"

"We've also analyzed traces of the agent from the hypo they used on the suspect. I think we've found the *Boy,* Carnegie."

"What boy?" Carnegie wanted to know. He found Johannson's obfuscation irritating.

"*The Blind Boy,* Carnegie."

"And?"

For some inexplicable reason Carnegie was certain the man *smiled* down the phone before replying: "I think perhaps you'd better come down and see for yourself. Sometime around noon suit you?"

Johannson could have been one of history's greatest poisoners. He had all the requisite qualifications. A tidy mind (poisoners were, in Carnegie's experience, domestic paragons), a patient nature (poison could take time) and, most importantly, an encyclopedic knowledge of toxicology. Watching him at work, which Carnegie had done on two previous cases, was to see a subtle man at his subtle craft, and the spectacle made Carnegie's blood run cold.

Johannson had installed himself in the laboratory on the top floor, where Doctor Dance had been murdered, rather than use police facilities for the investigation, because, as he explained to Carnegie, much of the equipment the Hume organization boasted was simply not available elsewhere. His dominion over the place, accompanied by his two assistants, had, however, transformed the laboratory from the clutter left by the experimenters to a dream of order. Only the monkeys remained a constant. Try as he might Johannson could not control their behavior.

"We didn't have much difficulty finding the drug used on your man," Johannson said, "we simply cross-checked traces remaining in the hypodermic with materials found in the room. In fact, they seem to have been manufacturing this stuff, or variations on the theme, for some time. The people here claim they know nothing about it, of course. I'm inclined to believe them. What the good doctors were doing here was, I'm sure, in the nature of a personal experiment."

"What sort of experiment?"

Johannson took off his spectacles and set about cleaning them with the tongue of his red tie. "At first, we thought they were developing some kind of hallucinogen," he said. "In some regards the agent used on your man resembles a narcotic. In fact—methods apart—I think they made some very exciting discoveries. Developments which take us into entirely new territory."

"It's not a drug then?"

"Oh, yes, of course it's a drug," Johannson said, replacing the spectacles, "but one created for a very specific purpose. See for yourself."

Johannson led the way across the laboratory to the row of monkeys' cages. Instead of being confined separately, the toxicologist had seen fit to open the interconnecting doors between one cage and the next, allowing the animals free access to gather in groups. The consequence was absolutely plain—the animals were engaged in an elaborate series of sexual acts. Why, Carnegie wondered, did monkeys perpetually perform obscenities? It was the same torrid display whenever he'd taken his offspring, as children, to Regent's Park Zoo; the ape enclosure elicited one embarrassing question upon another. He'd stopped taking the children after a while. He simply found it too mortifying.

"Haven't they got anything better to do?" he asked of Johannson, glancing away and then back at a menage à trois that was so intimate the eye could not ascribe member to monkey.

"Believe me," Johannson smirked, "this is mild by comparison with much of the behavior we've seen from them since we gave them a shot of the agent. From that point on they neglected all normal behavior patterns. They bypassed the arousal signals, the courtship rituals. They no longer show any interest in food. They don't sleep. They have become sexual obsessives. All other stimuli are forgotten. Unless the agent is naturally discharged, I suspect they are going to screw themselves to death."

Carnegie looked along the rest of the cages. The same pornographic scenes were being played out in each one. Mass rape, homosexual liaisons, fervent and ecstatic masturbation.

"It's no wonder the doctors made a secret project of their discovery," Johannson went on. "They were on to something that could have made them a fortune. An aphrodisiac that actually works."

"An aphrodisiac?"

"Most are useless, of course. Rhinoceros horn, live eels in cream sauce: symbolic stuff. They're designed to arouse by association."

Carnegie remembered the hunger in Jerome's eyes. It was echoed here in the monkeys'. Hunger, and the desperation that hunger brings.

"And the ointments too, all useless. *Cantharis vesticatora*—"

"What's that?"

"You know the stuff as Spanish fly, perhaps? It's a paste made from a beetle. Again, useless. At best these things are irritants. But this . . ." He picked up a vial of colorless fluid. "*This* is damn near genius."

"They don't look too happy with it to me."

"Oh, it's still crude," Johannson said. "I think the researchers were greedy and moved into tests on living subjects a good two or three years before it was wise to do so. The stuff is almost lethal as it stands, no doubt of that. But it *could* be made to work, given time. You see, they've sidestepped the mechanical problems. This stuff operates directly on the sexual imagination, on the libido. If you arouse the *mind,* the body follows. That's the trick of it."

A rattling of the wire mesh close by drew Carnegie's attention from Johannson's pale features. One of the female monkeys, apparently not satisfied with the attentions of several males, was spread-eagled against her cage, her nimble fingers reaching for Carnegie. Her spouses, not to be left loveless, had taken to sodomy. "*Blind Boy*?" said Carnegie. "Is that Jerome?"

"It's Cupid, isn't it?" Johannson said:

"Love looks not with the eyes but with the mind,
And therefore is winged Cupid painted blind.

"It's *Midsummer Night's Dream*."

"The bard was never my strongest suit," said Carnegie. He went back to staring at the female monkey. "And Jerome?" he said.

"He has the agent in his system. A sizeable dose."

"So he's like this lot!"

"I would presume—his intellectual capacities being greater—that the agent may not be able to work in quite such an *unfettered* fashion. But, having said that, sex can make monkeys out of the best of us, can't it?" Johannson allowed himself a half-smile at the notion. "All our so-called higher concerns become secondary to the pursuit. For a short time sex makes us obsessive. We can perform, or at least *think* we can perform, what with hindsight may seem extraordinary feats."

"I don't think there's anything so extraordinary about rape," Carnegie commented, attempting to stem Johannson's rhapsody. But the other man would not be subdued.

"Sex without end, without compromise or apology," he said. "Imagine it. The dream of Casanova."

The world had seen so many Ages: the Age of Enlightenment; of Reformation; of Reason. Now, at last, the Age of Desire. And after this, an end to Ages; an end, perhaps, to everything. For the fires that were being stoked now were fiercer than the innocent world suspected. They were terrible fires, fires without end, which would illuminate the world in one last, fierce light.

So Welles thought as he lay in his bed. He had been conscious for several hours, but had chosen not to signify such. Whenever a nurse came to his room he would clamp his eyes closed and slow the rhythm of his breath. He knew he could not keep the illusion for long, but the hours gave him a while to think through his itinerary from here. His first move had to be back to the laboratories. There were papers there he had to shred, tapes to wipe clean. From now on he was determined that every scrap of information about *Project Blind Boy* exist solely in his head. That way he would have complete control over his masterwork, and nobody could claim it from him.

He had never had much interest in making money from the discovery, although he was well aware of how lucrative a workable aphrodisiac would be; he had never given a fig for material wealth. His initial motivation for the development of the drug—which they had chanced upon quite by accident while testing an agent to aid schizophrenics—had been investigative. But his motives had matured through their months of secret work. He had come to think of himself as the bringer of the millenium. He would not have anyone attempt to snatch that sacred role from him.

So he thought, lying in his bed, waiting for a moment to slip away.

As he walked the streets Jerome would have happily affirmed Welles's vision. Perhaps he, of all men, was most eager to welcome the Age of Desire. He saw its portents everywhere: on advertising billboards and cinema marquees, in ship windows, on television screens—everywhere, the body as merchandise. Where flesh was not being used to market artifacts of steel and stone, those artifacts were taking on its properties. Automobiles passed him by with every voluptuous attribute but breath—their sinuous bodywork gleamed, their interiors invited plushly. The buildings beleaguered him with sexual puns: spires, passageways, shadowed plazas with white-water fountains. Beneath the raptures of the shallow—the thousand trivial distractions he encountered in street and square—he sensed the ripe life of the body informing every particular.

The spectacle kept the fire in him well stoked. It was all that will power could do to keep him from pressing his attention on every creature that he met eyes with. A few seemed to sense the heat in him and gave him wide berth. Dogs sensed it too. Several followed him, aroused by *his* arousal. Flies orbited his head in squadrons. But his growing ease with his condition gave him some rudimentary control over it. He knew that to make a public display of his ardor would bring the law down upon him, and that in turn would hinder his adventures. Soon enough, the fire that he had begun would spread. *Then* he would emerge from hiding and bathe in it freely. Until then, discretion was best.

He had on occasion bought the company of a young woman in Soho; he went to find her now. The afternoon was stiflingly hot, but he felt no weariness. He had not eaten since the previous evening, but he felt no hunger. Indeed, as he climbed the narrow stairway up to the room on the first floor which Angela had once occupied, he felt as primed as an athlete, glowing with health. The immaculately dressed and wall-eyed pimp who usually occupied a place at the top of the stairs was absent. Jerome simply went to the girl's room and knocked. There was no reply. He rapped again, more urgently. The noise brought an early middle-aged woman to the door at the end of the landing.

"What do you want?"

"The woman," he said simply.

"Angela's gone. And you'd better get out of here too in that state. This isn't a flophouse."

"When will she be back?" he asked, keeping as tight a leash as he could on his appetite.

The woman, who was as tall as Jerome and half as heavy again as his wasted frame, advanced toward him. "The girl won't *be* back," she said, "so you get the hell out of here, before I call Isaiah."

Jerome looked at the woman. She shared Angela's profession, no doubt, if not her youth or prettiness. He smiled at her. "I can hear your heart," he said.

"I told you—"

Before she could finish the words Jerome moved down the landing toward her. She wasn't intimidated by his approach, merely repulsed.

"If I call Isaiah, you'll be sorry," she informed him. The pace of her heartbeat had risen, he could hear it.

"I'm burning," he said.

She frowned. She was clearly losing this battle of wits. "Stay away from me," she told. "I'm warning you."

The heartbeat was getting more rapid still. The rhythm, buried in her substance, drew him on. From that source: all life, all heat.

"Give me your heart," he said.

"Isaiah!"

Nobody came running at her shout, however. Jerome gave her no opportunity to cry out a second time. He reached to embrace her, clamping a hand over her mouth. She let fly a volley of blows against him, but the pain only fanned the flames. He was brighter by the moment. His every orifice let onto the furnace in belly and loins and head. Her superior bulk was no advantage against such fervor. He pushed her against the wall—the beat of her heart loud in his ears—and began to apply kisses to her neck, tearing her dress open to free her breasts.

"Don't shout," he said, trying to sound persuasive. "There's no harm meant."

She shook her head and said, "I won't," against his palm. He took his hand from her mouth and she dragged in several desperate breaths. Where was Isaiah? she thought. Not far, surely. Fearing for her life if she tried to resist this interloper—how his eyes shone!—she gave up any pretense to resistance and let him have his way. Men's supply of passion, she knew from long experience, was easily depleted. Though they might threaten to move earth and heaven too, half an hour later their boasts would be damp sheets and resentment. If worst came to worst, she could tolerate his inane talk of burning; she'd heard far obscener bedroom chat. As to the prong he was even now attempting to press into her, it and its comical like held no surprises for her.

Jerome wanted to touch the heart in her, wanted to see it splash up into his face, to bathe in it. He put his hand to her breast and felt the beat of her under his palm.

"You like that, do you?" she said as he pressed against her bosom. "You're not the first."

He clawed her skin.

"Gently, sweetheart," she chided him, looking over his shoulder to see if there was any sign of Isaiah. "Be gentle. This is the only body I've got."

He ignored her. His nails drew blood.

"Don't do that," she said.

"Wants to be out," he replied digging deeply, and it suddenly dawned on her that this was no love-game he was playing.

"*Stop it,*" she said, as he began to tear at her. This time she screamed.

Downstairs, and a short way along the street, Isaiah dropped the slice of *tarte française* he'd just bought and ran to the door. It wasn't the first time his sweet tooth had tempted him from his post, but—unless he was quick to undo the damage—it might very well be his last. There were terrible noises from the landing. He raced up the stairs. The scene that met his eyes was in every way worse than that his imagination had conjured. Simone was trapped against the wall beside her door with a man battened upon her. Blood was coming from somewhere between them, he couldn't see where.

Isaiah yelled. Jerome, hands bloody, looked around from his labors as a giant in a Savile Row suit reached for him. It took Jerome vital seconds to uproot himself from the furrow, by which time the man was upon him. Isaiah took hold of him, and dragged him off the woman. She took shelter, sobbing, in her room.

"Sick bastard," Isaiah said, launching a fusillade of punches. Jerome reeled. But he was on fire, and unafraid. In a moment's respite he leaped at his man like an angered baboon. Isaiah, taken unawares, lost balance, and fell back against one of the doors, which opened inward against his weight. He collapsed into a squalid lavatory, his head striking the lip of the toilet bowl as he went down. The impact disoriented him, and he lay on the stained linoleum groaning, legs akimbo. Jerome could hear his blood, eager in his veins; could smell sugar on his breath. It tempted him to stay. But his instinct for self-preservation counseled otherwise; Isaiah was already making an attempt to stand up again. Before he could get to his feet Jerome turned about and made a getaway down the stairs.

The dog day met him at the doorstep, and he smiled. The street wanted him more than the woman on the landing, and he was eager to oblige. He started out onto the pavement, his erection still pressing from his trousers. Behind him he heard the giant pounding down the stairs. He took to his heels, laughing. The fire was still uncurbed in him, and it lent speed to his feet. He ran down the street not caring if Sugar Breath was following or not. Pedestrians, unwilling in this dispassionate age to register more than casual interest in the blood-spattered satyr, parted to let him pass. A few pointed, assuming him an actor perhaps. Most took no notice at all. He made his way through a maze of back streets, aware without needing to look that Isaiah was still on his heels.

Perhaps it was accident that brought him to the street market; perhaps, and more probably, it was that the swelter carried the mingled scent of meat and fruit to his nostrils and he wanted to bathe in it. The narrow thoroughfare was thronged with purchasers, sightseers and stalls heaped with merchandise. He dove into the crowd happily, brushing against buttock and thigh, meeting the plaguing gaze of fellow flesh on every side. Such a day! He and his prick could scarcely believe their luck.

Behind him he heard Isaiah shout. He picked up his pace, heading for the most densely populated area of the market, where he could lose himself in the hot press of people. Each contact was a painful ecstasy. Each climax—and they came one upon the other as he pressed through the crowd—was a dry spasm in his system. His back ached, his balls ached. But what was his body now? Just a plinth for that singular monument, his prick. Head was *nothing;* mind was *nothing.* His arms were simply made to bring love close, his legs to carry the demanding rod any place where it might find satisfaction. He pictured himself as a walking erection, the world gaping on every side. Flesh, brick, steel, he didn't care—he would ravish it all.

Suddenly, without his seeking it, the crowd parted, and he found himself off the main thoroughfare and in a narrow street. Sunlight poured between the buildings, its zeal magnified. He was about to turn back to join the crowd again when he caught a scent and sight that drew him on. A short way down the heat-drenched street three shirtless young men were standing amid piles of fruit crates, each containing dozens of baskets of strawberries. There had been a glut of fruit that year, and in the relentless heat much of it had begun to soften and rot. The trio of workers was going through the baskets, sorting bad fruit from good, and throwing the spoiled strawberries into the gutter. The smell in the narrow space was overpowering, a sweetness of such strength it would have sickened any interloper other than Jerome, whose senses had lost all capacity for revulsion or rejection. The world was the world was the world; he would take it, as in marriage, for better or worse. He stood watching the spectacle entranced: the sweating fruit sorters bright in the fall of sun, hands, arms and torsoes spattered with scarlet juice; the air mazed with every nectar-seeking insect; the discarded fruit heaped in the gutter in seeping mounds. Engaged in their sticky labors, the sorters didn't even see him at first. Then one of the three looked up and took in the extraordinary creature watching them. The grin on his face died as he met Jerome's eyes.

"What the hell?"

Now the other two looked up from their work.

"Sweet," said Jerome. He could hear their hearts tremble.

"Look at him," said the youngest of the three, pointing at Jerome's groin. "Fucking exposing himself."

They stood still in the sunlight, he and they, while the wasps whirled around the fruit and, in the narrow slice of blue summer sky between the roofs, birds passed over. Jerome wanted the moment to go on forever; his too-naked head tasted Eden here.

And then, the dream broke. He felt a shadow on his back. One of the sorters dropped the basket he was sorting through; the decayed fruit broke open on the gravel. Jerome frowned and half-turned. Isaiah had found the street. His weapon was steel and shone. It crossed the space between him and Jerome in one short second. Jerome felt an ache in his side as the knife slid into him.

"Christ!" the young man said and began to run. His two brothers, unwilling to be witnesses at the scene of a wounding, hesitated only moments longer before following.

The pain made Jerome cry out, but nobody in the noisy market heard him. Isaiah withdrew the blade; heat came with it. He made to stab again but Jerome was too fast for the spoiler. He moved out of range and staggered across the street. The would-be assassin, fearful that Jerome's cries would draw too much attention, moved quickly in pursuit to finish the job. But the tarmac was slick with rotted fruit, and his fine suede shoes had less grip than Jerome's bare feet. The gap between them widened by a pace.

"No you don't," Isaiah said, determined not to let his humiliator escape. He pushed over a tower of fruit crates— baskets toppled and strewed their contents across Jerome's path. Jerome hesitated, to take in the bouquet of bruised fruit. The indulgence almost killed him. Isaiah closed in, ready to take the man. Jerome, his system taxed to near eruption by the stimulus of pain, watched the blade come close to opening up his belly. His mind conjured the wound: the abdomen slit—the heat spilling out to join the blood of the strawberries in the gutter. The thought was so tempting. He almost wanted it.

Isaiah had killed before, twice. He knew the wordless vocabulary of the act, and he could see the invitation in his victim's eyes. Happy to oblige, he came to meet it, knife at the ready. At the last possible moment Jerome recanted, and instead of presenting himself for slitting, threw a blow at the giant. Isaiah ducked to avoid it and his feet slid in the mush.

The knife fled from his hand and fell among the debris of baskets and fruit. Jerome turned away as the hunter—the advantage lost—stooped to locate the knife. But his prey was gone before his ham-fisted grip had found it; lost again in the crowd-filled streets. He had no opportunity to pocket the knife before the uniform stepped out of the crowd and joined him in the hot passageway.

"What's the story?" the policeman demanded, looking down at the knife. Isaiah followed his gaze. The bloodied blade was black with flies.

In his office Inspector Carnegie sipped at his hot chocolate, his third in the past hour, and watched the processes of dusk. He had always wanted to be a detective, right from his earliest rememberings. And, in those rememberings, this had always been a charged and magical hour. Night descending on the city; myriad evils putting on their glad rags and coming out to play. A time for vigilance, for a new moral stringency.

But as a child he had failed to imagine the fatigue that twilight invariably brought. He was tired to his bones, and if he snatched any sleep in the next few hours he knew it would be here, in his chair, with his feet up on the desk amid a clutter of plastic cups.

The phone rang. It was Johannson.

"Still at work?" he said, impressed by Johannson's dedication to the job. It was well after nine. Perhaps Johannson didn't have a home worth calling such to go back to either.

"I heard our man had a busy day," Johannson said.

"That's right. A prostitute in Soho, then got himself stabbed."

"He got through the cordon, I gather?"

"These things happen," Carnegie replied, too tired to be testy. "What can I do for you?"

"I just thought you'd want to know: the monkeys have started to die."

The words stirred Carnegie from his fatigue-stupor. "How many?" he asked.

"Three from fourteen so far. But the rest will be dead by dawn, I'd guess."

"What's killing them? Exhaustion?" Carnegie recalled the desperate saturnalia he'd seen in the cages. What animal—

human or otherwise—could keep up such revelry without cracking up?

"It's not physical," Johannson said. "Or at least not in the way you're implying. We'll have to wait for the dissection results before we get any detailed explanations—"

"Your best guess?"

"For what it's worth ..." Johannson said, "... which is quite a lot: I think they're going *bang*."

"What?"

"Cerebral overload of some kind. Their brains are simply giving out. The agent doesn't disperse you see. *It feeds on itself*. The more fevered they get, the more of the drug is produced; the more of the drug there is, the more fevered they get. It's a vicious circle. Hotter and hotter, wilder and wilder. Eventually the system can't take it, and suddenly I'm up to my armpits in dead monkeys." The smile came back into the voice again, cold and wry. "Not that the others let that spoil their fun. Necrophilia's quite the fashion down here."

Carnegie peered at his cooling hot chocolate. It had acquired a thin skin which puckered as he touched the cup. "So it's just a matter of time?" he said.

"Before our man goes for bust? Yes, I'd think so."

"All right. Thanks for the update. Keep me posted."

"You want to come down here and view the remains?"

"Monkey corpses I can do without, thank you."

Johannson laughed. Carnegie put down the receiver. When he turned back to the window, night had well and truly fallen.

In the laboratory Johannson crossed to the light switch by the door. In the time he'd been calling Carnegie the last of the daylight had fled. He saw the blow that felled him coming a mere heartbeat before it landed; it caught him across the side of his neck. One of his vertebrae snapped and his legs buckled. He collapsed without reaching the light switch. But by the time he hit the ground the distinction between day and night was academic.

Welles didn't bother to check whether his blow had been lethal or not; time was at a premium. He stepped over the body and headed across to the bench where Johannson had been working. There, lying in a circle of lamplight as if for the final act of a simian tragedy, lay a dead monkey. It had

clearly perished in a frenzy. Its face was knitted up; mouth
wide and spittle-stained; eyes fixed in a final look of alarm.
Its fur had been pulled out in tufts in the throes of its cop-
ulations. Its body, wasted with exertion, was a mass of contusions. It took Welles half a minute of study to recognize
the implications of the corpse, and of the other two he now
saw lying on a nearby bench.

"Love kills," he murmured to himself philosophically and
began his systematic destruction of *Blind Boy*.

I'm dying, Jerome thought. I'm dying of *terminal joy*. The
thought amused him. It was the only thought in his head
which made much sense. Since his encounter with Isaiah and
the escape from the police that had followed, he could remember little with any coherence. The hours of hiding and
nursing his wounds—of feeling the heat grow again, and of
discharging it—had long since merged into one midsummer
dream, from which, he knew with pleasurable certainty, only
death would wake him. The blaze was devouring him utterly, from the entrails out. If he were to be eviscerated now,
what would the witnesses find? Only embers and ashes.

Yet still his one-eyed friend demanded *more*. Still, as he
wove his way back to the laboratories—where else for a
made man to go when the stitches slipped but back to the
first heat?—still the grids gaped at him seductively, and every brick wall offered up a hundred gritty invitations.

The night was balmy: a night for love songs and romance.
In the questionable privacy of a parking lot a few blocks
from his destination he saw two people having sex in the
back of a car, the doors open to accommodate limbs and
draft. Jerome paused to watch the ritual, enthralled as ever
by the tangle of bodies and the sound—so loud it was like
thunder—of twin hearts beating to one escalating rhythm.
Watching, his rod grew eager.

The female saw him first and alerted her partner to the
wreck of a human being who was watching them with such
childish delight. The male looked around from his gropings
to stare. Do I burn, Jerome wondered? Does my hair flame?
At the last, does the illusion gain substance? To judge by the
look on their faces, the answer was surely no. They were not
in awe of him, merely angered and revolted.

"I'm on fire," he told them.

The male got to his feet and spat at Jerome. He almost expected the spittle to turn to steam as it approached him but instead it landed on his face and upper chest as a cooling shower.

"Go to hell," the woman said. "Leave us alone."

Jerome shook his head. The male warned him that another step would oblige him to break Jerome's head. It disturbed our man not a jot; no words, no blows, could silence the imperative of the rod.

Their hearts, he realized, as he moved toward them, no longer beat in tandem.

Carnegie consulted the map, five years out of date now, on his office wall to pinpoint the location of the attack that had just been reported. Neither of the victims had come to serious harm, apparently. The arrival of a carload of revelers had dissuaded Jerome (it was unquestionably Jerome) from lingering. Now the area was being flooded with officers, half a dozen of them armed. In a matter of minutes every street in the vicinity of the attack would be cordoned off. Unlike Soho, which had been crowded, the area would furnish the fugitive with few hiding places.

Carnegie pinpointed the location of the attack and realized that it was within a few blocks of the laboratories. No accident, surely. The man was heading back to the scene of his crime. Wounded, and undoubtedly on the verge of collapse—the lovers had described a man who looked more dead than alive—Jerome would probably be picked up before he reached home. But there was always the risk of his slipping through the net and getting to the laboratories. Johannson was working there, alone. The guard on the building was, in these straitened times, necessarily small.

Carnegie picked up the phone and dialed through to Johannson. The phone rang at the other end but nobody picked it up. The man's gone home, Carnegie thought, happy to be relieved of his concern. It's ten-fifty at night and he's earned his rest. Just as he was about to put the receiver down, however, it was picked up at the other end.

"Johannson?"

Nobody replied.

"Johannson? This is Carnegie." And still, no reply. "Answer me, damn it. Who is this?"

In the laboratories the receiver was forsaken. It was not replaced on the cradle but left to lie on the bench. Down the buzzing line, Carnegie could clearly hear the monkeys, their voices shrill.

"Johannson?" Carnegie demanded. "Are you there? Johannson?"

But the apes screamed on.

Welles had built two bonfires of the *Blind Boy* material in the sinks and then set them alight. They flared up enthusiastically. Smoke, heat and ashes filled the large room, thickening the air. When the fires were raging he threw all the tapes he could lay hands upon into the conflagration, and added all of Johannson's notes for good measure. Several of the tapes had already gone from the files, he noted. But all they could show any thief was some teasing scenes of transformation. The heart of the secret remained his. With the procedures and formulae now destroyed, it only remained to wash the small amounts of remaining agent down the drain and kill and incinerate the animals.

He prepared a series of lethal hypodermics, going about the business with uncharacteristic orderliness. This systematic destruction gratified him. He felt no regret at the way things had turned out. From that first moment of panic, when he'd helplessly watched the *Blind Boy* serum work its awesome effects upon Jerome, to this final elimination of all that had gone before had been, he now saw, one steady process of wiping clean. With these fires he brought an end to the pretense of scientific inquiry. After this he was indisputably the Apostle of Desire, its John in the Wilderness. The thought blinded him to any other. Careless of the monkeys' scratchings he hauled them one by one from their cages to deliver the killing dose. He had dispatched three, and was opening the cage of the fourth, when a figure appeared in the doorway of the laboratory. Through the smoky air it was impossible to see who. The surviving monkeys seemed to recognize him, however. They left off their couplings and set up a din of welcome.

Welles stood still and waited for the newcomer to make his move.

"I'm dying," said Jerome.

Welles had not expected this. Of all the people he had anticipated here, Jerome was the last.

"Did you hear me?" the man wanted to know.

Welles nodded. "We're *all* dying, Jerome. Life is a slow

disease, no more nor less. But such a *light,* eh? in the going."

"You *knew* this would happen," Jerome said. "You knew the fire would eat me away."

"No," came the sober reply. "No, I didn't. Really."

Jerome walked out of the door frame and into the murky light. He was a wasted shambles, a patchwork man, blood on his body, fire in his eyes. But Welles knew better than to trust the apparent vulnerability of this scarecrow. The agent in his system had made him capable of superhuman acts. He had seen Dance torn open with a few nonchalant strokes. Tact was required. Though clearly close to death, Jerome was still formidable.

"I didn't intend this, Jerome," Welles said, attempting to tame the tremor in his voice. "I wish, in a way, I could claim that I had. But I wasn't that farsighted. It's taken me time and pain to see the future plainly."

The burning man watched him, gaze intent.

"Such fires, Jerome, waiting to be lit."

"I know . . ." Jerome replied. "Believe me . . . I know."

"You and I, we are the end of the world."

The wretched monster pondered this for a while, and then nodded slowly. Welles softly exhaled a sigh of relief. The deathbed diplomacy was working. But he had little time to waste with talk. If Jerome was here, could the authorities be far behind?

"I have urgent work to do, my friend," he said calmly. "Would you think me uncivil if I continued with it?"

Without waiting for a reply he unlatched another cage and hauled the condemned monkey out, expertly turning its body around to facilitate the injection. The animal convulsed in his arms for a few moments, then died. Welles disengaged its wizened fingers from his shirt and tossed the corpse and the discharged hypodermic on to the bench, turning with an executioner's economy to claim his next victim.

"Why?" Jerome asked, staring at the animal's open eyes.

"Act of mercy," Welles replied, picking up another primed hypodermic. "You can see how they're suffering." He reached to unlatch the next cage.

"Don't," Jerome said.

"No time for sentiment," Welles replied. "I beg you, an end to that."

Sentiment, Jerome thought, muddily remembering the

songs on the radio that had first rewoken the fire in him. Didn't Welles understand that the processes of heart and head and groin were indivisible? That sentiment, however trite, might lead to undiscovered regions? He wanted to tell the doctor that, to explain all that he had seen and all that he had loved in these desperate hours. But somewhere between mind and tongue the explanations absconded. All he could say, to state the empathy he felt for all the suffering world, was: *"Don't,"* as Welles unlocked the next cage. The doctor ignored him and reached into the wire-mesh cell. It contained three animals. He took hold of the nearest and drew it, protesting, from its companions' embraces. Without doubt it knew what fate awaited it; a flurry of screeches signaled its terror.

Jerome couldn't stomach this casual disposal. He moved, the wound in his side a torment, to prevent the killing. Welles, distracted by Jerome's advance, lost hold of his wriggling charge. The monkey scampered away across the benchtops. As he went to recapture it the prisoners in the cage behind him took their chance and slipped out.

"Damn you," Welles yelled at Jerome, "don't you see we've no *time*? Don't you understand?"

Jerome understood everything, and yet nothing. The fever he and the animals shared he understood; its purpose, to transform the world, he understood too. But why it should end like this—that joy, that vision—why it should all come down to a sordid room filled with smoke and pain, to frailty, to despair? *That* he did not comprehend. Nor, he now realized, did Welles, who had been the architect of these contradictions.

As the doctor made a snatch for one of the escaping monkeys, Jerome crossed swiftly to the remaining cages and unlatched them all. The animals leaped to their freedom. Welles had succeeded with his recapture, however, and had the protesting monkey in his grip, about to deliver the panacea. Jerome made toward him.

"Let it be," he yelled.

Welles pressed the hypodermic into the monkey's body, but before he could depress the plunger Jerome had pulled at his wrist. The hypodermic spat its poison into the air and then fell to the ground. The monkey, wresting itself free, followed.

Jerome pulled Welles close. "I told you to *let it be*," he said.

Welles's response was to drive his fist into Jerome's wounded flank. Tears of pain spurted from his eyes, but he didn't release the doctor. The stimulus, unpleasant as it was, could not dissuade him from holding that beating heart close. He wished, embracing Welles like a prodigal, that he could ignite himself, that the dream of burning flesh he had endured would now become a reality, consuming maker and made in one cleansing flame. But his flesh was only flesh; his bone, bone. What miracles he had seen had been a private revelation, and now there was no time to communicate their glories or their horrors. What he had seen would die with him, to be rediscovered (perhaps) by some future self, only to be forgotten and discovered again. Like the story of love the radio had told; the same joy lost and found, found and lost. He stared at Welles with new comprehension dawning, hearing still the terrified beat of the man's heart. The doctor was *wrong*. If he left the man to live, he would come to know his error. They were not presagers of the millenium. They had both been dreaming.

"Don't kill me," Welles pleaded. "I don't want to die."

More fool you, Jerome thought, and let the man go.

Welles's bafflement was plain. He couldn't believe that his appeal for life had been answered. Anticipating a blow with every step he took he backed away from Jerome, who simply turned his back on the doctor and walked away.

From downstairs there came a shout, and then many shouts. Police, Welles guessed. They had presumably found the body of the officer who'd been on guard at the door. In moments only they would be coming up the stairs. There was no time now for finishing the tasks he'd come here to perform. He had to be away before they arrived.

On the floor below Carnegie watched the armed officers disappear up the stairs. There was a faint smell of burning in the air. He feared the worst.

I am the man who comes after the act, he thought to himself. I am perpetually upon the scene when the best of the action is over. Used as he was to waiting, patient as a loyal dog, this time he could not hold his anxieties in check while the others went ahead. Disregarding the voices advising him to wait, he began up the stairs.

The laboratory on the top floor was empty but for the

monkeys and Johannson's corpse. The toxicologist lay on his face where he had fallen, neck broken. The emergency exit, which let on to the fire escape, was open; smoky air was being sucked out through it. As Carnegie stepped away from Johannson's body officers were already on the fire escape calling to their colleagues below to seek out the fugitive.

"Sir?"

Carnegie looked across at the mustachioed individual who had approached him.

"What is it?"

The officer pointed to the other end of the laboratory, to the test chamber. There was somebody at the window. Carnegie recognized the features, even though they were much changed. It was Jerome. At first he thought the man was watching him, but a short perusal scotched that idea. Jerome was staring, tears on his face, at his own reflection in the smeared glass. Even as Carnegie watched, the face retreated with the gloom of the chamber.

Other officers had noticed the man too. They were moving down the length of the laboratory, taking up positions behind the benches where they had a good line on the door, weapons at the ready. Carnegie had been present in such situations before; they had their own, terrible momentum. Unless he intervened, there would be blood.

"No," he said, "hold your fire."

He pressed the protesting officer aside and began to walk down the laboratory, making no attempt to conceal his advance. He walked past sinks in which the remains of *Blind Boy* guttered, past the bench under which, a short age ago, they'd found the dead Dance. A monkey, its head bowed, dragged itself across his path, apparently deaf to his proximity. He let it find a hole to die in, then moved on to the chamber door. It was ajar. He reached for the handle. Behind him the laboratory had fallen completely silent; all eyes were on him. He pulled the door open. Fingers tightened on the triggers. There was no attack however. Carnegie stepped inside.

Jerome was standing against the opposite wall. If he saw Carnegie enter, or heard him, he made no sign of it. A dead monkey lay at his feet, one hand still grasping the hem of his trousers. Another whimpered in the corner, holding its head in its hands.

"Jerome?"

Was it Carnegie's imagination, or could he smell strawberries?

Jerome blinked.

"You're under arrest," Carnegie said. Hendrix would appreciate the irony of that, he thought. The man moved his bloody hand from the stab wound in his side to the front of his trousers and began to stroke himself.

"Too late," Jerome said. He could feel the last fire rising in him. Even if this intruder chose to cross the chamber and arrest him now, the intervening seconds would deny him his capture. *Death was here.* And what was it, now that he saw it clearly? Just another seduction, another sweet darkness to be filled up, and pleasured and made fertile.

A spasm began in his perineum, and lightning traveled in two directions from the spot, up his rod and up his spine. A laugh began in his throat.

In the corner of the chamber the monkey, hearing Jerome's humor, began to whimper again. The sound momentarily claimed Carnegie's attention, and when his gaze flitted back to Jerome the short-sighted eyes had closed, the hand had dropped, and he was dead, standing against the wall. For a short time the body defied gravity. Then, gracefully the legs buckled and Jerome fell forward. He was, Carnegie saw, a sack of bones, no more. It was a wonder the man had lived so long.

Cautiously, he crossed to the body and put his finger to the man's neck. There was no pulse. The remnants of Jerome's last laugh remained on his face, however, refusing to decay.

"Tell me . . ." Carnegie whispered to the man, sensing that despite his preemption he had missed the moment; that once again he was, and perhaps would always be, merely a witness of consequences. "Tell me. *What was the joke?*"

But the blind boy, as is the wont of his clan, wasn't telling.

PERMISSIONS